SITTING BULL SPOKE

The chiefs sat around the council fire awaiting Sitting Bull's final instructions.

"Swift riders will go at once to every hunting band of Indians yet free upon the prairies. At the same time, riders will go to every agency of the Sioux, Cheyenne and Arapaho to the sunward of the Big Muddy River. The riders will whip their ponies hard. When the ponies stagger at last into the prairie camps and the agency villages, the riders will leap from their backs and will rip open the entry-flaps of each chief's tipi, speaking to him these words of Tatanka Yotanka:

"'It is war. Come to the camp of Sitting Bull which then will be at the big bend of the Rosebud River. Let us all get together and have one more big fight with the soldiers!'"

"Hun-hun-he!" roared the chiefs, deep ⟨voi⟩es bounding from the buffalo skins of the council l⟨odge⟩ ⟨Le⟩t us die as proud men, as freemen, as Indians—⟨…⟩

CUSTER

Will Henry

LEISURE BOOKS   NEW YORK CITY

A LEISURE BOOK®

August 1999

Published by special arrangement with Golden West Literary Agency.

Dorchester Publishing Co., Inc.
276 Fifth Avenue
New York, NY 10001

ISBN 0-8439-4569-9

The name "Leisure Books" and the stylized "L" with design are trademarks of Dorchester Publishing Co., Inc.

Printed in the United States of America.

Yellow Hair

HISTORICAL FOREWORD

. . . The energy and rapidity shown during one of the heaviest snowstorms known to this section of the country, with the temperature below freezing, the gallantry and bravery displayed, resulting in such signal success, reflects the highest credit on the 7th Cavalry . . . and the Major-General Commanding expresses his thanks to the officers and men engaged in the Battle of the Washita, and his special congratulations to their distinguished commander Brevet Major-General George A. Custer for the efficient and gallant service opening the campaign against the hostile Indians north of the Arkansas . . .

Text of General P. H. Sheridan's communique
announcing the Battle of the Washita,
November 27th, 1868

Custer's "signal success" along the Washita may indeed have reflected the "highest credit" upon his "distinguished commanding." But the tongue of White Man's history can be crooked. And the pens of Generals do not always travel in straight lines.

What actually happened that snow-shrouded, shameful dawn along the Washita has not been told.

Not the way Moxtraveto, the trusting Black Kettle of the Southern Cheyenne, would deeply mutter it. Not the way Axhonehe, the sinister Mad Wolf of the Cut-Arm Dog Soldiers, would angrily snarl it. Not the way Monaseetah, the legendary South Plains tribal princess, would hauntingly smile it. And certainly not the way Joshua Kelso, Custer's Indian-killing Chief of Scouts, would soft-spokenly remember it.

It has been told only in Brevet Major-General George Armstrong Custer's self-hallowed, heroic way.

Now it will be told in another way. Scarcely self-hallowed. Hardly heroic. Surely not distinguished. Nor highly creditable.

Now it will be told in *Yellow Hair*'s way.

W. H.

1. Plenty Kills

THE BIG DUN GELDING picked up the weary rhythm of his shuffling gait. His rider tensed, restless eyes quartering the darkened prairie beyond the nervous flick of his mount's ears. Shortly he relaxed, the softness of his voice belying the grimness of the nod which accompanied it.

"There she be, Wasiya. Broad as a squaw's bottom and twice as welcome. I allow we won't have no trouble makin' the fort by moonset now."

Ahead lay the Arkansas. Its broad trace glimmered ghost-white in the moonwash, bringing the smell of the first water since sundown. It had been a long, dry forty miles from Fort Larned back there on the branchwaters of the Pawnee Fork, and the gelding was thirsty. Black nostrils belling gratefully, the big dun went forward.

When the horse had watered, the man turned him to grazing, set himself to packing the bowl of his stone pipe with the bright shags of longcut Burley, alternating the precise slowness of the action with snakefast glances into the outer prairie darknesses. Apparently reassured, he struck the pocket flint to the shagcut, sucked the Burley into soul-satisfying life and settled on his heels to stare along the westward track of the wagon road down which, some forty miles now, lay his destination, Fort Dodge.

Although he was still those forty miles short of hearing Custer put it in his own words, a man already had a fair prime hunch what the palaver down there at the fort

was going to be about. And why the "General" had sent
that Osage scout to summon him to it. In his total years as
a man grown on the short grass, he'd never seen so many
warpaint hostiles as he had in his past week's ride. It figured to be sudden hell on the South Plains, mister, and
nobody but naked red devils stoking the furnaces.

The tall rider shook his head, knocked the emberless
dottle from his squat Sioux pipe. The quick, good sound
of his laugh echoed strangely, lifting Wasiya's curious
head from the belly-deep graze of the river swale. With
the laugh he was on his feet, moving with all the noise
and effort of a six-foot cat.

At his mount's side he paused, his hand checking
swiftly beneath the cinch-loosened saddleblanket to see
that the gelding was cooled out. Satisfied, he grinned
knowingly.

"Sure as sin's for sale in St. Louie, Custer's aimin' to
run them redguts off the Canadian once and for all,
come summer again. Once he's did that there's them
million skinny cows south of the Red River dyin' for a
mouthful of good grass. And them ten million fat Yanks
east of the Big Muddy dyin' for a mouthful of good
beef." He paused again, letting the grin sober with the
final nod.

"Old son, I figure any Texas boy with half a belly and
no brains can get rich bringin' them two appetites together!"

The gelding grunted to the sudden cinching of the
girth, skittered playfully to the mounting weight of the
rider. "Leastways," the thoughtful voice continued, "I
figure you and me can do it—"

He broke his words sharply off as his body stiffened
to the westward swing of his narrowed gaze. Straight
down the line of the wagon road, five, maybe six miles
west, the prairie sky was pinpointed by the rising stain
of a freshly lit nightfire. Grim-lipped, he heeled the gelding into a hammering gallop.

"Leastways we can, happen a few hundred South
Plains Cheyennes don't meanwhile lift our hair higher
than the stink of a stick-poked polecat!"

Big Coon Creek was ordinarily a decently dark and
quiet stream. But at 2.00 A.M. of the morning of November 13, 1868, it was anything but dark and quiet at
the confluence of the Big Coon and the Arkansas.

The bushel-sized blaze of the fire booming so cheerily
on the south banks of the Coon lit up the Santa Fe wagon road for hundreds of feet in either direction, limning
the four figures squatting to its broad glow. It bounced
ruddily off the high-sided army freighter whose corded
load of stovewood and three-span hitch of patient mules
formed the backdrop for the fireside group. Nor was the
unwonted illumination without its fit complement of
heartily raised human voices. The four soldiers were
making oral sign enough to be picked up by a stone-deaf
squaw listening eight miles off the trail and dead upwind.

First Sergeant Ben Henderson, Company B, Seventh
United States Cavalry, graciously passed the glazed clay
jug of Taos Lightning to his immediate inferior, Corporal Willy Hardermann. Having done so, he felt the time
was right for a rousing chorus of the "Battle Hymn of
the Republic."

Privates Toland and MacDougal fought valiantly, if
six keys sour, for the tenor lead while Corporal Hardermann took what was left, making the least of his coon-
hound bass in the effort. The harmony had struggled to
the point where the Lord was about to take a prodigious
whack at the wicked "with his turrible swift sword,'"
when MacDougal, the least saturated of the South Arkansas Woodhauling and Choral Society, broke off his
bid for first-tenor supremacy to gape up the firelit eastern reaches of the Santa Fe Trail.

The sight which dropped MacDougal's jaw easily war-
ranted the dislocation.

Take six foot-three and one hundred and ninety
pounds of bone-gaunt mountain scout clothed in
grease-blackened Cheyenne buckskins, add a slab-rock
face bristled with half an inch of hogwire beard and a
gimlet-mean brace of eyeholes bored alongside a nose as
horn-sharp as a bald eagle's, then blanket the net results

in a coating of alkali trail dirt deep enough to be turned with a moldboard plow and there'd be a middling idea of what MacDougal's jaws were ajar about. Especially if that apparition were mounted on a seventeen-hand giant of a Sioux gelding, unclipped since the past winter and wild-eyed and wicked-looking as a bull elk whistling up six strange cows.

The scout slid the lathered Wasiya into a stiff-legged stop that had his hocks burning horsehide. Without a word or look for the startled soldiers, he stepped off the gelding and went for the wood wagon. Seizing the five-gallon water keg, he lifted it from its leather moorings as easily as though it had been a backstoop dipper. In less time than it took MacDougal to get his molars back together, the offending blaze was drowned out.

"Don't you jackass jaspers know no better than to build up a bonfire in the bellyhole of Injun country?" The question hissed in over the angry spit of the drenched coals. "Happen I couldn't see you was new to the country, I'd swear you was some of Custer's outfit!"

"Yeah?" MacDougal's long legs were coming unwound. "And if we couldn't see you was all buckskin and no bath since last spring, we'd swear you was Custer hisself. The way you come bustin' in here with your fancy mouth flappin' a mile a minute—"

With the suspended observation, the bear-sized private stepped around the steaming firebed.

Fancy-mouthed or not, the newcomer knew when to stop talking. He came into MacDougal with a twisting cat turn. The first sensation the big soldier enjoyed was that of his right arm departing its shoulder socket. Followed a three-second flying journey through the Arkansas night air. Terminating his impromptu nosedive with a five-foot furrow of jaw-turned creek sand, MacDougal came to his feet fighting mad and fanning for his holster.

"Hold up, soldier." The flat warning came from behind the skinning knife which had appeared in the right hand of his adversary. "Right now I ain't gettin' paid to fight white men. You savvy?"

MacDougal, like all salt-worth fighting men, never

bucked the tiger. Not when it was nine steel inches long and trained squarely on his favorite navel. "All right, laddie buck, you're callin' the tune, suppose you strike up your fiddle. This here's a wood detail for Fort Coon, yonder up the crick there. Who the hell are you?"

"*Joshua Kelso*—"

"Joshua Kelso! Oh, sure!" The angry soldier's face relaxed to the sudden spread of the sarcastic grin, his accompanying nod going to his three companions. "Josh, I want you should meet Jed Smith, Jim Bridger and Charlie Bent. Of course you know me, Kit Carson!"

"I ain't goin' to straddle out here arguin' birth certificates with you." The big thumb slid suggestively along the edge of the skinning blade. "I'm Kelso and you'd best believe it. I'll tell you something else you'd best believe, too—"

"Sure. You can trust old Kit, Josh!"

"Shut your damn mouth, Jock." First Sergeant Henderson, moving forward over the smoking debris of the fire, was sobering fast. "He's Kelso, all right. I remember him from last summer when Hancock had him out Injun-huntin' with Custer. How you been, Kelso? What's up? You had Injun trouble up the trail?"

"I ain't had none and I ain't aimin' to have none. But *you're* goin' to. How far's this Fort Coon and how soon can you make it?"

The soldiers were no longer questioning the scout's identity. They were, in fact, doing considerable mental foot-shifting under the nervous impact of their new-found conviction.

Joshua Kelso, for his later day and time, had no less a name than the hairiest of the old Rocky Mountain Rough Brigade. Indeed, it had been Jim Bridger himself who, in recommending the young mountain man as a scout to Custer, had described him as "the Lew Wetzel of Wyomin'." When Old Gabe went that far and fancy in labeling a fellow fur trapper, a man didn't forget it. And as for becoming the enlisted man's hero of any garrison from Fort Huachuca to the Bozeman road, the

surest method was that employed by Joshua Kelso—
killing Indians.

"About six miles, Mr. Kelso." Private Bates Toland,
the teamster, furnished the respectful answer while the
others were still wrestling with the reality of meeting the
shadowy Ota Kte, face to face. "We can make it, come
daylight."

"I allow you'd best make it *come daylight.*"

The faint chill of the emphasis wasn't wasted. Privates
Toland and MacDougal, with Corporal Hardermann,
grabbed their stacked carbines and scuttled for the wood
wagon. Sergeant Henderson, half a jump behind them,
boarded his tethered mount and kicked him back toward
Kelso. The scout shot him a quick look, for the first time
noting the familiar red and white regimental insignia on
the issue saddleblanket.

"I might have knowed you was with the Seventh."
There was that in the disgusted grunt which went a full
set of ricepaper encyclopedias past the bare count of the
words themselves. "Beginning with Custer there ain't
none of you in that outfit that's ever learned to smell a
redskin with your nose less than six inches shy of his
stinkin' shirttail."

"Yeah?" The sergeant's little bid for dignity faltered
under the drive of the dark eyes. "Well, you civilian
scouts can't seem to quit smellin' them. Not even if
they're a hundred miles off."

"I wouldn't let that hundred miles comfort you none."
The grin was bobtailed as a bay lynx. "I just seen Mad
Wolf and three hundred Dog Soldiers not six hours ago.
Maybe forty miles north of where we set."

"Naw! You sure it was Mad Wolf?"

The big scout ignored the question, asked pleasantly,
"Sergeant, you got any good idea why them Injuns calls
me Plenty Kills?"

"You mean them wholesale yarns Custer tells about
how you've killed more of them than the smallpox?"

"Somethin' like that." The voice was still easy. "It's
been overdid by Custer, like most everything he puts his

hand or mouth to. I ain't took to killin' squaws and kids yet, like you army boys."

The trooper set his jaw to the old service insult, wisely chose to give it passing room. He let his question come as his uneasy glance divided itself between the towering scout and the disappearing tailgate of the wood wagon. "What's that to do with you seein' Mad Wolf and them Dog Soldiers?"

Kelso shrugged the answer as quietly as though he'd been asked the time of day. "Somehow Mad Wolf found out Custer had sent for me again. Right off, he tooken himself a personal pledge to put me under before the new grass comes. That's next spring the way they figure things, the same time they allow the Seventh will start after them again."

"Well, them Injuns is always talkin' big."

"Not this one, mister."

"Damn it, Kelso, I sure hope you're wrong."

"I ain't." The noncommittal grunt came as the scout reined Wasiya around. "You'd best get along after your boys. I allow Mad Wolf hisself will foller me. Anyhow, I'll do what I can to lead the main pack of them off'n you. See you downtrail, soldier."

"Cripes Amighty!" the trooper's delayed realization checked his departure. "You mean to say him and *all* them Dog Soldiers is follerin' you personal?"

Once more the dry flick of the grin kicked up the dust track of its passage across the dirt-powdered jaw. "If he ain't, and if he ain't been since first I snuck out'n the Bayou Salade six days gone, I been seein' double a hundred and fifty times over."

Before the sergeant could begin to unravel this bit of prairie arithmetic he found himself staring into nothing but South Arkansas darkness, no longer hearing either the fading clip-clop of the Sioux gelding's unshod hoofs or the hurrying trot-jangle of the wagonmules' trace chains. He was suddenly and unquestionably alone, alone with the muttering Arkansas and the muddy swirl of Big Coon Creek—and maybe three hundred of Mad Wolf's Cheyenne Dog Soldiers.

With a startled imprecation which echoed more of
present Cheyenne panic than prior Indian-proof conviction, First Sergeant Benjamin Franklin Henderson,
Company B, Seventh United States Cavalry, surrendered the field and fled without shame or evident shred of
regimental regret toward the dubious sanctuary of sod-
roofed Fort Coon.

2. Mad Wolf

THE EMBERS of the wagonfire still fingered the Arkansas
night air with the wan tendrils of their blue-wet woodsmoke when the quiet of the Big Coon confluence was
disturbed for the second time within the hour.

This time the noise was not so easily catalogued. Not
at any rate by a white ear. It was in fact a sound seldom
heard by fair-skinned settler or soldier lucky enough to
live to report it: the savage, animal-grunting sound of
three hundred Cheyenne war ponies slashing at a flat
gallop through the shallows of a South Plains tributary.

The greasy cloudfront of a storm building rapidly to
the southwest rolled the Arkansas moon in its leaden
wash, cut the light short off and made a nebulous blob
of the close-packed Cheyenne horsemen. There was still,
however, enough light to distinguish the faces and figures of the four Indians who rode forward to the soldier's fire.

The leader was of medium height, lean as a sun-dried
bone, dark-skinned as the smokehole of a Sioux hunting
lodge. His slender body, naked but for a doeskin
breechclout and wolfskin shoulder robe, was as muscle-

writhing as a prairie rattler's. His axe blade of a face was as high-cheeked as a Mongol Khan's, the tight leather of its skin entirely free of paint or charcoal. He wore none of the usual adornments of the horse-Indian warrior, his sole personal ornament being a gleaming Sun God medallion of Apache silver, pendant from a massive throat chain of the same metal. This was Mad Wolf.

Contrariwise, the first of his three henchmen was bedizened with every war-trail accoutrement: white eagle-feather bonnet, dyed horsehair shirt and leggin tassels, bear-claw necklaces, hawk-bone hair skewers and the like. He was a brute-faced giant, dwarfing the others with his great bulk, and his name was Etapeta, Big Body.

The third Cheyenne, Yellow Buffalo, was squat and pale-skinned. Also flashily beaded and feathered, he affected as his personal Big Medicine a war bonnet fashioned from an ocher-daubed buffalo skull.

The fourth horseman was very old. Dressed in the simple elkskin shirt and breeches of the rank-and-file Dog Soldier, he wore three black eagle feathers downhanging at the rear of his head—the ominous trademark of his illfamed lodge.

The dark-skinned chief signaled to Yellow Buffalo, who spoke gently to the old man. The latter swung down off his pony and as he did, the animal backed away, revealing the lead rope which attached it to the cantle ring of Yellow Buffalo's cavalry saddle. He, too, dismounted now, took the old man's arm and guided him carefully toward the fire's bed.

"*Hovahan hoesta!*" snapped the chief, the guttural bark of the Cheyenne tongue stinging like a lash. "Never mind the fire, you fool! I can see that from here. Take him to the tracks over there. Those are the marks of that yellow demon Ota Kte rides."

Heovhotoa, the Yellow Buffalo, nodded his horned skullpiece and led the old man quickly to a line of hoofprints clearly etched in the damp clay of the creek bank.

"*Hehe!*" Yellow Buffalo's shout was triumphant. "These

are his prints, all right. A blind man couldn't miss them.
Not with that crooked right forefoot!"

"*Nenano ononistahe,* shut your mouth and let a blind
man see them, then." The dark-skinned chief snarled the
order with a lip-lifted grimace which would have identified him even if his next words had not. "Mad Wolf is
followed by nothing but fools. Tell me, old one," the
ugly sound went out of the voice, "am I not right? Are
we not very close to him?"

Hokom-ooene, the Blind Coyote, let his thin fingers
run lightly over the rim of Wasiya's hoofprints. He
rubbed and blew upon the delicate members that they
might serve him yet more faithfully and felt, once more,
the inch-deep impressions of the Sioux gelding's prints.

"*Hehe,* Axhonehe is right. Ota Kte was here."

· "*Etoneeso?* How long ago?"

"A very short time. *Onehetto.* There were soldiers
here, too. I smell the iron on their mules' feet. *Vehoe-
map,* the smell of white man's whiskey is here on the
ground as well. *Hehe!*" the old man's cackle picked up
interest. "Maybe they left it behind. Maybe I can find it.
Let me smell around here—"

"How many soldiers?" The blunt question came from
the silent giant, Etapeta.

"Three, no wait, four. Yes, four." His answer came
from Yellow Buffalo. "One a big man like you, Etapeta.
They've gone up this stream, one riding a horse. The
other three in the wagon. *Hee-ahh,* father?" the anxious
query turned back to Blind Coyote. "Have you found
that whiskey yet?"

Mad Wolf scowled, whirled his roan pinto hard
around. "You go," he directed Yellow Buffalo. "Take
Etapeta and the old man with you. Many thanks, father," he called to Blind Coyote, accompanying the acknowledgement with the quick touch of the fingers of
the left hand to the brow, which was the Plains Indian's
sign of highest respect. "*Zeo notaseas,* I go from this
place now!"

It was Big Body's turn to scowl. "You are going after
Ota Kte some more now? Without Etapeta?"

Big Body was as simple of mind as a child, though hardly as innocent. He was a chief by virtue of his one talent—splitting white skulls with his four-foot war club, a piece of bois d'arc thick as a man's wrist and crotching a six-pound Navajo silversmith's anvil in its forked end.

Mad Wolf turned on him. "I'm tired of telling you. *Naseintamo,* I'm sick of you. Now hear it once more—" He threw his pony into that of the hulking brave, his words grating like a Conestoga axle long without antelope tallow.

"You were with us when we caught that Osage of Yellow Hair's. You heard him talk. You heard him tell us Ota Kte was ordered once more to guide Yellow Hair against our people.

"Then you heard my vow. You were there at the Sun Dance, remember, Emptyhead? I pledged myself to kill Ota Kte before the new grass came. Before he could again lead Yellow Hair into our camp. Well, that's where I'm going now, to kill him. *Ononistahe!*"

"Oh, yes. Good, good!" Big Body was virtually slobbering through the loose-lipped disfiguration which passed for a smile in Dog Soldier circles. "I'll go along with you. I want to see you do it. I want to work on his head with this, after you've taken his hair."

With the words, the big brave whirled the misshapen war club in a giant swing which came perilously close to decapitating his enraged leader.

"*Nonotovetto!*" Mad Wolf rasped at Yellow Buffalo. "Get this idiot away from me. Take him and leave in a hurry!" The Dog Soldier chief raised his rifle. "*Onehetto!* Go at once or I'll kill him where he sits."

Yellow Buffalo knew the sound of his chief's voice in terminal earnest. He knew that when Mad Wolf's ordinary snarl dropped into that deep growl, the time for tarrying was long past.

"We go," he signaled, hurriedly. "How many braves do you want us to take?"

"Take a hundred. Beat the ponies with your gun butts. You can catch the soldiers easily."

Yellow Buffalo hesitated, looking skyward. As he

'did, the last quarter of the moon foundered in the engulfing tide of the thunderhead, and the first fat spatters of rain exploded in the dust of the trail.

"I don't know, Axhonehe. It is pretty black now. How will we follow them with any certainty if we beat the ponies and go fast?"

"Follow the little stream," growled Mad Wolf. "Like I'm going to follow the big one. A white man will always ride along water when he can. *Nataemhon*, good hunting, brother."

With an impatient gesture, Mad Wolf wheeled his roan and raced down the Arkansas. Behind him, the hammer of eight hundred unshod pony hoofs drummed the deepworn ruts of the Santa Fe Trail.

The sound died aborning in the sudden cannonading of the South Plains thunder. The moon was completely covered before the first volley of the thunder echoed away across the Arkansas.

Thirty seconds later, the rain was sheeting down in a driving blackness six shades deeper than the pit.

3. Lieutenant Colonel Custer

MAD WOLF'S terse prophecy to the contrary, there *were* white men who did not "always ride along the water when they could," and Joshua Kelso was one of them.

It took a man fifteen miles out of his way to cut inland from Big Coon Creek to ride the dry route down onto Dodge. It was harder on a tired horse than the straightaway wet route along the river and tougher on a weary rider's saddle-aching seat.

But it sure saved wear and tear on a man's hair.

It was 5.00 A. M. when he topped out on the rearing bluffs which gave the first view of the Arkansas from the dry-route approach. The storm which had cut his tracks out from under Mad Wolf's Cheyenne trailers had grumbled on off toward the South Platte, leaving the prairie clean-washed and brilliant.

A mile south and east lay the straggling compound of board-and-batten barracks, Sibley tents and sutler shacks that was Fort Dodge. Another mile south, the rising smokes of the daybreak coffee fires, ash-gray against the dirty mushroom cluster of Pittsburghs and Conestoga freighters, located the Santa Fe teamsters' wagoncamp which always marked the spot where the wet and dry routes of the Trail came together.

It struck him that the freighters' spread was nearly ten times the size it had been last year, in spite of the fact it was late fall and past the peak of commercial travel along the old South Road.

Well, a man could figure that quick enough. Nobody but a slickbrain idiot would be staying out on the plains now. There looked to be no less than five hundred people shantied-up down there below the fort and it didn't take a set of mountain eyes to see they were ninety per cent of them sod-hut farmer families driven onto the River by the Indian stir.

These things his slant gaze recorded in one compass-swinging glance. After that he let his eyes linger on a sight which always took a High Plainsman's heart no matter he'd seen it so many times before.

He nodded. The tension of his jaw muscles, tooth-set for the better part of the past week, eased.

If there was a God, and somehow a man didn't always feel for certain there was, this would be his country. Born to it, as he had been, he had still never been able to describe it until the past summer.

And even then it was a simple-souled Negro woman who gave him the proper words.

Custer had just come on from Fort Riley with his omnipresent body servant, Eliza, an ageless colored woman

who struck Kelso as being nearly as old as God and anyway half as smart. He and the little officer had taken the
round-eyed woman to the bluffs atop which he now
paused, and Custer had jokingly asked, "Well, Lize,
what do you think of Kansas?" expecting her to protest
the emptiness of the vast lands.

He smiled as the woman's answer nudged his memory.
"Well sah, General sah, when de Lawd made dis hyar
world he found out dat he'd made one mistake. Dat was
dat he hadn't made hisself no garden. So he jest went to
work and made hisself a garden and I allow we just calls
it Kansas!"

He shrugged off the brief picture and jammed his
moccasined heels into Wasiya's ribs. The smile was gone,
the alkali mask resettled in its place.

Three minutes later he was loping past an indignant
brace of maingate sentries, advising them if they didn't
like his precipitate entry they could take their troubles
to Captain Custer—with Josh Kelso's compliments.

The gate detail was still untangling these instructions
as he stepped off Wasiya and handed the sweat-stained
hackamore rope to a third trooper inside the compound.
The latter was the prompt recipient of some further sentiments along the same salty mountain line.

"Rustle up a groom for this hoss, soldier. And see
you put him in a box by hisself. He'll kill another hoss
quick as he'll look at him."

Turning to stride down the raw dirt street marked
"Hq. Co. 7th Cav.," he flung a parting crumb of advice
to the mouthhanging recruit. "And see you don't crowd
him none yourself, happen you enjoy army life in the
Far West. He ain't famous for limitin' his hostilities to
hossflesh."

Custer's name caught his eye at the third quarters.
But it wasn't the name which held him, frowning
thoughtfully. The last he'd seen of the "General" he'd
been operating under his permanent rank of captain and
having hell's own time holding on to that. Then word
got into the mountains he'd been court-martialed and
suspended from rank and command for one year. Some

tomfool business about having left his command bad fed
and busted up in Fort Wallace while he traipsed off to
Fort Riley to catch up on his homelife with Mrs. Custer.
And getting himself waylaid en route by old Satanta and
a flock of his Kiowa badbloods and losing a sergeant
and two men.

That had sounded like Custer, all right. But now, so
did that neat new sign pegged up there alongside his office door. By damn, you had to hand it to the little rooster. Rank-broke from brevet major general to captain,
two years ago. Then busted from captain to plumb nothing less than ten months gone. And now there it was,
fresh as porchswing paint and twice as sassy.

"Lt. Col. G. A. Custer, Cmdg."

Josh turned into the little path, so precisely bordered
with its whitewashed creek stones. It was perhaps thirty
feet long, no more. But when a man's mind wants to, it
can move a long ways in a short spell. Especially backward.

As he walked, he was balancing his surprise at the
General's five-grade promotion against the growing total
of his own doubts.

Adding what he'd heard all summer about the South
Plains tribes being out to what he'd seen of the big drift
of warpaint hostiles he'd just ridden through, a man had
to allow there must be close to seventy-five hundred
warriors camped astride the Santa Fe Trail and daring
the whole army to come along out of Fort Dodge and
move them off of it.

Given that much of a fill-in, a man didn't need to be
any redskin genius to reckon what was in store for him
beyond that office door yonder. Not if he knew Custer
the way Josh Kelso knew him.

For all the long-haired cavalryman had a War-Be-
tween-the-States reputation second only to Little Phil
Sheridan's, a man who'd scouted for him had to admit
that when it came to Indian-savvy the "Boy General"
wouldn't have ranked a chevron higher than a two-stripe

corporal. Naturally, you couldn't help liking the crazy-eyed little devil. He was a sure enough he-coon for all his buckskin fringes, cowboy gauntlets, red silk sashes and special-made big black hats.

But he-coon or no, to Josh's careful way of figuring such things Custer was always a sight too quick to set his dandy foot into the buffalo chips before looking to see if they were still fresh-wet.

The backsweep of his thoughts tightened his jaw, slowed his hand as it started toward the weathered door panels. A moment, only, the hand hesitated, then descended with plank-bouncing force.

"Come in, come in! That door will open quite readily, sir! You don't have to beat it through. It's equipped with excellent hinges."

Josh grinned. That was Custer for you. It made no never-mind to him *who* was knocking. It could be Private Jed Jones, General Sherman, Mad Wolf or God Almighty. The idea was, come in, state your business and don't slam the door on your way out. The "General" was a busy man. No matter that if he was as busy as usual it would be in scribbling one of those ten-page, two-a-day letters to his precious "Libby," or to old General Walter Scott Hancock, running on about how come he hadn't quite got around to shagging Black Kettle and Satanta and the whole Cheyenne and Kiowa Nations clean into the North Canadian.

He lifted the latch and stepped in.

Custer was at his desk writing furiously. He didn't bother to put a comma to the galloping scrawl, much less look up from it. All the scout got was a head-jerked, "Be with you in a minute, Sergeant. As you were——"

He took the "sergeant's minute" to eye the Colonel's new quarters and found them a faithful tintype of the studied bareness of the ones he'd had as a Captain at Fort Riley.

The same tired pictures backed the big desk: his much worshiped wife as "Elizabeth Clift Bacon, age 14," prim and schoolmarm-pretty in a French lace kerchief and starched Pilgrim collar; "Brigadier General G.

A. Custer, 1863," left hand jammed Napoleonwise into the double-buttoned dicky of his Union dress tunic; "Elizabeth, Custer and Tom Custer (standing)," with the great man as a two-star major general and young Tom as a one-bar second lieutenant.

The same Spartan row of straightback chairs stood at attention along the wall siding the desk. On another wall were the familiar big-framed chromos of Sherman and Sheridan, the Boy General's patron saints in the War Department. And there on the floor was the same mangy white buffalo robe—the one Satanta, the White Bear of the Arkansas Kiowas, had given him as an eternal peace offering last summer—two weeks before ganging up with the Cheyenne Dog Soldiers to knock loose his boyish backside down on the Cimarron.

Coming to the General himself, a man couldn't see he'd changed much.

Maybe his hair was a mite longer and not so yellow. Maybe his forehead had gained another inch in pushing back the skirmish line of his scalp against his famous curls. Maybe, too, his jug-handle ears stuck out more than ever and his needle-long nose twisted itself more and more to the left. But his twitching, woman-small mouth still hid under a sunbleached droop of haystack mustache and the little ambush of beard on his chin still did its damndest to make him look like he wasn't weak-jawed as a pocket gopher. Top all that with the fact that his varmint-close eyes were as wild and coyote-looking as ever, and a man had a fair idea of the way the "Boy General" sat that present morning of November 13, 1868.

"Joshua, by Heaven!"

The expletive, strongest in a vocabulary religiously disciplined to the proper desires of Mrs. Custer, broke with the quick, friendly flash of the widely spaced upper teeth which hallmarked the famed Custer grin. It came backed with a catlike step around the desk and the firm grip of his small hand.

"I hadn't an idea in the world you would make it before the fifteenth. But it's good you did, sir, it's good you did! Sit down, sit down. What on earth were you riding, Joshua, a Cheyenne relay?"

"Well uh, nope, General, same old hoss—"

He found himself floundering in the backwash of schoolboy awkwardness this man always set up in him. He stood there grinning and arching his back like a tabby-cat getting her tailroot tickled. Damn it all, anyway. A man could sit around all winter hating the little gamecock's innards and vowing he'd never cinch a saddle in his service again. Then the minute he grabbed your hand and broke out that pegtoothed grin, you were dead. You'd not only follow him to hell and back, but kiss his foot for the chance.

"Do you mean to say that same scabrous yellow monster?" Custer was galloping on. "That slab-sided, slatribbed Sioux Percheron? That spavined excuse for a misbegotten jackass with which you won every enlisted dollar in Kansas Territory last summer? What was it you called him? Blizzard Boy? Snow King?"

That was Custer for you again. Talking faster and fancier than a hardshell Baptist preacher unselling a flock of sodbusters on sin. Asking six questions a second, before a man could get a civil answer in sideways.

"Winter Giant," Josh managed. "*Wasiya*, in Sioux."

"Ah yes, that's the horse—Winter Giant. Well, no matter, Joshua. You've won your last wager with him in my command!"

The big scout smiled. He couldn't remember the General ever having called him Josh or Kelso. Always "Joshua."

"No sir, by Heaven," Custer thundered on. "Not another dollar for you and that Prairie Pegasus! I've just got an Arab racer from Sheridan. Most magnificent buffalo horse mortal man ever sat to. I'll match you either on a killing run or a marked mile. Yesterday, Major Coates and myself—you remember Coates, my assistant surgeon? Well, yesterday Coates and I ran twelve straight in the afternoon alone! All bulls, mind you. No cows or heifers. Ah, you'll see, Joshua, you'll see—"

"Beg pardon, General," he fumbled the interruption,

"but I'm bound to report a mite of trouble downtrail before we get onto old times. You've got a sergeant and three men standin' hipdeep in Dog Soldiers down yonder to Fort Coon."

"What the devil, Joshua?" There was the second choice in the General's aseptic selection of strong language. "Why didn't you say so instead of standing there baiting me about buffalo horses?"

Josh cut the inner grin loose once more. Trust Custer. He didn't mean it to be that way but he could lie himself off any spot you could corner him on and swear over signature he'd trapped *you* there!

"What's the trouble down there? That was a wood detail, eh? Let's see—Fort Coon—ten men and a sergeant there—plus Henderson and my three—" He broke the thought abruptly. "What Indians, Joshua? How many? How long ago?"

Josh rattled it to him not forgetting a moccasin print of what had passed since he received Custer's message, his own mind as sharp for "red" soldier incident as was the officer's for white. He concluded his report with a jawthrust postscript for the Osage scout.

"That's about it, General, savin' for one thing. You better bury that infernal Osage of yours pretty deep in the woodpile. I mean the one you sent out to bring me in."

"How's that, Joshua? He found you, did he not?" Custer's voice showed the nettle it always did when the question was called on him or any under his orders. The tall scout took the nettle in stride, not even wincing as he stepped on it.

"He did, and quick."

"Well, sir?"

"Well sir, he found Mad Wolf a shade quicker."

"What the devil do you mean, man?"

That "man" was another tip for you. The General was bridling for sure now. He had a temper shorter than a stepped-on polecat's patience and nobody had better reason to remember it than Josh Kelso. But for the moment his own store of restraint was tolerably short-stocked.

"Them damn Dog Soldiers got wind of me comin' back to work for you. That's how come Mad Wolf tooken hisself that lodge oath to put me under. You can bet I didn't tell them!"

Custer frowned, his keen mind prying at the full sense of the scout's words. "I see. You're saying that Short Bear did then? Is that it?"

"Whatever his name is, yeah."

Custer nodded, temper subsiding with the soft agreement. "Well, perhaps he did at that, Joshua. He isn't back yet."

Josh's eyes tightened. "Sometimes I talk too much," he grunted. "The poor devil. I allow I had him wrong." He paused, then added grimly. "Well, he talked anyhow. But likely he done it with his feet in a fire and his face in the flashpan of a pistol."

The officer's pale eyes flared. His tongue flicked the surface of his lower lip. "What's this 'flashpan of a pistol' business? Something new?"

"Not for Mad Wolf. He's got one of them old single-loadin' Henry Derringers, with a primin' pan big enough to drink coffee out'n. He piles her up with Du Pont and triggers her off in your ear. She spits flame enough to roast a rack of hump ribs and belches loud enough to jar a ten-pound rock off a shelf. Time he's cut loose with that dose enough times, a man would tell the devil where God lived."

Custer swung to the door, whipped it open, bellowed for the corporal of the guard. When the wide-eyed trooper had raced off down the company street with the orders for Fort Coon's relief, he turned on Josh, dismissing him as curtly as he had greeted him effusively.

"All right, Joshua, I'm glad you're here in time for the fun. You'll excuse me now. Check with Captain Benteen after you've cleaned up. He'll bring you up to date. We've got a fine red fish due in Dodge tonight. You can watch me fry him!"

"What you aimin' to fry him in, General?"

The question, for all its apparent innocence, was not

lost on Custer. His answer came with the obvious relish of high confidence.

"A kettle, sir! A splendid, big *Black Kettle!*"

Josh chucked his head, threw the little half salute he reserved for Custer. "All right, General. Any special chef's directions for me?"

"I told you, man. Check with Benteen. Check with Benteen—"

Custer was at his desk scribbling again, the pen scratching across the rough paper at a hell-for-leather clip that would have done full justice to a rush call for all the reserves west of the Big Muddy, his thoughts as far from Joshua Kelso and Mad Wolf's Dog Soldiers as the distance by express courier from Fort Dodge to Fort Riley—and Mrs. Custer.

Josh watched him a moment, then eased out the door to stand with his broad back to the closed panels. Shortly he shrugged, and moved quickly down the rock bordered pat.

All right. If Custer wanted to have himself a Cheyenne fish fry, that was his business. But when it came to dropping a High Plains lunker the size of Black Kettle into the greasepot, a man better stand plenty far back from the fire.

He'd better, happen he didn't want to get splashed his sudden death of hot Indian fat.

4. Bad Medicine Night

CAPTAIN FREDERICK W. BENTEEN, Custer's executive and fifth in command, was a plain-faced, quiet man and as cautious and head-steady as his illustrious senior was rash and flighty. He received Josh, not as an old buffalo-hunting or horse-racing crony, but as an officer of the United States Army briefing a hired civilian professional.

"Come in, Kelso. Glad to see you. You've talked with Colonel Custer, I gather."

Josh took the proffered hand. "Thanks, Captain. Yeah, I seen him. Didn't learn nothin' though, savin' what a peecuttin' new buffalo hoss he's got. He don't change none."

"Unfortunately." The officer's agreement was meant just the way it sounded. "I suppose you've been sent to me for the bad news."

"Somewhat, I reckon. All I know is he called me in. I allow he wouldn't have, happen he just wanted to race buffalo hosses."

"You 'allow' right, Kelso. Here, sit down, man. Have a cigar. We might as well be comfortable."

"By damn, they're pure Habanas!" The scout removed the big Corona Corona from the cedar box with a reverence reserved to a breed brought up on Burley, buffalo chips and broomstraw. "Lookit the color of that baygold leaf!"

"The Colonel's compliments." The officer's smile broke a little wearily. "General Sherman keeps sending them to him though he knows as well as you and I that Custer never smoked in his life."

"Nor chawed, nor swore, nor guzzled," added the scout. "He's sure enough a rare-clean bird, ain't he, Captain?"

"Yes, Kelso, I really believe Colonel Custer is the most moral man I ever knew."

"Uh huh—" The fleeting sunbreak of the grin winked at the stolid cavalryman over the edge of the Habana's blue cloud. "Maybeso, Captain. All the same I'll wager Missus Custer's got her work cut out for her!"

"I beg your pardon, Kelso?"

Benteen wasn't sure whether an *entendre* had been doubled or not. Was taking no chance on the distaff side of the Seventh having been insulted.

"No offense, Captain. I was just thinkin' the General's got a bad eye for three things. Two of which is fancy hossflesh and flashy women. A man's got to do somethin' with his talents."

Benteen nodded, satisfied the honor of the Colonel's lady was secure.

"What's the third thing you say he's got a bad eye for, Kelso?"

"Walkin' into *wickmunkes*," growled the big scout, the smile long gone from his dark eyes.

"That's an Indian word of some sort—"

"It is," said Josh. "It means 'traps.' "

"Indian traps, eh?" Benteen shook his head slowly. "I know what you mean, Kelso. My God, I know what you mean." The hopeless feeling of the gesture was compounded by the tension in the tired voice. "He'll get us all killed, one day."

"Not while I'm scoutin' for you, Captain."

The denial was flat and quick. It held no hint of boast or joke. It was just a proud, child-simple statement of professional fact.

"I appreciate that, Kelso. And I'll remember it." Benteen played the cards of his confidence face up, embarrassing the scout.

"Uh, sure, Captain. I know. Thanks. Uh, what's the details on this here thing?"

Benteen stubbed his cigar, leaned quickly forward, once more the impersonal executive officer.

"The situation here has altered rapidly since you left. This spring General Hancock was relieved and Sheridan succeeded him in command of the Department of the Missouri. That's us, Kelso."

The big scout cocked his head attentively, and Benteen continued.

"Last January, prior to his dismissal, Hancock negotiated a good treaty with the Indians at Medicine Lodge Creek, guaranteeing them, through the Indian Bureau, one million dollars for immediate relief as well as arms and ammunition for the spring buffalo hunt. It looked to most of us here as though the worst was over."

"However, the minute Sheridan took over he had the appropriation cut in half and its administration turned over to the War Department. In direct treaty violation, he withheld all arms and ammunition from the Indians and, since Hancock had burned their main camp and all their supplies the previous fall, they were soon desperate.

"At this juncture, Agents Wynkoop for the Cheyenne and Leavenworth for the Kiowa succeeded in forcing the Department to grant them discretion in issuing limited arms—"

The officer paused as Josh frowned and spat disgustedly. He relaxed and continued only when the scout's lancing spittle rang the bell of the office spittoon.

"On August first, Wynkoop made the first of his issue, not to his Cheyennes, but to Little Raven's Arapahos; a matter of one hundred Lancaster Rifles, two hundred pistols, fifteen kegs of powder and twenty thousand caps. Bear in mind now," Benteen pointed the emphasis with his frayed cigar, "that not one weapon was issued Black Kettle's Cheyenne, the principal belligerents, you will recall, of last summer."

"I never thought so," said Josh, levelly. "Black Kettle ain't a *bad* Injun, and never has been. Them buzzards give us all that hell last summer was old White Bear's

Kiowa and Mad Wolf's Dog Soldiers. You boys ain't never learned to tell a regular Cheyenne from a Dog Soldier."

"We won't argue that point again, Kelso."

Benteen's too-quick reprimand deepened the scout's frown.

By God, they would never learn. Let a hundred hottail bucks hit the warpath and the army would jump the nearest meat camp full of friendly squaws. Let that damned White Bear or that hatchet-headed Axhonehe get out a few-score renegade Kiowa or three-feathered Dog Soldiers and go to killing settlers along some out-prairie stream, and Custer would pile his cavalry into the closest big village of peace-treaty Indians, killing everything they caught in their sights, down to and including kids and camp dogs.

No man hated a bad Indian better than Josh Kelso. But every time you killed a good Indian you made ten bad ones. Nobody knew that better than Josh Kelso, either. But the damned army—

The angry scout's thoughts were checked by Benteen's continued briefing.

"Now, then. The night of August seventh, Black Kettle came into Fort Hays to protest his great friendship. I have here the transcript of that masterpiece if you'd care to see it."

Josh nodded and Benteen passed him the document. His wide lips moved haltingly as he deciphered the precise army penmanship:

A LETTER OF TRANSCRIPT, FROM MOXTAVETO, BLACK KETTLE, CHIEF OF THE SOUTHERN CHEYENNE, TO THE OFFICER COMMANDING:

Fort Hays, Kans. Terr.,
9:00 P.M., Aug. 7, 1868

COPY TO:
A.A.G., F. B. Weir,
Fort Harker, Ind. Terr.,
Hq. Dept. of the Missouri,
P. H. Sheridan, Lt. Gen. Cmdg:

> *. . . Black Kettle loves his white soldier brothers and*
> *his heart feels glad when he meets them and shakes*
> *their hands in friendship. The white soldiers ought*
> *to be glad all the time, because their ponies are so*
> *strong and because they have so many guns and so*
> *much to eat. All other Indians may take the war trail*
> *but Black Kettle will forever keep friendship with his*
> *white brother. . . .*

M/SGT. J. EDWARDS,
CO. A,
SEVENTH CAV.

A. J. SMITH, COL. CMDG.

"Well? That sound like a bad Injun to you?" The big
scout returned the pathetic paper to Benteen's desk and
sat back to draw on his faltering cigar.

"Well!" echoed the officer sarcastically, "three days
later the Cheyenne began to kill on the Solomon. Fifteen
settlers killed and five women carried off. There's no
question in our minds that it was Black Kettle, and no
question that he got the guns from Little Raven. *Sic
semper Moxtaveto!*"

It was clear from the little hand flourish with which
the officer signaled his conclusion that he was pleased
with his success at phrase-turning. Josh wasn't impressed.

"What's that 'sick simper Black Kettle'?" he drawled.
"Latin for 'never trust a Cheyenne.' "

"My sentiments, precisely," grunted the lean-faced
scout. "Providin' you know what Cheyenne you're talkin' about. What else you got?"

"That's about it. When Sheridan got the report on
that raid, he moved his headquarters to the terminus of
the Kansas Pacific at Fort Hays. He has been there since
September building up his command and setting up a
big field depot about one hundred miles south of here
—place called Camp Supply."

Josh had never heard of the place, reckoned he never
would again. That he would, indeed, hear of it again, and
in fact live to wish he never had heard of it in any way,

shape or form, was naturally beyond his knowledge of the moment.

"Looks like they mean to make an end of it once and for all. That it, Captain?"

"That's it. Custer's pushing Sheridan for immediate command, and of course he'll get it. I don't have to tell you where that leaves us."

"Nope. You follerin' him and me leadin' him," grimaced Kelso. "And seventy-five hundred hostile Injuns waitin' for him to waltz us into their blue-ribbon *wickmunke*, come spring and the new grass."

Benteen stood up, signaling the end of the interview. "Right, with one small exception."

Josh caught the inflection, returned the officer's steady gaze. "So? How's that?"

"You recall last year Custer pooh-poohed your warning not to try fighting a summer campaign?"

"Naturally. You can't catch an Injun, much less kill him, when his ponies is grass-sassy and his own belly and the whole damn prairie is full of fat cow."

"Naturally," Benteen echoed. "Well, three weeks ago I transmitted Custer's request to Sheridan for the winter campaign you insisted on last year. Sheridan and Sherman have both approved it."

"Good, by damn!" His first reaction was genuine, his last, hard-grinned. "Of course the General gives me full credit for the idea?"

Benteen, never one to multiply a meaning, no matter how obvious, ignored the knowing grin. "I really don't know, Kelso. It wasn't in the transcript I prepared. Suppose you ask him?"

"Thanks, Captain." He slid his bone-weary buttocks off the split-oak seat of the office chair, headed for the door, then paused thoughtfully.

"Say, what's old Black Kettle comin' in again for? Make another peace spiel?"

"Undoubtedly."

"Hang it, what's the matter with the General that he would leave him do it? Can't he see he's never goin' to get anyplace talkin' to them one day and killin' their women the next? Is he plumb blind?"

"Just in *one* eye."

The officer's quiet emphasis caught and held his narrow stare. He let the little silence fatten ahead of his short challenge.

"Which eye, Captain?"

"One of your 'three bad ones,' I'm afraid."

"Such as?"

"There's a girl—"

"Not an Injun, for hell's sake?" The scout's question leapt with the quick denial of its own statement. "By God, I don't believe it. It ain't possible!"

"It is with this girl, Kelso."

The sober-faced officer paused, mustering his inadequate vocabulary reserves for the effort.

"Kelso, she is the most fantastically beautiful woman I have ever seen!"

The scout watched him, suspicious he was essaying a clumsy sally outside his accustomed fort of stodginess. He decided, short quick, that he wasn't.

"You been away from white women too long, Captain." The knowing headchuck put the smile to the words. "You know what they say when the squaws start lookin' good to you."

"I beg your pardon, Kelso!"

"Sorry, Captain." He respected this officer and knew the feeling was mutual. He intended it should stay that way. "You figure the General will actually give the old chief another chance to talk tonight?"

"In a manner of speaking, yes. You know how he loves to display that bright mind of his. He's been drooling over the prospect for the past week. He'll let the old man talk himself out, then he'll cut him to pieces, Custer-style."

"Maybe, maybe not," Josh shrugged. "Pretty hard to chop up a good Injun kettle when it's as old and smoke-black as Moxtaveto."

"We'll see. Leave the door open, Kelso."

"She's open. See you downtrail, Captain—"

With a nod, the scout was gone. His gaunt, high shoulders hunched nervously to the swift, loose swing of his narrow-hipped gait, leaving the officer to stare after him and wonder how a man could sound and talk so like a man—yet look and walk so like a wolf!

Josh finished his inspection of the quarters granted Wasiya in the officers' stableyard. Finding them superior to those furnished the men in the enlisted barracks, he promptly chose to sleep with his horse in preference to Custer's troopers—a not uncommon selection for his soldier-sensitive breed.

He slept like a six-foot sawlog, awakening eight hours later to the eye-squinting demand of the sun slanting over the sill of the boxstall door. After saddling Wasiya, he swung up and guided him across the parade yard toward the sutler's store, his refreshed mind once more taking up the backtrail to his present position.

He had come down to Dodge expecting a repeat of Custer's performance of last summer. After all, it was standard army procedure. There would be five winter months of rest at the respectable scout-pay rate of seventy-five dollars a month. Then a pleasant six months of Indian-chasing and buffalo-hunting across the friendly plains of the South Arkansas. A man would wind up with his hair a year longer and as safe as money in the Mastin Bank of Kansas City. He would, too, have had a government-guided tour of the best rangelands in the Indian Nation. And could have taken his own sweet time to pick out just the stretch of grass suited to his personal cow-purposes, protected all the way by six troops of prime grade U.S. Cavalry. Plenty of chance and to spare, any way you figured it, for a half-smart Texas boy to set himself up in the North Canadian cow business.

That was the picture that had popped into his head the minute the General's Osage had found him over in the South Park country. But what Benteen had just slapped to him was a horse of a far-off color. The way the wind set now, a man would be damn lucky to collect three measly months' pay and save his cussed hair.

He turned Wasiya in at the hitching rack in front of Bob Wright's Store. Seeing the half-dozen horses standing, rein-looped at the sun-blistered hitching rail, he grunted his satisfaction. Good, by damn. Those were mountain horses, and they meant that inside there would be at least four or five sons who could give him more information in a minute than Custer and Benteen could in a month. He recognized Bill Wilson's broken-down bay, Jim Hickok's fancy black Morgan, Apache Bill's glass-eyed calico stud and that stringhalted crowbait of California Joe's. Good again, by God. Boys like that could fill a man in quicker than a cat could wink.

So, all right. Maybe the situation wasn't as bad as it looked.

In the ensuing half-hour with his fellow professionals and in the clay jug of Taos Lightning always party to any such gathering of the curdled cream of the frontier, he found his hopes well justified. The situation *was not* as bad as it looked.

It was a hell of a lot worse.

The whole short-grass country from old Fort Harker to Fort Lyon at the mouth of the Picketwire where it emptied into the Arkansas had been a battleground all summer. The Kiowa, Comanche, Arapahoe, Cheyenne and Apache were out, and making like they aimed to stay out. Charlie Bent, the two-timing Cheyenne breed, was keying-up the whole mess by running guns and powder to Mad Wolf and the Dog Soldiers who, as Josh knew, were spearheading the rebellion.

The Barlow Sanderson Stage Line, running from Kansas City to Santa Fe, had abandoned its route in early May. Come late June, the Butterfield outfit had had to close out its Smokey Hill run and route its California traffic through southern Texas. All told, counting in close to two thousand northern Hankpapa Sioux and Wind River Arapahoe who had drifted down to help their southern brothers run the last of the "white buffalo killers" back to St. Louis, Apache Bill and the others fig-

ured there were some eight thousand hostile bucks
swarming the plains south and west of Dodge.

Josh scowled bitterly at this estimate, backing as it
did his own guess of seventy-five hundred, and counter-
ing Custer's confident claim that he had no more than
twenty-five hundred of Satanta's Kiowas and Black Kettle's Cheyennes to put down.

He was still scowling when, an hour later, his head
full of red figures and his belly full of raw white whiskey, he door-banged his way out of Wright's emporium
to climb on Wasiya and head him for the council
grounds, word having just come from Benteen that
Colonel Custer requested the presence of his scout
corps. The approaching Indian column had been sighted
winding up the Arkansas.

It was 7.20 P.M., Friday, November 13—a wineglass-
clear, dead-quiet fall evening. The yellow of the departed
sun still eerily lamplit the floor of the broad valley. Long
shadows backed the endless ranks of the ridges stretching
south from the fort to the far horizon.

It was the kind of an evening a mountain man didn't
like. Too quiet. Too clear. Too smoke-still. The pure
hush of it put a man's nerves on edge. Kept his eyes
working the prairie constantly, and his ears straining for
the first sound that would read Indian trouble.

It was a Bad Medicine night, and Josh Kelso could
smell it just as sure as he could the stink of a sick dog.

5. Bright Hair

BY THE TIME Josh, with Apache Bill, California Joe and the rest of Custer's regular scouts, reached the main gate, the Colonel was already mounted up and sitting impatiently at the head of his reception committee.

Josh's disturbance increased the moment he saw the nature of that committee—Captain William Thompson's Troop of the Seventh, fully armed with booted Spencers and heavily belted with regular field issues of ammunition.

Damn the General anyway. The way Indians saw such things a man didn't come to a peace palaver with his weapons polished. Not if he was a white man and his heart was really big for peace. Of course it was only natural for an Indian to bring along *his* war tools, but that was another matter. An Indian lived by his gun and would no sooner appear in public without it than without his breechcloth.

Custer, however, gave no opportunity for debate, and waved Thompson the "forward ho!" when the scouts rode up.

Minutes later, the command was drawn up on the level plain midway between the fort and the river, awaiting Black Kettle's mission. The nature of that mission served only to deepen Josh's scowl. For a solid half-mile the far bank of the Arkansas was clouded with the rising dust of the Indian cavalcade.

Moxtaveto was coming in force.

As the white forces watched, and while the enemy

caravan was yet a mile distant, a single horseman detached himself from its ranks and spurred his pony toward them.

He drew up before Custer with a flourish of South Plains horsemanship and a shower of Arkansas sod for the indignant Colonel that brought a hard grin flicking through Josh's scowl. The Cheyenne then barked out the stock Indian request; that the meeting take place *within* the fort.

Josh, as the sole member of the General's scout force who fully understood the complexities of the Cheyenne tongue, the most difficult of the Plains Indian languages, was waved forward by Custer. Translating the brave's demand, Josh's momentary uplift of feeling was brought hard down by the commanding officer's peremptory refusal.

"Tell the heathen rascal we'll do no such thing. Tell him we'll meet right here or not at all. If he comes in peace, that is one thing. But if there is the least demonstration advise him we are armed and ready."

The big scout nodded abruptly, turned to the waiting brave and shrugged apologetically. "Yellow Hair says he is sorry. He cannot see his brothers in the fort. He says it is better right here where all may sit like men in the open and unafraid. *Nahoxtahan!* Tell that to Moxtave-to."

The Cheyenne warrior's face darkened. Josh listened intently to his angry objections, then repeated them to Custer. "This boy ain't happy, General. He says Black Kettle doesn't like to meet at night. It makes him suspicious. He says that always before they've met in the fort. He doesn't want to tell Black Kettle these things. Says better you should wait till morning and talk in the fort."

The scout paused, dropping his voice. "I reckon maybe he's right, General. You know what I've told you about these Plains redskins not liking to do business after sundown. The dark is bad medicine for a Cheyenne."

Custer's spaced-tooth grin momentarily straightened the droop of his mustache, then was gone.

"Never mind your cultural lectures on the mores and

manias of the noble red man, Joshua. I'm quite as well
acquainted with them as you are. Please repeat my conditions, sir."

"Beg pardon, General. You meanin' to say you're
cornerin' them in the dark, a-purpose? Makin' them
goosy, deliberate?"

This time the mustache didn't lift, but the voice did.
"Oh, come now, Joshua. You're getting soft in your old
age. Get on with it, man. Of course I've planned it this
way!"

Josh knew that voice when it began to get high, and
that wild light that began to get into those pale eyes
when the General was strung-up. Benteen had been
right. For some reason, Custer was mortal hot to talk to
the Cheyenne. There was sure as hell something cooking
in his tricky mind beyond just baiting old Black Kettle.

When he had given the Indian Custer's second refusal, the brave wheeled his pony without a word, and
raced for his own lines now drawn up on the far side of
the river.

Custer took advantage of the interval to rearrange
Thompson's troopers.

"Column ho, by the flank, right! By the flank, left!"

The order, gauntlet-flung to Thompson, was passed
on by that officer. The men reined their mounts smartly
into a halfmoon line flanking Custer and his little knot
of officers and scouts.

Josh caught the look Benteen shot him and scowled
his wordless agreement.

Everything was right on schedule. The Boy General
was getting high-mighty and huffy before one word had
been said. The other officers, too, Major Joel Elliott,
Custer's second-in-command, Captain Miles Keogh and
young Lieutenant Tom Custer, looked to be as bit-
champing and shoulder-chipped as the General.

"Carbines at the ready, Thompson." The terse order
fell on the heels of the first. "I don't like the looks of
that mob over there. I'll not be intimidated within sight
of my own command post."

As the youthful captain repeated the order, and while

the short Spencers were still being snaked from their
saddle boots and cross-barred athwart the horses' withers, Josh was at Custer's side.

"Say, General, them naked guns ain't goin' to promote no spirit of sweetness and light, are they?"

"I trust not, Joshua." The peg-toothed grimace was
more smirk than smile now. "That brash rascal is here
to put on a show of force, precisely as I anticipated. He
knows he can't talk real peace to me again. He's simply
trying to bluff me into it this time. Can't you see that,
sir?"

"Can't say as I can, General." The shrug was noncommittal. "The boys at the store tell me they think the
old buzzard really means to tame down happen you give
him the chance. They figure he's got some kind of a deal
to offer for ridin' Injun-herd on the real bad ones."

"Oh, nonsense, Joshua. Don't try to sell me those
Dog Soldiers again. You and the rest of the scouts have
got Mad Wolf on the brain. We know who's behind all
this trouble and it's not Charlie Bent and the Dog Soldiers, by Heaven!"

"Listen, General," Josh's plea was dead straight,
"give them a chance this time. They've got wind of all
them troops Sheridan's gatherin' over to Fort Hays.
They may be simple but they ain't stupid. I know them
Cheyenne, General. I can smell a bad Injun far as the
wind can carry his stink. I think this Black Kettle's all
right."

"Yes, you've always thought so," the officer's voice
was rising again, "but let me remind you, sir, that I
haven't!"

"All the same, General," his voice dropped even lower, "I've got a hunch this is your last shot. I reckon I'd
give them their chance happen I was you."

"They've had their chance, by Heaven," snapped
Custer, that bad, quick light Josh had learned to distrust
lancing his pale eyes. "They'll not get another from me,
nor from Sheridan."

"Why talk to them, then?"

Josh's cool question, though it trod the touchy bor-

ders of insubordination as easily as if he were querying a
squad corporal about the way to the latrine, brought, surprisingly, nothing but a quick return of the wide-toothed
grin.

"You'll see, Joshua, you'll see! Don't bother me now.
And don't worry. I've got them this time and I don't
mean to let them up!"

The tall scout frowned, not missing the peculiar excitement. He knew his man well enough to realize Custer was fairly bursting with some new yellow-hair brain-
storm, and that further questioning was as out-of-order
as a skunk at a school picnic. He had no time, in any
event, to push the issue.

Across the river, the Cheyenne were on the move!

The savage caravan, snaking out of the desolate sandhills beyond the Arkansas and splashing on into the
shallow stream to bear down on Custer's nervous huddle
of troopers, was an awesome sight.

First rode one hundred garishly painted Dog Soldiers,
the military tribal police of the broad-faced southern nomads and the roughest cut in the whole card pack of
South Plains hostiles, including their blood cousins the
Kiowa and Comanche.

Josh's first thought upon identifying the vanguard as a
Dog Soldier unit was for Mad Wolf. But search as he
might, nowhere could he single out the familiar axe-
blade face of his self-appointed exterminator. Quite
clearly and for reasons not calculated to quiet the white
stomach, Axhonehe had chosen to absent himself from
this tribal peace program.

Behind the leaderless Dog Soldiers rode the solidly
packed, color-splashed mass of the regular Cheyenne
warriors numbering, to Josh's rough count, no less than
five hundred vermilion-smeared braves. To their rear
straggled a mixed horde of travois and pack ponies
bearing the motley complement of deadpan squaws,
big-eyed children and yellow-toothed oldsters of Black
Kettle's tribal village.

The minute he made out the squaws and pony-age
youngsters, he kneed Wasiya to Custer's side.

"Better have them troopers boot them carbines, General. This ain't no war party. Last thing an Injun will do is bring his women and young ones on a paint spree."

Custer nodded but made no move to implement the suggestion. "You'll never learn, Joshua. There's no end to their trickery. You cannot trust an Indian, sir."

"I don't trust them, I *know* them."

The flat emphasis froze Custer's small mouth, brought the ever-ready temper breaking through its thin crust of control.

"Are you saying I don't, sir? Look at them come, man! Don't be a fool."

Josh, his eyes never off the approaching flower of the Cheyenne Nation, swallowed his answer and set his long jaw. It had, indeed, become a moment to try the tension on the trap springs of any man's nerves.

As the Dog Soldiers splashed out of the Arkansas to come thundering down on the thin line of troops, the black-feathered pack of them howling fit to lift the neck hairs clean off a man's nape, Josh, as he so touchingly put it to Apache Bill, who had joined him at Custer's side, "didn't know whether to spit or holler uncle."

What made it so tough was that horseback Indians always came down on a camp that way whether they meant to be friendly or to cut your guts out, leaving it to you to decide if they aimed to kiss you or kill you. The big scout, flicking his glance down the line of troopers and seeing the tight-faced youngsters raise their Spencers to sweep the front of the advancing red wave, did his deciding hard and sharp. Having done so, he threw rank, face, form and military foofooraw squarely out the prairie window. He paid Custer the sole courtesy of holding his advice down so that the officer, alone, could hear it.

"By God, General, you tell them boys to boot them carbines. Them bucks ain't goin' to ride into us, but by damn happen one of your youngsters shakes off a shot, we're all of us deader than a bull-tromped wolf!"

Custer whirled on him, sunbleached mustache lifting to the angry mouth corners. Josh beat him to the outburst, buttering his suggestion with the little half-salute he saved for such occasions.

"Damn it, General, you do it now. I ain't never steered you wrong."

There were perhaps three people alive who could buck George Custer and get away with it. The first two were Mrs. Custer and Phil Sheridan. Custer indicated the third with his angry order to young Thompson. "Boot your carbines, Captain. On the double now."

With the repeat of the order and its fumbling compliance by the apprehensive troopers, the hostile rush had closed to a short hundred yards, its crazy pace unabated.

It was now Josh's turn to put the cinch to his shrinking stomach.

With the yelling Dog Soldiers fifty yards out, he began to figure he'd missed his call, and tensed to swing his own Henry repeater onto the leading chief. At thirty yards he was no longer figuring, he was dead certain he'd missed. Then in the last second the ten years he'd spent fighting the full cousins of these people paid off.

Forty feet from the mount-rearing line of Thompson's Troop, thirty from Custer and himself, the careening charge came to a halt.

All human sound ceased. As Josh sat watching, he was conscious only of the snaffling and shifting of the Indian ponies and of the clinking of the arms and harness of their riders. Without awaiting Custer's direction, he raised both hands, palms out, toward the Indians. It was the universal, prairie handsign of peace. Behind it he sent his deep voice, rapidly intoning the heavy Cheyenne gutturals.

"*Vahe, nomoto, nomoto,* you are welcome among us." He slashed his right hand down and across his left forearm in the handsign taken from the Cheyenne custom of cutting off the left arm of their enemies. "Yellow Hair says this to you. You are welcome in this camp. Our people are at peace with yours. *Heovemeaz,* Yellow Hair, has said it."

The Dog Soldiers made no sign they had heard the overture, but the bulk of the regular warriors had now

come up to crowd the rear of their line and among them
a ripple of friendly *"hau, hau's!"* was heard.

Josh waved gracefully, ignoring the Dog Soldiers to
address his remarks to Black Kettle's followers. *"He-
hau, he-hau,* who is chief among you? Which of you is
Moxtaveto?"

The big scout had never seen the notorious hostile.
Knew him only by reputation as the head chief of the
Cheyenne village slaughtered in peaceful camp at Sand
Creek four years earlier by the crackpot Colonel Chiv-
ington and his Colorado Militia. He knew, by this same
token that here was one Indian who had every right on
God's green prairie to despise the white brother.

He was, accordingly, scarcely prepared for the answer
to his question.

A wrinkled chief clad in the simplest of white elkskins
and armed only with a three-foot ceremonial pipe, urged
his potbellied mount forward.

"Hau, I am chief, here. I am Black Kettle."

The deep voice was soft as new snow, the placid face
behind it calm as a mountain lake at sunset. Josh's upset
was obvious.

"You are Moxtaveto, father?"

"Aye, and you, my son?"

"You know me, father—"

For the first time in his life, he felt ill at ease before
an Indian. The simple dignity of the old man was overpowering. It made a man feel all wrong inside and made
him hate to put his name into the harsh Sioux words
that were infamous among these people. He scowled,
angrily fighting his weakness. Yet still he heard the halt
in his voice.

"—I am Ota Kte."

He had known the old man knew him, just as the
bulk of his dead-still followers must have known him.
Nevertheless, he was jolted by the ugly murmur among
the Dog Soldiers at the sound of his hated name.

"Hau, I know you, my son." The surface of the old
man's face didn't alter a wrinkle. "Your heart is bad for
my people."

"Only for those whose hearts are bad for my people. You know that, Moxtaveto."

"Your heart is bad. You have killed too many."

The white scout shrugged and turned to Custer as the latter, realizing the talk was running overlong, bluntly interrupted.

"Tell him the Dog Soldiers must return beyond the river. They have no business here and I shall not talk to him so long as they remain."

Josh repeated the order to Black Kettle and the old-chief at once issued the required command. With the Dog Soldiers jogging sullenly toward the Arkansas, Custer abruptly stated his second condition.

"Tell him to bring his subchiefs only. Have them come to the tent over there. All the others will remain where they are."

His peremptory gesture swung Josh's eyes toward the fort. The scout was surprised to see the big Sibley which had been erected just beyond the stockade, and to note the rising glow of the fire being built before it.

Well, that was Custer. Not the bucko, the Boy General, to squat in the dark and wrangle with a batch of heathens. Hell no, not him. Bring the rascals in front of an issue tent. Throw a big fire on them. Rank the troopers up solid, all around. Set the stage, proper. Make the red sons know they were talking to the United States Army, Lieutenant Colonel George Armstrong Custer commanding!

Starting to give the order to the waiting Cheyenne, he found Custer suddenly at his side, voice held down to play under the ear range of Major Elliott, Benteen and the others.

"And, Joshua. Tell him he must bring Monaseetah. Do you hear, sir?"

"I got you, General."

His next query, offhand idle, produced an odd vehemence in Custer.

"Who's Monaseetah? He's a new one on me."

"Black Kettle's interpreter. Just do as I say, Joshua. I've had enough of your infernal questions, man. Jump

to it now!" Impatiently, he wheeled his horse, shouted
to Thompson, and with Benteen and his staff galloped
off through the growing darkness.

Black Kettle understood considerable English. Having
easily followed the first part of the conversation, he had
turned away to assemble his subchiefs. The remaining
Cheyennes were beginning to dismount and set up camp
as Josh came up to him with the remainder of the order.

"All right, father, let's go. Yellow Hair wants you to
bring your interpreter, too."

"How is that, my son?" The puzzlement in the old
chief's voice was genuine, causing the scout's eyes to
narrow quickly.

"Monaseetah was the name he gave me—"

The dusk was deep now, but a man couldn't miss the
dark flash which for the first time broke the wrinkles of
the Indian leader's face. *"Havsevestoz, nivehohavo—"*

The Cheyenne phrase narrowed the scout's gaze yet
further.

"Why do you say that, father? Why do you say it's a
bad thing and you don't like it?"

In answer Black Kettle called into the darkness.
"Emoonesta, come to my side!"

Josh translated the name as he watched one of the
Cheyenne swing aboard a small paint mare and move
away from the main camp. *Emoonesta,* Bright Hair.
That was a pretty tame name for a Cheyenne Cut-Arm.
A man couldn't see much to that, save how the General
had messed it up. As a matter of fact, a man couldn't
see much to the whole business. Couldn't see what the
tarnal sin was needed with another interpreter with him,
Josh Kelso, fronting the council fire. Couldn't see—

His difficulty in "seeing" vanished almost before he
got well started grumbling about it. His lean jaw suddenly slacked open and his eyes widened.

The settling dark opened to admit the approach of the
paint pony and its slender rider. The hush of the Arkansas evening fell apart to the powdery caress of a low
voice.

"I am here, father. Let us go."

Josh didn't hear the old chief's answer, nor his invitation to him to join them in riding to Yellow Hair's fire. He just sat and watched them pass in the purple dusk, his whole body, from elkhide footskins to shoulder-long hair, tight-strung as a war bow with the spine-jarring evidence of his startled eyes.

And when the prairie blackness had closed behind them and his unbelieving mind had fought itself to a standstill for a thought or a single iota of an idea on how to say it, there was still no way to beat Benteen's straight-out, eye-wide honesty.

That girl *was* the most *fantastically beautiful* woman that ever drove a mortal man's heart square through the roof of his dumb-open mouth!

6. The Sacred Pipe

THE COUNCIL got under way at 8.00 P.M. The full shade of the prairie night had drawn itself across the western horizon and outlined the leaping flare of Custer's bonfire and the close-packed half circle of savage red figures seated crosslegged before it.

Custer himself, with Josh and Benteen, was seated in the opening of the Sibley, Custer and Benteen in campchairs, Josh squatting on the ground to the latter's left. In the tent, three staff noncoms sat by the light of a hurricane lantern, rough paper and turkey quills in hand, waiting to transcribe for a hero-worshiping posterity the pathetic minutes of the last formal peace talk of a great Indian Nation. What they would write would be the literal wording of a palpably honorable hearing. What they would sign would be the dishonorable death warrant of a proud and ancient people.

At the moment, however, none of its principals, save perhaps Benteen with his painful knowledge of his superior's true character and his full access to the latter's prior exchange of plans with Sheridan and Sherman, had the least suspicion of Custer's motives in accepting the final meeting with Black Kettle's Southern Cheyenne!

Least aware of all of the possible presence of War Department intrigue and overly ambitious field-commander infamy was Joshua Kelso, Custer's Indian-hunting, court-favorite scout. Indeed, infamy, intrigue and overweening ambition were the furthest subjects from his mind.

For after ten years of safely dodging every lethal shaft winged his way by a succession of slant-eyed red women, Josh had been shot, dead center, by a pagan Cheyenne Cupid.

He was not only arrow-struck through the middle of his heart, but the shaft had wedged its barbs so solidly in his broad back it would quite likely kill him to cut it out.

Fortunately, or unfortunately, he was as unaware of this disaster as he was of the one about to be fashioned over Custer's council fire. For the moment, he only knew that his stomach was wrapped around an eight-pound rock, that his back and belly muscles were so tight he could scarcely breathe, and that his heart pounded like he was backpacking a bull elk, broadside, up the front of Pikes Peak.

He shifted uncomfortably, gulped in another mouthful of Arkansas night air, scowled at Custer and Benteen. Hang it all, why couldn't they get on with it? Custer just sat there grinning and folding his arms like a heathen Chinee, trying to force the Cheyenne to lose face by making the first talk.

And why couldn't he, Josh, learn not to mix civilized sowbelly and trade whiskey after living all winter on fresh cow and mountain water? His belly felt like it was full of placer gravel. By Cripes, a mountain son had ought to know better than to—

Yeah, that was right; he *had* ought to know better. To know better than to sit there horsing himself. Than to sit there breathing deep and holding his belly and blaming Custer or Benteen or Bob Wright's bad-fried fatback.

Where the hell was that God-beautiful Indian girl!

He'd seen her start for the tent. He hadn't been more than a hundred yards behind her and old Black Kettle on the way over and yet he hadn't seen simple sign of her since riding in to side Custer and Benteen by the fire.

God Amighty, but she was a looker. She had to be, to put rocks in the belly of a son who hadn't exactly set any records for backing away from free and fancy females. By God, she must be out there, somewheres. The infernal fire carried out about two or three rows of bucks, then a man couldn't see anything but prairie dark and—

His irate inner wanderings were cut off. Black Kettle arose, stepped slowly forward, a smoldering ceremonial pipe cradled in his arms. The Fort Dodge Council was in session.

The white scout watched, fascinated. He had sat to more than a few informal, horseback palavers between the Indians and the Army. But this was his first full-dress meeting. It presented a disturbing picture, which burned itself deep into his mind and created the first foothold for a thought which had been working at him ever since meeting the Cheyenne patriarch earlier in the evening. What were his *real* feelings toward these strange red nomads? Were they warmer than he believed? Did he rightly know *what* they were?

He shook off the shadow of the thought. He shed it with an angry start like a man would shuck a blanket that he'd pulled up in the dark and found crawling with gray-back lice. His jaw was in its old set as he waited for Black Kettle to conclude the pipe ceremonial.

The compelling figure of the aged Cheyenne held his audience in silence. He stood for perhaps ten seconds, the copper parchment of his face upturned to the still-ness of the Arkansas stars. Then he drew upon his pipe, blowing the smoke first east, then west, north and south, intoning between puffs the sacred peace prayer of the Cheyenne Nation. After that, he stepped forward quick-ly, placed the pipe on the ground between himself and Custer, and squatted crosslegged to face the army com-mander.

As the full light of the fire fell on the pipe, Josh's eyes widened. His words, sidemouthed to Benteen, were tense.

"The pipe! That's *the* pipe, Captain. Their Holy Medicine Pipe!"

Black Kettle now began to toll off the sonorous peri-ods of his last plea for peace along the Arkansas, but Benteen, sensing the excitement in the scout's whisper, asked sharply:

"What do you mean, Kelso?"

"When he came into Fort Hays to talk peace this summer, did he use that pipe?"

"I don't think so. Why?"

"By God, Captain, when they trot out *that* pipe, they ain't horsin'."

Benteen did not follow his excitement and let him know it with the quickness of his response.

"*That* pipe, *this* pipe, what's the difference? They al-ways lie."

Josh's eyes caught the officer's. His voice was short and bitter with worn-thin patience.

"Not over that pipe they don't, mister! It's their sa-cred medicine. Each Nation's got one; Sioux, Arapaho, Cheyenne, all of them. *Captain, that old man means to make peace this time!*"

"Better tell the Colonel." Benteen was at last dis-turbed by the scout's intensity. "I don't believe he's no-ticed it."

"Hoss feathers. He knows that pipe. He had his hands on it at Medicine Lodge Creek. By damn, Captain, I don't cotton to the smell of all this!"

His complaint was cut short by Custer's sudden ges-

ture, summoning him to his side. Pointing to Black Kettle, the General demanded: "Where's the girl, Joshua?
Plague it, man, I told you to have him bring her!"

"I told him, General."

"Well, tell him again, right now, sir!"

Josh shrugged. Turning to Black Kettle, he gave the
order. The old chief nodded to one of his braves, who
departed into the darkness to return shortly with the
girl. As she moved into the fire's full light and took her
place at Black Kettle's side, Josh's eagerness for his second sight of her was brought up sharply by his simultaneous marking of Custer's obvious agitation.

The General was leaning forward tensely in his chair.
His slender hands clutched the oak arms. His pale eyes,
diamond-bright, followed the girl like a man bewitched.
Noting the fact, the big scout scowled darkly.

With the scowl, however, he noted a second fact and
took what small comfort he could from it. The little
officer wasn't alone in his spellbound regard of the Indian girl. Every eye in Thompson's troop and in his own
staff glittered just as hard and bright as the General's.

And not without cause. A man had to admit that,
jealous or not.

Monaseetah was as slight and slender as a willow
wand and she moved with the grace of a mountain reed
in a spring breeze. She was clad in the single-piece doeskin camp dress of the unmarried Cheyenne woman, her
small knees, curving calves and slim ankles, as well as
her rounded arms and hollowed shoulders, copper-na-
ked in the shifting firelight. A man would just have time
to get that body-glance of her, before his eyes fixed on
her face and nothing else.

Unlike most Cheyenne women, her face was oval and
delicate. It was as perfect and unreal as an Egyptian
temple carving. Her cheekbones were high and slanting; her eyes narrow, oblique and fire-black; her nose,
straight-bridged and short. Her mouth was square and
full, and the underlip pouted in a moist, curving way
that made a man want to smash it and get his teeth into
it and grind the warm life out of it.

Josh was fighting for his breath when Black Kettle resumed his peace talk, breaking the spell the girl had put upon him and the officer corps of Custer's Seventh, and returning the council to order. With the old chief's remarks concluded, he waited for the girl to come forward with her translation.

To his surprise, Custer broke his stare from Monaseetah and snapped at him. "Well, what are you waiting for, sir? What did he say? Same old drivel?"

Josh eyed him, for the first time wondering what kind of an interpreter the girl was. He shrugged finally, putting the thought of the girl aside. After all, damn it, she was only an Indian!

Curtly, he repeated the sense of Black Kettle's statement.

"He says this time there's got to be peace. He's seen the soldiers at Fort Hayes. The Agents have told him why they're there. He says there must be no winter war. I allow he means it, General. That's the Big Pipe he's put on the ground. You know what that means."

"I know what it's supposed to mean. Is that all he said?"

"That's all. General, I think he means it this time. I allow you'd—"

"Thank you, sir. I'll do the thinking. Tell him exactly what I say, Joshua, and see that you don't change any of it."

The scout listened to the instructions, then turned to Black Kettle.

"Father, I believe you. I see The Pipe. I know it is holy. But Yellow Hair will not see it. He says he won't look at it any more. He says you are guilty. That you did those killings on the Saline River. And those on the Solomon."

"That's not a true thing, Ota Kte. You know who did those killings. You know who does all the killings. Tell him who it is."

Josh nodded solemnly. "I have told him, father. Many times. He will not believe it. He thinks you use the Dog Soldiers to excuse your own young men. He won't listen any more. He says the Agents have told him your Indians did it. Wynkoop says Satanta did it. Leavenworth says Black Kettle did it. I'm sorry, father."

Custer, drumming the arms of his campchair, interrupted demandingly. "What's he saying, Joshua? Come along, man, we haven't all night here."

"He says he didn't have nothin' to do with them Saline and Solomon killin's. Says the Dog Soldiers done it."

"Nonsense, sir! Tell him I'm tired of that lie. Tell him—"

"Beg pardon, General," the words stated the apology but the dark eyes denied it, "but I reckon it ain't no lie. What killin's the Dog Soldiers don't do, you can lay to Satanta's Kiowas. Black Kettle's a pretty good Injun, as Injuns go. I allow Mad Wolf's your boy, all right."

"Tell him," reiterated Custer, bluntly ignoring the scout's suggestion and rising dramatically to boom out the offer in his best Surrender-at-Appomattox style, "that I assert, and all candid persons familiar with the subject will sustain the assertion, that of all classes of our population the Army entertains the greatest dread of an Indian war and is willing to make the greatest sacrifices to avoid it."

The big scout frowned, his mind twisting to the task of cramming the highflown peace-feeler into simple Cheyenne, his heart glad, all the same, that Custer was accepting the old chief's proposal.

Right now, with the old man bidding and the Boy General buying, he could see his cow ranch in the Nation floating off down the North Canadian. Somehow he didn't give a damn, was actually relieved and maybe even a little tickled about it. He showed it, too, with the little grin he gave Black Kettle.

"Father, uncover your ears. I have a good thing to tell you. Yellow Hair says you lie about the Dog Soldiers, and he doesn't want to hear that lie again. But he wants peace, father. He says the white soldiers want to avoid war with the red brother. He says he is ready to do anything to bring peace along the Arkansas. It is up to you."

Black Kettle slowly raised the fingertips of his left hand to his forehead, sweeping them in turn toward Custer. "Tell Yellow Hair that Black Kettle hears his words and his heart is full. Tell him my people go home now. Tell him there will be peace and that we are going home."

The Cheyenne leader paused, nodded thoughtfully to Kelso. "I do not understand you, Ota Kte. You kill my people, yet I heard you speak to Yellow Hair and I heard him reply to you. Your heart was better than his."

Josh felt the strange thrill of the words but his eyes and thoughts were no longer on the problems of Black Kettle or any part of the Cheyenne Nation save that slender portion thereof so maddeningly wrapped in clinging doeskins. The girl, in turn, was all slant, black eyes for him. As their eyes met, her full lips curved into a haunting trace of a smile.

"I don't understand myself, father. Not any more—" The delayed words went to Black Kettle but the dark eyes remained with the Indian girl until the old chief broke the spell by moving forward to retrieve the pipe.

Replacing the sacred relic carefully in its foxskin cover, Black Kettle turned to apprise his subchiefs of the mission's success.

"Yellow Hair says the soldiers want peace too. There will be no war this winter. And no more war after that. The Pipe is blessed. We can go now."

The subchiefs were already swinging aboard their ponies when Custer strode forward.

"Hold on, hold on! Tell him to wait a minute, Joshua."

Josh was a little slow in complying with the directive and Custer, noting the cause of the delay, barked angrily. "By Heaven, sir, mind your business! I'm not paying you to ogle Indian wenches. I don't countenance that in this command and you know it. Do you understand, sir?"

Josh, too far down the travois-track of infatuation to

feel the lash of lesser emotions, grinned. "Yes sir, what'll you have, General?"

Still irritated, Custer rapped it to him.

"I want to know where these Indians are going to winter. Ask them where their camp will be. *Exactly.* Do you hear? I want to know the river and the specific part of it they'll be on. Carefully now, you understand? I don't want to alarm them."

The big scout's grin faded. The General appeared a shade too heated up. A sight too tensed for a man that just wanted to know were his red friends were going to spend their Christmas holidays. But then, hell. Likely, it wasn't the General that was too heated up. Likely it was him. What with the glare of the fire and those long, smoky looks the girl was giving him—

He put the thought aside, turned again to Black Kettle.

"Yellow Hair wants to know where his brothers will camp. Where they will be when the snow comes. So that he may know they are well and safe."

"On the Ouachita," replied the old Cheyenne unhesitatingly. "South a short day's pony ride from the first fork. It will not be hard to find. That's the first fork of the Canadian now, Ota Kte. The one the soldiers call the Wolf. In the Antelope Hills down there."

Josh touched his left fingertips to his forehead. "Yellow Hair thanks his brother. *Nataemhon*, good hunting father."

"*Nataemhon*," grunted Black Kettle and swung up on his pony to join Monaseetah, mounted and waiting. "Ride in peace, Ota Kte. We will meet again."

"Aye, father, we will. And you, girl," the tall scout's eyes abandoned Black Kettle, sought out Monaseetah, "*we* will meet again!"

"*He-hau, veho-hetan!* Yes, white man," the girl's words, softer than the smile behind them, carried clearly through the darkness, "we *will* meet again. *I swear it*—"

Before he could answer, the prairie blackness closed behind the departing Cheyenne. He was still staring after them when Benteen touched his elbow.

"Colonel Custer wants to know where that camp will be. What did the old devil say?"

He noticed that the commander was busy in the tent, sheafing through the staff noncoms' transcriptions, his quill scratching furiously as he added the high color of the Custer touch to the official recordings. "On the Washita," he grunted to Benteen. "Fifty miles south of Wolf Creek. The Antelope Hills country."

"Well, that ought to be close enough even for Custer. The poor devils!"

The way he said it stepped squarely on the bait-pan of Josh's still-puzzled mind. The jaws of his lingering doubt sprang ringing about. He twisted around, his Sioux-dark scowl hard as the core of a rifle barrel.

"How was that, Captain Benteen?"

"Just like I said," he let his lips shrink, the taste of the words too bitter even for a Regular Army mouth, "'the poor devils.' The Seventh is moving out in forty-eight hours—for Camp Supply."

"*Camp Supply?*" rasped Josh.

"Indian Territory," echoed Benteen acidly.

"And from Camp Supply?" he continued hard-eyed.

"To the Washita, 'fifty miles south of Wolf Creek. The Antelope Hills country.'"

There was no mistaking the deliberate mimicry of his own translation of Black Kettle's freely given directions. No misreading the naked disgust of the irony. Nor the brutal reason therefor.

Custer had set a white *wickmunke* for Moxtaveto, the Black Kettle of the Southern Cheyennes.

And the child-simple old warrior had walked straight into it.

7. The Devil's Brand

WITHIN MINUTES after the Cheyenne rode away from the council fire, Custer struck his tent and pulled out. In the flicker of the dying coals the two scouts smoked and talked quietly.

"Ten gets you twenty, Josh," nodded Apache Bill, "that this here palaver never gets writ into the Official Records."

"How so, Bill? Them sergeants was scribbling hard enough."

"Makes no difference. If I've sat to one with the General, I've sat to a dozen talks like this here one tonight. None of them got writ into the records that I know of. Sheridan will get a letter and maybeso Sherman. That'll be as far as she goes."*

"Could be, savin' for one to Mrs. Custer too. She'll get a ten-pager out'n this, you can lay."

"Yep, I allow. It beats all how crazy he is about that woman. I never seen a married man so constant. Reckon a man has to give him that much anyhow."

The remark led squarely into the worried hand Josh had been attempting to reshuffle in his mind for the past hour. "Bill," he drawled, trying his best to make it

---

* Apache Bill was right. The November 13 meeting with Black Kettle does not appear in the War Department records. Nevertheless, the fact of its occurrence persists both in the first hand accounts of such historical figures as California Joe, and in the tribal lore of the Arkansas Cheyennes and other South Plains bands involved in the campaign of 1868.

sound careless, "how *about* the General and this here Injun gal?"

"Oh, I dunno." The other scout made it careless without trying. "Course he did have her right along with him in the field this summer. Near onto six weeks, as I recollect. But he got shut of her in one hell of a tall hurry, you can bet!"

"How so?"

"Heard Mrs. Custer was comin' on from the east. Mister, you never seen a son shuck a squaw so sudden in your life."

"You sayin' he was squawin' with her?" The labored carelessness was long gone. "By damn, I don't believe it. Not of the General, I don't."

"I ain't askin' you to." The older man made cautious note of his young comrade's jawthrust. "And I ain't sayin' he was, neither. Hell, boy, nobody that really knowed him would. But, plague it, Josh, you know them senior officers. They're worse than a bunch of biddy hens catchin' their cockbird courtin' a duck. I reckon that outside of Captain Benteen and his own brother, young Tom, there ain't a commission in his command that wouldn't kick dirt on him happen they wasn't scared to death he'd catch them scratchin' it up. Course you can't entirely blame them."

"What do you mean?"

"This here tomfool 'interpreter' business."

"I'm waitin'."

"You needn't be. That gal don't neither speak nor understand a cussed word of English."

Josh drew three times on his pipe and let the smoke come slowly through his teeth.

"You still think there's nothin' to it, Bill? No matter he had her with him so long last summer?"

"I said so. I reckon I ought to know, too, happen anybody does. I was with him and her twenty-four hours a day—and forty-eight on Sundays."

"But—"

"But, hell, Josh! Lookit the gal, that's all! Wouldn't you like to have her around? Just to look at? *Wouldn't* you? By God, wouldn't I? Wouldn't any man that was a man? Hell, you seen them officers givin' her the hard eye just now. Why, she rightly pulls the breath square out'n you. I can't help that she does, you can't help that she does. And sure as hell, Custer can't help it no more than you and me can. Why, boy, she can't even help it herself. She's just that kind of a woman, Josh!"

"Yeah, I reckon—" The agreement was unwilling and still a little uncertain.

There was no answering uncertainty in Apache Bill's heated ultimatum.

"You reckon right. Damn it all, boy, you know how he is about Mrs. Custer! A man couldn't love a woman no more than the General does her. He'd likely die sooner than he'd do her any dirt. He can't help seein' what's in that Injun gal no more than the rest of us. And he'd want to see all of it he could, too, same as us. But comes to touchin' any of it, I say he ain't! I don't want to talk no more about it, you hear me, boy?"

"I hear you, old hoss," the young scout's relief was as evident as the grin which came with it, "and I'll remember it."

"See you do," grunted Bill. "You told me yourself that he's got a hard eye for a proud hoss or a prime woman. In this case I reckon he don't see no more in the one than he would in the other. You can remember that, too, when the time comes."

"I will," nodded Josh soberly. He stared into the fire a moment longer, before continuing thoughtfully.

"Bill, you was sayin' that the General's boys are just as set again him as they was last summer. I thought he'd cleaned all that up when he got his commission back."

"Hoss feathers," grumped the older scout. "That's nothin' but Custer-talk. There ain't a more unpopular field officer in the whole lousy army, and he knows it. Happen he didn't have Sherman and Sheridan frontin' for him, he couldn't get the command of a latrine detail, let alone a big outfit like the Seventh. Hell, they overslaughed five officers on his own staff to put him on top this here dungheap at Dodge."

"Yeah, I know. How in tarnation does he do it, Bill?"

The grizzled scout shrugged. "Only him and God knows, Josh, and neither of them's tellin'. He's already been through a court-martial and two General Reports that would have busted a four-star general to a buck private. You recollect the ones I mean. Them two affairs down in Texas where they called him up for rough-handlin' his men and abusin' his command?"

"Yeah, I believe I heard. Seems like he can lead a sanitary detail through a ten-foot trench of bull chips and come out smellin' like a rambler rose."

"He can. I allow he's the luckiest one army buzzard that ever broke a good officer for cussin' on Sunday, or ordered a batch of homesick recruits shot as deserters for runnin' away from dog-rotten food and billets a sick rat couldn't sleep proper in."

Josh nodded thoughtfully. "Maybe you're right, Bill. I reckon he ain't got a real friend in the world that ranks less than a general officer."

"Savin' yourself, he ain't." Apache Bill's headchuck was half agreement, half challenge. Josh picked up both the look and the averment and handed them back abruptly.

"How about you, Bill? And California? And the others?"

The older scout shook his head. His answer was as genuinely puzzled as the frown which went with it.

"By God, I dunno, Josh. Somehow, a man will leave fat cow and prime fixin's to foller him on moldy biscuit and blowflied fatback. I done it, you done it, we all done it. But how come the tarnal hell we done it? That's what's got me chasin' my tail. By Cripes, I jest can't figger it, Josh."

Josh took his time, his answer coming in that low, slow way a western man will take when all the bluffs are in and the last raise called.

"I allow I *can*, Bill. Custer ain't like other men. He ain't the same breed. He don't think he is, and he ain't.

There's men that allows no man's as bright as them. It ain't that it's so, mind you, but just that they *think* it is. And for them, that makes it so.

"They can answer any question. They can tot up any sum. They can rassle any bear and pin any bull. There ain't nothin' can beat them and no way they can lose. Not in their own minds, there ain't.

"Custer's that way, Bill. It ain't bred in a man, neither. Take his brother, Tom. Tom is out'n the same mother and he's by the same daddy, but he ain't the same man. He ain't no more like the General than you nor me. Tom's human and you and me are human.

"The General ain't, Bill.

"I allow it's some kind of almighty lightning strikes a man to make him like Custer. It don't strike often and it don't never strike in the same place twice. When it strikes a man it sets up a fire in him that'll burn him plumb to death before he's done. And it'll burn plenty of them that's standin' too close to him too. But all the same, when the Big Dark comes and such as you and me ain't no more than them dead coals there, the General will still be burnin' bright enough to see from here to Kingdom Come."

The young scout paused, seeking words.

"He's got the devil's brand on him, Bill, and you and me and all the others of us that's wild inside will foller him till hell freezes over!"

Bill, his simple mind stumbling along in bewilderment behind this outpouring from a man he'd never before heard string more than twenty words together, was still several strides off the pace when Josh, a little embarrassed, knocked out his pipe and rose with awkward haste to stride away into the cover of the prairie night.

It was a little after 9.00 P.M. when Captain Frederick Benteen looked up from his desk and cursed irritably.

"Damn it all, Kelso, I do wish you'd learn to knock!"

"Sorry, Captain. A man gets out of the habit in the mountains. There ain't no doors in a cowskin tent."

"Well, all right man, what's on your mind? As if I couldn't see it as clearly as you're standing there. Custer and those double-cross orders, eh?"

Taking his cue from the officer's brevity, he made it short. "Captain, I want to see them orders. I know it ain't regulation but you and me are more or less in the same mudhole. Leastways we are happen them orders is writ the way you said."

"They are, Kelso. What's the matter with my word for it?"

"It ain't your word, Captain Benteen." It was perhaps the third time the officer had heard him use the full address. He knew at once that the scout was deadly serious. "It's just that I can't believe the General would hoodwink them poor devils that way."

The officer looked at him. When his answer came, his voice was harried and nerve-thin.

"Now listen, Kelso, I can't do any more for you in this matter. I've already told you enough to get myself broken. Perhaps as you say we're in this thing together, but the thing you have to remember is that first, last and always I'm Colonel Custer's executive. As such, there are limits to any association you and I may have, and this is one of them. If you want to see those orders, you'll have to get them from Custer. I'm sorry. And for God's sake man, don't mention me in connection with them!"

Benteen was on his feet, the brief interview clearly at an end. "I'll give you some advice, however. I wouldn't bother him now if I were you. He was in here not twenty minutes ago filing his reports on tonight's affair. He mentioned you. Something about did I think, or had I noticed, you going soft on the Indians all of a sudden."

"The gal, eh?"

"Possibly. As a matter of fact, probably. In any event I wouldn't push him on those orders. Not tonight, you understand?"

Josh stepped back, eyeing him steadily.

"I aim to see them orders, one way or another," was all he said before turning away.

8. Sheridan's Orders

MOVING UP THE PATH to Custer's quarters for the second time that day, Josh's mind was in more of a tangle than ever. Damn it all. It was one thing to take a free shot at a running buck. But to put out a bait-set for him and then drill him when he came up to sniff at it was something else again. Something a mountain hunter's belly didn't sit well to. Not, anyway, as long as there was the chance of a doe coming along to that bait-set with the buck, and not if that doe was a black-eyed Cheyenne beauty named Bright Hair!

The thought of the girl and of the stab of her sudden, sweet smile brought him to a stop. A man needn't have watched the Army fight Indians as long as he had, to know the way they went about it. And to know that when the Seventh's band started blowing "Garry Owen," the General's own regimental song, and the first companies set their horses bombarding down the village streets it was every Indian for himself and the Spencer carbines take the hindmost—which in nine cases out of ten were the squaws and toddle-age kids.

Standing there on Custer's stoop at Fort Dodge, he could see the beautiful body of the Indian girl flying off that little paint mare to the smack of the .54-caliber slug in her soft belly, as clearly as he could the bright splash of lamplight coming from the Colonel's window.

Shaking his head, he reached for the door. Remembering Benteen's acid complaint, he held up and knocked loudly.

"Come in, Joshua. I've been expecting you—"

The surprise served only to lift the angle of Josh's hackles.

Damn him, anyway. A man hadn't even had the chance to open his mouth and there he was already cutting the ground out from under you! He kneed the door open, strode in and stood truculently before Custer.

To add to his surprise, he found the commander in definitely level spirits.

"Well, Joshua, out with it. What's eating you, sir? I've been watching you. You can't get around me with your surly mountain ways, man. Something's had your wind up all evening. The girl, I shouldn't wonder. Am I right, sir?"

The way he said it, clear-eyed and quick, with the old pegtoothed smile backing it all the way, wet a man's powder before he could strike his flint. It made you wonder how you could ever have suspicioned he would have anything to do with Monaseetah, much less with plotting a cold-blooded trap for Black Kettle.

"Well yeah, I reckon, General. Her and the old man. Mostly him right now. Way things was goin' out there tonight, I reckoned you was workin' to peace-talk the old devil square into a set trap."

"What makes you think I wasn't, sir?"

The smile was gone. Seeing it go, Josh set himself for a blasting. He got instead a friendly hand on the shoulder.

"Joshua, you and I are going to come to an understanding. I was just talking to Benteen about you and I'm worried."

There it was again. His mind was shiftier than a once-trapped dog wolf's. He had already smelled out that you were going to brace him about his having told Benteen you were going soft on the redskins. Not only had he smelled out your brace but he was beating you to it by admitting it before you could jump him about it.

Josh sought awkwardly for his answer. "I allow you needn't be," he said, at last.

Having said it, he wanted to kick himself. Now, why

had he said it, goddammit? He'd come in here to raise a stink and he was still aiming to raise it. Yet there he was standing there and assuring the General he wasn't!

"All the same, Joshua, I am." Custer said it softly, like a man that meant it. "I am, and I want you to speak freely. Ask your questions right out, sir. You'll get your answers the same way. You know that."

Now the big scout's jaw came forward. His dark eyes grew still.

"All right, General, I've got a couple. First off, what orders have we got comin' up immediate? I mean relatin' to them Cheyenne we just talked to."

Custer's intense expression didn't alter as he strode to his desk and seated himself. Pulling out an order file, he motioned to Josh. As the latter moved to the desk and sat down, he took up the first paper.

"This is the last General Policy Directive from Sherman. It is under date of October fifteenth, the present year. It reads in pertinent part, as follows:

> . . . as for extermination it is for the Indians themselves to determine. We don't want to exterminate them or even to fight them. The present war was begun and carried on by the Indians in spite of our entreaties and in spite of our warnings, and the only question is, whether we shall allow the progress of our western settlements to be checked, and leave the Indians free to pursue their bloody career, or accept their war and fight them. We accept the war.
>
> I shall do nothing and say nothing to restrain our troops from doing what they deem proper on the spot, and will allow no general charges of cruelty and inhumanity to tie their hands, but will use all the powers confided in me to the end that these Indians, the enemies of our race and of our civilization, shall not again be able to begin and carry on their barbarous warfare on any kind of pretext they may choose to allege . . .

"Now then," he tossed the paper aside, "that's number one. Any questions?"

"That apply generally," Josh grunted, "or just to the Cheyennes?"

"The Cheyennes, specifically. The Kiowas and Comanches south of the Arkansas are in the department of Colonel Hazen at Fort Cobb."

Josh shook his head, still trying to untangle the double-talk in Sherman's statement. "We don't want to fight them," and then, "We accept the war." "It is for the Indians themselves to determine," and then, "I shall use all the powers confided in me to the end that these Indians . . . shall not again be able to begin and carry on their barbarous warfare."

Read it anyway he wanted, a man could spell it out clearly enough. All the hostiles south of the Arkansas were going to be cut out of the fight by a trumped-up peace quarantine. Then Sherman's boy, Yellow Hair, was going to move in and murder every arms-age Cheyenne north of that stream. The only question remaining was, when was he going to make that move?

"Uh huh," he said at length, his noncommittal grunt not matched by the directness of his query, "now how about them orders?"

Again Custer held his silence. For his answer he fished a second document from the file and tossed it to the scout.

"That's Sheridan's of the fifteenth, immediately subsequent to Sherman's announcement of the same date." He paused. "It's the order," here a little return flash of the smile, "which certain desk-dreamers in the Indian Bureau are pleased to refer to as 'the notorious General Order of October fifteenth.' Read it, please, Joshua."

The scout began frowning his way through the opening body of the order, concise and official looking over Little Phil's sprawling signature. Suddenly his eyes skipped to the last lines of the brutal document.

. . . you are thereby ordered to proceed south in the direction of the Antelope Hills, thence toward the Washita River, the supposed winter seat of the hostile tribes; *to destroy their villages and ponies; to kill or*

*hang all warriors and bring back all women and
children . . .*

"And that, Joshua," the little commander's eyes
caught Kelso's as they swung up from the order, "is
number two. Any more questions, sir?"

"I reckon not." Josh was on his feet. "You knowed
you was going to hit them when you let them come in to
talk peace. Even if they brung the Sacred Pipe, your orders was writ when you talked to them." He paused, eying the famous officer, letting his final charge come quietly.

"And it so happens I know, General, them orders
wasn't writ by Sherman or Sheridan. *They was writ by
you!*"

"Those orders, sir," Custer was standing now, too, his
pale eyes narrowed, "were written by Black Kettle, the
day and hour of August seventh when he began to kill
on the Saline and Solomon Rivers!"

"I know better, General," was all Josh said, as he
turned away.

"Where do you think you're going, sir?" The officer's
too-quiet question came as the big scout moved for the
door.

It was in Josh's mind not to tell him, but in the end he
could no more lie to Custer than he could to himself.

"After the girl, General. I ain't goin' to let your boys
blow her guts out when they jump that village."

"Joshua—!"

It was a command. He heard it and understood it,
and deliberately ignored it. His big hand reached for the
latch.

"I'm sorry, General. You played an Injun trick on
me, gettin' me to ask her people where their winter
camp would be. Now I'm playin' one on you. I'm quit-
tin' you flat."

"If you walk out that door, Joshua, you will regret it
to the last day of your life." Custer was coming around
the desk, the usual quick-rising anger in his voice
strangely missing.

"You do not understand this situation. Neither you nor any of your mountain kind can ever understand it. I know you. You have, all of you, no matter that you profess it otherwise, a secret and abiding admiration for the Indian. You no less than the others, Joshua, despite your reputation."

He stopped in front of the towering scout, long curls back-flung as his intent gaze sought the face above him. "You are all halfbreeds in a sense, your feelings for these people entirely ambivalent. You profess to fight them. But you fight them like a scattered legion of mountain-demented Don Quixote's. You keep looking for something decent, noble and chivalrous in them, which is not there to find, even as you jab halfheartedly at their buffalo-hide windmills."

Custer stepped back and drew himself up.

"I do not ask you to understand that, Joshua. I only ask that you take my word for the fact that I do."

Josh hesitated. For a moment something in what the little officer had said had come will-o'-the-wisp close to clearing the confusion which had been his since the Cheyenne council. But even as he hesitated, the haunting face of Monaseetah was before him and he could only shrug, hard-faced.

"Could be, General. All the same, I'm goin'."

"Joshua—I ask you not to do it. I need you here—"

There was that in the voice which he'd never heard there; a dead earnestness, a sudden unabashed disregard of rank and relative position, a naked admission of long-hidden loneliness.

A man found it hard to believe but he couldn't miss it. Custer was asking him to stay, not as a paid scout or hired Indian hunter, but as the one thing he needed above all else. The one thing his headlong career had never given him time to make, nor his overpowering ambition to earn.

A simple friend.

Confusion growing with each silent second, Josh hesitated again.

"By God, General, I can't help it. I got to go to that

gal. I'd sooner eat boiled buffalo dirt than run out on you, but I can't help it. I got to do it!"

Custer's attitude shifted suddenly. He had won and he knew it. He lost no time in abandoning the uneasy ground of his impetuous revelation and retiring to his prepared position of the Colonel commanding.

"You've got to do no such thing, man. There is no question of harm to the women and children of that camp. You read those orders, sir. They are explicit: 'to bring back all women and children.' That means to bring them back *alive*, sir. You will get your girl, Joshua. You have my word on it."

"I can't get it out of my mind about me askin' them where the village would be, after promisin' peace. That ain't the way I fight Injuns, General."

Custer was beside him then, small hand finding the broad shoulder once more, the old smile flashing its wide-toothed wizardry.

"You've let the girl unsettle you, Joshua. Remember those orders you just read, man. They locate the village as clearly as did old Black Kettle himself. Your question to him was nothing more than a confirmation of something we already knew. No odium can attach to you from it and it can have no possible bearing on an outcome which was in any event inevitable. Our course was determined weeks ago by the Indians themselves. It is contained and irrevocably stated in Sherman's own word —extermination. There is nothing you nor any man alive can do to alter that course. You must see that by now, sir."

He was trapped. There was no way out for him now. And if there was, it wasn't through that door. His hand fell slowly from the latch.

There was no gainsaying the General's claim that he knew beforehand where the camp would be. Nor the dead certainty of Sherman's directive, nor Sheridan's General Order. When it was put to a man that way, he had to admit it. He had to admit, too, the truth of Custer's shot about the girl. There was no question she had him unsettled and going soft on her relatives.

Head down, sunbrown hands clenched, the big scout surrendered.

"I'll stay, General—"

He heard the dull acceptance in his voice and knew that once more the Boy General had him mired in the bull wallow of a bad decision. He knew, too, that he had to let him know it.

"But I got to say one thing." As Custer waited, pale-eyed, his deep voice dropped, the accusation in it flatly quiet. "I used to think that killin' Injuns was *my* business. Right now, I reckon it's yours!"

Custer stood motionless while the heavy seconds stalked the eye-locked silence. Finally he moved, strode wordlessly to the desk, removed a second file and took from it a succession of reports.

Without further notice of Josh, he began to read:

"August 7th, instant, Saline River: 300 Cheyenne moving along a 20-mile path, killed 15 settlers and carried off 5 women . . .

"August 11th, instant, Solomon River: same war party, crossing from the Saline, killed 6 settlers, scalped another alive . . .

"August 18th, instant, small Cheyenne band raiding along the Pawnee Fork, dismembered a settler alive, in front of his wife, later killed, and his two children, subsequently carried off and to date unreported . . .

8th September, instant, Cimarron Crossing: war party identified as Sand Creek Cheyenne entered a wagon park to trade. Seized 17 white teamsters whom they subsequently burned amid the contents of their train . . .

"9th September, instant, Fort Wallace: wood hauling detail attacked. Six U. S. contractors killed, scalped and mutilated . . ."

The officer's voice moved ahead, ignoring Josh's hand-waved remonstrance; the precision of his diction never varied, his eyes flicked from manuscript to listener as he discarded each report in turn.

"1st October, instant, Spanish Forks: large band tentatively identified as mixed Arapahoe and Sand Creek Cheyenne killed 4 men and outraged 3 women, the last of whom was violated by 13 Indians then scalped in front of her 4 small children, the children then murdered one at a time. Investigating detail found axe still in woman's skull. Certain identification of weapon as Southern Cheyenne . . .

"3rd October, instant, Fort Dodge: 12-month report children carried off, this district: 14 known to have frozen to death while captive in hostile camps. Two camps identified, High Bear's and Roman Horse's, both Cheyenne . . .

"6th October, instant, Fort Lyon: party of 60 Cheyenne raiding along the North Canadian surprised 5 haycutting contractors. All mutilated. No survivors."

Custer paused, then leaned forward over the desk. "There is one more of these little items, sir. One with which, lest memory fails me, you enjoyed some small personal connection!" The bitterness of the cynicism was heavily troweled-on, the harsh acid of its spreading forbade interruption.

"It is here, sir, in my hand." He waved the crumpled sheath of reports. "But I shall not trouble to read it for you. It is recent enough, you will permit me the liberty to assume, for even your abbreviated remembrances. Allow me, sir, to *recite it* for you, from memory—*and to the comma!*

"14th November, instant, Fort Coon, Kansas Territory: Relief squadron from Fort Dodge arriving on above date under Lt. Wm. Cook, found Sergeant

L. C. Woods and ten troopers of his outpost detail under hostile attack. The Indians, positively identified by the survivors as Arkansas Cheyenne, withdrew in the face of the relief's advance . . . six men wounded, four dead. The latter group, a wood detail from Fort Dodge under 1st Sergeant Ben F. Henderson. They were found scalped and mutilated two miles east of the guard outpost on Big Coon Creek. Sergeant Henderson was unrecognizable."

Custer stood up, watching Josh for a full five seconds. At last, he nodded.

"Yes, *Kelso!*" It was the first and last time he ever used the name. "You 'reckon' correctly."

The following words fell so softly Josh's keen ear barely caught them. They came backed, nonetheless, with a sudden flaring of the pale eyes which seared them into his memory.

"Right now, killing Indians *is* my business!"

9. *Black Kettle's Tipi*

Josh TOSSED restlessly. For a fall night getting on into winter it was uncommon hot. The cussed hay appeared bent on jabbing a man every time he turned. On top of that the drumming and chanting from the Cheyenne camp beyond the stockade was keeping Wasiya gingered up.

After an hour he gave up and admitted it wasn't the gelding stomping around that was keeping him awake. It was the girl. He cursed silently, remembering his pledge to Custer.

Followed another ten minutes of bed-punching, and
that was it.

When a man was used to sneaking around situations
where any noise lustier than a mouse sneeze could mean
his hair, it wouldn't be any trick to slide in and out of
this camp. What Custer didn't know wouldn't hurt him.
Besides, happen a man had in mind to see that Indian
girl again he'd best be about it. The Cheyenne camp
would be clean gone come daylight.

Fort Dodge was built in a halfmoon, the two points
based on the Arkansas. Back from the river a ways was
a twenty-foot bluff where the main barracks of the enlisted men were dug in and sod-roofed over. Once down
that bluff and past the sod shanties Josh had only to hit
for the river, drift south a spell and then cut back in
across the open prairie.

Ten minutes later, he was skirting the Arkansas willows.

Minutes after that he was shadowing in on the Cheyenne camp. The only trouble he'd encountered had been
with a bunch of night-grazing cavalry mounts being held
outside the fort under herd guard. He'd had to pass so
close to the horses he'd been able to identify them when
one of the troopers struck flint to his midnight pipe—
Captain William Thompson's troop of the Seventh.

Ahead of him now, he had the Cheyenne pony herd.
It was placed as always by these red nomads between
themselves and the potential enemy: in this case and in
spite of all the palaver and pipe-smoking, Yellow Hair
and his Cheyenne-chasing Seventh Cavalry.

Josh nodded grimly as he noted the old chief's caution. Then wondered whether it was really caution or
something else. Something else spelled a lot more like
suspicion. Or maybe downright information.

The pony herd was nothing. He had been too long in
the South Park country to smell like a white man. His
buckskins were deep-cured with the woodsmoke of ten
years of tipi fires. He floated past the Cheyenne remuda
without lifting a solitary roman nose from the rich graze
of the Arkansas uplands.

Then his troubles began.

The camp was a big one. It spread over a quarter of a mile of open plain. There was nothing to draw a bead on save the big cowskin cone of Black Kettle's lodge. Outside of that, there wasn't a tipi in the whole layout, so a man's approach was about as private as a sow grizzly crossing a snowslide.

Right now a man began to wonder what he was doing out there. Sure, he could call out and make an open walk-in. That way he'd be safe enough as far as the Indians were concerned. But just let him show himself in front of the whole tribe and the General was certain to hear of it. Next, he could belly around the camp hoping to spot the girl and signal her out, risking in the process getting gutshot by some spooky horse guard. Or lastly he could smarten up and light a shuck right back where he'd come from, forgetting the whole thing.

But as long as he was hell-bent on seeing the girl—

Setting his jaw, he dropped to his knees and began snaking toward the silhouette of Black Kettle's lodge. He was careful to keep it squarely between himself and the light of the dance fires.

At the rear of the lodge he thought once more about how badly he wanted to see Monaseetah. The guttural barking of dancing braves, not forty feet from him, stiffened the hairs on his neck. Gritting his teeth, he lifted the rear covers and went under.

He was luckier than any white man who would deliberately belly-sneak in on five hundred celebrating Cheyenne had any right to be.

"*Niva tato?* Who is that?"

A deep voice muttered the challenge from behind the glow of a pipe not six feet from his nose.

"*Nanehov, nihoe*, it is I, father!" Recognizing the voice, he let his breath go gratefully. "Your friend, Ota Kte."

"Ota Kte!"

Josh's eyes adjusted to the darkness of the tipi and he could see Black Kettle now. He could see, too, the steady muzzle of Black Kettle's carbine.

"Aye, father. Gently there, with the Holy Iron! I have come to seek your help, Old One. As a son to a father."

The old Cheyenne nodded, motioning him forward.

"You are very foolish to come into this camp in such a way. I could have shot you. The pony guards could have shot you. Yellow Hair would have called it murder."

Josh squatted crosslegged on the buffalo robe, facing the old man. He returned the nod soberly. "You could, and he would," he agreed succinctly. "But I could not let Yellow Hair know that I came here. He has my word that I would not do it."

"Your word is no better than that, Ota Kte?"

"What do you think, father?"

"It is the girl then." The old man's statement fell softly, startling Josh with its certain insight.

"Now why do you say that, father?" he countered awkwardly.

"*Haheneeno.*" The Cheyenne leader shrugged. "A man knows these things. When a young brave is not at war there are two things he will risk his scalp or his honor for. Food in his belly. A woman in his blankets."

"I must talk to the girl, father. You understand these things and I am glad. When I saw her today my heart was big and my eyes full of joy."

"Hah!" The snort was eloquent. "You mean your eyes were big! I didn't notice the heart. It's all the same when you're young though."

"You will bring her then? Here to the tipi? I ask it, father. My fingers are touching the brow."

"Only a moment, yes. The squaws will be returning from the fires soon. It is late and we travel early."

He waited in the half-gloom of the lodge. Seconds seemed to grow into hours before the old man's form again blotted the entrance flaps. Behind him was the girl. At the sight of her Josh felt the thick blood hammer in his wrists and temples.

"*Vahe Veho!*" Her low voice went through him,

leaving him suddenly weak. "You are welcome, White
Man. You make my eyes glad again."

He struggled for an answer. Before he could find
words, Black Kettle's warning mutter was falling.

"Talk quickly now. You have only a moment. The
dance is ending. I will be outside. Remember, my heart
is good for you. When you hear the grass hawk whistle,
you will know the squaws come."

With the admonition he was gone, leaving only the
darkness of the tipi between Josh and the Indian girl.
She moved toward him, and he arose to meet her. She
spoke first.

"We have no time, *Veho*. Listen to me. I know that
what is in my heart is also in yours. When you look at
me I do not think of Ota Kte, the killer of my people. I
think only of the White Man I see. Such a *Veho* as I
have never seen before—"

"You listen to me, girl!" His interruption stumbled
uncertainly; his mind whirled at the implications of her
words. "We can't talk of these things now. Not in this
place. I came here that you might tell me how I can find
you when your people leave this camp. You told me at
Yellow Hair's fire that we would meet again. I came
here that you might tell me when that will be. And
where, Bright Hair."

"I have not forgotten, *Veho*. Had you not come, I
would have sent for you."

With the thrill of this new promise, the girl hurried
on.

"I will wait for you the second sun from tonight,
when that sun is sinking. There is a place on the South
Road beyond the Arkansas. A spot near the river where
the spring flows. It is heavy with willows and cottonwoods there. Do you mark that spot, *Veho*?"

"Middle Spring," he said tensely. "On the Cimarron.
Past the Dry Crossing, past the Jornada. Is that the
place, girl?"

"That is it, *Veho*. Monaseetah will be there. We will
talk and you can show me with your hands what I have
already seen in your eyes!"

The way she said it, the words low and fierce, brought
Josh to his feet. In two strides he was across the darkened lodge. He seized the roundness of her arms, high
up, and his thumbs tensed to the swell of her breasts.
His wide lips smashed downward upon the demand of
her parted mouth. His hard body cradled the eager, forward thrust of her soft one—

The long-drawn quaver of the nighthawk's whistle
broke the brutal kiss in mid-demand. The girl backed
away from him and ducked, shadow-swift, through the
tipi flaps. And he stood there with two last-minute memories: the perfume of her body against his buckskins,
the salt and the blood of her torn mouth against his lips.

For a moment he remained motionless. Then he
dropped and rolled under the rear skins of the lodge. He
came erect outside, listening intently. Within, deep
grunts announced the arrival of Moxtaveto's squaws.

For the first time in twelve hours, he allowed himself
the luxury of a grin. He was still enjoying it when he
turned and slid away toward the protecting shadow of
the pony herd.

If it was a laugh Josh Kelso meant to have there back
of Black Kettle's lodge, it was as well it was a silent one.

For with a Cheyenne, as with any Indian, the last
smile went to the one who took the scalp. And Emoonesta, the Bright-Haired One, was a Cheyenne.

She was still smiling softly, long after the peaceful
pony herd had closed behind the form of Ota Kte, Indian Killer.

10. *Captain Thompson's Horses*

SHORTLY AFTER MIDNIGHT Josh, starting upwind around Captain Thompson's grazing horse herd, ran into the trouble he had spent the past hour begging for.

His first warning was a tremble of the ground under his feet. He knew the sign. In the next second he dove headlong for the only cover, a six-foot gullywash in the prairie level.

His instinctive thought was that the Cheyenne horse herd had winded him and begun to run. But by the time he got his eyes back above the lip of the gully, he knew better. They were Cheyenne ponies all right and they were running. But they weren't stampeding. Astride each crouched a slit-eyed savage.

Much has been written, and will be, about the war-whooping, bloodcurdling cries of an Indian assault. About the heathen war screaming and caterwauling of the red warrior as he rides down upon his enemy. But any High Plains scout worth his salt could tell the writers something about that.

Any time the hostiles meant real business and were not just whooping it up for the benefit of some delegation from the Indian Bureau, they rode with no more noise than the churn of unshod pony hoofs and the grunts of cayuse ribs being caved in by barrel-swung rifle butts.

It was the classic pattern of the High Plains raider on profit bent. The profit these particular raiders were bent on taking was the choice cavalry herd of Captain Wil-

liam Thompson's G Troop. They were going to take it
too. A man could see that plain as prairie moonlight.
Josh saw something else as well, before ducking his head
and letting them thunder past. He saw three chiefs riding neck-and-neck in the van of the hostile swoop: a
lean, hawk-headed devil in the middle, a towering blob
flanking him on the right and a skull-adorned buzzard
hugging his left.

Aii-eee, brother! Those were the Dog Soldiers out
there. A man better remember it and keep his head hard
down.

There was nothing wrong with Josh's memory. And
he could tuck his neck tighter than a sleeping sagehen,
happen the cover was scant and the sign read Cheyenne.
By the time he dared take a second look over the edge
of the gully, the Dog Soldiers had driven the cavalry
horses past the fort and were hazing them for the river.
He watched them long enough for the thrash of the
stampede to hit the water, telling him the raiders were
driving wide around Black Kettle's camp. With that, he
was up and running.

Damn their lousy hides! There was a typical Indian
trick for you. A white man would never get on to the
ways of their crazy minds. Let five hundred of them ride
in and make a decent peace and fifty of them would ride
out and start a war. Let a troop of cavalry make a suc-
cessful palaver and the hotheads of the tribe would immediately figure the way to get back at the white sol-
dier-brother would be to run off the selfsame horses he
had sat on at the council.

Damn the red idiots again. If there ever had been a
chance Custer would get cooled down by old Black Kettle's peace talk, that chance was now as gone as Captain
Thompson's horses.

Cuss them as he would, though, a man needn't pretend they were as dumb as they acted. Mad Wolf had
failed to come into that council for a good reason. And
such of his boys as had come into it had come knowing
they would be booted out by Custer. Black Kettle wanted peace and he thought he had made it. Mad Wolf had

thought the same thing. But the Dog Soldier chief wanted war, not peace. And, come blue norther or slush-thaw chinook, he was going to have it!

Particularly when getting it was no more trouble than running off a prime horse herd within sight and rifle shot of the biggest Pony Soldier camp west of Fort Riley.

He redoubled his silent curses as he called out his identity to the main gate sentries and loped past them toward Custer's quarters.

The lousy, no-good, settlement-raiding red sons. They'd fixed it now so's old Moxtaveto would get the full credit for the horse herd run-off and guaranteed that war would come to the Washita right on Sheridan's dirty schedule. They'd spoiled any last chance he or anybody else might have to talk Custer out of a winter campaign. They'd ruined any outside shot whatever of a regular spring and summer chase whereby a man could figure to earn the pay he needed for starting that North Canadian cowspread. They'd fixed it, too, so he'd likely never again lay eyes on that beautiful Indian girl.

Goddam that mangy Mad Wolf clean to hell, and all his murdering Dog Soldiers with him. If it was the last Indian Josh Kelso ever killed, he was going to put *that one* under for keeps!

Knowing none of the troopers guarding the cavalry herd had beaten him into the fort, he was surprised to see the lamplight in Custer's office as hard at work as it had been three hours earlier. The surprise didn't slow his knock, nor the boot of his moccasin-toe against the door planks.

He came into the commander's office narrowing his eyes to the brightness of the lamp. As quickly as his eyes narrowed, they widened again.

"Gabe, for Cripes sake! If it ain't the old he-coon hisself!"

With the shout, he was belaboring the old mountain man. Jim Bridger, protecting himself as best he could, backed off complainingly.

"Blast yer hide, ye slabfoot mountain ox! Whut ye aimin' to do, tromp a man to death? Lay off now, you hear me, dang ye? I didn't sashay all the way out here to git put under by no White Comanche!"

Custer sat back, giving master and apprentice time to get over, mountain-man style, the fact they hadn't seen one another since the older scout had given up fighting Blackfeet and Mormons in the days of his beloved Fort Bridger. When the assorted greetings and Green River insults had quieted down, he lost no time in updating Kelso on what had brought his famous tutor back to the frontier.

Aged and infirm, the old Indian fighter had made the long overland trip from his Missouri homestead to urge Custer to abandon his plans for a winter campaign. Bridger felt the cavalry could not survive in the field the rigors of the High Plains blizzards. He had come in by army ambulance from Fort Larned within the past hour. His pleas, passionately made, had already been denied.

Josh remained quiet until Custer had gotten that far. Then, before Bridger might again take up the argument, he brought the meeting to present order.

"Well, Gabe, I allow this here winter campaign was my own little brain shower, but that ain't neither here nor there right now. What's here, is the General all gingered up to fight Black Kettle. What's there," the young scout pointed the prairie beyond the south stockade, "is Mad Wolf a'runnin' off every last head of Captain Thompson's hosses."

"What the devil are you saying, man?" Custer was on his feet, thin face livid.

"I already said it, General. The Dog Soldiers just run off G Troop's hosses."

"By the Lord, sir, I don't believe it!" The officer's face clouded, his voice dropping. "Who told you, Joshua?"

"I never take nobody's word for nothin'. I reckon you know that."

"You've been outside, sir?"

"Somewhat."

"With the Cheyennes?"

"More or less." The shrug was noncommittal. "You want to hear about my life with the Injuns, General, or what happened to Thompson's hosses?"

"By thunder, sir, I had your word. I want to know what you were doing outside the stockade!"

The second shrug compounded the indifference of the first. "I didn't cotton to the way Mad Wolf hid out on the council today, nor the looks on such of his boys as he sent in, when you sent them packin'. I figured old Axhonehe was up to somethin'. Figurin' same, I took myself a *pasear* over the wall just now and cussed near got myself run down. They come by me hand-close on the first pass. I seen them, you can lay."

"You're sure?"

"I said I seen them. Mad Wolf, Big Body, Yellow Buffalo, the lot of them. I told you Black Kettle wasn't mixed in with this bunch."

Before Custer could vent the spleen this defiant claim deserved, or the silent Bridger get started to questioning it, the door crashed open to admit the bug-eyed front runner of Thompson's troopers.

"Beg pardon, Colonel Custer, sir, but them lousy Cheyenne just run off our horses!"

"What horses, Corporal?"

Custer's query was as matter-of-fact as though he were questioning the trooper on the condition of his carbine. Again, Josh wondered at his capacity for control in front of troops. He could rave and rant like a rotten-spoiled kid so long as nobody military was within earshot. But just let the lowest buck private on the post step into range and he was all at once Lieutenant Colonel G. A. Custer, Commanding, and don't let anybody forget it!

"Captain Thompson's, sir." The trooper's reply came over Kelso's thoughts. "Every last head of G Troop, as we had 'em on graze just south of the fort."

"Did you see any of the Indians, Corporal? That is, to identify them with any certainty?" Custer was eying Josh, not the flustered soldier.

"Yes sir, they was the Cheyennes. Rode down into us right from their camp yonder."

"Did you recognize any individual? Any of the Indians who were at the council this evening?" The questions came deliberately. "Was there moonlight enough to see reliably by?"

"Yes sir, there was, and yes sir, I did. I seen old Black Kettle hisself, a'ridin' right up in front and a'leadin' the whole shebang!"

"That's a damn lie, soldier!" Josh was towering over the trooper, dark eyes blazing. Custer's voice cut in between them.

"That will do, Joshua. I'll not have you bullyragging the men. I want this boy's story and I'm quite competent to get it without your help."

"This 'boy,' " the scout nodded acidly, "better get his own story—and get it straight! I don't aim to stand by and listen to no more rot from a green-bellied cavalry boot. Not when it comes to Injuns, by God. I seen them Cheyenne, General. They was Dog Soldiers!"

The trooper, sensing his commander's sympathy, fought back defiantly.

"They was from the camp, Colonel, sir. We seen 'em comin'. And I seen that there Black Kettle too, clear as day!"

"I've had it, General. You can—" He was starting for the door, starting to say that Custer could draw his pay, when he had to step back to avoid being run over by the rush through the open doorway of the corporal's fellow herd guards.

"Beggin' your pardon, Colonel, sir," the spokesman for the three took up the corporal's claim, "but we seen them Cheyenne comin' from that camp and we seen Black Kettle too. And Smitty here, he seen somethin' else!"

"All right, Smith, what did you see? Out with it, man."

"Yes sir, well sir, I was the last one away, bein' on the far side of the herd when they struck us. As I legged it in, I looked back toward the Injun camp and they was

pullin' out, sir. Headin' smack for the Arkansas, fast as
they could mount up and make off!"

"Good! Good!" Custer's pale eyes were snapping as
he wheeled on Josh. "You hear that, Joshua? What do
you say now, sir?"

The big scout, still seething, was nevertheless glad he
hadn't gotten to ask for his pay. He had had time in the
ten-second interval to think once more of Monaseetah,
and to realize his best chance of ever seeing the Cheyenne girl again was in sticking, burr-tight, to Custer and
the Seventh Cavalry. Regardless, he was bound to speak
his professional piece.

"I say, figure it this way. Happen you was the old
man, what would you do as soon as your own hoss
guards run in and told you the Dog Soldiers had just lifted some of Yellah Hair's hosses? He knows you, General, remember that. And he knows what damned liars
your men are. He figured it just as sure as he was standin' here listenin' to us, that you'd blame him for the
run-off. So he just up and got shut of you as far and fast
as he could. Naturally."

"All right, Joshua—"

That "Joshua" didn't fool a man for a minute. Custer
was hopping mad and holding down only because troops
were present. A man knew that, and he didn't need the
little rooster's next words to prove it.

"You may go, sir. I shall want you back here at four
A.M., and I suggest you bring some better manners and a
quiet mouth when you come. That will be all, sir."

Josh turned without a word, paused only to shake
hands with the embarrassed Bridger.

"Sorry, Gabe. Didn't aim to drag you into any family
ruckus thisaway. See you tomorrow, old salt."

"Sure as shootin', boy. You grab yourself some sleep
now, hear? You're edgy, Josh."

"Yeah, I reckon." He managed a shade of the old
grin. *"Nataemhon,* old hoss."

"Good huntin', boy—" The aging scout echoed the
old Cheyenne phrase as he moved to follow his tall
protégé to the door.

Josh moved out and away from the lamplight. He
paused, as he did, to look back quickly. The forlorn picture of the old mountain man, rheumy-eyed and gaunt,
his goiter-misshapen throat bulging past the frayed col-
lars of his settlement shirt, his trembling hand lifted to
wave uncertainly from the yellow frame of the doorway,
brought a sick, slow tug to his heart.

Somehow, he knew the old man was saying goodbye.
He hesitated, accordingly, while the lamplight still picked
out his own youth-lean form. Flicking the fingertips
of his left hand to his forehead he spread them swiftly
with the point of his long arm, in parting salute to the
lonely figure in the doorway.

He waited only long enough to see by the return sign
that the old man understood, then turned away, soft-
footed, to vanish in the outer darkness of the parade
yard.

It was the last time he ever saw Jim Bridger.

11. *Young Tom Custer*

THE THIN GRAY of the four o'clock, false dawn put the
hunch of its chill in the saddled back of Wasiya where
the gelding stood in front of Custer's office. Presently
the Sioux pony lifted his nose, cocked an ear to the
flood of light released by the opening door, and whickered softly to the familiar, gaunt figure of his approaching rider.

He was rewarded, shortly, by a kick in the ribs and
some suitably terse directions.

"Hump it, hoss." Josh's weight settled in the saddle.

The tone of his grunt let the gelding know he was in for a rough day. "We got a damn diaper detail to wetnurse. Howsomever," the voice lifted to the chronic, quick grin, "happen we're pure lucky we won't lose no more than a night's sleep out of it."

Following his rider's knee-guide, Wasiya swung out of the street and headed for the main gate. He broke into a lope as he caught and passed the little column of mounted troopers already moving out of the fort. Josh reined him in alongside the youthful officer heading the column.

"Mornin', Tom. The General tells me he's lettin' you get your feet wet today."

"Yeah, Josh," Tom Custer grinned the reply with a proper return of the scout's sloppy salute, "and sending you along to see that I don't get them damp above the knee, eh?"

He nodded, receipting the boy's rich grin with one of his own dry specimens.

Tom was as different from the General as they came. He was a head taller, six heads handsomer and anyway three heads more human. He was friendly as a spaniel and not too much smarter. If the boy had a brain he'd never gotten the chance to prove it, the way the General mother-henned him. Besides, the kid was that convinced his older brother was the greatest cavalryman since Jeb Stuart that he made his own life a looking glass for the General's, reflecting every claim, idea, order or afterthought the former might see fit to hold or hand out.

Withal, though, he was normal as rain in April. And just weak enough in his worship of his brother, to leave off of it short of wearing it thin. Tom would take a stogie quick as the next and his addiction to the occasional cup was as well known as his famous brother's hatred of the habit. A man wouldn't want to say young Tom was a drunk but he could allow the boy had a fair start to getting as sopped as the rest of the Seventh's staff, than which no officer corps on the frontier had a worse or wetter record.

"Yeah," he broke the pause to agree with the youngster's probe, "I reckon that's so. But you needn't get huffed about it. Happen I hadn't convinced the General there wasn't no more than thirty head of hostiles in the bunch what run off Thompson's hosses, you wouldn't have got the detail, boy."

"Come along now, Josh!" The infectious grin was spreading again. "You're not hinting you deliberately mislead the General so that I'd get the chance to chase these redskins?"

"Somewhat. Course there *was* only thirty of them actually run off the hosses. But I happen to know there's another two hundred and seventy of them where that thirty come from. I allowed if the General knowed it was that big a bunch he'd have wanted to go after them hisself."

"I don't follow you, Josh." The boy's smile faltered with the words. "Are you saying you went out of your way to keep the General from going after these Cheyenne?"

"I am."

"I don't believe I like the sound of that, Joshua." The smile was gone.

"Like it or lump it, boy, but get it straight. I'd rather chase three thousand ordinary Injuns than three hundred Dog Soldiers. Had the General come along I couldn't have held him off of them. With you I figure I can. And boy, when we get out yonder and the tracks start gettin' prime hot, you remember that. So long as you and your eighty lads don't want to wind up with your hair hangin' down a Cheyenne lodge smokehole, you hold up when Josh Kelso tells you to. You hear me now, Tom?"

The youngster shot an uneasy glance back toward his small column. It looked much smaller now that Fort Dodge was falling so rapidly to the rear. He turned with a sober nod to the waiting scout.

"Sure, I hear you, Josh. You don't have to worry, man. I've got my orders too, you know."

Josh was at once concerned, thinking Custer had slipped in some dangerous instructions in briefing the youngster before talking to him. Watching him carefully, he said, "What you mean by that, boy?"

" 'You are, sir,' " Tom Custer mimicked the Seventh's C.O. perfectly, " 'to do precisely what Joshua proposes in any given situation. And you are not, sir, to use your own judgment in any case. Is that clear, sir?' "

Josh picked up the concluding grin and tossed it back. "We'll get along, boy." His accompanying thumb-jerk went quickly over his shoulder toward the following troopers. "Tell them to pick it up. We ain't got all week."

The youthful officer's "forward ho!" rang out immediately. The column responded by moving from a trot to a lope as it swung left to cross and move away from the Arkansas, bearing almost due east into the trackless grass of the open prairie.

It had been 4.30 A.M. when Josh had turned the column away from Fort Dodge and across the Arkansas. Ten hours later they had seen no more sign of Captain Thompson's stolen horse herd than the wide track of its passing which now, as at the crossing, stretched clearly away eastward.

Frowning, he pulled Wasiya up and grunted to young Custer to wave the halt to the following column. Pointing to the high swell of prairie confronting them a half-mile ahead, he spoke quickly.

"Well, Tom, what you want to do? Past yonder rise you get into a bad batch of sandhills. We ain't even seen herd dust yet and I don't cotton to the looks of things."

"Hell, Josh," the youngster didn't share his brother's restraint of vocabulary, "we're not well started yet. Besides, the lack of dust doesn't mean anything, does it? We've been on buffalo grass all along. That keeps the dust down, doesn't it?"

"It does," nodded the scout. "It keeps it down so you don't know whether they're ten miles or two hundred yards ahead of you. Gettin' into them hills like we will be now, you can't see far enough ahead to even take a guess, neither."

"I'll take one. My guess is that we're still way behind them, Josh. Let's move along. We've got lots of time. Remember, we don't have to get back to the fort."

He was remembering just that, and scowling as he remembered it. Custer's orders had been to trail the raiders as long as possible, then, failing a contact, to swing south and west to join his Camp Supply column in the field. This last was exactly what he wanted to avoid. No army scout, least of all Josh Kelso, admired spending a night in the open with a green lieutenant and eighty raw recruits. Not, at least, when that open was inhabited by three hundred Cheyenne horse raiders.

Still, a man knew young Tom was right. They did have lots of time and no good reason for turning back.

"All right boy, let's do it this way. You and me takes twenty troopers and tops out on yonder swell. The rest waits here. That's a bad country past that ridge. I got me an idea we'll be glad we didn't poke our whole nose past it."

Tom Custer agreed at once, leaving the main column with Lieutenant Edward Law and moving for the high ground ahead after arranging with Law to move up on signal should they find something.

Two minutes later he and Josh were atop the ridge and had indeed "found something."

As the latter had predicted the ground sloped sharply past the crest of the rise. Beyond the slope lay a level saucer of grass. Beyond that began the precipitous channels of the Kansas sandhills. But what widened the eyes of the young officer was not the slope, nor the saucer, nor the sandhills.

It was Captain Thompson's horse herd standing peacefully in the middle of the open grass below, unattended save by half a dozen sleepy Cheyenne guards.

"By God, we've got them, Josh!" He was turning to wave the "forward ho" when his companion seized his unflung arm.

"Not quite, youngster. Wait up now."

The disgruntled officer wheeled on him but was given no chance to get started.

"Look, Tom boy, use your head. You see how close them hosses is bein' held to them sandhills?"

"Certainly. What of it?"

"Them hills could hide the whole Cheyenne Nation, let alone three hundred hoss raiders. Check them hair-braids and three feathers on them guard bucks. Them's Dog Soldiers, son!"

"A trap, eh Josh?" The boy smiled a little weakly, realizing the situation belatedly. "Using our own horses as bait—"

"Yeah, Tom. But I allow this is one trap that's set just right to get back-sprung!"

Catching the rare excitement in his scout's voice the young officer questioned him quickly. He got his answers in the same vein.

"Signal Law to come up and lay low just this side of the ridge. After that me and you and our twenty boys will ride on down like we didn't smell nothin'. When they jump us we cut and run back for the ridge, leadin' them up and over and smack into eighty cavalry carbines. You got that boy?"

Custer got it. The preparations were carried out. A noncom was sent racing back to instruct Law's troops who were now moving forward. The rest of the troopers on the ridge nervously kneed their mounts down the slope after their commander and his hard-faced scout.

When they were three hundred yards from the herd the sleepy horse guards came awake. Turning, they fled for the sandhills as thought there weren't another Indian to aid the horse guards in Kansas Territory. Then, when they were fifty yards into the hills, they came racing back out of them as though they had miraculously found every hostile south of the Arkansas. Which indeed it appeared they had.

Mad Wolf's three hundred ambushed Dog Soldiers came belching out of the hidden gullies with such a rush they very nearly swallowed up Josh's counterbait before the scout could get the startled troopers turned around.

Once the race stretched out, however, the big cavalry horses opened up the distance between themselves and

the scrawny mounts of the Dog Soldiers to a hundred
yards. This space was widened to nearly two hundred by
the time the slope was surmounted and the counterbait
party had wheeled its mounts into position with the
waiting line of Law's men.

The rest was easy the way such things went.

There never was the Indian, Dog Soldier or otherwise, who would linger around to argue about odds of
less than three to one on well-mounted and well-led
white soldiers. Josh had figured on that.

The hostile horde came pouring over the crest of the
ridge in typical Indian order, the fastest ponies and
boldest riders well in advance. These startled vanguards
threw their ponies on their haunches the minute they
saw the waiting cavalry line. Their following companions piled over the ridge and into them at full speed.

At the moment of maximum snarl-up, Josh nodded to
Tom Custer and shouldered his Henry carbine. The
steady bark of the repeater was seconded by the timed
volleys of the eighty Spencers behind it.

Josh counted twelve ponies down in the first volley.
By the time the second was ripping into the retreating
hostile rear, no less than twenty Cheyenne ponies were
struggling on the ground. But with the usual Indian alac-
rity and of course the superb Cheyenne horsemanship,
the disorganized Dog Soldiers managed to scoop up
most of their wounded as they fled the ridge in the face
of the immediate charge led by Tom Custer.

One brave, alone, lingered too long in attempting to
aid a wounded fellow, letting Wasiya bring Josh down
on top of him.

The scout drove the giant Sioux gelding into the
scrubby Cheyenne pony, knocking the little animal
sprawling. Before the warrior could recover Josh had
him in a South Park bearhug with his skinning knife
planted above his right kidney.

"Don't move, cousin. I'm not going to kill you."

The guttural Cheyenne assurance was superfluous.
The terrified brave had already assumed from the identity of his captor that his time was overshort, and was be-

seeching Maheo, the Cheyenne Almighty, to witness that he died without fear and in pursuance of his sacred duty of killing Pony Soldiers.

By the time Custer returned from his short pursuit of the Dog Soldiers, driving the recovered horse herd ahead of him, Josh and his skinning knife had struck up a speaking acquaintance with the Cheyenne buck.

An acquaintance not painful to the red man alone. Adding it all up now, as he hung back to outride the column's rear against any surprise return of the routed Dog Soldiers, the white scout wrinkled the unburned bridge of his nose with considerable anguish. He grimaced savagely as he scowled his unspoken curses through the rising dust of the recaptured cavalry herd. No matter how a man turned it, it came out the same.

Somebody had tipped off Mad Wolf about him having been in the Cheyenne camp the night before!

And had done it fast enough for the Dog Soldier to bring his boys down onto that herd of Thompson's before he got back to the fort. It didn't seem possible they could have moved that fast but it had to be that way.

The captured Dog Soldier had made that clear when he's said that Mad Wolf had ordered the raid by telling them Ota Kte was passing close to the herd and would thus be named to scout for whatever soldier party set out after the raiders. It was hard to swallow but judging from what the brave said, the whole thing had been set up and run off on the outside chance of drawing him away from the fort with a small pursuit party.

That much of it didn't bother him. He'd known all along the Dog Soldier chief was after him, and that he was idiot enough to try anything to get him. But the one thing which jolted a man was that *somebody* had told Mad Wolf that he'd been in, and just left the Cheyenne camp.

That somebody had to be a Cheyenne.

There were only two Cut-Arms in that camp who'd known he was in it. Black Kettle for one. Monaseetah for the other.

From there a man could twist it some more, and all he wanted. It still came out one answer.

There was no sound reason on God's green prairie why the old Cheyenne chief would put the Dog Soldiers onto him and that horse herd. It would be the last thing the old man would want, to get Custer riled in any way. Especially in any way that would associate him with the Dog Soldiers.

A man could set his jaw all he wanted to, and scowl his damndest through that horse-herd dust. And cuss in Cheyenne, Sioux, Comanche or Arapaho. There was one Indian, and one alone, who could have set Mad Wolf onto him in such a hurry last night.

Her name wasn't Black Kettle.

12. Middle Cimarron Springs

ON JOSH'S RECOMMENDATION Lieutenant Custer abandoned his plan to head west in attempting to intercept his older brother's column on its line of march over the Jornada or Dry Crossing between the Arkansas and the Cimarron. The scout warned that young Custer's own column, without water for the horses since leaving the Arkansas the morning of the 14th, would have to strike a stream by noon of the 15th or be in serious trouble.

He chose, therefore, Josh's suggestion of the longer course of following down the Lower Crossing of the Jornada to strike the Cimarron and move up that stream's channel to join the General's column at its first nightcamp out of Dodge—the Lower Spring of the Cimarron.

The column, moving at a forced walk-trot, the best

gait possible in consideration of the large herd of loose stock being driven with it, cut into the Lower Crossing road about 6.00 A.M. It turned south along the ruts of the abandoned wagon route, forcing the pace for another three hours. There was no sign of following hostiles.

Ten o'clock brought them to the Cimarron and the unpleasant fact of having Josh's prediction it would be dry at this season borne out. The last of the water in the men's canteens was employed in washing the clotting dust from the horses' nostrils and in squeezing a few precious drops into each mount's swollen mouth.

They pressed on at once, a four-hour, horse-killing ride bringing them in distant sight and water-smell of Lower Spring about 2.00 P.M. They were camped, and the last head of stock watered-out and on graze by three o'clock.

Tom Custer, soldier enough to know when he had missed a bad blunder by a few hours, and man enough to admit it, called Josh aside and expressed his gratitude. The taciturn scout quickly shrugged the compliment aside, but not that quickly his keen mind didn't think about how differently the other brother would have handled the same situation.

In his entire association with the older Custer he couldn't remember having once been thanked for a good job well done. Plenty of praise and promise beforehand, always. But let the affair be well or brilliantly brought off, no matter there might be reward and to spare in it for all concerned, the General always managed to somehow wind up with his own thumb in the middle of the plum.

Shortly before dusk, the senior Custer's column moved in along the main road of the Middle Crossing. Josh was amazed at its size—twelve full companies of the seventh, together with an ammunition and supply train of over forty wagons. Among the officers he recognized Majors Joel Elliott, Gibbs and Tilford, Captains Benteen, Keogh, Hamilton and Yates, Lieutenants Moylan, Brewster, Longan and Cook. The selection let him know the Boy General had handpicked his companies

with dangerous care. Outside of Benteen, Joe Tilford
and Miles Keogh, with maybe Billy Cook among the
juniors, the officers of the Camp Supply column were all
pretty much cut to Custer's own slapdash pattern. Particularly was this true of Joel Elliott, the Colonel's second-in-command.

He knew the senior major nearly as well as he did his
commander. Elliott was not alone Custer's second-in-
command but was as well, to the scout's rueful knowledge, his chief's camp-favorite and boon buffalo-hunting companion. A man could guide out many a long
column of Indian chasers without being backed by a
better combination of bad-reckless commanders. True
enough, there wasn't a brace of field officers on the frontier to match them for guts and go-ahead. But when a
man could read military brands as certainly as Josh
could, he had to know that Major Joel Elliott was as
flank-marked for trouble as ever his long-haired commander.

Custer's present spirits reflected his scout's uneasy
presentiments. His main column had seen no hostile sign
and although its scouts, California Joe, Apache Bill, Ben
Clark, Jimmy Morrison and the Mexican, "Romeo,"
insisted the lack of sign was "bad doin's," Yellow Hair
was in his usual Indian fettle. Which would be to say, in
Josh's short way, "he was ridin' high, smilin' wide, and
seein' bad."

Tom Custer's report did nothing to diminish the Little
General's optimism and before the cook fires had made
a decent bed of coals a man could choke himself on the
smoke of overconfidence fogging that Lower Spring camp.

Despite his professional misgivings, Josh was pleased
enough to find his primary employer so well taken with
himself. And with the auspicious outlet of his campaign
to put himself and his Seventh Cavalry back on the military maps. And back, too, on the front pages of the eastern newspapers which so assiduously printed those maps
when the "fiendish" quarry was dark red of skin and the
"heroic" huntsman bright yellow of hair.

A man needed to catch Custer just right happen he

aimed to get any special favors. The General was one who liked to keep his scouts in close where he could accompany them and better their advice with his own. Josh Kelso had no intention of being "in close" to either the column or its commander, come sundown of the following day. Whether a man really thought that plush-bodied Indian girl had double-crossed him or not, he couldn't get the powder burn of that kiss off his lips.

Come the hell or high water of Custer's disapproval or otherwise, he was going to be in that cottonwood grove at Middle Spring of the Cimarron "when the sun was low" tomorrow afternoon.

He'd get his answer out of the girl as to how Mad Wolf had found out about his visit to Black Kettle's lodge. But before he got that out of her there was something else he aimed to get. Something the thought of which put the blood thick and dark in his face.

If he never got another thing in his life, he was going to get the rest of that kiss. He was going to get it or die trying.

He was suddenly conscious of nothing but the remembered press of the Indian girl's body in the darkness of Moxtaveto's tipi. Impatiently, he sought out Custer's orderly.

The young trooper soon returned with the word that the Colonel had dined, dismissed his staff and would indeed be most pleased to see his favorite scout and fellow buffalo hunter.

Once with the ebullient officer, he eased into what he'd come for as gracefully as he could, being first forced to sit still to the rambling narrative of the buffalo seen on the way down, in particular one herd of bulls spotted in an enclosed valley just south of the Arkansas.

"By Heaven, Joshua, I had the glasses on them twenty minutes. Counted no less than fifty record heads, sir. There's plenty of grass and water in that draw and they're unquestionably there for the winter. We shall have a time of it, sir, believe me, once we've gotten this cursed Cheyenne camp cleaned out."

"Yes sir," he made deliberate use of the rare respect,

"I imagine we will, sure enough. Right now, though, General, I've got somethin' else in my craw. Can't seem to get it down, neither. I'm hopin' you can help me, as usual."

"Why certainly, Joshua. You know I follow your recommendations wherever possible. What's on your mind, sir?"

"Me and the boys have been talkin'. Joe and the rest of them agrees with me that things is too quiet. But they also agrees with you that it's best for the bulk of us to stay right with you so's you can keep your personal eye on the looks of things as we move along."

He placed his little load of bushwa very carefully in the vulnerable lap of Custer's vanity. He was relieved to note the commander fold his slender hands over the neat pile with obvious relish.

"That's quite right, sir. Now come along, Joshua, what's working in that Cheyenne mind of yours?"

"I want to go on ahead, General. Tonight, I reckon. Aimin' to scout your track between here and Middle Spring. I got it in mind them Dog Soldiers me and Tom brushed with ain't so bad hurt they wouldn't think of swingin' wide and tryin' somethin' fancy at the spring."

"Good idea, Joshua." Custer surrendered to the scout's back-scratching. "Matter of fact, I was going to suggest just that. Old Hard Rope and my Osage scouts joined us yesterday so I can spare you overnight. See you're back with the column by tomorrow noon, however. And don't spend any of *my* time looking for your Cheyenne light-of-love. I'm paying you to pursue Indians, to be sure, but not amorously, sir!"

He put his peg-toothed grin behind the sly remark as Josh, rising to go, returned it with a sober nod.

"Why, I ain't thought of her since last we talked, General," he lied, straight-faced. "Leastways, not so's you could notice it."

"That's a confounded falsehood, sir. On both counts. No man could help thinking of that girl, least of all a mountain elk like you. And you needn't think I haven't noticed you doing so, sir!"

The grin was still behind the good-natured innuendo and Josh, clearly relieved, took it at face value.

The General might be a lot of things but there wasn't a small bone in his body. Nor, when it came to white man's morals, a bad one. A man knew now, if he hadn't all along, that there'd never been anything body-wise between Custer and Monaseetah. A man of his make-up might make light of many an ordinary confidence but he would never joke with another man about a woman both might have known. Apache Bill had been right. The time had come and he was remembering what the older scout had said. The General admired that Indian girl as he would a proud-fine piece of horseflesh—just that straight-out, clean-minded way, and not one damn way more.

"I allow you shot me center both rounds, General. You ain't lost your aimin' eye, by Cripes."

Turning to go, he returned Custer's friendly wave. "See you downtrail, tomorrow, happen Mad Wolf don't see me first."

He rode only far enough out of the cavalry camp to be well clear of it for an early start in the morning. A man wanted his eyes and ears sharp for tomorrow's ride. The best way he knew to whet both was with about eight hours' good sleep. Unsaddling the gelding, he picketed him close in to the river. In a matter of seconds he was deep into the trained-soldier-sleep of the professional frontiersman. He came awake around 4:00 A.M., saddled up and moved out.

He saw nothing in that morning's wary ride, stopped to water and graze Wasiya about ten o'clock, mounted up and moved on.

It had turned off blazing hot for a November day, the way it will freakishly do in the Cimarron country, and between him and Middle Spring now, the river cover was so thin it wouldn't decently shade a short lizard. By the time he sighted the cottonwoods and willows of the spring he was sweat-hot and ready for water.

Scouting the perimeter of the grove, he rode in to find

Middle Spring as inviting as ever. The gushing spring
and eighty-foot pool of river water footing it could not
have been better designed to strike a desert-wilted mountain man as prime fixings.

He was purposely an hour early for his "appointment" with the Cheyenne lady, aiming thus to avoid any
outright traps she might have set up for him. It was clear
from his preliminary scout that no such plan was in op-
eration. The grove had been too still and peaceful to
rate a second look. After enough years at it, a man developed a feel for things like that stretch of brush. The
hell with it. Right now everything was sitting pretty at
Middle Spring of the Cimarron, and he could tend to
himself for a change.

Following a long drink from the spring, he dragged
Wasiya's saddle over to a handy sunny clearing, loaded
his pipe and stretched out on the short curl of the buffalo grass.

Ah, that was more like it, mister! Nothing like a
stone bowl of shagcut and a twenty-minute catnap to lift
a man's troubles.

Or, better yet, his scalp. . . .

13. The Holy Iron

THE FIRST HINT he had that all was not well along the
Cimarron was when a chance, sleepy-eyed glance showed
him Wasiya flaring his curious nostrils towards the far
edge of the clearing. Six foot two of nerve-strung white
scout came rolling to his feet.

It had to be Indians coming, even though he'd padded

a circle around that grove as cautious as an old dog lying down in tall-grass snake country. So what the hell did a man do now? Sprint for his gun? Stand there with his arms folded, hoping they'd take him for the second coming of Anpetuwi, the Sun God? Or go diving into the nearby brush where he could get ten seconds to think?

It wasn't much of a choice. Josh dove.

The shade in the brush clump was as cool as the laugh which came with it.

He whirled, plastering his back to the nearest sapling, sunblinded eyes squinting to adjust the shadows. The laugh came again and with it, this time, some words in a guttural tongue he had cut his second teeth on.

If he had thought Monaseetah looked good in the prairie dark of Black Kettle's tipi or in the uncertain flicker of Custer's council fire, he had a second think coming in the cool daylight of Middle Spring grove.

She was a little thing, less than armpit high to Kelso, very light copper in color, with level eyes and that rare, mahogany-bright hair you sometimes saw in the Southern Cheyenne. Her features were as regular as a high-bred white woman's and her figure, hardly damaged by the cling of the thin elkskins, was like none you'd ever seen on a white woman, high- or low-bred. A man needn't have crawled through as many tipi flaps as he had to know those rising breasts and shifting hips under that tanned elk were as bouncy-firm and juicy as a winter apple.

"*Vahe, Veho!*" She repeated the snowflash of her smile, bringing his wandering gaze back to her face. "Welcome to my tipi, White Man."

Josh began to demonstrate his skull was stuffed with something sterner than the pap he'd been using for brains the past half-hour. He watched her closely, answering in Cheyenne.

"It's easy to talk pretty words. I want to know what is in your heart. Why have you come here? What do you want of Ota Kte?"

"I did not come to talk pretty," said the girl, "but

only to look pretty." She stared at him full-eyed, the
dazzle of her smile doing nothing to give the lie to her
answer.

"Aye," he nodded, tough intentions melting under the
heat of her regard, "it's a true thing. Your tongue is
straight. You are very beautiful."

It was her turn to hesitate. *"He-hau,"* she smiled, de-
murely, "the *Veho* is pretty too. *Hoko hotao!*"

He thought this last remark over, the translation leaving him at once man-proud. To be standing in front of a
beautiful young girl, no matter she was only a red Indian, and to have her running her eyes up from your toes
to your scalplock and not missing anything in between,
either, was addling enough. Add to that that she looked
you square in the eye and told you you were a "real bull
buffalo," and any man was heading himself into a stampede.

Sternly fighting down his thoughts, he put his unwilling mind once more to his present position.

"Listen, girl, I'm in a bad country here. There is
much danger for me." He watched her again, hard-eyed.
"Where are the Dog Soldiers, Bright Hair?"

"There is no danger for you, *Veho.*"

"You lie," he said flatly. "And keep this in your
mind. If your tongue is not straight, the snout of this
Holy Iron is." He patted the Henry barrel. "Where are
the Dog Soldiers?"

"My tongue is straight, *Veho.* There is no danger.
The Dog Soldiers are two suns east, driving the horses
they stole from the soldier camp."

The fact she knew about the horse herd run-off
quickened his suspicions. *"Ame vita!"* he snapped. "That's
a pile of pure fat!"

"No *Ota Kte,* no!" The smiles were gone. "My tongue
is straight!"

"Remember, Bright Hair, the Holy Iron is watching
you."

"Let him watch something else." The girl's plea came
with the supple gesture, pushing the rifle bore away

from her stomach. "His eye in my navel makes me nervous!"

Josh nodded, the shade of a smile chasing the frown lines for an instant. After all, maybe it made sense. She could know about the horse herd run-off. Indian news had a way of traveling faster than any white man could ride. And apparently she didn't know the herd had been recovered. That stood in her favor.

"All right, girl. Let's talk about something else. Like you and me, perhaps—"

With the words he moved toward her, his ears suddenly closed to all danger, his eyes seeing nothing but the full-bodied look of her standing there staring at him.

She stepped back, the smile playing again, her mood shifting as quickly as a prairie breeze.

"Do you swim, *Veho*? As good as a Cheyenne?"

The impish suggestion stopped the scout, catching him without an answer, making him stammer.

"I don't know. How good can a Cheyenne swim?"

"This good, *Veho!*"

Her answer was muffled by the upsweep of the elk-skin dress as it went off over her head to be carelessly flung on the grass. He gasped as the red blaze of the late sun struck the girl's body.

From the high-pointing breasts to the slim insteps of the dainty feet, she stood stark, pagan naked.

He was kicking off his own moccasins then, shucking his leggins, skinning out of his shirt and diving cleanly after her into the river pool of the Cimarron. But it was no contest.

His natural elements more closely associated with the proximity of his britches to a horse's back, or his moccasins to the feel of prairie grass, Josh was not at home in the water. After a minute he gave up his losing pursuit of the Indian girl and hauled out on a midstream sand-spit to watch her gleaming body knife around the shelving bank of the spit.

By damn, here was a woman. The man on the sand-spit was beginning to know that.

Ride, shoot, build a fire. Just let a man name it, she

could do it. No doubt she could bead a moccasin, gut game, mend a buckskin shirt, tan a robe, pound pemmican and boil dog too. But what the hell? Was that against her? Was it, happen a man was thinking of setting up a cow ranch right in her backyard? And thinking, too, maybe, of asking her in as a fifty-fifty partner?

Josh found himself thinking it wasn't. Doubtless all along God had cut him to size for an Indian girl. He just hadn't been brainy enough to see it. Likely they would make it down the trail pretty fair, him and Monaseetah.

Presently, the girl had had enough of the water.

Flushed and smiling she came to him, sitting cross-legged in front of him with the request he try his clumsy hands at a task they must, as any proper Cheyenne husband's, become accustomed to: the care of his woman's hair.

Her simple request, along with its innocent implication of her future being accepted as that of his woman, brought a loneliness and longing into him he had never known. Such as the poignant feeling was however, he did not let it interfere with the business to hand, that of the braids.

When he had gotten them undone with a deftness which well might have led the Indian girl to wonder how much practice he had had, she shook her head to fluff the hair, speeding the process with quick, flinging motions of her hands. In a matter of seconds the bright mane shone like burnished metal against the tiger glow of her skin.

Now, when Josh would throw his lean arm behind her neck and bury his teeth playfully in the hollow of her shoulder, she wriggled free, jumping to her feet, glancing apprehensively at the angle of the sun and counseling a prompt return to shore.

He arose, taking her offered hand. Her voice came softly.

"Carry me, Ota Kte. I do not wish to wet my hair again."

Nothing loath, he picked her up, not just exactly thinking about the softness of her buttocks on his forearm, nor the firm thrust of her bare breasts against his chest, but just the same knowing he had something better than just any bag of bones and hank of hair in his arms.

She for sure knew it too.

That crossing was so shallow she could have forded it on her hands and knees without wetting a braidtip!

Ashore, he put her gently down on the short pile of the buffalo grass and remained standing over her a moment, his hand still holding hers. She looked up at him, squeezing his hand, with the curving smile. He returned the little pressure, still standing awkwardly, suddenly now, and for the first time, feeling unsure of himself. Feeling shy. And clumsy. Schoolboyish, almost. And certainly, beyond any invitation of the wicked smile and gleaming body of her, very much in love.

Suddenly then, she sensed his hesitation, and guessed, instinctively, its shift of meaning. Without realizing that it had done so, she let the impulse of this swift knowledge remove the bold sensuousness from her smile, replace its wanton lure with a softer curve. A curve of quick, responsive tenderness. A curve, almost, though fleeting and quickly hidden, of haunting sadness.

It will be no different, the world over. It never has been. A maid may seek a man with every provocation of moistly beckoning lips and bold, demanding weave of wanton, soft-fleshed body. And a man may answer to that seeking with the drive of his passions hammering harshly and brutally within him. But only up to the old, old point. The oft-told, time-tried, unfailing moment. The inevitable instant. The particular, unpredictable, capricious minute of passion's progress where love, actual, awkward, of-the-spirit and wondrous "first love," steps unbidden to the fore.

It is in that little fragment of remarkable time that lust becomes worship, passion gives way to adoration, and a kiss becomes a pledge, not a demand.

Josh Kelso was knowing that moment, and knowing it with a poignant, all-pervading sense of bewilderment and heart's confusion which his simple mountain man's

tongue could not, in a million years of untangling itself,
have intelligently stated.

And Monaseetah was, in her own turn, feeling the
first uneasy approach of a real love. Not so deeply as
Josh. And not yet so completely and confusingly.

She came to her feet, the tenderness of her smile
growing. She moved into him, standing on tiptoe to
reach his lean cheek, kissed him lightly and quickly, and
as quickly moved away. By unspoken, thoughtless consent, she retrieved her elkskin camp dress, and he his
buckskin leggins.

Returning to the sand, she drew him down beside her.
They talked slowly at first, and with that halting defer-
ence which comes in the wake of desire turned aside for
spiritual exploration.

Even now, Monaseetah said little, but the talk, once
unleashed, tumbled out of Josh like a mountain stream
in full spring thaw. It was the talk of a lonely man, long
without anyone who would listen, or who would care to
listen. It was soon enough done with his dark and solitary past, and coming swiftly now to the Indian girl and
to his suddenly born dreams for their future together.
But as he would speak, at last, of his love for her, Monaseetah pressed her slim fingers to his lips, bidding him
nay with the troubled shake of her small head. Her soft
arms were around his neck then and he was holding her,
and feeling the burn and quick run of the tears against
his naked shoulder.

He stroked her hair, soothing her with tender, deep-
voiced Cheyenne love-words, cradling her in his arms
like a child, repeating again, and then again, his no
longer awkward promises of their life to come. When
she had at last stilled her sobs and lay in easy-breathing
quiet within his arms, the shade of the cottonwoods had
crept forward to hide their trysting place, and the sun
was only an orange-pink ball tipping the western horizon.

14. Ota Kte's Trap

THEY RESTED, fully dressed now and side by side. The girl's coppery hair was outflung on the scout's buckskinned shoulder. The remaining heat of the earth came up through the muscles of their bodies, flushing them with the slow waves of long relief. Josh idly fingered the beaded waist of Monaseetah's camp frock, then let his big hand seek and find the warm pressure of her slim bronze one. He continued to stare, long and thoughtfully into the gathering gloom of Middle Spring grove.

Presently he spoke, voice soft with the hour's memory. "I am far from my camp, Bright Hair, and the day is going. I must travel soon."

"Aye," the girl whispered, her bright smile fading with strange swiftness, "the moon will be fat tonight. The trail will be good. I am grateful to you, Ota Kte, but you must hurry now. *While there is yet time!*"

Josh, his head full of the coming moonrise and the just-past sunset, missed the peculiar emphasis. His mind was confused now and his heart hopelessly confounded. His tongue remained obstinately mute. He thought a moment, trying to form his words so she wouldn't get any too-fast ideas on what he meant.

A man always felt different afterwards. Like maybe he'd said too much already. You had to watch these Indian women. Like you had to watch a lost dog. One pat on the head too many, and they were apt to follow a man plumb home. He wasn't in any position to be followed right now. Maybe not even of a mind to be fol-

lowed, now or anytime. Damn it all, a man didn't know.
He just didn't know—

"I'll remember you," he said at last and lamely,
knowing that wasn't what he'd meant to say at all.

"To remember is nothing," she said quickly, down-
cast eyes sweeping up his buckskins to hold on the
tanned granite of his face. "To forget, though, that is
something."

"I won't forget you either, girl—"

He clamped the words off, not meaning to have let
them out. Damn it, why couldn't a man just let it go?
Just get up and out of there like he had with others like
her? Or were they like her, by damn? Maybe that was
the rub of it. Maybe a man had best quit horsing himself. Had best admit this little Cheyenne squaw had
winged him with an arrow he'd never break off.

"*Veho*," her voice blocked the growing trail of his
confusion, "when I came to this grove my heart was not
as it now is. I had not looked upon you with my true
eyes. I had not had your great hands upon me, nor your
true love-words in my ear—"

Something in the way she said it took the softness of
the ground from under him.

"What are you trying to say, girl? I don't like the
sound of your voice now. Something is wrong."

"May Maheo forgive me," the girl muttered, "Moxtaveto and my people never will!"

"What do you mean?" He caught the sudden glance
she eye-tailed around the edge of the clearing behind
them. The hackles of fear rose in him now, straight as
the hair on a strange dog's back.

"Lie down, Ota Kte, here by me!" She dropped back
onto the grass, her whisper coming to him fiercely.

"Damn it, gal—"

"You fool, Ota Kte! Do as I say. Down here by my
side, quickly!"

He dropped then and he dropped fast, his lean belly
shrinking at the crowding tumble of her words.

"I have lied to you, Ota Kte, but listen that you may
know my tongue was straight at last. I love you, *Veho*.

As Maheo is my witness, I love you now! But it is too late. I have plotted to trap you here—"

"I knew it! By God, I knew it!" He heard his own thick whisper, shifted instantly from the hissed English to the growl of the Cheyenne. "You and what other one? Quickly now, girl!"

"Axhonehe, my promised one."

Mad Wolf! This beautiful girl and that filthy murderer promised to one another? Working together all along to trap him in cold blood?

"Moxtaveto knew nothing of it, I swear." Her whisper raced savagely ahead. "Oh, hear me now, Ota Kte, my true love. I would die to save you now. You who have honored me with your heart. You who have asked me to be your woman. To share your fire. To—"

"Hekotosz! You stinking red vixen!" The vicious curse came, breath-low. "Where are they?"

"Do not move to arise, Ota Kte!" The soft warning came with the smiling lips which reached for his neck. "They are behind you. They are just coming up through the grove. They will wait for you to see them before they move upon you. If you will play at the love-motions—pretend we are in a lovemaking—they may hesitate yet a moment more!"

Appreciative as he was of his unseen enemy's predicted forbearance, Josh had no intention of taking advantage of Mad Wolf's generosity. While awkwardly trying to comply with the girl's order to make strategic love to her, he shot an eye-tail glance over her shoulder.

Aii-eee, brother! Monaseetah's tongue was straight now!

Guiding their gaunted ponies toward the clearing's edge, and being hawk-shadow-still about it, were a baker's dozen of Cheyenne Dog Soldiers. God Amighty, here was a salty enough set of chaperons for any chief's daughter! A man could see the first twelve of the approaching hostiles qualified as such, without hardly he had to look at them. The thirteenth, without he had to look at him at all.

It was Mad Wolf!

Well, there was one way to go. A man could roll

away from his make-believe embrace with the girl, taking up his rifle on the roll. Then he could snapshoot Axhonehe in the belly. That way, no matter the rest of them rode him under and got him down the next minute, he'd at least have paid off his pledge to get the murdering red son. And he'd have left Monaseetah a suitable wedding present to boot.

Half a second before he made his move, he checked himself. By God, yonder came a longshot chance! Knock-kneed, maybe, and cowhocked for sure. Arrow-scarred and splayfooted, too, and mud-yellow and raunchy as a Kansas City alleycat. But by God, a chance!

Muzzling the tender browze of the riverside grass, wandering his carefree way out of the encircling timber and along the bank of the Cimarron directly toward the waiting scout, came Wasiya.

The Dog Soldiers paid scant heed to the big pony. The dramatics of the situation were too diverting.

Vahe, Veho! By the Gods this little she-fox, this Bright Hair, this tiny squaw-to-be of Axhonehe's was a clever one. What a wonderful way to *wickmunke* a pale-faced sneak. *He-hau, he-hau!* This was one time Plenty Kills was going to give a scalp instead of taking one.

Aye, by Maheo, but hold the guns now. Don't use the Holy Irons, just the arrows. Feather him just a little, not too much. Keep the shafts low and into the legs only. Just get him down. Remember, Axhonehe has said he wants this one alive!'

While the grinning Dog Soldiers hesitated, Josh didn't. His lightning roll and bent-double race for Wasiya caught them off guard. There was no time to nock an arrow, let alone draw one. The belated rage of their war cries blended with the echo of Josh's Sioux shout at the gelding. Their scrubby ponies churned the dry dirt of the clearing in the eagerness of their start after the fleeing Winter Giant.

But no sowbellied Cheyenne scrub was going to catch that big Hunkpapa pony in the first forty jumps, nor in the next eighty. Wasiya had Josh out of arrow range before the Dog Soldiers' ponies got their scrawny haunches well under them for the first leap.

Ahead of the scout, across the river, lay a hundred miles of wide open, waterless short grass. To his right up the river lay a rocky cut up-country bad for running and leading no place but right where the Cheyenne would love to have him go.

His best chance was along his own back-trail. He took it without undue debate. Swinging the gelding hard left, he sent him belly-skimming down the open bank of the Cimarron.

He didn't trouble looking back to glory over his tactical brilliance. Rifle slugs were now whistling close enough to give a man pleurisy just by the draft they set up, and if that wasn't hot pony breath blowing on his backside it would do till some came along. Mad Wolf's warriors had their ponies that close to Wasiya's rump they could have spit spang over his crupper happen the wind had been right.

In response to his rider's inspired Sioux yelling Wasiya flattened out, gradually opening the twilight between himself and the Cheyenne mounts.

Josh grinned. To be certain sure, he was a long spell from home. But the deer-fast yellow gelding had him well on the way. Failing any one of thirteen chances they'd yet get winged by a stray ounce of Indian lead, him and Wasiya had it made.

Turning to throw a final shout of derision at the pursuing Dog Soldiers, he felt the sudden, jarring wrench in the powerful withers and heard Wasiya's desperate neigh. He knew one of the reaching forefeet had found and driven through the thin crust of a prairie dog hole, and tried, too late, to throw himself clear of the falling gelding. The blinding shock of the ground came into the side of his twisting head.

After that, he knew only a long cool blackness in which there was no slightest sound, no least hint of further feeling or body motion. . . .

15. Dead Mule Mesa

WHEN HE REGAINED CONSCIOUSNESS there was enough of the early moonlight to let him see he was still in Middle Spring grove. And to let him see a few other things.

Not ten feet from him stood Wasiya, apparently none the worse for his fall. It was the way with those cussed gopher-hole stumbles. Either a horse broke his leg or his damned neck, or he didn't get a scratch. Yonder there, past the spring, Mad Wolf and his Dog Soldiers were girthing-up their mounts. Squatting guard over Yellow Hair's late favorite scout was Etapeta, Big Body, the bore of his Sharps' breechloader wandering the region of Josh's temple. Nowhere in the whole of the moonbright clearing was the least sign of Monaseetah.

Beyond these facts, he had only time to ascertain that his head felt as cracked as a yard-egg, and that he was bound hand and foot. Then Big Body was hoisting him up and dumping him across Wasiya's withers.

To this insult was added the injury of lashing his hands to his feet under the gelding's sweaty paunch, to keep him, in Big Body's touchingly solicitous words, "from falling off and hurting himself."

The head-hanging, spine-jolting start from the grove was now made. Mad Wolf and Big Body led the little column with the latter towing the unwilling Wasiya. Josh's return to consciousness lasted for perhaps half a mile before the blessed darkness once more reached up and folded him in.

When he came around for the second time it was early daylight, the Dog Soldiers having made their night camp and being now in the process of departing it. Recognizing the familiar snaggle of cottonwoods protruding through the riverbank's blistered gums, Josh was surprised to realize they were no more than ten miles past Middle Spring grove. Apparently, for a reason not clear at the moment, the Cheyenne raiders had moved on only far enough to avoid Custer's immediate advance.

Before his aching head could make anything of this the column was on the move once more. Its start brought the second surprise of the morning when Mad Wolf ordered Wasiya led up alongside his own gaudy piebald stud. There he directed Big Body to untie the scout that he might join them and "ride like a brother."

As an afterthought it was decided to bind his feet beneath the big gelding's belly, but to all outward appearances he was now a member of the expedition in good standing. Here, again, the reason for the move escaped him. But not for long. Twenty miles down the trail it became as clear as South Park sunshine.

So that was the way the march strung out: Mad Wolf with Josh and Big Body making the dust for the rest of them to eat; Black Dog, a subchief who with twenty new braves had drifted into the camp sometime during the night, along with the scowling Yellow Buffalo and the original dozen Cheyenne bucks bringing up the rear.

Josh, his head clearing and his strength returning, kept his eyes on the surrounding country and the way of the trail through it, his mind turning ceaselessly on the problem of escape. So far they were following the main track of the Camp Supply road up which Custer and his main column must soon come. Well and good. When and if a man could make his break he'd have no trouble hooking up with the troops. But Amighty God, what a country to make a break in!

The naked plains waved away in endless bulges fit to make a man seasick with their monotony. Off west the vague mountains shimmered in the uncertain sunglare. As far as a man could see or hear, it was a vast, dead,

empty land, the only noises those of its present human
and four-legged trespassers.

Hour after wordless hour the hostile column bore
southwestward. Noon halt came and passed. Still the
savage caravan jogged steadily on, the restless, constant
swing of Mad Wolf's eyes telling Josh the Dog Soldier
chief was looking for something.

It was perhaps 2.00 P.M. when he found it.

Suddenly the hostile leader jerked his pony's head
around, spinning the wiry beast to a stop. Josh's eyes
were only a flick behind the chief's in spying the cause
of the halt. The six black dots floating in the sunbake
ahead steadied down and stopped swimming, then came
sharply into focus.

Men. Mounted men. Four of them Indians and mule-
mounted. The other two, white men and horse-mounted.

Across the prairie now, he saw the six dots pull into
one. He knew from that, and was glad that his white
brothers and their red companions had spotted the
Cheyenne. If it was going to be a fight it would leastways be one, and not a dry-gulch slaughter.

And a fight it was, or in any event Mad Wolf made it
look like one.

"Let's go, cousin." Big Body's purring voice reminded
him with a shove of the Sharps' muzzle. "I don't want to
miss this. I want to see it. And Axhonehe wants it to see
you!"

The scout missed neither the leer nor the words it un-
derlined. He had no time, nonetheless, to ponder their
meaning.

From the way the four mules of the trapped men lay,
their heads outflung at grotesque angles, he knew their
riders had forted up by cutting the throats of the animals. The surviving two horses were down with the men
behind the dead mules.

"Hold yer fire now, Bill. Easy, old salt. Leave the Osages shoot fust."

The white voice carried clearly past the sandhill behind which the Dog Soldiers had taken cover. Josh's recognition of it was no quicker than Mad Wolf's.

"Yellow Hair's scout, Yellow Hair's Big Scout!"

The Cheyenne chief's snarl and the gloat of triumph in it was instantly seconded by Yellow Buffalo's nod, as the voice of the second white man was heard answering the first.

"I gotchy, Joe. Hold yer boys down, Hard Rope. Wait till the black-feather jaspers get in good and close now."

"*He-hau!* You hear that other one there?" Yellow Buffalo's grin spread itself another six teeth. "Him Yellow Hair scout, too. Him damn Apache Bill, you hear?"

The scout's belly pulled in. Yonder past the hill were California Joe and Apache Bill. With old Hard Rope and three of his Osage scouts. Out looking for him, Josh Kelso. Just exactly as Mad Wolf had figured them to be.

Too late, he saw the full depth of the Dog Soldier's cunning. It wasn't just as simple as trapping him in that grove back yonder. That was only part of it. If Mad Wolf had used Monaseetah to bait him, he was now using him to bait his fellow scouts. To draw them out and away from Custer's column. To cut them off, trap them, kill them. To put out Yellow Hair's eyes and stop his ears before ever the Camp Supply column got halfway to the Washita!

But if Josh thought he had guessed the entire scope of Mad Wolf's crazy planning, he had a second guess coming.

Dismounting, each of the Dog Soldiers now took a short horsehair rope from behind his saddle, braiding it hurriedly into the tangled mane of his nervous mount. These ropes, about six feet long and looped on the free end, were new to him. He watched their adjustment with professional interest.

With the ropes in place, Mad Wolf instructed Big Body to expose himself on the hilltop with the hapless Kelso. He added that should Ota Kte feel called upon to so much as open his mouth or lift a hand in reply to his fellow scouts' recognition he was to be shot through the kidneys.

With that, Mad Wolf got down to business. He

paused only long enough to make sure his guest fully appreciated the situation.

He-hau, was it clear now? They were going to kill all those scouts over there except one of the Osages. He would be left to carry the news to Yellow Hair that Plenty Kills was riding like a brother, and of his own free will, with the South Arkansas Dog Soldiers.

"Vahe, Veho!" He concluded the address with a friendly wave. "Welcome to our lodges, White Brother!"

With that and with nothing else save their rusty trade muskets, looped horsehair ropes and thirty-one bellies full of rash, red guts, the Dog Soldiers followed their slit-eyed chief down upon the waiting army scouts.

Josh had only time to hear Apache Bill's shout of recognition as the latter saw him top the hill with Big Body. Helpless to return the call, he could only improve this moment by adding to his Indian education the adept use of the Dog Soldier "war rope."

Coming in rifle range of Custer's scouts each of the hostile riders kicked one foot through the looped end of his horsehair thong, hooked the heel of his other foot across his mount's whipping spine and threw his body behind that of his pony. The maneuver left the desperate army scouts nothing to shoot at but crazily galloping horseflesh.

And horseflesh does not go down so easily.

The trapped scouts' six shots disappeared into the closing savages without visible result. The garishly painted ponies thundered straight in. Thirty yards from the slaughtered mules it looked as though Maheo, God himself, could not have stopped the Dog Soldier ponies.

But Maheo doesn't smell like a dead mule.

Where the Cheyenne Almighty might have found himself hamstrung, a few quarts of mules' blood moved with startling effect. Twenty yards from the dead animals the leading ponies broke and split around the mule fort, the hated smell of the mule blood sending them into a frenzy of bucking and pitching.

Mad Wolf was bright enough to feel the jab of the

lancehaft of hard luck when it had been shoved into him and broken off. Before the army scouts could get in their second shots he drove his scattered warriors back under the cover of Kelso's hill. They had indeed shot down both of the white men's horses, but it was not enough. The state of affairs clearly called for a council of war.

Black Dog, a medicine man of reputation, urged an immediate return to the attack, quoting a vision he had just received from the holy navel of Maheo. Mad Wolf, a saner military mind and an agnostic of long standing, briefly instructed him to take his vision and replace it in God's bellybutton.

Oxahos! Dry pony dung! It was no time for prophecies.

Still, because of the fanatical Dog Soldier hatred of all whites and because of the latent prestige in lifting the hair of California Joe, Yellow Hair's official Chief of Scouts, Mad Wolf yielded to the insistence of his followers, agreeing to wait until darkness might make a sneak-in possible.

Yellow Buffalo at once protested that nighttime knew no color, that it would hide a white man as well as it would a red. "We wait, they get away," he complained bitterly, again using the broken English of which he was so proud. "Goddam now, you see!"

But the other braves had had enough of the white scouts' daylight marksmanship. *Oxahos!* They were just lucky somebody hadn't been killed as it was. Four ponies had been hit and Gray Bird's mare would never travel again. Hawk Man had a bullet crease across his skull you could see the bone through and Little Elk was sitting there with a hole in his rumpcheek big enough to stick your thumb in. *Nohetto!* Enough was enough.

The decision to wait for a cover of darkness stood.

Through the intolerable hours of sunblaze and flybiting, the Dog Soldiers squatted on their side of the hill, the trapped scouts suffered on theirs. There was no shade in either camp, and no water. When night came at last, the hostile chief and his fellows moved around the hill and carefully toward the now invisible mule fort.

Halfway there, they crouched in the darkness, gathering themselves for the charge, sharp ears tuned to the location of the dead mules. It was well to take a last-minute pause, making sure their approach was so far undetected. Those cursed white scouts out there were not the ones you came up on with impunity—even in the dark!

Josh, his ears tuned as strainingly as the Cheyennes', at once wondered if the silence out by the dead-mule fort wasn't unnaturally heavy.

Apparently it was. Yellow Buffalo came to his feet.

"*Eoxeoz*, it stinks. Too quiet out there. Him damn Apache Bill gone. Him only wait for darkness too. Him smart. Yellow Buffalo told you. You go, we see." His angry growl, going to Mad Wolf, was answered in kind.

"*He-hau*, I think Heovhotoa says a true thing. Let's go and see."

And go and see they promptly did, Josh and Big Body along with them. California Joe and Apache Bill, along with Hard Rope and the Osages, were clean gone. And gone, clean. They had taken nothing with them save their guns. The Dog Soldiers had waited five minutes too long. Yellow Buffalo stood vindicated. The night, indeed, knew no color.

Pursuit short of daylight was questionable and Mad Wolf would have none of it in any event.

"There is no time," he grunted in response to Black Dog's demand that at least some of them follow the escaped scouts. "Yellow Hair is too close and the plan is even better this way. Yellow Hair might not have believed the Osage that Plenty Kills rides with us like a brother, but his ears will be open to the white scouts. Mad Wolf goes now."

Shortly, their ponies sagging under the added carry of the scouts' fine saddles and rich food packs, the impatient band was pounding for the main Dog Soldier camp at Willow Bar twenty miles up the Cimarron.

Mad Wolf, with Josh and Big Body back in their places at his side, held a hard pace; 10.00 P.M. and the full light of the rising moon found them topping out on

the broad granite swell overlooking Willow Bar. The
Dog Soldier chief had ample cause for his grunt of satisfaction. It had been a fine day. *Nataemhon,* good hunting indeed. The very best in a long time.

16. Axhonehe's Hospitality

IT WAS A BIG CAMP, the shadowy flood of the moonlight
letting Josh count no less than two hundred and fifty
lodges strung like dirty, cowskin pearls along the sil-
vered rope of the Cimarron.

The hair-raising buffalo wolf howls by which, after
the time honored custom of the Cut-Arm People, Mad
Wolf announced his arrival on the long granite ridge
overlooking Willow Bar had the big camp crawling with
three-feather Cheyenne bucks in less time than it took
the returning Dog Soldiers to slide their weary mounts
from the ridge to the level of the river.

Even as the scout was making terse mental note of
the comparative scarcity of squaws and young children
among the gathering hundreds of Axhonehe's followers,
Mad Wolf was speaking.

The ensuing remarkable account of the dead-mule
fiasco struck Josh as a work of pure Indian genius. His
deep voice barking angrily the lean chief strutted for his
faithful, the weird shift of the victory fires serving to
limn the drama of his exultant posings in a manner
which had even the white scout's hardened jaw dropping.

". . . *Eahata!* Listen to this! With my trap I caught
Yellow Hair's scouts in the open, even as I planned.

Killing them would have been like stoning rabbits. But the cursed blood of their mules made our ponies wild. Faster than Maheo's lightning then, a new plan came to Mad Wolf. Let them all go. Let them all tell Yellow Hair they had seen Ota Kte among us. Riding right with us. Watching us attack his white brothers. Not answering a word when they called out to him.

"In this way will begin our vengeance on Plenty Kills, making all his white brothers remember him as a traitor to his own people. And in *this* way will it end—"

The dark-skinned chief paused, eyes sweeping the spell-bound ranks of his followers.

"I have given my sacred pledge to kill Ota Kte for you. I will do it, my brothers. I will *burn* him.

"When I am the true chief of all the Cheyennes, I will do this. When Moxtaveto is destroyed by Yellow Hair and when we have killed all the Pony Soldiers, then I will burn Ota Kte.

"And so we shall have our war. We shall have it until the last white man is driven from our lands. Mad Wolf has spoken. May Maheo bear me witness. *Remember my words . . ."*

As Axhonehe concluded his snarling diatribe, Josh grimaced bitterly.

Remember his words? How in God's name could a white man ever forget them?

There it was now, his whole rotten-bellied scheme. Right out in the open at last. Let Custer knock off Moxtaveto and his peaceful Cheyennes. Let Axhonehe and the Dog Soldiers seize power over what was left, guaranteeing to keep the war going so long as there was no bad-medicine buck to follow the Dog Soldier flag.

Never mind, now, the fact he meant to put Josh Kelso under along with old Black Kettle.

Never mind his Indian-crazy plan to make Custer think his pet scout had turned Cheyenne.

Now more than ever, the big thing was to break loose and get to the General. Happen a man could get away, knowing what he now knew—could get to Custer before it was too late to stop his slaughter of Black Kettle's

guiltless tribesmen—could convince the General as he
now felt he could that the Dog Soldiers were the whole
culprit—could bring the full force of the Seventh Cavalry down on these murdering outlaws instead of on Black
Kettle's good Indians—could somehow—

The big scout's racing thoughts were broken off bluntly.

Having built his bonfire, Mad Wolf was giving over
its blazing stage to Black Dog and his howling braves.
He himself was retiring in slit-eyed triumph to the sanctuary of his lodge, there to seek food and such other
comforts as his present three wives might see fit to provide for the next tribal chief of the Southern Cheyenne
Nation.

In this latter pursuit he insisted on the unhappy company of his "guest."

Preceded by Yellow Buffalo and dogged by his constant shadow, the hulking Big Body, the puzzled scout
followed Mad Wolf into his tipi. Big Body remained
outside to, in his own loosely grinned words, "Look at
the moon a while yet—"

Ducking through the entrance flap, Josh gasped. The
kingly aura of Mad Wolf's lodge was overpoweringly beyond description.

About all a man could do was say that if you took a
dozen green buffalo hides, buried them in sick-pony
dung till spring, dug them up and sewed them into a
twelve-foot cone, then let four or five unwashed savages
live and cook and breed and belch and break wind inside for six months, you might begin to get a whiff of
the idea of Axhonehe's home.

If the Dog Soldier chief's abode was a cesspool of
stinks, his habits and morals fitted the incredible smell
ounce for foul ounce. He and his chief hireling, Yellow
Buffalo, sat to the iron pot of boiled dog contributing a
running fire of double-ended flatulence as their main social effort, letting the solicitous squaws tend the selection of a flow of choice dog cuts for their mighty menfolk.

Josh, never having acquired the taste for fricassee of
man's best friend enjoyed by the majority of white

mountain men, tactfully refused the readily identifiable
puppy's head offered him on the point of a Green River
knife by one of Mad Wolf's squaws. Instead, he sat back
in the shadows of the sideskins, chewing a shag of dried
buffalo beef and letting his weary mind hammer at the
dimming hopes of his sole remaining aim—escape to
Custer.

An interminable half-hour later, Mad Wolf stood up
to announce that all would forthwith retire.

"I am sleepy," he grunted. "We will all of us sleep
now."

With the words and with that peculiarly Indian quirk
of courtesy which demands equal treatment for the
doomed captive of unquestioned bravery in war, he
waved graciously toward Josh, indicating to him the
third squaw, a rotten-toothed harridan who was clearly
verminous if not downright venereal.

"You sleep with Little Fawn, Ota Kte. She is good.
Old. Knows everything."

The grinning squaw started toward him as he found
his feet.

"No! Ota Kte says No!" he blurted awkwardly,
seeing Mad Wolf's face go blacker than a strangled
Ute's with the blunt refusal.

"*Oxahos!* Pony dung! Ota Kte dares to say No to my
woman?" The Dog Soldier chief was on his feet, staring
challengingly across the cooking pot. "How does he say
it then? How does he mean it?" The delicate balance of
the question teetered on his slow reach for his hand-
somely engraved rifle.

"*Aii-eee!*" disclaimed Josh hastily. "The woman is all
you say. More, much more. Fragrant as first mare's
milk. A real fawn. But curse the luck, it is a devil's fate.
I cannot sleep with any woman just now!"

He shrugged, feigning an embarrassment that was
false only in its claimed origin.

"I am sick, *here.*" With the eloquent gesture, he
pointed the source of his hurriedly invented contagion.

"*Mavetoxz!*" exclaimed Mad Wolf, patently pleased
with the depth and sensitivity of his social perception.

"As you say, it is a devil's fate. You will excuse us then?"

Josh's agitated agreement ended the whole matter. Mad Wolf grunted a sober acknowledgement of his white guest's thoughtfulness and summarily dismissed the no longer required Little Fawn. With the squaw's departure, he and the impatient Yellow Buffalo at once joined ardent forces and turned their delayed attentions to the remaining squaws. This action shortly put the nervous white scout as far from the four red minds as the distant craters of the moon.

Josh's hopes, burning almost out but a moment before, flared quickly. By Cripes, maybe this was it! Maybe, hell. It *was* it. A man could sense that now. This was the time, the place, the prayed-for moment.

The excitement of it put every last nerve in his body on vibrating edge. His slant glance whipped toward the slightly parted tipi flaps. One look was enough. The way was clear in that direction!

Easing along the sideskins as slowly as a sun shadow at high noon, the big scout inched toward the entrance. Belly-flat and breath-held, he made the last three feet unnoticed, thankfully poked his pale face into the clean, free air beyond the flaps.

To the east the stars were fading in the milky haze of pre-dawn. The light was not yet strong enough to carry a man's eyes much past the end of his anxious nose. But there was enough of it to show him that short as the remaining darkness might be, he was going to spend it right where he was.

Just beyond the parted flaps, his gross body hunched against the morning chill, squatted the lump-still Etapeta.

"*Pave vona*, good morning, cousin," grinned Big Body. And viciously drove the iron-heeled butt of his buffalo rifle full into the white scout's peering face.

17. *March of the Dog Soldiers*

"NASEHAOHO!"

Big Body illustrated the order to arise with a shove of his Sharps' barrel. Josh, mind groping once more toward consciousness, stumbled uncertainly to his feet.

As the full light of the morning sun struck his eyes, he raised his hand to shade them. The slight touch of the hand brushing the battered face brought a wince of quick pain and a sudden flash of returning memory.

Behind him the side skins of Mad Wolf's lodge were being rolled off the rib poles by two of the chief's squaws, the third stacking them into the travois behind a droop-headed pack pony. All over camp the process was being repeated. The Dog Soldier camp was on the move again.

Down on the bank of the Cimarron, athwart the willow-bristling sandbar which gave the place its trail name, Mad Wolf was haranguing a gathering of the braves.

Evidently the dark-skinned chief and the main village were going to part company. Mad Wolf and a party of picked braves were to continue under forced march up the Cimarron and across to the Canadian for the Washita, and the village was to move by regular stages for the same objective. The primary object of Axhonehe's detour was to combine business with pleasure by horseraiding along the lower Santa Fe Trail. Fresh mounts were badly needed for the coming clash with Custer and

118

the raiding band might, with luck, encounter an out-of-season herd being driven up from Mexico.

No sooner had the Dog Soldier chief announced how it would be than he began telling off those who would accompany him. As each name was called, the brave would step forward, strike his breast proudly with the flat of his right hand and growl deeply. "I hear my name. *Vahe,* let's go to fight!"

When Mad Wolf had called his last man, the remainder put up a rolling mutter. *Eoxeoz!* No good. It stank. When a Plains Indian had earned himself coup ratings of half a dozen eagle feathers he clearly didn't care for being left behind among the old men and boys. Their leader put down this grumbling quickly enough.

"*Hekotosz!* Be quiet, all of you! There will be fighting enough for all when we join our Arapaho brothers in that *wickmunke* for Yellow Hair. Do you hear me now?"

It was the first time Josh had heard that the Dog Soldiers had a definite trap worked out for Custer, let alone the fact the Arapaho were in it with them.

"*Hau! Hau!* We hear you. We all hear Axhonehe!" The warriors' deep answers rode in over his thoughts.

Mad Wolf turned and stalked haughtily toward his war pony. Josh nodded and wheeled to follow him. Here was something a man in his moccasins could afford to remember. Happen there was any outside chance still left of his getting away, he would do well to smell out the details of that trap before leaving. That kind of information would go a long way toward convincing the General his boy Joshua hadn't wasted his time among his self-appointed "Cheyenne brothers." And happen Joe and Bill had pushed it to him about seeing him with the Dog Soldiers, the General was apt to take just about all the convincing a man could conveniently hand him.

Swinging up on Wasiya to follow the horse raiders out of camp, the big scout nodded once more. The track was getting hot and the time, short. And Custer was halfway to Camp Supply!

Mad Wolf made his noon halt at Battle Ground Bend of the Cimarron.

The hostiles took no food on their noon halts, only stopping because a horse is no Dog Soldier and needs to breathe once in a while. Twenty minutes and they were on their way again, holding the ponies to a jingling walk against the unseasonable blast of the dropping sun. Two hours and ten miles later they hit Upper Cimarron Springs, the last wagon camp on the Camp Supply road.

With darkness and the ponies rested, the red horse-men took the trail again. They still followed the regular military route, going the five miles up the Cimarron to Cold Spring and leaving the river there to head south-west into the second desert crossing and the thirty dry miles to the North Fork of the Rabbit Ear River. When they forded the North Fork at midnight Josh would have sworn half the mounts in the caravan were three hobbles from going down. Yet with barely a ten-minute pause to blow and water they hit the trail again, holding a rolling canter until dawn and four-thirty found them another twenty miles south and just entering into the main track of the Santa Fe wagon route.

Here the first real hills encountered since leaving the Cimarron thrust their brown backs up out of the naked desert. Striking a winding stream within the first range, the Dog Soldiers swung down off their staggering mounts and called a halt. Every warrior in the group, save one, was asleep in five minutes.

For all his weariness, Josh fought against joining them. But presently, seeing that Etapeta remained as awake and watchful as himself, he shrugged and gave in. The hell with it. He wasn't going to try any more early-morning sneaks on that big buzzard. About one more working-over with that Sharps' butt and a man wouldn't know himself in the mirror. He was asleep almost before the thought faded.

Two hours later, with the seven o'clock sun bouncing off the tops of the Rabbit Ear Mounds, the trail name of the hills in which they had made their dawn halt, the Dog Soldiers were off again. And an hour after that,

they found what they had apparently been looking for
—their field commissary!

Josh allowed that Cibolero buffalo camp was something. Swarming with coffee-colored women and soot-
eyed youngsters, squealing Mexican curs and wandering, gaunt-flanked oxen, the whole disorderly sprawl
seemed strung together with endless ropes of drying buffalo beef.

From what Big Body had grudgingly to say while he
and his captive charge joined their comrades in stuffing
themselves with Cibolero beef and bread, these happy
nomads were the Mexican version of the white market
hunter. Their full lives were spent roaming the Canadian
River uplands in their wood-wheeled oxcarts, killing and
jerking buffalo beef for the trade in Santa Fe and Taos.
They were the friends, perforce, of the red and white
wanderer alike, this popularity bought and paid for by
their willing offer of fresh bread and meat. The bread
was brown as beanmeal, hard as bedrock, tasteless as
trail dust. But it was bread, and to white travelers weeks
without anything but fatback and cornmeal it was hardly
less welcome than to the gluttonous Cheyenne.

As a Texas border boy Josh had of course heard of
the fabled Ciboleros. Nevertheless, he sat quietly to Big
Body's growling discourse on their manners and habits,
hoping that by giving the subchief enough lingual rope
he might get him to hang himself with some kind of *real*
information.

When Mad Wolf's band had eaten to the point where
a dozen of them had had to walk out of the feeding circle and vomit, the Dog Soldiers got up off their haunches and caught up their ponies. Bidding the Ciboleros a
belching farewell, they pounded hell-bent for the next
stop.

This proved to be at five that afternoon when Black
Dog, riding back from scouting ahead, reported the end
of their search. Six white men with a herd of five
hundred horses were coming north along the Trail.

How were the horses? *Vahe!* Real good. Spanish,
they looked to be. Coming up from Chihuahua for trad-

ing in the eastern settlement. *He-hau!* They were top horses, no doubt of that. Just the thing they were looking for to mount the jaws of their *wickmunke* for Yellow Hair. Just what they needed now that their own ponies were winter-thinning.

Josh's alert mind pounced on the remark. But his easy query, going at once to Big Body, was as casual as a man excusing himself to make water.

"If your friends could open a trap as easily as they do their big mouths, brother, old Yellow Hair would be a dead soldier right now—"

"He *is* a dead soldier, cousin!" The vacuous Big Body snatched greedily at the carelessly flung bait. "And the mouths of our traps have big teeth. *Aii-eee,* cousin, and lots of them. Three thousand, maybe more. Do you hear?"

"Oh, sure, I hear your big mouth."

The studied insult brought the giant Dog Soldier's pony shouldering into Wasiya.

"Listen, *Veho,* you know that big bend of the Ouachita? And how Moxtaveto's camp sits on this side of it?"

"Of course," Josh lied evenly. "What fool wouldn't."

"Well, do you know what will be around that bend when Yellow Hair rides into Moxtaveto's tipis? Right around on the other side, hidden by that big hill where Yellow Hair will never think to expect it? Aha! You guessed it, cousin. The whole of Little Raven's Arapaho, better than *two thousand* of them. And all the Dog Soldier Lodge, too, even some Northerns who have come down to help out. You hear, cousin? More than one thousand of us, every one wearing the three black feathers."

The big brave paused triumphantly, his slab face leering into Josh's.

"Now how does that strike you, Ota Kte? Let's hear how big *your* mouth is now, cousin. I'm listening!"

Josh's reply was cut off by Mad Wolf's orders for the approaching horse herd. But even as he watched the Dog Soldiers ready their ambush his mind was detailing the full import of Big Body's revelations. The end-product of that detailing was blank-wall certain. If Custer wasn't warned in time, he was just what Etapeta had labeled him. *A dead soldier.*

Axhonehe's pack, ambushed in waiting, rushed the white caravan the instant it showed around the trail-bend. Five minutes after the shooting broke out the entire herd of five hundred horses had been swept away. Not a shot was fired by the white herders in defense of their property; a piece of discretion which beyond certain question accounted for the fact they reached Custer's column to report their loss.

The Dog Soldiers drove their stolen herd ten miles down the Santa Fe Trail, intercepting the North Fork of the Canadian River shortly before sundown. Here they halted, watered the ungainly herd and split up.

Mad Wolf, with Josh and Big Body and six chosen braves, picked fresh horses from the Spanish herd and pushed on at once. Their course, as nearly as the captive scout could determine from the set of the early stars, was almost due east, swinging south of the Canadian and straight out toward the waterless panhandle of his native borderland.

Noting the direction, the weary scout nodded grimly.

The time for questions was done. The red die was cast and the compass point of its casting could be told by the way the North Star was falling away behind a man's left shoulder. The way those ponies were pushing they would raise the headlands of the Dry Fork of the Washita with first light—the southern flank of the Antelope Hills by dusk—the Big Bend of the Main Washita by midnight. It was journey's end for Joshua Kelso.

Mad Wolf was going home.

18. Moxtaveto's Mettle

SOME TIME BEFORE MIDNIGHT of the nineteenth, Mad Wolf's advance party struck the main Washita thirty miles west of that stream's entrance into the Antelope Hills.

Josh was, as always, amazed at the homing instincts of the nomad raiders. They had traveled thirty-six straight hours across a land as featureless as a brown-grass billiard table. Unguided save by a handful of prairie stars and the wide swing of the Arkansas sun, they had nonetheless come in off the trackless short grass within one mile of their first landmark and a half-hour of their final objective.

A short while later, moving eastward down the widening valley of the Washita, they struck the first group of lodges. There were no more than sixty of these, their distinctively symboled side skins designating them as Cheyenne. Josh, on the point of dismissing them as the guard camp for the immense pony herd through which they had ridden the past ten minutes, took sudden note of the big black lodge centering the group. He'd seen that set of skins before, and not long before. It was Black Kettle's.

Mad Wolf halted his lathered command in front of the chief's abode, the yapping of the half-dozen camp curs worrying at the ponies' heels announcing his arrival. A handful of sleepy-eyed squaws answered the canine summons but there was no sign of the tribal headman.

Mad Wolf upended his carbine and levered four shots, the Cheyenne Good-Medicine Number, over the ridge-poles of Moxtaveto's tipi. His boastful challenge rode in over the impromptu fusillade.

"Ho, you, Moxtaveto! Come out now. See what Axhonehe has brought you. The war is on, old man, and we have counted the first coup!"

For Mad Wolf, Josh reckoned the greeting was one of rare good humor. He awaited Black Kettle's response to it with considerable interest.

The response came neither in good humor, nor did it come from Black Kettle. It came instead from Antelope Woman, the old headman's elder squaw and one Cheyenne, quite clearly, who feared neither the devil nor his Dog Soldier advocate.

"May Maheo curse you, Axhonehe!" Her dour greeting preceded the emergence of her craggy features through the parting entrance flaps. "Take your stinking soldier dogs and be off! You know as well as you sit grinning there on that runted stallion that Moxtaveto is not in his lodge."

Mad Wolf refused to depart from either his good humor or his present position. Sensing something peculiar about any mood but his normal bad one, Josh watched the Dog Soldier closely.

"Come now, woman, don't tell us the mighty Moxtaveto is not at home? Don't tell us he isn't in the camp of his people when the enemy threatens!"

"He is where you sent him, you skinny whelp of misfortune. Out counseling the Kiowas and Comanches to return. Out bringing them back from where your scouts chased them with their big lies about Yellow Hair coming to destroy us. Ride along, mad dog. You will see their empty lodges down the river there. You will see how well your lies have worked. Be gone. May Maheo spit in your eye when your hour comes to face him!"

With the curse the Indian woman wrenched the tipi flaps closed and disappeared. For the first and only time in Josh's memory, Mad Wolf laughed. With the laugh he turned triumphantly to Big Body.

"You see, Etapeta? You see what a brain your chief has, brother?"

"Aye, it worked." Big Body added his thick-lipped grin to his leader's. "I never thought it would. Those scouts you sent ahead to spread the fear were a good idea."

"Ten Bears and Lone Wolf are afraid of war. I want no Indians who are dreaming of peace in this camp when Yellow Hair comes. Just old Moxtaveto, that's all."

Josh whistled silently.

This damn Axhonehe was crazy like a coyote. Ten Bears was the top-dog Comanche chief. Lone Wolf was second only to Satanta among the Kiowas. To have gotten them both out of the way to soften old Black Kettle up for Custer was a stroke of pure-red military genius.

"Now listen in there, old woman!" Mad Wolf's interrupting shout was sent to the silent lodge. "When Moxtaveto comes in you tell him I have captured Ota Kte. You hear that, woman? Old Plenty Kills himself! Tell him I am going to burn him for our people. Like I promised in my pledge to the Lodge. You hear me?"

There was no answer from the lodge and the Dog Soldier, his short string of humor exhausted, wheeled his pony.

"She heard me all right. Let's go. I'm thinking now it may be well to burn this white dog *before* the old man gets back."

"Aye, then the old devil can't stop us." Big Body's agreement was instant. "But all the same I'd rather work on him with this skull club. Of course I mean after you've taken his hair."

"Be still, you fool. Come on, let's go."

With the order Mad Wolf put heels to his mount, his braves racing to follow him. Big Body grinned and turned to Josh.

"Well, come along, cousin. When the next War Chief of the Cheyenne says something, it's best to listen." With the advice, he slashed Josh's mount across the rump

with the butt-swung barrel of his rifle, jumping the nervous beast into a wild gallop.

"*Hii-yee-hahh!*" The red giant's thundering shout was
abetted by the simultaneous discharge of his rifle toward
the listening stars.

"Let's go, cousin. Let's go to war!"

The approach of Mad Wolf's returning raiders had
the Cheyenne main camp in an uproar minutes after
they rode in sight of Black Kettle's lodge. Josh was un-
ceremoniously dumped into the noisome shelter of the
tipi of Stone Calf, Black Kettle's deputy chief. There he
was left to ruminate on the little pleasures inherent in
an army scout's life in Indian Territory.

Meanwhile, a booming council fire was lit just outside
the tipi's parted flaps and the name chiefs of the sprawling camp got down to serious discussion. With no other
heritage available Josh perforce fell disgruntled heir to
the sum and substance of that discussion.

Its offhand bequeathal shortly lifted his ears very
nearly clear of his aching head.

In ten minutes he had as unpretty a picture of Dog
Soldier dirt as the intriguing hand of Mad Wolf could
paint. Translating the grunts and handsigns of the con-
sulting Indian a man got the unhappy impression that
the string of his future was shorter than a bitten-off
bear's tail. And that Colonel George Armstrong Custer's
number wasn't anyplace but way up.

In the first place, with his trusting tribal chief well out
of earshot, Stone Calf was wavering toward the cause of
the Dog Soldiers. Josh had always figured Black Kettle's
second-in-command for a bad Indian, a judgment now
born precisely out. In the second place Little Raven, the
number-one Arapaho, was clearly with the Dog Soldiers, confirming Big Body's earlier boast. In the third
and unpleasantly final place, while there was still some
little argument as to the wisdom of attempting to trap
the justly feared Yellow Hair, there was none at all re-
lating to the deserving justice of an immediate end to
Ota Kte. His past crimes against the people were a total

indictment. The slip-eyed jury presently hearing his poor
case was bound to come in with Axhonehe's requested
verdict: guilty of Indian murder in the first degree.

The sentence would be automatic—death at the burning pole.

There were some other minor informations disclosed
to the sweating scout. Chief among these was one relat-
ing to a Cheyenne he had sudden cause to recall; Monaseetah, his one-time lady love.

The girl, whose absence he had not had time to remark, was away from the camp traveling with Black
Kettle. Following her return and Mad Wolf's seizure of
power, and of course the sometime-in-between burning
of Plenty Kills, the nuptials of the Cheyenne princess
and the Dog Soldier heir presumptive would be duly cele-
brated.

The idea proved at once attractive to the attending
chiefs. It would weld the erstwhile peaceful faction of
the tribe to the hostile element. It would strengthen the
entire Nation for its coming Holy War with the Pony
Soldiers.

For the hundredth time since his caputre, Josh tested
his bonds. For the hundredth time he cursed them and
subsided. When these South Plains butchers trussed up a
bird they didn't short any corners. A man couldn't have
gotten out of that spider net of braided horsehair picket
ropes with one hand free and a four-foot cavalry saber
in his hip pocket.

For perhaps the first time in his life he turned his red-
dened eyes skyward. He stared long and thoughtfully
through the open smokehole of Stone Calf's lodge. Presently he had himself a few well-chosen, soundless words
with the white man's Maheo. Nothing like the heat of a
hostile council fire and the upcoming stench of singed
scout-meat to make a settlement Christian out of a
South Park heathen.

Happen God Almighty didn't soon call for a hand in
the deal, Josh Kelso was cashed in.

The following morning, even while the red-painted,

twelve-foot length of the cottonwood burning pole was being planted beside the Washita, Josh got a last-minute reprieve.

It came in the angry person of old Black Kettle jogging his lathered pony into the midst of the preparing festivities shortly after sunrise. The appearance of the aging chief created a furor well calculated to test the mettle of any savage commander.

The quiet-faced Cheyenne had no base iron in the veining of his character. He was old and the once total grip on the loyalties of his guileless followers was slipping with every mile Custer's column put beneath the advancing feet of the Seventh's horses. But he was still the headchief of all the Southern Cheyenne.

He now put the cold steel of that prestige squarely up to the infuriated Mad Wolf.

The Dog Soldier demonstrated his own dangerous alloy by cannily refusing the showdown. It was too soon. Everything was coming his way. There was a good seven suns yet before Yellow Hair could be expected to reach the Washita. The Pony Soldier chief had not yet reached Camp Supply. There was time, lots of it.

With a flowery covering speech about his sacred vow to kill Kelso, and about his thoughtlessness in not awaiting Moxtaveto's blessing on its termination, Mad Wolf made his temporary peace.

As Josh wondered at this change in tactics, the reasons for it came riding up the Washita from the direction of the recently deserted Kiowa and Comanche lodges. The moment he recognized old Ten Bears and the furtive-eyed Lone Wolf he had his answer. The Kiowa and Comanche warrior strength was back in camp and with it the precarious balance of power had teetered back to the old Cheyenne.

Even so, with Indians, where a face has been lost, part of it at least must be restored.

Mad Wolf pressed his advantage to wring from a clearly unwilling Black Kettle his blessings on the mating of his beautiful niece and the plotting Dog Soldier.

Black Kettle wasn't through bargaining. In return for

this concession he demanded and got the replacement of
Stone Calf with Magpie, a lifelong friend, as deputy
chief, and the immediate release to him of the captive
scout Ota Kte.

There was a wave of angry growls at this latter insistence but the old chief made it stick, covering it by playing his trump card.

"Listen, my people—" the old Cheyenne's voice quieted
the muttering ranks of his followers, "I have returned
with hopeful news. Ten Bears says that at Fort Cobb
there is a new Peace Mission. He says that Colonel Hazen,
the soldier chief there, has orders to give sanctuary to all
peaceful Indians, and much money to buy us food."

The silver-haired old man paused, weathered hands
sweeping eloquent accent to his plea.

"Do not take the war trail, my people. Wait for me to
return. I go now to treat with the soldier chief at Fort
Cobb. He will let us come in. We will go there and be
safe. Only those whose hearts are big for war will stay
and seek out Yellow Hair.

"I will return and you will know whose tongue is
straight. I ask you to wait for me."

Black Kettle's speech had a marked effect on the
main body of the Cheyenne. The whole camp fell into
an uneasy quiet to await his return from Fort Cobb.

The news of Colonel Hazen's orders to provide sanctuary against the approaching threat of Custer's campaign of extermination cut the ground from under the
exhortations of the war leaders.

He-hau, it was no time for fighting. The ponies were
already thin and the snows would come any day now.
Vahe, let there be peace. Let Moxtaveto return from
Fort Cobb and lead them into its protection. Hazen
Chief had a good heart, everybody knew that. The
words of the old chief were always best. Wait for Moxtaveto. *Nohetto,* let that be the end to it!

Thinking swiftly, Josh still couldn't untangle the
hopeful surprise of the Hazen mission. He was as set
back as any of the Cheyenne to hear of the unprecedent-
ed "sanctuary order." Not that it wasn't a hell of an

idea. It for sure made good sense. In fact, so good a
man could scarcely believe it. Not, at any rate, a man
who knew the way the army operated and who with his
own eyes had read Sheridan's orders to Custer not ten
days gone. True, Hazen's district was a separate and distinct command from Sheridan's, but somehow a man
couldn't bring himself to think even the Army could be
that balled up on its own orders.

Something smelled wrong about the whole setup. Big,
bad-medicine wrong.

All through the endless hours of the 21st, 22d and
23d, Josh paced the confines of Black Kettle's lodge
awaiting the return of the chief's mission to Hazen.

He was no longer bound hand and foot, at least not
by rawhide and horsehair. But Mad Wolf wasn't
whelped yesterday, or the day before. He had Big Body
and a guard-changing shift of Dog Soldiers strung so
tightly around old Black Kettle's lodge that a grayback
louse couldn't have crawled twenty yards from it without being stepped on and squashed by a patrolling Dog
Soldier's footskin.

With dusk of the 23d, while he was squatting outside
the lodge with Magpie for his evening's airing, he heard
the wolfcall of the Cheyenne tribal signal echoing in
over the darkened prairie from the east. Ten minutes
later Black Kettle rode up to Magpie's supper fire,
flanked by the tribal chiefs who had accompanied him.
These were Stone Calf of the militant Cheyennes, Ten
Bears of the Comanches, Lone Wolf of the Kiowas and
Big Mouth of the hostile Arapahos.

But the composition of Moxtaveto's retinue was lost
on Josh as his eyes alighted on the figure at the old
chief's side.

He had not seen Monaseetah since Middle Spring
grove. But anger, treachery, hate and heartpain combined had not been able to keep the picture of her face
from his mind. She had ridden with him every weary
step of the way from that love-trap on the Cimarron.
Now here she was again, as hauntingly beautiful as ever.

His eyes, however, sought the return of hers in vain. The Indian girl sat her calico mare staring blankly over his head, her gaze as straight and stony as any in the dark-faced company around her. By not so much as a long black lash flicker did she recognize the living presence of her betrayed white lover.

Turning bitterly from the girl to the faces of the peace mission, his jaw clamped.

If a man could read a face, he could read a red one as quickly as a white. On any face in that hard-eyed group, from the mahogany-dark frown of Little Raven to the pale, pockmarked scowl of Stone Calf, one word and one alone was written: *disaster*.

Seconds later the silent group, accompanied by the expressionless Monaseetah, had turned its ponies past Black Kettle's fire to file into the darkness toward the main Cheyenne camp and Josh, seated with Moxtaveto in the flap-closed interior of the old chief's lodge, was listening to the fateful terms of that disaster.

19. The Burning Pole

GNARLED HANDS moving swiftly, voice held low, Black Kettle tolled off the deathknell of his people.

"I am too old, my son. I have lived too long. I see the end of it all now. Hazen Chief cannot help us. Yellow Hair will come and Axhonehe will have his way."

"Are you sure, father?" Josh's questions fell tersely. "Is there no chance left? Are you certain Hazen Chief is powerless?"

"I told him I had tried to make peace with Yellow Hair but that my scouts had since brought me word that he was coming against me. I told him my camp was on the Ouachita, forty miles east of the Antelope Hills, and that Yellow Hair knew where it was. I told him I had only one hundred and eighty lodges and that I spoke only for my own people. Even so he would not hear me."

"What did he say? Perhaps there was a misunderstanding, father."

The old man shook his head.

"There was no misunderstanding, Ota Kte."

"What were his words, father? Exactly, I mean. Do you remember them? Perhaps there is yet time if you have mistaken his meaning. Perhaps I might go with you, to him. Or you with me, to Yellow Hair."

Again the aged chief shook his head.

"I remember his words. They will stay in my heart like a riverstone, never wearing away. The Cheyenne are lost, my son."

"Quickly, father. There is little time. His exact words now—"

Wearily the old man recited the military requiem of his tribe, the words Hazen's, the last and lost-hope inflections his own.

" 'I am sent here as a peace chief,' Hazen Chief told us. 'All here is to be peace, but north of the Arkansas is General Sheridan, the great war chief, and I do not control him, and he has all the soldiers who are fighting the Cheyennes and Arapahos. Therefore you must go back to your country, and if the soldiers come to fight, you must remember they are not from me, but from that great war chief, and it is with him you must make your peace. I cannot stop the war but will send your talk to the Great Father, and if he gives me orders to treat you like the friendly Indians I will send out to you to come in; but you must not come in unless I send for you, and you must keep well out beyond the friendly Kiowas and Comanches. I hope you understand how and why it is that I cannot make peace with you.' "

"Was that all, father?" He put the question softly, as Black Kettle's voice trailed off.

"No!" There was quick bitterness in the denial.

"When Hazen Chief had spoken, Lone Wolf and Big Mouth betrayed me. They told him my heart was good but that I could not speak for my young men, and that my young men were big for war. Then Stone Calf, that son of a sick she-dog, made their words sound true."

"You mean he talked war in front of the soldier chief? Deliberately, father?"

"Aye, deliberately, to show Hazen Chief that Lone Wolf and Big Mouth spoke the truth. He struck his chest there in front of the soldier chief, and he said he could see no point in a truce of a few moons only. Next spring, he boasted, the Sioux and Northern Cheyenne would come down and help us clean out the whole of the Arkansas. Hazen Chief fed us all and treated us like chiefs, but Stone Calf and the others, all save old Ten Bears who is my friend, they rode off muttering because he would not give us everything in the fort."

He paused, weathered hand shaking as it struck the flint to the blackened bowl of the stone pipe.

"It is the last smoke of Moxtaveto, headchief of all the Southern Cheyenne. Ten Bears has told me he must take his people to Fort Cobb. Lone Wolf will follow him, no matter his brave talk in front of the soldier chief. Even now the lodges will be coming down. The Kiowa and Comanche will depart, and Moxtaveto will wait for Yellow Hair alone."

Josh watched the smoke drift upward, let his words come soft and bitter.

"We are dead, father, you and I. I say goodbye now, and I touch the brow for the last time. My heart is good for you."

With the words, he lowered his head, touching the left fingertips quickly to his forehead. He was on his feet then, the softness long gone from the harsh bark of the Cheyenne syllables. His muscular arm reached for the chief's rifle.

"Give me that gun, old man! I am going now. It is better to die than sit here waiting for Axhonehe. *Zeo notaseas!*"

Black Kettle seized the gun, sweeping it away.

"No, my son. You must trust me. Moxtaveto is dead but Ota Kte will live! I have arranged it."

"Give me that gun, father!" His voice turned ugly. "You cannot arrange anything. Your power is gone, here. You know that. You have said it yourself. Axhonehe will be down on this lodge within the next breath."

"Aye," the smile was strangely happy, "my power is gone and Axhonehe will be here even as you say. But in here, my son," he tapped his head significantly, "I am still chief over that Dog Soldier cur. You will see!"

"You're wrong, father—" Josh moved, wrenching the weapon away from him. "I'm not waiting to see. I'm going presently. *You* will see, old man. When Axhonehe appears in front of this tipi, he is a dead Dog Soldier. I have made a vow, *too, Moxtaveto!*"

The sudden snarling of the tribal drums barking the news of the returning peace mission's arrival in the main camp downstream rolled up the Washita to break the silence. Black Kettle shrugged eloquently.

"You can die by your own way, or live by mine. The decision is yours, Ota Kte. I am waiting, my son."

Josh was waiting too, his wavering mind spurred by the building tide of sound racing up the Washita.

Mad Wolf was on his way. Black Kettle's power was broken by the failure of his mission to Fort Cobb, and Axhonehe was coming to redeem his pledge to the Dog Soldier lodge. The compelling vision of the bright red burning pole flashed through the moment of his indecision. Swiftly he turned on the silent headchief.

"All right, father. I'm listening."

"Listen well, my son. Axhonehe is upon us!"

He had no real need of the admonition. The muttering rush of the old chief's following words, startling and hope-building as they were, scarcely had time to reach him before they were ridden under by the turf-showering halt of Mad Wolf's braves beyond the tipi flap.

Black Kettle was rising then, the muzzle of his returned rifle burying itself in the crawling region of Josh's kidneys. The sudden look of hate and contempt suffus-

ing his patient face was as genuine as any South Plains
thespian ever affected.

"Out the flap now, Ota Kte. Quickly before he has a
chance to call out!"

"I am your prisoner, father." The bone-dry grimace
managed a trace of the old grin. "Deliver me to your enemies like the weakhearted old traitor you are. *And may
Maheo forever bless you!*"

Lying in the familiar blackness of Stone Calf's tipi,
Josh reflected at uneasy leisure on the tallow-smooth
working of the first part of Black Kettle's promise. Outside the lodge, the hostile yelp and yammer of the second preparation for the burning of Plenty Kills went forward apace.

The old chief, acting the loyal white-hating Cheyenne
to the last proud feather in his seven-foot war bonnet,
had succeeded in his wily gamble to beat Mad Wolf in
the primary move. He had emerged from his tipi to surrender Josh to the Dog Soldiers at the end of a patently
sincere rifle barrel. Outmaneuvered, Mad Wolf had angrily accepted the prisoner. He had then vented his
spleen by throwing a cordon of tribal police around the
big black lodge, leaving the old man a virtual prisoner in
his own camp. Even at this late hour the Dog Soldier
was taking no chances of a last-minute emotional appeal
by Black Kettle to his changeable tribesmen. Nothing
must now stand in the way of the much delayed burning
of Ota Kte.

Knowing the customary hour for such festivities, Josh
added the three hours which had passed since his
"treacherous" delivery by Black Kettle to the time of
that act's happening—around eight o'clock. *Aii-eee,*
brother! Plenty bad arithmetic! Happen a man could
still tot a simple Indian sum, that made it close to eleven
now, and left him a thin-poor hour for the rest of the old
chief's far-fetched pledge to come about.

The thought of that second part added another pint of
perspiration to his already sopping backbone.

It was all well and good for Black Kettle to have told

him, even though he'd refused to reveal his identity, that
he still had one loyal friend among his fellow tribesmen.
And that that friend would manage Ota Kte's escape
sometime before midnight. The bad part was that a man
didn't have to guess much as to who that mysterious
"one loyal friend" was. And having guessed it, he had to
admit that old Magpie, staunch friend or no, was a pretty rickety warhorse upon which to throw much of a
hope-load.

Not that the old rascal might not try. But suspicious
of him as the Dog Soldiers would naturally be, Black
Kettle's best friend had about as much chance of getting
close to Stone Calf's tipi as a coyote to a mother-guard-
ed buffalo calf.

Still he was all the chance a man had left and happen
the old coot showed up, he wasn't going to let his senili-
ty stand in the way of his following him as far and fast
as his creaky legs could lead.

Two things were in favor of a getaway.

Trussed up as tight as they had him and with the
whole danceground swarming with drum-crazy Dog Soldiers, they'd put no actual guard in front of the tipi. Beyond that Stone Calf had thoughtfully pitched his skins
to back up on a thick stand of river willows that reached
clean to the water's edge.

His nerve-tuned reflexes jumped to the sound of the
knifeblade slashing the rear of the lodge. Fascinated, he
watched the slim blade lance through the taut cowskins.
The next minute he was stifling a gasp of recognition.

That small head and slender arm following the knife
through that opened tipi wall were a long way from senile or shaky!

Monaseetah came to him, shadow-swift, the soft
crush of her lips on his warning back all questions. The
knifeblade flashed faster than a man could follow it. He
was free and following the Indian girl back out the slitted skins thirty seconds after her wordless appearance.

A three-minute sneak brought them to the banks of
the Washita, Josh careful to see that his following moccasin prints stepped into and obliterated the girl's. At

the river there was no pause. Monaseetah slipped into
the darkened flood and let the current carry her down
and away from the flaring reflections of the dancefires.
Behind her, the tall scout bumped the guiding drive of
his legs against the shallow bottom, his dark head cutting the surface only inches behind the girl's.

Ten interminable minutes later their combined swimming and floating had carried them a quarter-mile
downstream of the camp.

They came out of the water on a long stratum of slab'
rock leading to a growth of cottonwood saplings back
from the river. On the naked rock their tracks dried and
disappeared as they entered the screening brush. He recognized the high withered shadow of the gelding even as
the girl's first words were coming to him.

"It is your Winter Giant, my love. Take him and ride.
Do not stop to talk. Goodbye, Ota Kte. My heart rides
with you—"

Her words were broken off by the hard smash of his
kiss.

"God bless you, girl," he muttered. "You know where
my heart rides."

"Aye, Ota Kte, always—"

She clung to him a moment then, her lashes wet not
with river water alone. When she broke away, her voice
had gone harsh. The Cheyenne gutturals hissed at him.

"Go now, *Veho!* Before I am missed!"

"Before *you* are missed, girl?"

"Yes. Don't argue, my love. I must be in the camp
when they find you gone."

"I won't ride without you, Bright Hair." The refusal
was flat, final.

"You will have to. If I am missed they will kill Moxtaveto. They will know he planned this if I am not there
for them to see. There is no other way, Ota Kte."

He cursed viciously. She was right, of course. Happen
those Dog Soldiers got it in their minds Black Kettle had
arranged the slip-out, they'd kill the old chief, sure.

"Suppose you do get back? They'll find those cut
ropes in the lodge—"

"They will find nothing!" With the denial, the girl reached in her dress, pulled out the slashed piece of the horsehair ropes. "You see, I have them here. I will bury them on the way back. They will never know how it was done. I saw you covering my tracks with yours back there."

Her old sunbright smile flashed suddenly, stabbing him like a knife in the heart.

"The escape of Ota Kte will still be a miracle when our children's children are telling the old tales!"

Like it or not, a man had to buy it. He had his chance to get back to Custer now, and he couldn't refuse it. Not after the girl had risked her life to give it to him. Besides, there were too many more lives beyond his and the Cheyenne girl's mixed up in the rest of that miracle of hers; the remaining slim bet that Wasiya could still get him clean away from the Washita.

He had to go, and to go fast. The last, best chance for all of them was in his getting to the General and stopping him short of Black Kettle's winter camp.

"I'll be back, girl," was all he said before swinging aboard the restless gelding. *"Zeo notaseas!"*

"Zeo notaseas," she echoed softly. "I'll be waiting for you, Ota Kte—"

20. The Winter Giant

HE KEPT WASIYA down to a swinging walk the first two miles. They followed the south bank of the Washita, taking advantage of the outcrops of bare sandstone featuring that side of the river.

Across stream the prairie lay open and swampy, the
soft turf of its bottomlands setting a perfect track-trap
for the man who would be tomfool enough to ride a
twelve-hundred-pound gelding across them. The late
moon was climbing fast and within an hour the whole
plains would be a blaze of near-white light. With that
damned Blind Coyote and his guiding hand, Yellow
Buffalo, up front of the Dog Soldier pursuit, a man
couldn't be too cautious where he left his barefoot pony
prints.

Wasiya was one horse in a score of hostile pony herds
but the rib-gaunt old devil had been ridden down to his
hocks in that crazy march from Middle Springs, and
four days on winter grass hadn't gone halfway to putting
the spring back in his pasterns.

Fifteen minutes downstream of Black Kettle's camp
he brought the gelding up, slid off him and cocked a
primely interested ear back toward the dancing war
camp.

He was still close enough to catch the bounce of the
dance fires off the night sky over the Big Bend. The
wind lying where it did, light and warm from the Southwest, would let a man pick up any ear-sign of a ruckus
in the hostile celebration. Ten seconds of listening
brought him nothing but the swirl of the Washita and
the dying rustle of the night breeze among the leaves of
the riverbank cottonwoods.

Wagh! All was well in Mad Wolf's firelit front yard.
The red sons hadn't yet spotted his getaway. By now the
girl would be back in Moxtaveto's lodge.

Unknotting the muzzle-wrap Monaseetah had so
properly installed on Wasiya to keep the gelding from
whickering before he had his rider out of Cheyenne earshot, Josh took one last look and listen toward the Dog
Soldier camp.

Half a held-breath later he was piling aboard the startled Wasiya and kicking him through the shallows of the
Washita.

A deaf-mute with both ears plugged and buggy-blind-
ers on couldn't have missed that commotion. There was

enough unhappy Dog Soldier yapping going on in that camp to raise new hair on a scalped Sioux's head. The boys had come to Stone Calf's tipi to pick up their trussed white bird and had found him long flown.

Across the river lay the open prairie and a ninety-mile night ride to swing wide northeast then straight west to intercept Custer on his line of march from Camp Supply. It was 1.00 A.M. of the 25th and the General had been scheduled to leave that field base on the 24th. Knowing the General the way he did, a man could gamble that what the orders called for, Custer would come up with. It was 100-to-1 he'd left Camp Supply on the exact hour of his orders and was already in the field heading for the Washita.

That left a man in his footskins with three options.

He could make his wide swing to hook up with Custer, taking his chances Mad Wolf would figure him to do just that and would head the Dog Soldiers straight north to cut him off halfway around his big circle.

He could hold his own line due north from the Washita, not swinging back west to join the General at all, but just keeping on pounding Wasiya's rump until the gelding had him due east of Camp Supply. Then all he'd have to do was ease west and home-out, scalp-safe, on that powerful base.

He could take the simplest way of all. Just give the gelding his head straightaway down the southeast valley of the Washita and come out a short seventy miles later in the "peace sanctuary" of Colonel Hazen's commission at Fort Cobb.

He hesitated, the trail-taking howls of the Dog Soldiers nudging his natural regard for the shoulder-length Kelso locks.

He owed Custer next to nothing. The vain-crazy Indian killer had refused to open his ears to every warning he'd offered him. He had laughed or snapped off every level-headed suggestion put to him. He would by now have heard California Joe's report of seeing him with the Dog Soldiers on Dead Mule Mesa, and would more than ever suspect him of going soft on the Cheyenne.

Like as not, he would turn him over to a guard detail and route him back for Camp Supply the minute he struck the column.

Still, a man had his loyalty to think of, and when the hostiles were howling a scant six miles off his backside and the burning pole was still waiting for him back along the Washita a man had sudden reason to remember which side he was on.

He had reason, also, to remember what he knew about the Arapaho-Dog Soldier trap waiting for Yellow Hair back there in the Big Bend. And about the fact the General thought he had no more than eight or nine hundred of old Black Kettle's "peaceful" Cheyenne on his hands once he got his troops to the Washita.

In the end a man had a last thought. It was a thought which set his jaw stiff as lake ice in January, and put his hand to jerking Wasiya's halter rope so hard around it nearly took the gelding's head off.

It was a thought which had to do, first off, with a Cheyenne face, yellow-toothed and grinning evily with its Dog Soldier vow to put Ota Kte under and wed-up with Moxtaveto's niece. It was a thought which had to do, second off, with a remembrance of a wrinkled red hand touching a weathered brow in final respect and farewell to an enemy white man whose loyalty had in the last hour of trial surpassed that of any of his own tribesmen. And a thought which had to do, last off, with a memory neither in his mind nor in his eye, but in his heart.

The picture of Monaseetah smiling up at him in the hurried dark of the downstream cottonwood grove—the refeeling of the quick burn of her hungry mouth on his —the tearwet caress of her dropped lashes—the quiet promise of her parting promise, "I will wait for you, Ota Kte," brought the final curse.

"Hee-yahh, little hoss! Custer's ninety miles away and we got a *wickmunke* to report! And sure as hoss sweat stinks, old son, a howlin' 'Mad Dog' Soldier to shoot!"

The harsh words were seconded by the vicious drive

of the moccasined heels into the gelding's flanks. Wasiya
jumped into a hammering gallop. The drumfire of his
unshod hooves faded quickly and was gone.

Once again the sum of one of Josh's Indian arithmetic
problems added up.

As he drove Wasiya northeastward across the Washita uplands, the sounds of the Cheyenne pursuit dropped
away behind. Within another five miles they were lost
altogether and he pulled the lathered gelding down to a
ground-eating shuffle trot, the natural trail gait of the
plains-bred saddle pony.

But as Wasiya's gait slowed to a trot his rider's
thoughts picked up to a gallop. Second guesses were
coming fast and with them some hard facts which didn't
add up as smoothly as the simple hunch that Mad Wolf
couldn't hold his exact trail once he was well away from
the Washita.

First, a man had to admit that his plan to outride the
Dog Soldiers with a ninety-mile swing-around would no
longer hold.

Next, he had to realize his only chance of coming up
to the Camp Supply column in the field short of its Big
Bend destination, was to cut due west right now.

But the country ahead for half a day's ride in any
direction was flatter than an old squaw's chest. With daylight, a mounted man would stand out on that short grass
as black as a two-thousand-pound bull buffalo in the middle of a forty-foot wallow. And with Dog Soldier patrols
crawling the country between him and Custer thick as
sowbugs under a turned-over cowcake, a man wouldn't
have a Chinaman's chance. He'd be spotted before the
sun was two hours high and scalped before it was three.

Still a mountain jasper in his saddle had about as
much choice as a Kansas darkie in a Kentucky Klan
meeting.

The flint of the scout's grin struck its light briefly.

Such as the Arkansas Option was, a man reckoned
he'd have to take it. And take it mortal fast. Happen he

aimed to get to Custer he'd never make it riding the red
fringe of Mad Wolf's north-flung gauntlet.

Once more Wasiya spun to the head-jerking demand
of the halter rope. Spun hard left and jumped obediently
to the hammer of the sweat-stained moccasins. Spun
hard left and pointed the roman ugliness of his sooty
nose as due west as the sink of a six o'clock sun.

An hour before dawn the southwesterly breeze faltered and died. The prairie became grass-rustle still.
Wasiya swung his muzzle nervously, searched the dead
air and whickered softly. Josh stirred in the saddle, adding his own uneasy grunt to the gelding's complaint.

When ten days of unfailing southwest wind, bearing
up from the parch of south Texas and old Chihuahua
the dry desert breath of the longest November hot spell
he could remember, suddenly quit blowing, a man could
begin to worry. He could in this infernal country. The
wind never quit unless she was fixing to switch, and a
man could sweat a little until she decided to let him
know which way she meant to switch.

For the next hour and until the leaden daylight came
filtering eastward across the empty reach of the plains,
Josh sweated. But twenty minutes after the first sick
light of the twenty-fifth began to grow, his perspiration
was shut sharply off.

The unnatural hush and humidity of the past hour began to move. Slowly at first and not direct enough for
a man to mark it. Then Josh, watching the unfailing ba-
rometer of the buffalo grass, saw the delicate nap of the
prairie carpet wave and rustle away into the southwest.
A moment later the first south-spreading ripple of the
grasses was succeeded by a second, and a third. Less
than a minute after the first warning wave, the full
lengths of the brown grama stems were holding far over
and steady due into the southwest.

With the flattening of the grass the temperature began
to drop. In a matter of half a mile his shirt, damp-wet
since leaving the Washita, was frozen to his broad back,
the creak and pop of its adjustment to his hunching

muscles putting more than the mere chill of its own discomfort into the tightening small of his spine. Another half-mile and the caked trail lather lacing Wasiya's steaming flanks was crusted solidly over by a quarter-inch rime of hoar-frost. And still the wind was no more than a mouse-rustle in the buffalo grass.

But it was that kind of mouse-rustle which put a High Plainsman's prairie instincts straight on edge—along with the clamp of his hard-set teeth.

There weren't many things Josh Kelso figured to be afraid of. That creepy ghost-rustle through the panhandle short grass was one of them. When the grama started to stir where there was no wind; when it rustled and whispered and lisped at a man as though ten million tiny mousefeet were moving invisibly through it; when it lay all flat in one direction and that direction, pointed by the restless gibberish of its crowding stems, lay dead and due southwest; it was full time for a man to pucker his gut and admit he was plain, damn, scared stiff.

Again Wasiya whickered, the uneasy swing of his belling nostrils now steadied directly away from the south pointing press of the grass. Josh, his nervous gaze following the gelding's, cursed silently.

Well there it was, mister. Him and the gelding had had it. Mad Wolf, Custer, Monaseetah and all the rest of them could make it out among themselves. It was Josh Kelso and his horse against Waniyetula, the Blizzard God of the North Plains Sioux now. All bets were off and the Dog Soldiers were a deader issue than last year's Agency beef.

That greasy cloudbank crouching northeast up there past the Main Canadian wasn't any summer shower. The way it was bellying and mushrooming down across the prairie hush; the way it was shutting off the daylight quicker than a man could watch it go; the growing minor key hum of its god-awful power building in the dead air all around him; the pure, raw, snowstink of its winter-rotten breath, let a man know once and for all straight where he was riding.

And where he was riding was dead into the hollow
gut of a Blue Texas Norther.

The smash of the snow's storm-howl roared and
crashed against the staggering gelding, clogging his rolling eyes and clotting his close-pinned ears. Atop the
failing pony, Josh fought the snow away from his own
mouth and nose, gagging and cursing at the breath-kill-
ing strangle of it. His arms were like frozen clubs now
and in the clamp of his long legs around the gelding's
ribcage there was no longer any feeling below the knee.
In the shelter of an eight-foot cutbank he halted the
gelding and forced his numbing mind to the last decision.

For four hours they had fought the white hell of the
Norther, the scout trying always to keep the full blast of
the wind on his right shoulder, hoping thereby to hold a
rough course westward.

But in the belly of a High Plains blizzard the compass
point of the storm's fury swings crazily as a rudderless
sea wreck. Four times alone in the past twenty minutes
it had shifted the drive of its giant's fist, smashing him
and the gelding now north, now east, now south, now
west. And in the black bowel of a blue-ice Norther no
way is north. None east. South, nor west. A man loses
all sense of time and direction under the constant blood-
cry and yammer of its incredible noise.

And shortly he loses his other senses. The eyes first,
from the stark blindness of straining through the serous
drying blast of the ice slivers. The ears next, their drums
ruptured by the incessant high-level scream of the hurricane wind. And lastly, the whole feeling in the body
goes, the tortured flesh and bone no longer able to trans-
mit the last warnings of the freezing skin.

As the scout huddled in the lea of the tiny cutbank,
his final senses fought their ways into the frost waste of
his slowing mind.

His hearing was gone and he had not been able to see
the black flick of Wasiya's ears for the past hour. Trying
now to move, thinking to dismount and give the gelding

a last respite, he found he could not bring his off-leg over the ice glaze of the saddlehorn. He knew, the next instant, that God hadn't intended him to. Happen a man had made it down off that pony he'd have legged over his last saddle. He would never have remembered to try and mount back up and he would never have made it had he remembered.

It was the last hour he and big horse had ahead of them, and *he* was done. Blind, deaf, powerless to move, three quarters frozen, he'd made his dead-end human effort. It was up to the horse now.

Up to twelve hundred pounds of steel-tough, Sioux buckskin. Up to a mud-yellow bundle of bad nerves and bellows-sized lungs. Up to a high-withered North Plains horse who in the seven years since he'd quit sucking his wild dam's leathered udders, had never been ridden down to the baserock of his bottom. Up to a rattailed, burr-maned pony whose last ride would tell a man how well his Sioux breeders had named him.

Wasiya . . . the Winter Giant . . . it was up to him.

Josh leaned clumsily forward. The effort cracked the set-ice gluing his buttocks to the frozen cantle of the saddle and broke the sleet glaze covering the blue of his barely moving lips.

"It's your head, little hoss. Fight it off, goddam you, fight it off—"

Wasiya rolled the whites of his wicked eyes and swung his muzzle toward the mutter of the cracked voice. Blowing the clotting snow from his sooty nostrils, he nuzzled briefly at the hanging arm of his rider. He shook himself like a great yellow cat as the grunting reassurance of his soft whicker went to the no longer listening scout.

Moving out from the shelter of the cutbank the big gelding swung sharply to his right. As he went, he heeded no shift of the hammering wind, heard no siren voice of the Blizzard God's angrily beckoning howls. Instead, he drove powerfully and arrow straight along the needle-point of his instinct-chosen compass.

The yellow-gelding was neither deaf nor blind and his long-forgotten Sioux herdsman had named him well.

Wasiya, King of the Big North Snows. *Wasiya*, The Real Winter Giant. . . .

21. Canadian Crossing

THE FACE ABOVE HIM seemed floating in the empty air, now drawing closer until it almost touched him, now receding swiftly until it was lost in a distance as far and hazy as some outer star. Still he knew it. Recognized it as surely as he would his own. The bleached droop of the haystack mustaches, the compelling glare of the coyote-wild eyes, the petulant set of the small mouth. Diminishing or rushing up at him, whirling, fading, star dim or suddenly moonbright, there was no mistaking that face. It was Yellow Hair's.

The fire ran into his mouth, spread racing down his throat and balled up in his stomach to explode like a burst of grapeshot.

There were more faces above him now and with the fire one of them sprang into clear, hard focus, pushing the others back into the nebulous fringe of the outer group. Dr. Coates. Thin-jawed, fierce-eyed Major "Scalpel" Coates, Custer's buffalo-chasing Assistant Surgeon.

The fire ate down his throat again and now he felt the slop-over trickle of it running across his jaw and down his chest. And he smelled the raw, familiar, god-blessed stink of it. Whiskey, by Christ!

He sat bolt upright, his shoulder catching Coates and knocking him halfway across the tent. The next instant he was on his feet, tottering for the flap-laced entrance.

"Catch him, boys, he's going down!" Coates's sharp order came as the big scout staggered. "All right, get that cot and that damned snow out of here. Bring me half a dozen blankets and a bucket of hot coffee. On the double now!"

Minutes later Josh was sitting up in the warm bundle of the blankets, gulping the steaming coffee and forcing the story of his capture and escape through the unwilling stiffness of his lips. When he had concluded, Custer merely nodded.

"You're lucky to be alive, Joshua. That muckle-dun Percheron of yours brought you in. The good Lord knows how. Probably found the river and followed it up to strike our camp."

"What river, General?" His question blurted awkwardly, the cracked, frost-burn blackness of his lips still refusing to function properly. "By God, not the Washita?"

"The Canadian, Joshua."

"The Canadian! Goddam it, then you're almost on top of them. Listen, General—"

"You listen, sir. Coates says you're not to talk any more. He's had you packed in snow for three hours and you can thank him you still have arms and legs. I think we owe him the courtesy to do as he asks. Do you hear me?"

He nodded weakly, the sudden return of his strength all at once failing. He sank back into the reaching warmth of the blankets, hearing the dim mutter of Custer's voice asking Major Coates how soon he might expect him to be rational and ready to talk, barely hearing the Assistant Surgeon's replied estimate of four or five hours. Then he neither knew nor heard any further sound.

When he once more awoke, the tent was dark and warm, its only light the faint glow from the smoking wood stove. Such as the illumination was, it was sufficient to make out the lone orderly stationed by the entrance flaps.

"Call the Colonel, soldier, and hop your butt about it. I ain't got all winter."

With the scowling order and the trooper's quick agreement to it, he was out of the blankets and toeing into his stove-dried moccasins. Shortly, the familiar, light, quick step crunching the snow outside the tent announced Custer's arrival.

"Well sir, by thunder this is better. All right, orderly, outside. Now then, Joshua—"

Josh grinned, frost-cracked lips or no.

By God, you just couldn't put this little bantam down. Let him get caught in the wide open with a full field column of green troops by the worst blizzard in ten years and he still had guts and gall enough to rattle on like he was sitting snug and safe back of the stockade at Dodge.

"Yes sir, General." The grin let itself out another stiff notch. "I reckon you want the story of my life with the Dog Soldiers again."

He didn't miss the quick clouddrift of the frown, and wasn't fooled by the peg-toothed grin which supplanted it.

"No sir, I believe I got that before."

With the short nod Custer read it back to him, from Monaseetah's Middle Spring trap to Wasiya's miraculous finding of the Cimarron Crossing camp. The too-bright way he rapped it to you made it sound like something he'd read in a Ned Buntline penny-dreadful, and let you know that, scoutwise, you and G. A. Custer had come to the end of the trackline. His own grin died.

"You don't believe it, is that it, General?"

"I *do* believe it, sir. That's the whole trouble. And in the face of it I can no longer trust you with the Cheyenne."

"By God, General, that's not so!"

"I'm afraid it is, Joshua." Custer's contradiction came quietly, Josh noting his voice wasn't high and flighty like it was when he was tempered-up. "It's the girl, you understand? I assume you were taken and held by force and I further assume your complete loyalty to me. But I do not assume the continuing quality of your judgment under the circumstances."

"I don't foller you."

"My entire point," said Custer soberly. "You cannot follow me. You may indeed owe *your* life to Monaseetah and the old chief. But what *I* owe them and every one of their murdering tribe north of the Arkansas is something else again. You cannot, Joshua, repay your debt to them at the same time you are guiding me in the action I intend taking to collect mine. I'm sorry, sir. California Joe will take the column in from here."

Expecting it or not, the jolt of the dismissal hit a man like the flat of an open hand. Josh shook it off, the apparently easy idleness of his reaction taking Custer off guard.

"General," he might have been speculating on the number of snowflakes crusting the little officer's collar, "how many hostiles you figure you got waitin' for you yonder?"

"Perhaps a thousand, you know that."

"And you got how many troops with you?"

"Eight hundred and fifty, you know that too. What are you getting at, sir?"

The simple bareness of the questioning was beginning to penetrate Custer's impatience, making him hold up and think. Josh stepped softly into the holdup.

"Countin' the full strength of the Dog Soldier Lodge at close to one thousand, you got better than three thousand five hundred hostile bucks squattin' down there in that Big Bend waitin' for you to poke your long nose past it."

"By Heaven, that will do, sir!"

"They'll let you come in on Black Kettle's lodges, pitched like they are on the near side of the Bend." Josh was thinking out loud, ignoring Custer's bristling order. "Then once you get your troops strung out across the open flat of the Bend going for the main Cheyenne camp on the far side of it, the Arapahoe and Dog Soldiers and Stone Calf's hostile Cheyenne will pile in on you from three sides. It can't work no other way, General, the way I got that camp set in my mind. I could draw you a map of it that wouldn't miss six pony steps from bein' accurate down to the last hoss apple."

Custer, quick anger bridled, was listening now, his soldier's mind caught up by the scout's terse detailing of the military picture awaiting him along the one-day distant Washita. His determination wavered, began to fail.

"If I could only be sure of you, man, that map would be priceless. But hang it all, Johua—"

"Listen, General, you ain't got no choice but to be sure of me. You lead them boys of yours into that camp the way you're aimin' to and you're goin' to get the biggest headlines in them eastern papers you ever dreamed of. Only it's going to be a bad dream, General, and the printin's goin' to be plumb black."

"I've heard enough of your impudence, sir!"

" 'CUSTER KILLED ON THE WASHITA,' " he intoned, the dead level of his voice unheeding of the officer's rising tones. " 'COMMAND WIPED OUT IN INDIAN TRAP.' 'NO SURVIVORS IN CHEYENNE MASSACRE OF SEVENTH CAVALRY.' "

He paused, shrugging laconically. "How do they sound to you, General? Take your pick."

During the naked seconds of the grim tolling off of the big scout's predictions, Custer's anger had flared, been fought down and brought under control. With no further reaction than an understanding nod, he stepped toward the tent flap.

"Orderly."

"Yes sir, Colonel?"

"I want Major Coates up here, please."

"Yes sir. Right away, Colonel, sir."

With the clearly disgruntled Assistant Surgeon dragged from his warm billet and crowding in through the snow-billowing flaps, Custer's quiet directions continued.

"Give this man an opiate, Coates. He's more nearly done in than we thought. Not yet rational, you under-

stand? Orderly. Mount a guard detail out front. No one
is to come into this tent. Is that clear?"

"My God, General, wait a minute!"

Josh's desperate outburst was countermanded by the
quick touch of the slender hand on his shoulder and by
the too-ready assurance of the old, bright smile.

"Easy now, Joshua. Take Coates's pill and let that be
an end to it for tonight. Let's call that an order, sir."
Here, the irresistible broadening of the famous grin.
"You've got to rest if you're going with me in the morning!"

With the surprise announcement of the reinstatement,
Custer strode from the tent.

Josh, left to the irritated insistences and sugar-coated
laudanum tablets of Major Coates, offered no resistance
to either.

He was suddenly tired again and tomorrow was another day. Plenty of time yet to make his map of the
hostile layout for the General and to sweet-talk him into
following it in his approach to the Cheyenne camp.
They were still a long day's march from the Washita and
the drowsy, warm feel of the blankets and the wood
stove smoke-smell was more than a played-out mountain
jasper could argue with.

He lay down, letting the leaden ease of the drug push
him back and keep him there. Major Coates's face
pulled away, got fuzzy, floated around the tent a spell,
then drifted peacefully out the flap.

Beyond the thin canvas walls old Waniyetula, the
Sioux Blizzard God, still yammered wildly. But in the
big Sibley it was close and warm, and the waiting Washita was thirty safe miles away.

Who was there to blame the dozing scout if he failed
to hear the sudden, crafty change in Waniyetula's angry
howl? The change which put the old devil's harsh voice
from frustrated, baffled screaming to sudden mock-hol-
low laughing. . . .

22. Custer's Compass

JOSH CAME AWAKE. He frowned up at the unfamiliar gray of the tent cover, the lethargy of the opium still slowing his mind. Presently it occurred to him that the gray of that light filtering through the dirty sidewalls was a mite too strong for nighttime. Then, in harsh succession, other things began to cross his quickening thoughts.

That was daylight-gray, well along into morning. Custer wasn't the commander to sleep late on a campaign ride. The storm had let up and it was almighty quiet outside. Way too quiet for a field camp of eight hundred and fifty cavalrymen.

He was at the tent flaps then, sharpening instincts halting him short of ripping them open and blundering out. The big hand parting the flaps moved them no more than a chance breeze.

Outside the air was still, only a powderflake fall of snow still sifting down. It was nothing like enough to mar a man's eyesweep of the Canadian Crossing campsite.

The overcoated silhouette of the lone trooper patrolling the twenty-foot beat in front of the tent overlay the rest of it. Beyond the trooper's path the story read as clear as the race of a South Park creek.

The long, horse-appled tramplings of the empty picket-lines. The black smudges of the dead-coaled cookfire spots. The silent rows of the parked supply wagons and spare field ambulances. The back-hunched lines of the nosebagged mules. The lonely scatter of the deserted Sibleys. The handful of heavily bundled troopers tending the feeding of the wagonstock. The stark, ironshod staring of the broad path of snow-held horse sign leading into the near side and out the far, of the ice-clogged Canadian.

Add it all up, even in the half-breath it took you to sweep it in. Divide it, multiply it, tot it back up any way you would. It came out the same. There wasn't a Seventh Cavalry saddleblanket in sight.

Custer was gone. And he'd left Josh Kelso behind under armed guard and camp arrest!

The big scout wheeled like an arrowshot bear. Plastering his broad back to the tent flaps, he let the hiss of his held breath go.

Goddam the lousy little scut. Smearing his soft-smiled bullcrap right in a man's teeth. Letting him have the cow-cake of his stinking shoulder-pat and making him eat it too. A man could forgive a lot of things about the General, and forget a lot more, but not this. This a man would remember. He'd remember it as long as he would that buddy-up shoulder squeeze. And then, after that, a hell of a lot longer.

There was only one way a man could go now. That prairie compass had only one needlepoint for a man in his skins. And it wasn't east, nor west, nor north. It was due south.

But it had to be worked so no troopers got shot, and no civilian scouts either! It had to be worked slick and smooth and above all, fast. A man had to have some information first, along with a good, warm issue overcoat. He rolled back into the blankets, let his voice waver out weakly.

"Hey, soldier. Gimme a hand here, will you? I can't seem to make it to my feet."

He heard the answering crunch of the sentry's step on the snow, tried to set himself to look as pale and puny as a hundred and ninety pounds of muscle-tight mountain man could manage.

"Sure, buddy. How you feelin'?"

The trooper's smile was friendly, his behavior hand-made to Josh's urgent order. The boy-simple way he laid that Spencer down when he reached for the expiring scout couldn't have been better planned. Josh had his knee in his kidneys and his arm barred across his trusting throat before the stupefied youngster was aware the blankets had so much as rustled.

"All's fair in war, soldier." His grin came as his free hand scooped up the carbine. "Make certain sure you don't yammer when I ease off'n your windpipe."

He stepped away from him just far enough for the snout of the carbine barrel to stay embedded in his sucked-in stomach.

"Now then, boy, talk fast and you won't get hurt. How long ago did the General leave?"

"Five o'clock. It's most eight now."

"Where-a-way is his line of march? Dead south?"

"Yes sir!" The boy threw a salute, in his belly-shrinking fluster.

"All right. Good. Where's the saddlemount picket? What's left of it."

"Yonder past that near line of wagon mules."

"You know hosses, boy? To pick one out?"

"Yes sir—"

"Well, pick one."

"The gray mare. She's Major Coates's buffalo pony. He didn't want to risk her down yonder."

"Arab mare? Dishface blaze? Sockfoot, steel-gray?"

"That's her, yes sir."

"By God, that's somethin' anyway. What's left behind here otherwise? How many men? What officers?"

"The Colonel didn't take nothin' but seven wagons of ammunition and one ambulance. There's near thirty of us left here. Only one officer though, Lieutenant Mathis. He's—"

"All right boy, turn around."

His flat interruption brought a hesitating, white-faced obedience. The youth turned carefully with his hands half raised. As his back came around, Josh stepped in. The just-right tunk of the Spencer barrel took the trooper behind the right ear. He went down like a hand-dropped sandbag and Josh apologetically rolled him into the cover of the blankets.

"Sorry, youngster. You won't need this coat. You'll be real cozy here. And just long-quiet enough to get me and that mare clean across the Canadian."

For the first six hours the snow held off, the wind, uneasily down. The clouds were still low, sometimes lying flat to the ground so that a man had to feel his way for a mile at a time. But generally there was light enough to see and Custer's column was leaving a heavy track. Where a man couldn't see it he could smell it, working slow and following the sharp sting of the horse-dropping smell.

Before long he had closed the gap to where a Sioux-trained hand, held close and steady, could detect the radiating core-warmth of the freezing apples. Within half an hour more, he didn't have to squat to put a hand to them. The thin wisps of the bowel-heat smoke, yellow-gray against the white of the snow, told a mountain eye they were only minutes old.

But another mile along the freshening trail and the wind was moving in. A quarter-mile farther, the snow was driving dead level with the flat of the plain. Five minutes more and the rounding snow dimples of the filling hoofprints disappeared. Custer and his eight hundred and fifty men and mounts could have been four hundred yards away and still no nearer than the far side of the Rocky Mountain moon.

Josh felt the sink in his belly.

Son of a bitch. He fought down the fury that rose in him. To have gotten fresh-apple close to them! To miss them by twenty minutes of up-sudden snowhowl!

Or was it snowhowl, by God? The more a man listened to the new noise of it, the less it sounded like howling. And the more like idiot-simple, cracked, crazy laughing.

He set his long jaw, clamping back the unreasonable fear that wanted to come up in him.

Let the old devil laugh. This time Josh Kelso was going to get the last cackle. This time, by God, a man had a trick or two left!

He was riding a fresh horse. The wind, flat and noisy as it was, hadn't switched yet. Old Waniyetula had blown his guts out in his yesterday's try to get him. His bluster was still big and noisy but it didn't have the dead cold in it any more, nor the wild, ever changing swing of the wind. The old villain was trying but a man could tell that he was just blowing and snowing now, and running almighty fast out of real breath.

That wind was coming down off the Canadian as true north as the pole. As long as it held steady he could drift with it and figure he was hitting roughly south. Going that way, if he didn't come up with something else meanwhile, he was bound to sooner or later come up to the damn Washita itself. He could hole up there in the river-bank timber and weather it out, Custer or no Custer.

But what a man actually expected to hit before he hit the Washita was the broad track of the old east-west Indian trail over which the Dog Soldiers had brought him into Black Kettle's camp. Now if he could hit both that trail and Custer too—

Not over half a mile of humpbacked drifting later, the gray mare turned "whiffy."

He brought her up at once and sat watching the work of her muzzle and ears against the crossdrive of the wind.

When a horse that's cavalry-bred and barracks-raised turns all at once whiffy on a man, it isn't that she's smelling Indian ponies or red soldiers. Not when she was as sharp-nosed as this mare. And as eager whiffy. A horse could get scared whiffy too, but any son that had worn out the best part of six leggins' seats polishing them on the cantle of a Texas saddle could spot the difference wink-quick.

This mare was winding friendly. And she wasn't blowing any smell but Seventh Cavalry horse sweat out of her flared open nostrils.

He gave her her head, compounding the generosity with a drive of his moccasins which nearly caved her aft ribs in. Within a handful of snowblind minutes the gray mare had blundered squarely into the storm-turned rumps of Custer's picketlines.

The Colonel had halted his command in a wide-snow-filled wash, the low walls of which gave some protection from the wind. Such as this shelter and that of the seven ammunition wagons was, the men of the Camp Supply column were making the miserable best of it.

The one tent, a big Command Sibley, was pitched to the lea of the field ambulance, and toward it now Josh guided the Arab mare. The windrows of huddling troopers seeking the shelter sides of the ammunition wagons or the animal warmth of the picketlines paid him no more heed than had he been one of their own number which, bundled in the high-collared bulk of his late guard's overcoat, he indeed appeared to be.

At the tent he pulled the mare up, grinning his satisfaction.

From the cut and color of the ponies hunching their backs in front of the General's Sibley, a man could rightly guess that a full-out council of war was in progress within. And that the star witnesses and chief hell-getters thereof were California Joe and Apache Bill, along with the rest of Custer's famous string of hired scout-hands.

Stepping off the mare, he paused outside the opening, eying the confirmation of his guess through the slit in the billowing flaps.

If there had been a carpet in that damn tent, his late fellow scouts would have been standing squarely on it. Joe was heading the bunch, backed by the rest of them: Apache Bill, Ben Clark, Jimmy Morrison, the Mexican "Romeo," and old Hard Rope. The General, sided by his brother Tom and by his three field majors and Benteen, was putting the screws to his head-hung scout corps.

"Well, gentlemen," the thin voice was sour as swill, "I suggest that despite your vaunted reputations you've gotten me as thoroughly lost as though I'd hired one of Black Kettle's Cheyennes to do the job. We have left the trail entirely and had it not been for my own use of the compass we would not even know as much as we do, which is simply that we're eight hours south of the Canadian. Any questions on that, gentlemen?"

"None at all, General." California Joe wagged the black brush of his beard soberly. "We're just as lost as Bo-Peep's sheep. Bill and me ain't bin in this Washita country much of late and Ben and Jimmy been up among the northerns pretty much since 'sixty-three."

"That's mortal true," nodded Apache Bill, his own excuse for not knowing the local terrain thinner than any of the others. "Way this cussed Washita country lays, the land so flat and all, a man can't rightly keep long in his head what little landmarks he's got. There ain't a tree high enough for a runt coyote to hoist on, nor a doghill big enough to let a tall gopher see more'n forty yards."

The other scouts nodded wordless agreement with Bill's lament, Hard Rope, the Osage, adding the lone postscript to the majority opinion.

"Me no good, find village," he shrugged. "Me plenty good, *you* find village."

The remark, addressed to the scowling Custer, brought the quick flit of Josh's grin.

The old rascal wasn't talking through his beaver hat. These Osages weren't somehow worth a tinker's damn, come to locating a village of their cousins. But just let a white scout find it for them and they woke up sudden. Nobody could beat them at sneaking in close and spying out the layout of a bunch of lodges. They smelled right to the hostile ponies and even the village dogs wouldn't bark at them.

While he was still enjoying his grin and as he was reaching for the tent flap, a reply to Hard Rope's cryptic observation was coming from the officer group. The nature of that reply, along with its stolid-faced source, checked his hand and shortly widened the spread of his grin.

"Well, Colonel," Benteen's slow voice went to Custer, "here we are. We've got everything but what we came after—Black Kettle's village. And we left the only man who could take us straight to it back there with the baggage wagons. No offense to you other boys," his nod to California Joe and his group was sincere, "this snow is hell. There's no blame on any of you. But I, for one, wish we had Josh Kelso here."

"You ain't wishin' no harder than the rest of us, Captain!" California Joe's fervent affirmative was backed by the soberly agreeing headnods of his fellow scouts. No group of repentant buckskin sinners, mute as they might be, ever echoed a louder or more unanimous "Amen!"

The simple eulogy brought an awkward flush to the listening hero's grin.

A man better get the hell in there and put a stop to those nominating speeches before they had him set to run for President. Especially if he didn't know too much more about where they were than the other scouts did!

But Custer's voice was staying his reaching hand this time, and for a long spell he was glad he'd let it do so. A man was forever selling the little General short, only to have him up and buy his way back into your heart just like he was doing now.

"Gentlemen," the statement was given in one of Custer's rare moods of self-admission, "you can include me in those wishes. But if wishes were horses, we wouldn't need oats along.

"Boys," his short nod went to the scouts, "Joshua was a sick man. I purposely had Dr. Coates drug him so he would not be further depressed by our departure. I believe I regret that action now. I, too, wish we had that thick-headed Mountain Moses here to lead us out of this blizzard's bullrushes. But he is *not* here, and wishing he were is not going to bring him through those tent flaps!"

Josh couldn't resist it. A man could stand outside all winter and never get a better chance to bust in. He took his big grin with him as he bent his tall form through the tent opening.

"Oh, I dunno, General. Depends on how hard you wish—"

His quiet words, preceded by the high flight of the Custerian prose, broke the meeting as wide open as the appearance of any Moses, mountain or biblical, could ever hope to do. In a matter of seconds the backslaps of his fellow scouts and the unabashed handshakes of Custer's worried staffers were completed and the commander ordered the tent cleared save for himself and his prodigal ex-favorite scout.

Josh nodded grimly.

Jealous as always where he smelled the chance for a big decision or a clean-cut military move, the little General was not about to share with his staff any distinction which might result from his scout's disclosures. What Josh might have to tell him about their present location in relation to that of Black Kettle's Big Bend camp, along with any success which might obtain from following up that information, was going to belong to Lieutenant Colonel G. A. Custer, Commanding.

And any history book title or credit for getting the Camp Supply column unlost and heroically led out of the blind gut of that November 26th snowstorm wasn't going to get split up with California Joe, Josh Kelso or any other living soul.

It was going to stay with Custer and his precious compass!

23. *The Lonely Hill*

THE MARCH of blundering events put in dangerous motion by Sheridan's notorious General Order of the 15th, now gathered the final speed of inevitability.

It was 5.00 P.M. by Custer's big gold watch, that religiously held instrument which shared the hallowed vestry of his breast pocket with the sacred compass, when the little General ordered his staff to leave following Josh's dramatic arrival. For the next hour the pacing silhouette of the column commander's thin figure moved across the lamplit walls of the big Sibley. In the far corner of the tent Josh's shadow crouched over the Colonel's war chest, the only movement in it the scratchy laboring of the turkey-quill pen.

While the crude map of the Washita grew under the scout's awkward hand and glass-sharp memory, Custer fired at him an abrupt round of questions concerning the last-minute strength and disposition of the hostile forces.

Was he sure the Kiowa-Comanche camps were largely deserted? Was he convinced the Arapahoe meant to fight? Did he realize that such a gathering of lodges as he described would cover no less than five miles of riverbank? Would house over four thousand Indians? Could he with certainty put the column onto that east-west Indian trail leading into the open side of the camp? Was he positive Black Kettle's lodges were isolated from the main camp? Could they definitely be struck first and, by a bold move, cut off from the others?

To these brief queries Josh's grunted asides provided even shorter answers.

The Kiowa and Comanche were gone, giving the excuse of buffalo-hunting over on Rainy Mountain Creek. The Arapahoe would fight, Big Mouth would see to that. The stretch of the hostile lodges along the Washita reached nearer ten than five miles. There were closer to seven thousand than four thousand Indians clustered up in that Big Bend. He could find the trail. Black Kettle's lodges were right where he was inking them in. They could be cut off in five minutes.

Presently Josh's looming shadow grew tall on the tent walls. The map, the questioning, the answering, were done. Providing the snow eased off they could move with first light tomorrow. Six hours would see them on the Washita. It was up to Custer now.

Seizing the map from his slow reach, Custer studied it for two full minutes which seemed to Josh to crawl on their bellies like snowfrozen molasses. At last the little General laughed, handed the map back to him, the bad-wild light in his eyes beginning to grow.

"Keep it, Joshua. Show it to your children. I've got it now."

Josh took the map*, folding it carefully into his coat pocket. He knew Custer's high-voiced excitement was no idle boast. Given half the time he'd used on your rough scrawl, he could six months later draw it for you from memory, not missing a flyspeck nor an inkblot, and drawing it a sight better than you had in the first place.

"I'll get Benteen and the others in now," Custer's tones showed no lowering of his Indian Fever, "and run

---

* *Author's Note: Kelso's map of the Washita:* Kelso's map of the Battle of the "Ouachita," drawn for Custer in the field and from memory, contains significant errata: (1) there were no hostile lodges north of the Washita, (2) Custer reported his retreat exactly followed his advance from the east, (3) his own account of the action listed four, not three, attack columns; the fourth under Capt. Wm. Thompson, (4) Col. Edward Meyers, not Major Alfred Gibbs, commanded the column on Custer's right.—C. F.

over the approach with them. You get over to the commissary and put something in that long belly of yours. I won't need you right away, and Joshua," there was that old shoulder-squeeze again, "when you're done, see that you come back here. I won't have you out in this weather. You're sharing the General's tent tonight, you understand?"

He nodded, understanding several things now. Primarily, the business of handing him back the map and telling him to stow it away. No use showing the staff something somebody else had done. Not when Yellow Hair could give it to them cleaner and quicker in his own way, and at the same time make it sound like his personal opinion and private idea.

Moving for the entrance, he found the little officer there before him, parting the flaps to put in his impatient call for Benteen. The half-frozen trooper outside never got the order. Custer's eyes widened as the flap opening revealed the night sky. Eyes glittering, thin lips suppressing his excitement, he wheeled on the big scout.

"By heaven, Joshua, we've got them now! Look at that sky, man!"

Josh was over his shoulder then, his belly pulling in as his dark eyes narrowed.

As far as a man could see, he was looking at nothing but clear air and clean, black starlight. There wasn't a wind whisper or a snowflake stirring south of the Canadian or north of the Washita. And within two hours there would be moon enough to read a handwritten letter by.

"Don't you do it, General!" He was reading the book of Custer's mind a page ahead. "Your boys have already got eight hours of bad trail behind them. They ain't had no hot food. The hosses is wore down fightin' ground-snow. By God, General, you can't—"

"Orderly!"

"General, for Christ's sake, listen—"

"Orderly. Get Captain Benteen up here. Major Elliott, Gibbs, the rest of them. Instantly sir, you hear?"

"Yes sir, Colonel! Corporal of the Guard ho! On the double!"

"General—"

"By thunder, will you be still, Joshua! You've done your work, man. Now get out and let me do mine. Get out, sir! Do you understand?

"I understand, General," was all he said, before stepping through the flaps to stand bitter-eyed and silent, watching the wild race of Custer's orders break the huddling camp from its snowbound bivouac.

Within minutes the troops would be on the last, grim southward move. Within miles Josh Kelso and the coming harsh white moonlight would be guiding them toward a trail no mountain man could miss. And within six short, frost-clear hours that trail would have them topping out on the mile-long, naked crest of the last ridge overlooking Moxtaveto's tipis.

The Camp Supply column stood committed. The Washita was waiting, and Yellow Hair was coming.

The light within the lodge came only from the pipe-bowl's smolder, the alternate rise and fall of its copper glow highlighting the old chief's impassive face. Across from him the girl crouched in thought-held silence. Outside, the wind, quiet for the first time in three days, let the blackened cowskins hang slack and still along the gaunt ribs of the lodgepoles, gave no hindrance to the incessant thunder of the scalpdance drums from the restless camp below.

There was good cause for the silence and the thought-holding.

Two days gone, the last Dog Soldier patrol returning from its pursuit of Plenty Kills had reported hearing rifle fire along the Canadian. Its members had thought, until reaching camp to find theirs the last party in, that it had been one of their own groups shooting buffalo. Last night Red Bird, a loyal Cheyenne, had come back from a scout to report seeing through the snow a long dark line of marching figures south of the Canadian. The light was bad, too much snow. They had looked like buffalo at first but their line was very even. They could have been soldiers. This morning two of White Bear's Kiowa, moving east with a band of stolen Ute horses, had passed through the camp with a tale of having crossed the snowtrail of many ponies wearing iron shoes. And yes, the trail was lying to the south, almost where Red Bird had seen the buffalo.

Black Kettle stirred, palmed the cold ashes from the long pipe, nodded to the waiting girl.

"Bring the ponies now. Tie them outside. I am uneasy. My heart is bad within me."

"Magpie has been on watch since sundown." Monaseetah's words came with her understanding gesture. "It is time he was relieved, uncle. Who shall I send?"

"Double Wolf. He can be trusted. Send him."

The lithe figure of the girl moved quickly through the flaps, leaving the darkened lodge to the last thoughts and long-cold pipebowl of Moxtaveto, the tired Black Kettle of the Southern Cheyenne.

The dry cottonwood logs of the downriver dancefire were piled swiftly higher. *Aii-eee*, cousin! This was turning into a *real* dance!

From the northeast, within the hour, two big parties of new Dog Soldier braves had arrived. Both from Kansas, where they had been raiding even while that senile Moxtaveto had been whining and pleading with the soldier chief at Fort Cobb. Both big for war. Both led by real chiefs. Black Shield, cousin! And Crow Neck! *Wagh!* Real chiefs indeed. And they had white scalps, fresh ones, twenty-three of them. Now they *would* have a scalp-dance.

The drums thundered the news. The cracked voices of the old criers, running the village streets of all four tribes, summoned a fresh wave of dancers from the farflung scatter of the hostile lodges. A scalpdance, brother! Come running now! And bring your squaw or sweetheart. This is the time you dance with her.

It was true. In the strict social order of the South

Plains tribes, the scalpdance was the sole ceremonial in
which the braves and their women were allowed to
touch each other's bodies. It was a rare occasion, cousin,
and a wild one!

Every warrior old enough to straddle a pony smeared
his broad-boned face with the black charcoal paste of
victory, seized his chosen one and bound her tightly to
him in the folds of a single blanket. A wheeling circle
was formed, the paired-off dancers facing inward and
shuffling from right to left. Their close-packed shoulders
and hips left scarcely room to twist and shift to the
quickening throb of the wardrums.

The squaws, their squat features blazoned with ocher
and vermilion, their skinning knives or butchering
blades belted on the outside of their flaring doeskins,
bore proudly aloft the war weapons or hunting shields of
their menfolk. The annointed few among them exhibited
the matted tangle of the fresh scalps, starkly upheld on
slender trophy rods of peeled willow. As they moved,
the black-faced braves grinningly bound their rawhide
lariats around their bodies and those of the couple next
them, that no dancer might quit the circle from the simple excuse of fainting with exhaustion.

Hour after hour, the driving chant of the drums went
on. The glaring rise of the Arkansas moon served only
to heighten the frenzy of the naked bodies beneath the
tight-bound blankets. Ten o'clock came and was pounded under by the drums. Another hour passed. Another
began.

On the lonely promontory west of Moxtaveto's lodge,
Double Wolf pulled the heavy shroud of his buffalo
robe closer. Curse this midnight chill. But then, *wagh!*
The dance was going well below and all was still to the
west. It was a good clear night and the moon let a warrior see a long ways. All was quiet. There was no use
huddling here and freezing. His lodge was only a few
steps down the hill. There were the warm embers of a
fire in there, and maybe a little of that boiled dog left in
the cooking pot. Moxtaveto was an old woman. And it

was getting colder by the minute on that cursed hilltop.
Nahooxz! It was time to go home.

Seconds later, only the moonlight guarded the glistening snow of Black Kettle's watchtower.

24. *Garry Owen*

JOSH KEPT THE GRAY MARE close in hand. Beside him, Hard Rope held down the chopping gait of his paint gelding, his slant eyes narrowing as Josh pointed the long ridge ahead.

Behind them a scant hundred yards moved Custer and the rest of the scouts. While another hundred yards behind the little General came the snake-long column of the Seventh Cavalry. The snowsqueak and harness jingle of its cautious advance carried clearly to the tense scout and his Osage companion.

He reined in the mare and flung up the warning signal of his long arm. Custer, catching the prearranged gesture, waved it on to the following troops. The Seventh came to a hoof-shuffling, uneasy halt, the steam clouds from the sweated flanks of its mounts rising arrow-straight in the dead-calm air.

Another wave from Josh and Custer was dismounting the scouts. With them he moved swiftly forward on foot to join Josh and Hard Rope. Leaving two of the Osages to handclamp the muzzles of Hard Rope's paint and Josh's gray, the little group inched up the moonwhite slope of the ridge.

At its crest, belly-flat in the snow, his propping elbow

touching Custer's, the big scout let his sidemouth whisper come short and tooth-set.

"You're in luck, General. They ain't even got a sentry posted."

"How can you tell, man? I can see nothing but snow."

"That lone hill yonder. The one that sticks up just this way of the main jumble of them ridges. You see it?"

"Yes, what about it?"

"That's Black Kettle's watch-out. They had a sentry on it twenty-four hours a day when I was with them. You can see it's bare as a new baby's butt."

"Good Lord, Joshua, you don't suppose they've gone!"

"They ain't gone, General." He put the frost of his hard grin to the remark. "They just ain't as crazy as you are. They'd never figure you to come down on them in a snow like this."

"I can't believe there's a war camp beyond those hills, sir." He didn't say it like he was asking any questions. He was stating a fact and his next words nailed it down. "We'll move on down the river. You've missed your marks, man."

Josh's rejoinder was to suggest that before ordering a pony-muscle moved, the column commander accompany him, California Joe and Hard Rope to the deserted top of the watch-hill. He added the dry prediction that he's be mortal happy he had, once he'd shoved his belly across the snowcrown of *that* hill. And he'd be tolerably pleased, as well, that Josh had had him hold the column up back where he had, instead of letting it crunch right up to the last lookout. After all, even "Yellow Hair" wouldn't try to walk eight hundred and fifty iron-shod cavalry horses square up to Moxtaveto's front door across any such loudpoppy snowcrust as they were moving over!

Custer peg-toothed his appreciation of the reminder and put the quick squeeze of his small hand to the scout's bulging bicep.

"All right, Joshua, let's get up there. We can't give the troops time to get on edge."

The four black-furred dots glided down the slope of the ridge, picked their way warily across the open snow of the level separating it and the watch-hill. Within minutes they had again ceased to move, motionless smudges now, on the crest of the distant hill.

The four sets of slitted eyes atop the abandoned silence of Double Wolf's sentry post strained through the puddled darkness of the scene below. Their anxious stares were defeated by the rough tumble of small hills, shelving cutbanks and nebulous blotches of river timber. Custer could see nothing, hear nothing. Josh and California Joe fared little better. But Hard Rope had Indian eyes. And ears.

"Me hear dog bark."

The deep grunt swung the eyes of the listening white men in his direction.

"I didn't hear a living thing." Custer's nervous whisper went to Josh. "And I can't see a living thing!"

"Hold up, General. I got the dog just now. You catch it?"

Custer nodded. There was not only *a* dog barking, there were several of them. And not any mile away either. Those barks were coming out of that right-hand stretch of riverbank cottonwoods, not six hundred yards from where they lay!

"Me see ponies. This side river. You see?"

"Where, Hard Rope?" Custer's glance swung to follow the point of the Osage's arm. "Why, bless you, man, those are trees—or buffalo—yes, by the Lord, they're buffalo! Good heavens, there must be a thousand of them. By thunder, Joshua, you were wrong, sir, you were wrong!"

"There's a thousand of them, all right, General," his voice dropped with the nod, "but they ain't buffalo. And hold your talk down. We can't afford to spook the crazy devils. Happen we work it right, we can gather them in on our way into camp. Happen we work it wrong, the bastards'll stampede and roust out every ear-poundin' buck for fifteen miles down the Washita. Let's go, General. *Them's ponies yonder.*"

"I'm not satisfied, Joshua. I remain confident those
are buffalo down there, dogs or no dogs. I think your
Indians are gone, sir, leaving a few of their curs behind
as they always do."

"No buffalo—ponies," grunted Hard Rope.

"If they're buffalo," grinned Josh, "I'd sure as hell
like to know who hung the bells on them!"

Custer's quick scowl died aborning. Up from below,
tinkle-clear from the ghostly movement of the big herd,
came the unmistakable jangle of a grazing bell. It was
overlain by the answering music of a second. And a
third.

"As you said, Joshua," Custer's light-quick smile
fought the moonlight to a standstill, "let us go."

The smile faded in the moment of its flashing, the pale-
eyed stare which replaced it putting the gray iron of
carbine-close reality to the grim conclusion.

"And may God have mercy on Black Kettle's soul. I
shall not!"

Beyond the mile-long shelter of the first ridge, Custer
readied his column.

The lean ration of coffee and hardtack for a single
day, per man, brought from the base camp on the Canadian, was dumped on the Washita snows, to be followed
by the saddlebag of oats each man had brought for his
mount. There was to be no turning back, no counting on
any source of supply whatsoever. When the troops of
the Seventh Cavalry were committed, they were to understand *they were committed*. Each trooper was allowed
to carry only his ammunition issue of one hundred
rounds and his unbooted Spencer carbine. Even the
heavy field overcoats were ordered stripped off and
added to the mingling trample of oats and coffee, the
huddled men waiting in their issue shirtsleeves for the
final "forward ho!"

There was to be no company talk, no shouted commands, no bugles blown ahead of the coming advance.
Smoking was completely forbidden and the man who

struck a flint or match within the ranks did so in the face of a field-order death sentence.

To Josh, waiting tensely, the sibilant muttering of the hundreds of white tongues sidemounting their frightened whispers in nerve-strung defiance of the "no talking" order to the hand-close comfort of some fellow trooper or perhaps the hard-bitten understanding of a trusted and battle-tried noncom sounded loud enough to be heard in the last Cheyenne lodge down the river.

But a man shook it off, knowing the whole course of the harsh discipline and hand-signaled maneuvering of realigning squads, platoons and companies was going forward with remarkable silence and efficiency. And knowing, too, that when a man knew as much as he did about what was waiting beyond that frozen watchtower of Black Kettle's there was a limit even to his own gut-tough nerves.

He could see the new commands forming up now. Moving the gray mare closer to Custer's staff group, he was able to catch some of the Colonel's low voiced orders.

There would be four attack columns, proper, two of them to move as a unit under Custer. Of the two distinct commands Major Elliott would have one to swing wide around the camp to the south and to come back up and attack from the east. Major Gibbs, or was it Colonel Meyers, there, would have the other, to swing off on Custer's right and between him and Elliott and attack from the south. The third column under Captain William Thompson would move on Custer's left and in direct conjunction with the commander, to attack from the present or western position. The ammunition wagons would be left on the ridge.

Elliott's column moved out first, Gibbs's holding up for fifteen interminable minutes, then following off in planned succession. Custer, sitting his bay buffalo horse in absolute silence, sided by himself and Captain Thompson, watched the slow crawl of the minute hand on the big gold watch, glanced presently toward the paling

gray of the eastern starfields, nodded quietly to young
Thompson.

"All right, Captain, let's go. Hold to a walk until
we're given away."

The double column of Custer's and Thompson's four
hundred troopers split like a snake's tongue around the
narrow base of Black Kettle's watchtower. On the far
side, they converged toward the dark cone of the single
tipi flanking the hostile camp's side of the hill.

Double Wolf's woman, out with the dawn to scrabble
firewood for her breakfast pot of pemmican, dropped
her cottonwood faggots to stare in unbelieving terror.
The next instant she had slipped into the screening
brush and was scuttling for the lodge.

Double Wolf, still sleepy from his night's vigil, was
rubbing his eyes when the woman entered. He saw her
seize their two small children and drag them whimpering
through the entrance flap, and heard the warning of her
single, guttural growl, "Soldiers!" The next moment he
was grabbing his rifle and wrenching back its sidebuilt
percussion hammer.

Stumbling outside, still heavy with sleep, he watched
the squaw fade into the nearby brush. He turned in time
to see the hated silhouettes of the Pony Soldiers topping
the rise behind him.

Double Wolf was a "peaceful" Cheyenne. But he had
been at Sand Creek and seen his other squaw and four
young children ridden down and riddled with carbine
slugs. He saw, now, their blood on the snow again, and
forgot in its red blindness the insistent order of old
Black Kettle to raise the white rags if the soldiers came.
Instead, he raised his old percussion musket and fired it
with his war cry into the advancing troops.

His twisting body was nearly torn in two by the answering hail of soldier lead. His last memory was of the
clarion blare of Yellow Hair's bugler sounding the
charge. The instantness of his death spared him the ig-
nominy of hearing the echoing of its blatant signal by

the brassy notes of Custer's omnipresent regimental mu-
sicians blasting away at "Garry Owen," the war song of
the Seventh Cavalry.

The Battle of the Washita was begun.

25. *Death of a War Chief*

CUSTER'S COLUMN splashed through the waist-deep
Washita and sent its horses scrambling up the opposite
bank, atop which stood the cluster of perhaps fifty
lodges which had chosen to remain camped with Black
Kettle. As the General's troopers topped the bank from
the northwest, the first of Gibbs's cavalrymen dashed up
from the south. Josh, riding ahead of the shouting Custer, saw Black Kettle's squaw run from the big lodge to
race for one of the two tethered ponies. A moment later,
the old chief ran out shouting and waving at the troopers.

Firing was general now and the few other braves,
running half naked from the surrounding lodges, were
beginning to go down. Only a handful of these were
armed and but one or two of them discharged his piece.

Black Kettle had had no time to seize his faithfully
prepared flag of truce. The surprise was too great. The
panic memory of the Sand Creek Massacre, too overwhelming. The pathetic tatter of the dirty white feedsack
laced to its peeled willowpole was later found within his
lodge, trustfully stacked alongside his buffalo-hide war
shield and White Horse Lodge ceremonial lance.

Seeing his frantic gestures unheeded, the old man
turned and stumbled toward Antelope Woman, the bul-

lets of the laughing, cheering troopers kicking and whining around his heels. The tethered ponies, wild with
fear, were lunging and rearing at their halter ropes,
defying the efforts of the squaw to approach them.
Black Kettle seized the mane of the nearest pony and
vaulted to its plunging back. Slashing the picketline with
his knife, he whirled the squealing animal toward Antelope Woman, dragging her up behind him and spurring
the pony for the Washita.

Josh's shouts of protest to the milling troopers were
drowned out by the renewed burst of carbine fire poured
after the escaping chief. Custer himself rode him aside
in his fury to follow Black Kettle. Fighting the gray
mare free of the melee, he threw his glance back toward
the lodge in time to see a third red figure dart from its
entrance.

Somehow Monaseetah made it to the second pony.
She slashed the maddened animal free, made a running
mount and drove in a headlong gallop for the screen of
the riverside cottonwoods. He had no time to see if she
made it clear or not, the converging rush of Gibbs's
troops catching him up and sweeping him toward the
Washita.

There he was in time to see the miserable end of a
Plains Indian era.

Black Kettle's pony, both riders still mounted, had
miraculously run the ragged gantlet of the excited troopers' fire to reach the river's edge. And more, had managed to land upright in the shallow stream and keep
going for the far side. But that was all.

The pony staggered, hit and ripped from haunch to
wither by the simultaneous rupture of a dozen .54-cali-
ber Spencer slugs. He went down in a smother of gray
water and bloodfoam. Still he regained his feet, bearing
only the squaw now, and struggled on toward the opposite shore. He had not gone three lurching steps when
Antelope Woman screamed, threw her hands back to
her kidneys and slid off into the water. Her body
bobbed and floated, face down, not two yards from that
of Black Kettle.

Josh. had no time for the nausea and anger which welled up within him. Black Kettle was dead, shot in the back as he fled, weaponless and with his woman mount-ed behind him, before the senseless fire of the Soldier Chief with whom he thought he had made an honest and honorable peace. As the scout watched, the last miser-able coup was struck in the spurious name of that "peace."

Hard Rope, with his fellow Indian scouts, charged his rattailed pony down off the cutbank and into the Washi-ta. The braves piled off their mounts in midstream. One of them, reaching the sodden body of the murdered chief, felt under the snow-muddy current for the floating tangle of the gray braids, knotted his hand among them to lift the bullet-torn face above the water.

The knife did its shameful work quickly.

The red hand came away, holding triumphantly aloft the clotted honor-token of having counted the final coup on the last war chief of the Southern Cheyenne. Mox-taveto, the Black Kettle, had departed for the Land of his Ancestors, scalped and started up that shadowed trail by a wooden-handled army butcher knife and a vermin-dirty Osage buck who, in Indian life, would not have been fit to feed his poorest pony.

Josh turned from the river, wanting to vomit, and helpless for the moment to do anything but sit and watch the following slaughter.

Custer's military planning had been efficient. Thomp-son's troops commanded the south bank as well as the entry into Black Kettle's village from the west. To the south, below the camp, sealing it off from the main hos-tile strength, downriver, stood the two hundred and twenty-five troops of Major Alfred Gibbs.*

Yellow Hair had his Indians where he wanted them. 'And where he wanted them was dead.

The execution proceeded.

In the dead chief's isolated group of loyal lodges there

---

* Kelso was in error. These were the troops of Colonel Edward Meyers, not Major Gibbs.

were perhaps a hundred and seventy-five warriors and
teen-age boys, with half that many squaws and small
children. A group of eighty desperate braves, headed by
the ancient Magpie, reached the riverbank, slid over its
precipitous edge and began to fight its way downstream.
Magpie was killed in the first rush but the bulk of his
followers managed to get behind the cutbank and hold
the troopers temporarily at bay. The remainder of Black
Kettle's warriors, cut off by Gibbs from their pony herd
and by Custer from the river, was trapped.

Custer now stationed Lieutenant Billy Cook with forty
sharpshooters on the south bank immediately below
the village. He then swung around above the village and
drove east through it with his main command. As the
braves fled ahead of him, they ran into the withering
crossfire of Cook's sharpshooters on the riverbank and
Gibbs's troops to the south of the lodges. Those few who
managed to win through to the river were mowed down
by Thompson's rifles holding the opposite, or north,
bank. It was a complete carnage.

Josh's earlier estimate of five minutes for the cutting
off of Black Kettle's village could not have been exceed-
ed more than a handful of seconds before the last brave
left among the lodges was shot to pieces and the last
squaw and child captured.

Custer, with Josh back at his side, now turned his attention to the surviving group holed up along the Washita. Taking Cook's sharpshooters, he led them across the
stream and turned their fire into the flank of the Cheyenne. As the trapped braves broke and fled eastward
along the bank, Josh counted seventeen red bodies bobbing in the bank shallows or sprawled in the naked clay
of the bluff's base.

From the south bank now, and eastward along the
Washita in the direction taken by the escaping Cheyenne, came the heavy-throated booming of a full Spencer volley. Custer, light eyes blazing, whirled on Josh
with his first words since ordering the bugles blown.

"By the Lord, Joshua, that's Elliott down there! He's
got them. Good, good. Let's get down there and give

him a hand. That's the last of the red scoundrels, by Heaven!"

"We'd best get down there, all right," the big scout grunted, "but that ain't the 'last' of them, General. It ain't hardly the first."

"Now what do you mean by that, sir?"

"By God, General, I told you there was better than three thousand of them *below* the Bend. We ain't even hit the Bend yet. But Elliott has, providin' that's him firin' down there. He's right on it. Happen he goes a step farther, he's dead. We got to head him off, I reckon."

"All right, let's go, sir." With the words Custer was waving Cook's command forward, putting his bay buffalo horse back into the Washita, grinning back at the following scout.

"But I still think you've lost your touch, Joshua. We haven't yet seen a solitary one of your three thousand 'hidden braves.' "

"You'll see them, mister," Josh muttered to himself, and put the gray mare to breasting the croup-deep current.

Custer, rejoined on the south bank by his main command, lead the two hundred and fifty troopers down the Washita at a hard gallop, the absence of hostile resistance broadening the grin he flung at Josh. The scout took the grin and kept it, not bothering to give it back. And for a quickly evident reason.

Ahead now, the heavy firing of Elliott's command fell off. Seconds after the impact of this stillness reached Custer, he rode into the rear of Elliott's retreating troops. The column was in good order and a young lieutenant commanding the rear of it informed Custer they had caught and killed thirty-eight Cheyennes in a narrow ravine just ahead. Then the hills to the right and left of them had begun to fill with fresh warriors, apparently from the downriver camps. The lieutenant had not himself seen Elliott, but had assumed the retreat order had been given when the ranks in front of him began to fall back.

Custer, on the point of moving forward to seek out Elliott, felt Josh's big hand on his arm.

"Hold on, General, you'd best hold up here and let me mosey on ahead. I smell a rat here somewheres. Lookit yonder."

Custer, following the point of the long arm, saw the bobbing rows of war bonnets and rifle-barrel flashings beginning to sprout in the morning sun along the nearby hilltops.

"Arapahoe," scowled Josh. "We're in trouble, General. Best let me go on up while you unscramble these boys here."

"All right, sir." Custer's decision came with his second look at the growing clouds of warriors along the encircling hilltops. "Get up there and locate Elliott. Bring him back here at once, you understand, Joshua?"

Josh understood. He wasted no time in spurring the gray mare forward. A man could smell that rat for sure now.

It smelled *dead*.

Five minutes after leaving Custer, he rode into the abattoir in "Elliott's ravine."

He found the thirty-eight dead Cheyennes all right, along with something else the young lieutenant had neglected to mention—half a dozen mutilated white troopers. Among this number one man was still alive. He was off the mare and alongside him instantly.

He didn't bother moving him. A man could see the bullet hole going in through the belly just under the heart, and the three, lower down, coming out through the belly from the back. If that wasn't enough he could take a look at the half-scalped skull, the missing right ear and the lance-gashed thigh and shoulder. If this boy lived long enough to say goodbye, it would be a mortal wonder.

He got his arm under his head, and was rewarded by the opening flicker of the eyes. They were sane and quiet though the youngster couldn't be three breaths short of closing them for keeps.

"What's your name, soldier? What outfit? What happened here? Talk while you can, boy."

The soldier nodded, letting a man know he understood. His voice came clear and easy like a man's sometimes strangely will when he is shot to shreds and shouldn't even be alive.

"Harry Mercer, corporal, Company E, Major Elliott. Some of this Injun bunch here got away on down the river. The Major called for volunteers and went after them—" The boy's voice faltered, his eyes straining to focus on the scout's face.

"You're Kelso, ain't you? The General's scout?"

He nodded, seeing the eyelids sag, feeling the slump of the head across his arm.

"—Funny thing," the trooper muttered, just before the blood came, "them Injuns that made it off—they had that purty Cheyenne gal with them—gosh, but ain't she a looker though—"

This time there was no more movement of the eyes. The hemorrhage welled silently out of the slack mouth, and that was all.

He laid the boy's head down, stepped for the gray mare and swung up on her. There was no hesitation in the sharp turning of her head downstream. A man had his orders. Find Elliott and bring him back. Now he knew where Elliott was. Knew, too, that Monaseetah was still alive somewhere ahead of him down the Washita.

A mile along the river he found them both.

The unmistakable bullroar of the big-caliber Spencers broke on his ears as he rounded the last bluff before the open grass of the Bend. On the west bank of the little creek which was southern tributary to the Washita at the point, Elliott and his little band of volunteers had trapped the last of Black Kettle's Cheyennes. The dozen braves were dead before Josh could get the gray mare up to the creekbank, and the major's men were happily examining their four captives—Monaseetah and three of Magpie's small children.

Moving toward the girl, he caught the warning flash of her scowl.

"Do not speak to me, *Veho!*" she hissed. "The Dog Soldiers are all around us. They must not know. They must not see."

His surprise and any further exploration of it were cut off by Elliott's greeting.

"Kelso, by God. Glad to see you, man. How's the Colonel doing? Where is he?"

"Back yonder past the ravine. He sent me up to tell you to get on back. He's got his hands full of Arapahoe back there and you got nothin' but more of the same plus Dog Soldiers and Stone Calf's Cheyenne ahead of you. You'd best get the hell shut of here, Major."

"All right, Kelso. I believe you're right. I mean to go just beyond this creek to make sure we've cleaned them all out down here. Then we'll head back."

"I wouldn't do that, Major."

The blunt admonition went unheeded. The officer had already turned and was issuing his orders.

"Sergeant Kennedy!" A burly sergeant major moved forward from the gathering troopers. "Take this girl and these children back to the village. We'll follow on as soon as I've had a look across the creek."

"Major, you stay on this side." Josh kneed the mare toward the officer's mount. "I reckon we're already cut off even if we head back now. And don't send that gal off with the sergeant by hisself. He'll never make it in with them, alone."

"Nonsense," responded Elliott shortly. "We'll be right behind him. However," his nod was curt, "you may go along with him if you wish. I'll be all right here."

"I got my orders." He let it come flat and hard. "I was told to bring you in."

"Very well, suit yourself, sir. Here we go!"

Elliott and his eighteen men, Josh counting them across the little stream, forded the creek and pushed out into the open of the Big Bend grasslands. But not far. Just far enough, in fact, to clear the Washita timber and get a good look at what was swarming down off the crossbend hills, north, east and south of them.

Aii-eee! Josh winced, jaw thrust. Here came your three thousand "hidden hostiles," mister. Or at least the best, lousy part of them?

Too late, Elliott saw his situation and called out the order for the retreat back across the creek. As his men reached the banks that last avenue of retirement was cut off.

From the mouth of the little stream's channel through the southern hills, Mad Wolf led his howling Dog Soldiers down its west bank, the bulk of them holding up at its juncture with the Washita, a small band led by Mad Wolf sweeping away to the west to engulf the still visible figures of Sergeant Major Kennedy and his Cheyenne captives.

"We got one chance, Major." Josh's tight words hurried. "Gather your boys and try and ride through them right now. Whatever you do, for God's sake don't stop and hole up here."

"We'd never make it, Kelso. We'll have to stand in this high grass on this side. We can hold them off until the Colonel gets up. He shouldn't be long now."

"I tell you he's likely cut off hisself back there!" The reply was harsh with anger. "He'll never get up to you in time. Why, he don't even have any idea where you are. How the hell's he goin' to get to you?"

Once more the abrupt warnings went unheeded.

Elliott at once reined his horse for the heavy grass of the creekbank, shouting for his troopers to follow him. There he dismounted the men and to Josh's further dismay, ordered their horses turned loose.

Major Joel Elliott would do or die right where he stood.

Josh could not know that as the young officer had dashed off in pursuit of the ravine survivors, he had shouted to his volunteers, "Well, here goes for a brevet or a coffin!" But had the scout heard the famous phrase he could at the present moment have guaranteed the final nature of its grim choice without a second's hesitation.

Major Joel H. Elliott was standing in the shoulder-high side boards of his creekgrass coffin as of right now.

His men could see nothing. Their field of fire was point-blank zero. In the flat of the Bend ahead and to the right of them circled Stone Calf's Cheyenne. Behind them milled the black-feathered mass of Mad Wolf's Dog Soldiers. To their left the high hill across the Washita was alive with Arapahoe. Sergeant Major Kennedy was dead and with him the last hope of getting word to Custer. Unless—

"Major!"

It was a statement, not a request. He backed it by swinging up on the restive mare.

"I still got my horse and I aim to use her. Give me a burst for cover toward the river. If you can hang on here I'll try and make it to the General. Don't waste lead on long shots, boy. Save it for when they rush you."

He booted the mare out the riverside exit of the creekgrass before the officer could answer, his only remembered view of Major Elliott the bent-double glance he flung back in time to catch the officer's wave of understanding.

It was the last any white man saw or knew of Elliott and his men. All that was ever to be known of the manner and speed with which they died would come years later in the cracked voice of Roman Nose Thunder, one of the Cheyenne survivors, speaking from the time-distant removal of an Oklahoma reservation.

"The shooting was over then. All the soldiers were dead. The fight did not last longer than it would take a man to smoke a pipe four times."

GET YOUR 4 FREE* BOOKS NOW— A VALUE BETWEEN $16 AND $20

Mail the Free* Book Certificate Today!

FREE* BOOKS CERTIFICATE!

YES! I want to subscribe to the Leisure Western Book Club. Please send me my 4 FREE* BOOKS. Then, each month, I'll receive the four newest Leisure Western Selections to preview FREE* for 10 days. If I decide to keep them, I will pay the Special Member's Only discounted price of just $3.36 each, a total of $13.44 ($14.50 US in Canada). This saves me between $3 and $6 off the bookstore price. There are no shipping, handling or other charges.* There is no minimum number of books I must buy and I may cancel the program at any time. In any case, the 4 FREE* BOOKS are mine to keep—at a value of between $17 and $20!

*In Canada, add $5.00 Canadian shipping and handling per order for first shipment. For all subsequent shipments to Canada the cost of membership in the Book Club is $14.50 US, which includes $7.50 shipping and handling per month. All payments must be made in US currency.

Name_____

Address_____

City_____ State_____ Country_____

Zip_____ Telephone_____

If under 18, parent or guardian must sign. Terms, prices and conditions subject to change. Subscription subject to acceptance. Leisure Books reserves the right to reject any order or cancel any subscription.

Tear here and mail your FREE book card today!*

Get Four Books Totally F R E E* — A Value between $16 and $20

Tear here and mail your FREE* book card today!

PLEASE RUSH
MY FOUR FREE*
BOOKS TO ME
RIGHT AWAY!

LeisureWestern Book Club
P.O. Box 6613
Edison, NJ 08818-6613

AFFIX
STAMP
HERE

26. Yellow Hair's Way

ACROSS THE CREEK, the Dog Soldiers saw the gray dart of Josh's mare streak for the Washita. The burst of wolf howls this discovery sent up among them was instantly stilled by Mad Wolf's barking cry.

"He is mine! It is my vow. I claim the first coup on him. He cannot get away and he is mine alone. Who will deny it?"

Clearly, none of the Dog Soldiers were of a mind to rob their chief of this long awaited honor. It was true what he said, anyway. Ota Kte could not get away. Let Axhonehe have him. Across the creek were plenty of scalps for all!

Mad Wolf, not waiting to hear his challenge accepted or denied, was already plunging his pie-bald stallion into the Washita. Behind him his faithful returned their attentions to Elliott's command. It was perhaps only after three or four minutes of the resumed firing that Yellow Buffalo looked at Big Body and nodded.

The hulking brave returned the nod with loose-grinned understanding. Where Axhonehe went, there went his two lieutenants, whether he ordered it otherwise or not. Only of course it was just the better part of policy not to let him know he was being disobeyed. Unnoticed, the two subchiefs fell back from the lines, caught up their ponies and headed up the Washita after their leader.

But seconds before they departed, another of their relatives had taken the same course before them, and with even less notice.

As Yellow Buffalo and Big Body cursed their ponies forward, Monaseetah had already slipped away from the red ranks of her "rescuers" to swing up on her mare and race westward along the banks of the Washita, following the cross-river course of her white lover by the triumphant wolf howls of the close-trailing Mad Wolf.

Josh had exhausted his ammunition in his brief siding of Elliott's men. He had now between himself and the closing Dog Soldier his guts, his Green River knife, and Major Coates's fast-faltering Arab mare.

In the minutes of his brief race for freedom the deep-throated fire of the Spencers from the creek junction behind him had already begun to fail. Mad Wolf would be up to him in a dozen jumps and behind him not another ten minutes would come the main wave of the big pack now finishing off Elliott. If he managed by some piece of outhouse luck to down the Dog Soldier chief and to get on down the trail ahead of his following lodge brothers, he was still on the wrong side of the river. Ahead of him on the north bank were up to five hundred of Big Mouth's Arapahoe, engaged in holding Custer down. Back of him on the same bank, providing the rest of the Dog Soldiers didn't beat them to him, he had Little Raven and the main bunch of the Arapahoe which were presently helping polish off Major Elliott.

Custer, unless he got to him, was likely to move on down the Washita and into the same trap the hostiles had closed on Elliott. Monaseetah was with the Dog Soldiers and giving every sign she meant to stay with them. Totting it all up as he threw a snap glance over his shoulder to see that Mad Wolf's studhorse had the chief two jumps off the gray mare's rump, a man had to admit that likely Custer was going under. And for sure Josh Kelso was.

About all a man had left right now was his promise to himself to knock off that axeheaded son behind him if it was his last mortal act. Seeing that it was shaping up to be just that, a man might as well get on with it.

He timed it hair-close enough to suit even his particular mountain tastes.

As his eyetail showed him Mad Wolf's little stallion coming up even with the mare's croup, he threw the slender pony as hard left as he could, pulling her dainty head almost back to the saddlehorn and jerking her front feet out from under her to flatten her like a shoulder-shot elk.

As he felt her go, he flung himself to the right and as far free as he could. He hit the ground hard. But not that hard he didn't see Mad Wolf's stud pile into the mare and go, backside over appetite, right on over her. The Dog Soldier had seen it coming just soon enough to leg off his falling pony and hit the ground in a Cheyenne "shoulder roll." He was on his feet and coming for him before Josh got his senses well cleared.

He had grabbed enough over-shoulder glances during the short chase to know that Mad Wolf had not unbooted his rifle. He knew by that that the red son aimed to try it the hard way.

An Indian never could understand the white man's idea of counting coup with a rifle slug. There was no honor in that, no courage required and no credit coming.

If there was another thing the Indians never understood about their white brothers, it was rough-and-tumble fighting—mountain style.

Josh closed with the Dog Soldier, getting his left shoulder high up under the pit of his upflung knife arm, and knotting his hands behind the small of the brave's back. With the crushing pressure of the South Park bearhug, Mad Wolf's knife hand spasmed. The nerveless fingers lost the blade's haft and the weapon slid harmlessly over Josh's shoulder to the ground.

The big scout stepped back, kneeing his gasping victim out and away from him. Stooping, he seized the chief's knife and sent it whirling into the hand-close Washita.

"Get up, cousin," his grunt came in belly-deep Cheyenne, "I don't want to kill a chief on the ground."

Watching the Dog Soldier regain his feet, he saw the sudden widening of the slant eyes, read their message of triumph, too late. He turned only in time to see the grinning Big Body start the swing of the anvil-headed warclub. His reflex side-twist saved his skull from being pulped, and that was all. The crushing weight of the anvil smashed into his chest and across his shoulder with enough force to drop a buffalo.

The next instant the huge brave scooped him from the ground and barred his sapling-thick arm across his throat. He held him thus, belly out and helpless as a butcher-strung steer, awaiting the mercies of his chief's interrupted coup-counting.

He saw Mad Wolf take the knife which Yellow Buffalo held out for him, and start to move toward him and Big Body. He saw something else too, over there across the narrow channel of the Washita. At the same moment, the grinning Big Body also saw it. But Josh saw it the longer.

The amazed look of discovery was still on the subchief's thick mouth when the neat blue hole of the .44 Henry slug appeared an inch above his unbelieving eyebrow. He was dead instantly.

Twisting violently, Josh broke away from his slackening grasp and knocked up the barrel of Yellow Buffalo's rifle as it leveled on the slim figure of the marksman across the river. The bullet whined harmlessly over the southbank cottonwoods and Monaseetah, kneeling not forty yards away across the Washita, shot the second chief through the belly.

Josh wrenched Yellow Buffalo's rifle from him as the subchief fell. He turned with it in time to smash its barrelswung butt full into the face of the snarling Mad Wolf as the latter came at him with Yellow Buffalo's knife. The Dog Soldier staggered forward, Josh moving aside to let him fall. He hit the ground, writhed over on his side, raised his bloody face with a final blind effort, collapsed and lay still.

By the time he could turn away from him, Monaseetah had splashed the calico mare across the Washita. She swept on past him to catch up the trailing halter rope of Coates' mare, wheeled and galloped the led animal back to him.

"God bless you again, gal!" The awkward English stumbled out ahead of the swollen bruise of the big fist which sought and found her slim hand with the muttered Cheyenne transposition.

"May Maheo bless you, girl. And understand you, too. God knows," here he slipped grinningly back into the English, "Josh Kelso never will!"

"Maheo understands everything," smiled the Indian girl.

With the quiet words, she levered three shots from Black Kettle's beautifully engraved Henry into the belly of the still breathing Mad Wolf.

They crossed the river quickly, putting their horses westward along its south bank through the thick cover of the cottonwoods. Ahead of them in Custer's direction only the occasional black-powder boom of an Indian musket, with its scattered answer of Spencer carbine fire, could now be heard. Behind them, eastward along the Washita toward Elliott's creek, all sound of firing had ceased.

Keeping to the strangely deserted banks of the river they reached Black Kettle's village without incident. Josh at once reported to Custer on Major Elliott's situation and the certainty of its outcome.*

For some reason forever a mystery to the scout the little General treated the report with apparent unconcern, simply noting that Elliott was well able to take care of himself and would no doubt join back up in due order. There were at the time, he pointed out, no less than three other detachments similarly missing. Two

---

* Custer always claimed he did not know Elliott was missing until the column had retired from the Washita. It seems at least, viewed in its most charitable light, a peculiar military admission.

others, so absent, had just come in to rejoin the main column and there was no valid reason to believe that Major Elliott's and the remaining absentee units would not show up given good time. It was, after all, only just past 10.00 A.M.

The thing now, by Heaven, was to clean up the mess they had right here in Black Kettle's camp, and only then to move on down to pick up Elliott and take care of the rest of the hostiles should any of them be disposed to continue the issue which, in Custer's opinion, by thunder, was highly unlikely!

Josh changed that opinion no sooner than the Colonel had uttered it.

"Take another squint through them glasses, General. Yonder there on the hills where Big Mouth and them Arapahoe has been settin' all mornin'."

Custer raised the glasses quickly, and as quickly put them down.

"By Heaven, Joshua, there does seem to be a considerable number of them moving up onto that hill, at that."

"Not alone *that* hill, General. Lookit over here on the right."

Following the scout's direction the officer swung the glasses toward the southern hills.

"Good Lord! More of them! Aren't those the Dog Soldiers, Joshua?"

"They are." The agreement was succinct. "And they're warpainted just like yonder Arapahoe. These are all fresh hostiles, General, and Monaseetah tells me there's a thousand lodges of them spread for the next fifteen miles down the river. I reckon it's time we went home, General."

While Custer debated the advice, the sergeant left in charge of the abandoned overcoats and march rations beyond the first ridge raced his horse into the camp to report that huge numbers of Indians were swarming in from the west and had overrun the supply dump and taken off in pursuit of the fleeing ammunition wagons.

A momentary grim relief was brought by the present

appearance of the wagons around the shoulder of Double Wolf's hill. Their white-faced drivers slid them, brake-locked, down the steep snows of the Washita's far side and dashed crazily into the stream to bring them lumberingly across.

Josh's nod was understandingly short.

Once you got the little General in a real tight, the officer hadn't been commissioned who could outthink him, much less outfight him. If he had a genius for walking into traps, he had an equal one for cool-ordering his way out of them. The big scout relearned that now as he watched the sudden, murderous turning of Yellow Hair's way.

Throwing Cook's sharpshooters and Gibbs's unblooded troops between himself and the threatening thousands of Dog Soldiers and Arapahoes, Custer held them at bay while his own troops methodically completed the rape of the Washita.

His surprise attack on Black Kettle's village had netted him sixty captive squaws and their children. On the icy ground in and around the empty lodges lay the freezing bodies of the Cheyenne dead: a hundred and three warriors, sixteen women, eleven children.

Piled in final total before the big black lodge of the slain chief lay the naked fruits of Indian war: 241 saddles, 1123 buffalo hides, lodgeskins and robes, 82 rifles and revolvers, 425 war axes and lances, 4035 arrows and warbows, 2185 blankets, lariats and buckskin parfleches, 535 pounds of black powder, 1375 pounds of raw lead and molded bullets, and 700 pounds of tobacco plus the untold tons of winter-stored buffalo beef.

Even as Josh noted the wealth of the loot, Custer was putting the torch to it. He had come into the village with nothing but his men and mounts. He was going to leave it the same way. The harsh orders barked out.

Using the captured rawhide lariats, the hurrying troopers began pulling over the lodges and dragging them toward the growing mountain of cowskins east of the already burning loot pile. Shortly, to the flare of two hundred pounds of the captured powder, the winter homes of Black Kettle's murdered Cheyennes were adding their greasy smoke to that of the other camp plunder.

Calling Kelso and California Joe to him, Custer gave the final order—take Hard Rope's Osages and drive in the captured pony herd. There was one last, best chance to break the pressure of the hostile assault building against Cook's and Gibbs's delaying force. Kill a Plains Indian and two will spring to take his place. Destroy his pony and his heart for war drops dead within him.

There were by this time fully three thousand Arapahoe and Cheyenne clouding the surrounding hillsides. More were riding up by the minute. The situation, already grave, threatened to break out of all hand before the retirement could be begun. As for that retirement, Custer knew, no less certainly than did Josh, that were it not possible to speedily create some major diversion in its face, what might begin as an orderly retreat would become a disastrous rout.

The Indians were driving the holding forces back upon the village. If the movement were not stopped, Custer would join Elliott in his brevetless coffin on the Washita.

As the little General, completely oblivious to the hail of Indian lead, rode the flanks and center of Gibbs's and Cook's failing line, Josh spurred to his side.

"California's got them comin', General. Where do you want them?"

"What's the best place, Joshua? You know these rascals better than I."

"East of camp there," he pointed the spot, "on that clear strip of high ground along the river. The Injuns can look square down on it from them hills."

"Get to it, please." Custer's words were unhurried. "They're pushing us, sir."

Josh wheeled the gray mare to meet the advancing front of the wild-eyed Cheyenne pony herd. "Up on the point yonder, Joe!" The other scout returned his stirrup-standing wave. "Where the red sons can see them go down!"

In three minutes the scouts had the huge herd in a neighing, kicking mill on the high ground of Josh's choice. And in five, the butchering began.

Custer, throwing his entire reserve into the caving forward line, shouted to Cook to pull his sharpshooters out and report to Josh at the pony herd. Joining the scouts, the young lieutenant merely waved his hand in reply to the mountain man's signal. It was a little late in the day for formal orders, given or taken.

For a solid hour Josh's executioners poured their ceaseless crossfire into the screaming mass of the hostile ponies. Watching on the hillsides, the packed ranks of the hostiles grew hushed. The trampled snow around the herd became a fetlock-deep morass of blood slush and acrid, green manure. Still, and interminably, the roar of the short Spencers and the hollow cough of the mountain rifles snarled on.

The Indians were moving now, slowly at first and in small groups. Then more swiftly, by the dozens and the tens of hundreds. Eastward they moved, away and across the silent hills, down and along the crimsoning Washita. Their savage voices were stilled. The barrels of their forgotten rifles cold. Their wild hearts within them, gray and heavy as the river ice.

The war ponies were dead. And dead with them, the wills and minds of their nomad red masters.

No formal count of that pony herd was ever made. But in the minutes of its hurried rounding up, the practiced eye of California Joe had rough-guessed it at better than nine hundred. When the barking volleys of Custer's powder-grimed riflemen ceased, not a Southern Cheyenne pony was standing on the blood-frozen floor of Josh Kelso's Washita slaughterhouse.

Yellow Hair had had his way.

27. *Waniyetula's Blessing*

THE PARTING with Custer was abrupt.

The retreat to the base camp on the Canadian, under forced and fearful march, the men without rations or overcoats in the bone-chill of the Arkansas winter, the horses gaunted from forty-eight hours without feed or any respite long enough for a cinch to be loosened, was completed with nightfall of the fateful 27th.

No sign of follow-up by the overwhelming number of the Washita hostiles developed, Custer's concern they would sweep north around his flanks to destroy his undefended supply train at the Main Crossing proving unfounded. By 9.00 P.M. the last of the hollow-cheeked officers and men and the blanket-wrapped, bitter-eyed Indian women had recrossed Custer's Rubicon.

The following day the retreat was resumed, still under forced march. Camp Supply was reached sometime late in the afternoon of the 29th.

With the surviving regulars gratefully billeted in the long rows of stove-warmed Sibleys, the wounded under delayed treatment in the rough board hospital barracks, and the dead laid in staring-eyed, stiff-limbed state on the frozen dirt floor of a company woodshed, Josh sought out Custer.

His long-striding progress toward the plank door of the commander's sod-roofed quarters was rudely barred by the carbine of a pea-green guard corporal whose sole contribution to the Washita campaign had been the policing of the near-empty stables of the base camp during the Seventh's brief absence.

"Sorry, friend. Colonel's orders. He ain't seein' nobody."

"He'll see me. Tell him Josh Kelso's outside."

"No luck, friend. Sherman and Sheridan are both in there."

"It don't cramp me none if U. S. Grant's in there." The lean jaw moved out. "Tell him Josh Kelso wants to see him. Me and the Injun gal is leavin'."

"Listen, friend," the young trooper's tone turned belligerent, "move along now, see? There ain't nobody less than two stars ranks a break-in on the Colonel right now—"

The corporal's attitude underwent some hasty modification with his feet treading the empty air and the scout's hair-backed fist knotted in the upper blouse buttons of his issue blues.

"All right, mister, all right! You needn't go to gettin' sore about it. I'll fetch your message in to him."

"See you do," nodded Josh. "And don't drag your feet. I ain't got all winter."

The young soldier was back before Josh had more than time to hawk and spit disgustedly into the parade ground slush. His attitude had altered again.

"Colonel says he'll send for you," he smirked. "Says you ain't to worry about your pay, he'll see you get it."

The trooper paused, savoring the tidbit.

"Oh yeah—and he says the Injun gal stays here same as the other squaws. She's a prisoner, friend, and will go east with the others. You got any more billy-doos for the Colonel, friend?"

"Yeah, *friend*." The big scout's unsmiling grunt came as he turned to go. "Tell him Black Kettle and Josh Kelso said goodbye."

He moved quickly, the full dark of the Arkansas winter night coming down, blackly sullen and heavy, to screen his movement. It was no trick to slip around the huddled guard detail at the loose-stock horse herd. Nor to snake out old Wasiya and the girl's paint mare from

under their night-blind noses. After that it got a little
thicker.

All the same, he was shortly able to dig their two saddles out of the ruckpile of the Seventh's unloaded wagons. Then to smuggle his own and Black Kettle's Henry
repeaters out of the scout barracks and to rummage up a
sack of rolled oats and another of hardtack and army
dried beef. And finally to get the whole of the borrowed
plunder stowed safely away back of the last stable south
of camp, without anybody but himself and the horses
getting wind of it.

By a quarter of ten he was ready to move.

The captive Cheyenne squaws were being held under
a "loose herd" no more humane nor well tended than
that of their snow-covered ponies. Their guttering cook-
fires dotted the manure-stinking confines of an empty
corral just beyond the last stable building.

Getting Monaseetah out of that corral was no more
than a matter of waiting for the three troopers on duty
to finish one of their slipshod inspection rounds and return to the comfort of their own fire and battered tin of
boiling coffee.

The girl caught his grunting, perfect imitation of a
Cheyenne pony whicker. She looked up, returned the
rapid movement of his handsigns and slipped quietly
away from the tiny fire she was sharing with a dozen
older squaws. She joined him bearing the pathetic but
eminently practical total of her highborn Plains Indian
dowry: two calfskin sleeping robes retrieved from the
burning spoils of Black Kettle's lodge.

By 10.00 P.M. the double nightblack line of their
pony prints was three miles south of Camp Supply.
Eight hours later they had crossed the Canadian and
were safely camped in the stormproof shelter of the Antelope Hills.

To the north, sixty miles, Yellow Hair was being
routed from the 5.00 A.M. blackness of his conqueror's
bed, being unhappily informed that his pet scout and
prize Indian captive had departed in the unknown
hours. To the south and east, forty remembered miles,

Black Kettle was sleeping undisturbed, still and quiet with his faithful woman beneath the winter-calm waters of his native Ouachita.

Above it all, Waniyetula was again laying the thick white cover of his will. But the old God wasn't howling now, nor even bitterly laughing. He was chuckling as he carefully filled the telltale southpointing hoofprints of the Sioux gelding and the Cheyenne mare. And smiling as he drew the peaceful blanket of his friendly snows over the snug, dry resting place of Ota Kte and Emoonesta.

Bright Hair, his Indian child, had bested him. Even that rascal of a *Veho,* that puny, white-skinned villain of a Pony Soldier scout, had taught him a lesson or two. *Eszenistoz.* Give them a red God's blessing. They were well mated, those two!

Let them dream there under that snug bank. Let them rest now, their grateful voices low and tender with the moment, their tingling muscles easing to the long-sought fullness of the hour's union.

Aye, even hold one's breath a little stiller now, that she might miss no word of the *Veho's* vision. Of the vision of that promise of the endless herd of spotted buffalo he would bring to graze the rich, fat grasses of Moxtaveto's valley. Of how in the moons to come they would prosper, Emoonesta and Ota Kte, brightening the dead chief's homeland with the unfrightened voices of their many children.

And now stop the snow flurries altogether, that the fall of no least, wandering flake should disturb the softness of her answer. Let the listening *Veho* hear its every full-lipped whisper. Let him know that this was the way old Moxtaveto had seen it over the smoke spiral of his last pipe. Let Ota Kte know that this was the way, even exactly as he was telling it to her, that the aging chief had spoken it to Emoonesta that last night within the big black lodge.

Let Yellow Hair come, the old man had said. Let him have his wanton hour of shameful war. Give him the little minute of his willful, bitter pleasure. Then let him go, and let him come no more.

Let there be peace, not war, along the Ouachita. And let that peace come with the growing herds and the smiling, happy children of Ota Kte and Emoonesta.

Yellow Hair had had his way. Now let Black Kettle have his.

Nohetto. Let that be the final end to it.

Custer's Last Stand

For
Kin Platt
old friend
and true.

FOREWORD

This is the true story of General George Armstrong Custer and the Battle of the Little Big Horn. Known in myth and legend as "Custer's Last Stand," this battle was unquestionably the greatest Cavalry and Indian fight in the history of the American frontier. Yet its story has been told in more wrong ways than any other adventure of the Western past.

The events depicted herein are drawn from the actual documents of the times, and from eye-witness testimonies of the Indians who lived then, both Sioux and Cheyenne.

Certain conversations and descriptions have been supplied by the author where the silent tongues of the dead, red man and white, could not speak for themselves.

The essential facts are faithful, alike, to the heroic memories of the gallant officers and men of the Seventh U.S. Cavalry, and to the valiant red horsemen who rode against them in the name of freedom on that June day in 1876, in far Montana.

W. H.

Custer Battlefield
Little Big Horn
Montana, 1965

CONTENTS

Part Four—THE ROSEBUD

Part Five—THE LITTLE BIG HORN

PART ONE

THE WASHITA

1. THE CAMP OF BLACK KETTLE

The Seventh Cavalry moved toward the sleeping Indian encampment like a hungry wolf, silently in the dead of the winter night. In a snow-filled gully behind low hills, General Custer halted his command. The breaths of men and of horses rose in frosty silver columns in the biting cold. The jingle of harness, the squeaking of saddle leather—these were the only sounds.

Beyond the hills lay the Washita River and the tipis of the unsuspecting Cheyenne, Arapaho and Kiowa tribes gathered together there to spend the Time of the Deep Snows where all would be safe, warm, happy.

True, there had been bad fighting with the white Pony Soldiers that past summer of 1868. Nor did the red men deny their part of the blame. But all of that was behind them now.

Far to the north their Sioux brother, Red Cloud, had just touched the pen—made a new treaty—with the Great Father in Washington. The treaty promised peace. Word of it swept to the south, even to the banks of the Washita. Black Kettle and the other chiefs of the three tribes resting there gave thanks and prayed to their red gods in gratitude. They told their people that now all would be well. They might close their eyes in safety at last. The Pony Soldiers would come no more.

But beyond the low hills that black November night, the Seventh Cavalry lay waiting in the snow with no thought to the new treaty. General Custer had orders other than those of peace. He had been sent on this winter march to find the Indians when their ponies were

2

weak from lack of grass and could not escape the grain-fed strong horses of the cavalry troops. When he found the Indians, his orders were to destroy them, to scatter them, to drive them back upon the reservations —whatever he could do to them. But in no event was he to allow them to escape, to get away and go free.

The Indians were much at fault. They knew this. In August, on the Solomon River, they had killed fifteen white people. They had carried off five innocent white women. They had raided on the Saline River, killing more. They had also killed settlers on the Republican River. In September, they had burned a wagon train and seventeen men at Cimarron Crossing. They had murdered six men near Fort Wallace. At Spanish Fork, they had killed four men, outraged three women, brutally murdered four small children before their parents' eyes. These were terrible things—evil things. But many of the Indians said that they did them only because the whites had done so much evil to the red man. Others among them made no excuses, and were sad in their hearts, and guilty.

Doing evil for evil, they said, made all men bad.

For his part, General George Armstrong Custer was no Indian hater. He admired the red man. He said, always, that he was a brave and noble foe, and driven to many of his crimes by the misdoings of the white men in his lands.

But Custer was first of all things a soldier.

And a soldier obeyed his orders.

Now, to his dimly lighted tent, Custer called all of his officers and his scouts. Lieutenant Tom Custer, the General's younger brother, was there. Captain Benteen was there. And the names of the scouts read like a roll-call of frontier legends: Apache Bill, California Joe, Ben Clark, the Mexican half-breed "Romero," and the Osage Indian "Hard Rope." They were men who, as the saying went, "could track a hive of white bees through a blizzard." Yet, strangely, on this dark and stormy night they were all lost—or so Custer accused them of being when all had gathered and were waiting.

"Gentlemen," said the famous officer, "I want to suggest that not one of you knows where he is! All of your great and fabled reputations mean nothing. You are fortunate that your commander happens to own a compass, and knows how to read its arrow, even in the dark!"

Custer spoke with a nervous, quick grin. His voice was high and excitable. He was a friendly man, but severe on bunglers. Moreover, he was a very proud man and loved to demonstrate to others his own superiority.

"At least we know," he said, holding up the compass for all to see its needle, "that we are still on our due-south course, and cannot be overly far from the Indians."

Here the little withered Osage stepped forward. He held up his dark hand, shaking his head. "Compass no have ears," he said. "Injun do."

Custer knew that the small scout had more to say. The General was a keen student of the red man, and appreciated his ways.

"What do you mean, Hard Rope?" he asked.

"Compass no hear dog bark just now," replied the Osage. "Me do."

"What? In this wind and snow! Are you sure?" Custer was doubtful, but he felt his nerves tighten. The other officers crowded forward.

"Me hear dog bark," insisted the small man. "You come go follow me. Me show you."

"Where?" demanded Custer.

"Past him low hill over there," said Hard Rope. "You go along me, you hear dog, too."

"Gentlemen!" Custer's voice snapped with excitement. "I have a hunch Hard Rope is right. I am going with him. All scouts, forward with us! You—Benteen, Elliott, Gibbs—bring the men forward. Keep in column. No talking, no smoking. Do not get too far behind us, but maintain quiet at all cost!"

He was gone before his officers could discuss or

question the plan. He was Custer. He led. Others merely followed.

"I hope," said one of the staff, "that for a change he knows what he is doing."

"He had better know," said a fellow officer. "Somewhere off there in the night are old Black Kettle and a hundred eighty lodges of southern Cheyenne. That's at least three hundred fifty warriors right there, and the good Lord knows how many more Kiowa and Arapaho braves camped with them. I heard Romero guess at a thousand warriors."

"Well, you know the General," a third officer volunteered, uneasily. "He'll charge them if there's ten thousand."

"Some day," said Captain Benteen, who knew Custer better than any of them, "he's going to *find* his ten thousand Indians. Then we'll all wish we had decided to be something else besides officers and gentlemen in the Seventh Cavalry!"

"Oh, aren't you the cheerful one!" laughed a young lieutenant. "Personally, I think the General could whip those ten thousand redskins, if he ever found them. What do you think of that?"

Captain Benteen paused in the doorwary of the tent. He looked hard at the young lieutenant, then nodded sharply.

"Just what I think of Custer," he said. "You're crazy, too."

2. HARD ROPE HEARS
THE PONY BELLS

Custer held the reins tightly on his horse. Beside him, Hard Rope pointed ahead. The storm was lifting now. The stars glittered. The moonlight, where it shot through the ragged clouds, painted the snows a glaring white. Custer could clearly see the long ridge which lay beyond the low hills. He glanced back, slowing his horse. California Joe and the other scouts also halted. Behind them, two hundred yards away, the cavalry column had also stopped moving forward.

"Is that the elevation you want me to climb with you?" Custer asked Hard Rope.

"Village hide other side ridge," replied the Osage. "Me you climb. You see."

"All right," said Custer. "Come on."

They started ahead. With them went California Joe. The other scouts went back to tell the troops to stay where they were until the General returned.

Hard Rope led the way up the ridge. He went at a snow-crunching trot. Custer and California Joe had difficulty keeping up with him. Atop the ridge, the Osage beckoned for them to lie down beside him. They did so, all three men peering intently into the darkness below.

"I don't see a thing and I don't hear a thing," complained Custer nervously. "You've missed your way, Hard Rope. There's no big Cheyenne village down there."

"Be quiet," said the Indian, showing no fear of the

officer's high rank and his fame as a war leader of the white men. "Keep mouth shut, ear open. Aha! There! You hear him dog bark?"

Custer strained his ears. "I hear nothing!" he said. "And I see nothing except that jumble of small hills and river timber there in the big bend of the Washita."

"Listen more hard," commanded the Indian.

Custer started to say something in anger, but California Joe touched his arm. "Begging your pardon, General," the tall white scout said. "But Hard Rope is right. Listen."

This time Custer heard the bark. And then another. And another. Those *were* dogs barking, faint and thin, but very clear now. They could be nothing but Indian dogs in this distant and lonely place. Custer's whisper grew tense.

"But I still don't *see* anything!" he insisted stubbornly.

"You no look right place," muttered Hard Rope. "Me see Cheyenne pony herd right there. Look. Bottom this hill."

"Bah!" said Custer. "Those are buffalo down there!"

"General," said California Joe, "if them are buffalo down there, they're the first buffalo I ever knowed of to wear grazing bells hung on their necks."

"How is that, sir?" demanded Custer sharply. "Are you making fun of me?" His temper was as quick as his famous "peg-toothed grin." But California Joe was not joking.

"No sir, General," he said "Keep listening."

Suddenly, Custer was propping himself up on his elbows, high voice crackling with excitement.

"By heaven, man!" he cried. "I *do* hear pony bells!"

Hard Rope grunted something uncomplimentary in Osage, and came to his feet. California Joe turned to Custer.

"Come on, General," he said. "Bend low and don't talk so loud. We've found your Injuns for you."

The commander of the Seventh Cavalry obeyed the scout's warning. Crouching, he followed California Joe

and Hard Rope. But at the last moment he paused atop
the snowy crest, peering into the blackness which hid
the Indian encampment below. His words were spoken
so softly aloud that only the night wind heard them. And
only the glitter of the far, high stars lit the moment's
triumph in his thin face.

   "Sleep well, Black Kettle," he said. "Yellow Hair is
coming!"

3. DEATH COMES FOR DOUBLE WOLF

The men prepared for the attack, leaving everything they could behind. Into the snow went their rations of coffee and hardtack, and their saddlebags of oats for the horses. The troopers carried only fighting gear, their readied carbines, a hundred rounds of ammunition. Even their winter overcoats were thrown aside. The man who talked in ranks, now, faced death from the firing squad. The officers and scouts came to Custer's side when all was ready.

"Yellow Hair," as the Indians called him, spoke quickly.

There would be four attack columns. One, under Major Elliott, would swing wide of the Indian camp and attack from the east. One, under Colonel Meyers, would go to the right and attack from the south. Custer and young Captain Thompson would attack from the center, hitting the camp from the west. The river lay to the north and would serve to prevent escape in that direction. Were there any questions?

None of the officers said a word. They only saluted.

"All right," said the General. "Let's be about it, then." He turned to the young officer who would ride with him, his pale blue eyes ablaze with eagerness. "Captain Thompson," he said, "you will hold your command to a walk until we are discovered by the Indians. Good luck."

"Yes sir, General," said the young soldier. "Thank you."

The four hundred horses of the troops of Custer and Thompson started forward. They split in two lines, like

the fork of a snake's tongue, to go around the base of the
last of the low hills between the advancing cavalry and
the Cheyenne village. It was now early in the morning,
with the gray light of the new day just staining the
hilltops. There was still no sound from the village.

On the far side of the hill a lone tipi stood. From this
tipi to the top of the hill ran a narrow path. Up this path,
each dawn, went the camp's sentry, leaving his warm
guardpost-lodge and his wife for the frost of the daybreak.

All of the Indians knew that Yellow Hair and his Pony
Soldiers were somewhere in their country. Black Kettle
had said to keep a sharp lookout—had warned the sentry
warriors to go very early to their posts. Thus it was that
Double Wolf, faithful to his trust, had started up the hill
path when behind him he heard a fearful cry. It was his
wife.

Turning, he saw the woman come out of the tipi. She
was dragging their two small children, still half asleep.
She pointed frantically, first to the right side of the hill,
then to the left, and cried up to Double Wolf the
dreaded words.

"Pony Soldiers! Pony Soldiers——!"

Double Wolf unslung his rifle, as his woman commenced to run with the children through the snow
toward the village.

He could not yet see the cavalry, but he was very
much afraid. Double Wolf had been at Sand Creek with
Black Kettle in that other camp where the Pony Soldiers
of Colonel Chivington had come in the early morning
shadows. He had lost his first wife and four small
children in that terrible time. He knew the same dread
that his present woman did. And, in his great fear, he
forgot Black Kettle's firm orders not to fire on any
soldiers who might come to that camp. He forgot to raise
the white cloth and cry out for peace. Instead, he raised
his rifle.

When the Pony Soldiers came into his view, he gave a
start. The daylight struck the leader of those soldiers.

Double Wolf could see the long curls of red-gold hair cascading beneath the wide black hat. He saw the famous red neckerchief and the high polished boots of that most famous of Pony Soldier chiefs, and he cried out in the Cheyenne tongue, "*Heováe! Heováe!* Yellow Hair! Yellow hair!" And his woman, hearing him, nearly collapsed with fear, and froze in her tracks for a moment. Double Wolf, to protect her, fired directly at Custer. The brave warrior's body was almost cut in two by the answering hail of soldier bullets. Custer did not even look aside as the Indian's bullet whistled harmlessly past him, and Double Wolf died for having fired it. Instead the General calmly raised his hand and signaled the regimental band to commence playing "Garry Owen," the war song of the Seventh Cavalry; and thus it was that the Battle of the Washita was begun.

4.   YELLOW HAIR! YELLOW HAIR!

Custer's troopers drove their horses into and across the shallow Washita River. Before them, on the far bank, stood the first of Black Kettle's tipis. The camp was becoming aroused now. Beyond the tipis of the Cheyenne, those of the Arapaho and the Kiowa were stirring. Here and there half-dressed Indians were running out of the warm lodges into the snowy streets of the village, crying out to one another to learn what was wrong. Only the first lodges, those near where Custer now slashed across the icy river, knew that the camp was being attacked by Pony Soldiers. And, as those first few Indians came out into the morning darkness calling and crying out for friends and relatives who might be near, Double Wolf's widow tottered up from the riverbank.

"Yellow Hair! Yellow Hair!" she cried, and the panic of great fear at once swept downward through the entire camp.

Black Kettle, the old chief of peace and friendship for the white brother, stumbled out of his tipi. With him was his wife, also gray-haired and slow of step. They tried to reach some ponies tied nearby, and so escape. The old chief was able to mount a pony, and draw his wife up behind him.

Instantly, the blast of the Pony Soldier carbines struck at the elderly couple.

But the old chief had the heart of a grizzly bear.

He spurred the pony straight at Custer's soldiers, and by a miracle broke through them and drove on for the river.

Black Kettle had no rifle—he was not firing at the soldiers. His woman, too, was innocent of weapons. Both wanted only to escape with their lives. But the troopers of the Seventh Cavalry had had their orders, and the carbines roared again.

Down went the laboring pony, shot through a dozen times. Black Kettle never moved when he fell with the pony. His woman struggled to her feet and ran a few more steps. The soldier fire pelted into her back. She twisted about, came back to her mortally wounded husband, fell near him, crawled until she could reach out and touch his hand, then moved no more. The soldiers rushed on, leaping their horses over the silent couple.

After that, the Indian camp had no chance.

Custer had planned the attack too well. Everywhere that the desperate warriors and their families ran, soldiers were there before them. Most of the Indians were unarmed, having had no time to secure weapons, or to load rifles, in the surprise of the dawn assault. Women and children died with the fighting men. A soldier bullet screaming through the half-darkness of the early day could not see what it struck.

Below the camp, the soldiers of Major Elliott cut off the escape. To the south, Colonel Meyers not only blocked escape, but also had seized the entire Cheyenne pony herd, the greatest tragedy which might befall any plains Indian camp. Now all thoughts of flight must be of flight on foot. And who could run so fast as to outdistance a rifle's bullet?

The Indians understood then that they were trapped.

There remained but a single avenue of possible escape, and that was the riverbed of the Washita. If they might reach the stream's low banks of prairie clay, they could fight from behind those banks, as they moved downstream to try and unite with their Arapaho and Kiowa brothers.

Yet, once more, the dreaded Yellow Hair was before them.

He had seen that they must turn for the river. And

across the course of the Washita he had stationed a
picked troop of sharpshooters under Lieutenant Billy
Cook. When the terrified Cheyenne began running for
the banks of the stream, they ran directly into the heavy
fire of Cook's hidden sharpshooters.

The fleeing people fell among the rocks of the
streambed, or over the steep-cut banks, into the water
itself. Their bodies bobbed and floated, or lay half in,
half out, of the icy current. Still, by sheer courage, the
last of Black Kettle's warriors, a group of some eighty
wounded and smoke-blackened braves, reached the
shelter of the riverbank and began to fight their way
toward the camp of the Arapaho, next down the stream
from their own.

The heavy rifle-fire which had been coming from that
lower camp now commenced to slacken. Hearing this,
Custer threw up his gauntleted hand and shouted for his
men to hold their own fire.

"By heaven, boys!" he cried, high voice cracking.
"We've got them! That's Elliott slowing his fire down
there. The fight's over! He's got them on the run at his
end, too!"

But the fight was not over.

The little Osage scout, Hard Rope, rode his pony up
to the General. "No quit now," he warned. "Him soldier
down there no stop shoot on purpose."

"What?" shouted Custer, grinning through the dust
and gunsmoke which still swirled about. "Say what you
mean, you red rascal! But be quick. I'm going down
there and congratulate Elliott. What a day!"

"You no go down there," said Hard Rope, his wrinkled
face suddenly dark with uneasiness. "Me hear Arapaho
war-talk down there. Heap more Cheyenne, too. Something bad down there."

By this time California Joe was also growing restless.

"General, something *is* wrong down there. Listen—"

Custer and his officers who had come up to join him in
the moment of triumph, all fell still.

"You don't hear a one of our carbines bellowing," said

California Joe, ominously. "They got a deep sound. It
booms, sort of. All you hear down there where Major
Elliott went are sharp barks. Them's Winchesters talking
down yonder, General. Injun guns."

For the first time the flushed face of the Seventh's
leader grew pale. A chill not borne in the winter air
struck him.

Instantly, the atmosphere shifted from victory to
apprehension, as the crowding troops caught the scent
of fear.

But Custer was no coward.

"All right," he said quietly. "We must then take a
strong force and proceed at once past the big bend to
Major Elliott's aid. Recall Captain Cook and form up the
troops of Captain Thompson behind my own."

In a very few minutes, the troops were probing toward
the increasing stillness beyond the big bend. In another
few minutes they had reached the bend and gone
beyond it, halfway across a large open meadow toward
the camp of the Arapaho. But they went no farther.
Suddenly, California Joe, riding beside Custer in the
advance, reined in his pony. He seized the General's
arm and pointed to the hills which loomed above the
river where Elliott's fire had last been heard. The sun
was rising, now, just tipping the high ridges to the east,
sending its warming light into the meadow.

But Custer was not warmed by what he saw upon
those hills.

As far as the eye could reach, on both banks of the
Washita, the slopes were covered with warriors from the
lower camps. Their weapons glittered in the morning
sun. The eagle feathers of their warbonnets flashed
everywhere. These were not sleepy old men and squaws
and little children routed from warm buffalo robes and
running half-naked through the snow. These were full-
grown fighting men. And they were dressed for war, and
had their rifles and their ammunition belts, and were all
watching like a gathering of red wolves the halted
command of General Yellow Hair Custer.

"General," said California Joe, "all due respects to you
and the Seventh Cavalry, sir, but we'd best get out of
here *right now*."

Hard Rope, the Osage, moved his arm in a sweeping
circle, all about the meadowland.

"Look him tall grass," he said. "Grass no stop bullet."

Custer was a bulldog of a man. Once he had an idea in
his grip, he disliked extremely to let it go. He had
started out to find Major Elliott. He was not going to be
frightened off by any hillside full of feathered warriors.

"We will go forward," he said. "Bugler, sound the
advance!"

The trumpeter raised his horn to obey. But the call
never came. As if awaiting a signal, the hundreds upon
hundreds of Indians standing silently on the slopes
broke into deep and wild war cries. It was a sound to put
the fear of death in any white man. And, with it, the
painted warriors surged downward, toward the startled
troops of the Seventh.

"General," said California Joe, "you had better change
that order to the bugle boy. And mighty quicklike, too."

"But what about Elliott?" frowned Custer. "By thunder, man, we can't leave him over there!"

"General," replied the tall scout, tight-lipped, "wherever the major is, over there, or anywhere else, he's past
all help of ours. Unless you want your own men to join
his, you had best tell that bugler to blow retreat. And
right now!"

Custer took one last look across the meadow. The
advancing red men were into the tall grass now, weaving
through it like a horde of angry ants. The first of their
rifle-fire was beginning to patter and pelt like falling rain
into the meadow hay about the troopers of the Seventh
Cavalry.

"Trumpeter," he said, his pale blue eyes dark with the
shadows of shame and doubt, "sound the recall."

5. THE STILLNESS ALONG THE WASHITA

Before Custer's troops could get out of the meadow, they were joined by a large number of Major Elliott's men, led by a young lieutenant. This officer said Elliott's troops had killed thirty-eight Cheyenne and taken no great casualties of their own. But when questioned upon the major's whereabouts, the lieutenant showed surprise. He had thought to find Major Elliott with Custer. Where was the major?

No one answered the grim question, and the retreat resumed to the first village.

There Custer began his regrouping. The buglers continued to blow recall, and in response the various troop units began to come in. Before long, of the principal commanders only Major Elliott was still unreported. At this point, Custer believed that his own position was safe enough. He was trying to decide whether to retire from the field with what victory had already been his, or to march on down the river and clean out the Arapaho camp as well. It was in his mind to do the latter, as he would enhance his triumph considerably if he could add the scalp of the Arapaho leader, Big Mouth, to that of the Cheyenne chief, Black Kettle. But at the moment of issuing the order to re-commence the offensive, California Joe and Captain Benteen came up with the Osage scout, Hard Rope, and a captive Arapaho squaw. This woman, who spoke broken English, informed Custer that there were eight hundred lodges scattered along the next five miles of the Washita River and that for the soldiers to advance farther would be to invite a massacre of monstrous proportions.

Custer, of course, said that the woman was lying. She was attempting to stop the renewal of the attack, so that her murderous tribesmen might escape.

But the squaw, with an Indian's dignity, drew her blanket about her. She threw out an arm, pointing dramatically to the hills which surrounded the upper camp, as they did the lower meadow where Elliott had disappeared.

"Look, Yellow Hair!" she cried. "See for yourself. Me no lie. You want lose hair like Oak Leaf Chief?"

"Good Lord, sir!" broke in Captain Benteen. "Oak Leaf Chief is their term for a major's gold shoulder-leaves."

"Yes, yes, you fool," said Custer, irritably. "I know that. Say what you mean, Benteen."

"The woman is trying to tell us that Major Elliott is dead," answered the level-voiced captain. "And she is telling you that you will be the same, if you don't turn about and get out of here while the getting is good."

Custer glared at the other officer. He did not care for Captain Frederick W. Benteen, and the latter believed what he had told the young lieutenant in Custer's tent before the battle: that Yellow Hair actually suffered from delusions of great power, of invincibility, and that the famous long-haired general was not of sound mind.

"Benteen," said Custer now, in a cold voice, "do not interfere again. We will discuss your behavior at a later time."

"I'm certain that we will," said Benteen, returning the commander's angry stare with quiet restraint. "But right now let's discuss the behavior of those Indians gathering across the river."

Quickly, Custer and all the officers saw that the situation of the open meadow was about to be repeated. The number of the braves visible now was beyond hundreds, however. It was California Joe, the chief of the General's scouts, who spoke of this altered fact.

"General, I believe there's somewhat like fifteen hundred—mebbe two thousand—hostiles up there. I further believe they mean to charge us any minute. You've poked a hornet's nest, sir, and they're only beginning to swarm back at you."

Custer, for all his faults of rashness and thoughtlessness, had the mind of a fox. He saw at once that the scout was right. More importantly by far, he understood what he must do about it.

"Captain Meyers," he said calmly, "if your men and the sharpshooters of Lieutenant Cook will kindly keep those Indians away from us for half an hour, we shall be all finished here. Please commence firing at once, sir."

So it was that, under the protection of the best riflemen in the Seventh Cavalry, Yellow Hair set about the final destruction of Black Kettle's camp.

His treacherous attack on the Cheyenne village had brought him sixty captured squaws with their surviving children. On the icy ground about the lodges lay the bodies of the Indian dead. One hundred three warrors. Sixteen women. Eleven small children. Piled high between the lodges were the articles of triumph: 241 saddles . . . 1123 tanned buffalo hides . . . 82 rifles and revolvers . . . 425 axes and lances . . . 4035 arrows and warbows . . . 2185 blankets . . . 535 pounds of gunpowder . . . 1375 pounds of lead and bullets . . . 700 pounds of tobacco . . . Untold thousands of pounds of buffalo meat cured for the winter.

All of this plunder was now piled in one enormous heap.

To this vast pile were added all of the tipis, pulled over by ropes and dragged in by the troopers on their horses.

Over the now mountainous pyramid of Indian life-goods, the more than five hundred pounds of gunpowder were sprinkled.

"Stand away, men!" shouted Custer. Then, high-voiced to his waiting orderly, "You may go ahead, sir. Fire it."

The orderly, standing by with a burning brand seized from one of the Cheyenne tipi fires, hurled the flaming torch into the pile. There was a single moment's pause, then a belching roar of fire leaped upward, and the black smoke began to roll across the Washita. Custer, as calmly as though standing on the parade ground at Fort Wallace, turned to his scouts.

"Hard Rope," he said, "have your Osage braves bring over the captured ponies. Drive them out into the open by the river, where those Indians across the stream may see them."

"What are you going to do, General?" asked Benteen.

"I am thinking of an old Cheyenne proverb," responded Custer. "Kill an Indian of the plains, and two more will spring up to take his place; but destroy that Indian's pony, and his heart for war drops dead within him."

And so it was.

The Osage brought forward the beautiful herd of Black Kettle's people. The rifles of Lieutenant Cook's sharpshooters commenced to roar out their deep bellowing reports. Some say that it lasted for one hour. Some say much less, even so little as the thirty minutes Custer had promised.

But the result was the same, by either time.

When the last Pony Soldier carbine had boomed out, eight hundred seventy-five Cheyenne horses lay dead or dying upon the banks of the Washita. And Yellow Hair's proverb had come true.

Across the stream, the rifles of the horrified Cheyenne had been stilled for many minutes. The warriors could not fight while their beloved ponies were being destroyed. They withdrew upon the hills in silent hundreds. Then, without another sound, their entire number—California Joe always maintained there were three thousand of them—rode slowly from that terrible field. They went away down the river. No single further shot was fired by either side. No war whoop rang. No bugles blew. The troopers were as stunned, almost, as the broken-hearted Indians.

As quietly as the departing Cheyenne, Custer marshaled his Seventh Cavalry and left the field.

He went westward, back along his own tracks through the snow, abandoning brave Major Elliott and all other men not reported by that time. Behind him he left only the smoke and the drift of the ashes and the smell of death in the lovely Valley of the Washita.

That and the terrible silence.

The Cheyenne never forgot him, and they never forgave him. They vowed, as they rode away through that stillness on the Washita, that some day, along some distant trail, they would meet again with Yellow Hair beside another river.

PART TWO

THE PA SAPA

6.   RED CLOUD'S TREATY

The snows of two winters had fallen. It was 1870, and the Indians of the South Plains were quiet, their spirits defeated by Custer. For the most part there was peace. And for the most part the Cheyenne and the Arapaho obeyed their Medicine Lodge Treaty with the white man, staying on or near their reservations below the Arkansas. There was good reason they should. The buffalo were extremely fat that year, and there were a great many of them. Also, the treaty to which their chiefs had touched the pen at Medicine Lodge Creek —at about the same time the Sioux and the Cheyenne of the North were signing the Laramie Treaty of 1868 —that treaty promised the Indian that no white man might come south of the Arkansas River to hunt the buffalo, or any of the other of the Indians' game animals. So there was peace in the South, as in the North, and the white people across the land began to hope that the bloody wars with the red men were a thing of the frontier past.

They hoped far too soon.

In the North the great Red Cloud was preparing to travel to Washington, the mighty village of the Great Father. The Sioux leader rode to the east upon the Iron Horse, the white man's railroad. He saw in the great city of Washington all of the wonders of the white man. He realized how many of the enemy there were. He saw their huge cannon. He saw all of their thousands of soldiers, both Walkaheaps of the Infantry and Pony Soldiers of the Cavalry. Red Cloud was an intelligent

man. His eyes told him that the Indians could no longer
fight the white man. But his heart was heavy, all the
same, and there was a reason for that.

His people had told him that he must find out from the
Great Father in Washington exactly what that fine treaty
of 1868 had said. Many chiefs of the Sioux and the
northern Cheyenne, and of the Arapaho, said that the
treaty had promised the red man that, "so long as the
grass shall grow," no white man would come into their
lands, neither to travel through them, nor to hunt within
them, nor to build or camp or settle in any way upon
them. Yet the road of the Iron Horse had been built
where it frightened away the buffalo. The wagons of the
settlers going west still camped in Indian country, still
chopped down Indian trees, grazed out Indian pastures.
And now, most unhappy thing of all, even the beautiful
Black Hills, the sacred *Pa Sapa* of the Sioux, were being
violated by white hunters and wanderers. Such things
were wrong.

So it was that when his trip was nearly at an end, and
he was to be put once more upon the Iron Horse, Red
Cloud spoke to the great chiefs in Washington, saying
that he and his people must hear, at last, exactly the true
tongue of the New Laramie Treaty.

The Secretary of the Interior, a good man and one
who had some understanding of the simple, childlike
faith of the Indian mind, had the treaty brought forward
and translated, word-by-word, for the proud and
haughty leader of the Sioux.

For the first time in his life, Red Cloud was brought to
understand what he had done; was made to see what he
had signed away for his people when he touched the pen
for them.

There were three main things:

The treaty declared that the Indians agreed to leave
forever their wild free life hunting the buffalo and the elk
and the fleet antelope, and to settle down upon small
fenced places and to become peaceful farmers like their

white brothers who would soon come and plow up the
buffalo pastures.

The treaty stated that the Indians would peacefully
permit the building of railroads—as many as the white
man wished—across the buffalo ranges, and that they
would not attack the Iron Horse, nor tear up its steel
rails, nor bring down any of its telegraph wires, but stay
far away and do nothing.

And in its last, most secret term, the treaty said that
the Indians promised to retire to, and never to stray
again away from, the new reservations prepared for
them in the barren and gameless lands far eastward of
their high plains' homes, hard against the banks of the
Mini Sosi, the Big Muddy River, the Missouri.

Red Cloud had no guile to match that of the white
man. He was brave and he had pride as fierce as that of
the wild horse. It is said that, when the interpreters had
told him these things which he had promised in the
name of his people, the prairie chieftain uttered a great
cry and leaped to his feet. As swiftly, he drew from
within his blanket a pistol which he had carried there,
unknown to any, all of those days. He put the muzzle of
the weapon to his temple and would have killed himself,
except that some of his fellow chiefs sprang upon him
and took the gun away from him.

But, even so, his wild heart was broken.

He said that he would treat no more with the white
brother. He said that he would go home and tell his
people of the shame which he had brought upon them.

"But I will tell them," he cried, drawing himself to his
full height, and his voice growling like summer thunder
far across the plains, "that they must not believe this
treaty! I will say to them, 'Come, my brothers. We are
few and the white man is as many as the heads of the
grass. But let us fight him so long as our ponies live to
bear us forward, and let us keep on fighting him. He has
lied and made fools of us. He has made a fool and a liar
of me. There can be no peace with liars.'"

Here the angry chief paused. His muscular arm shot outward, menacing all of the Peace Commissioners.

"From this day," he said, "stay away from my people——!"

The good-hearted Secretary, and the well-meaning members of the Peace Commission—all of the Indians' friends who were present—made haste to quiet the chief's anger.

But in other parts of the nation's capital, the reaction was not so kindly.

Said crusty President Grant when informed of the uproar over Red Cloud's impassioned outcry:

"Nonsense; tell that Indian to go home and start plowing."

7. THAT THIEVES' ROAD

But the Indian Bureau would not take Grant's hard-headed advice. Its members persuaded Red Cloud not to go home, but to go to New York City and make one more plea for "understanding," one more appeal for "peace and brotherhood."

This time the Sioux chief had a far larger audience.

His speech was carried in all of the large metropolitan newspapers. It was picked up by the smaller papers and spread across the land. Red Cloud rose to soaring heights of Indian eloquence in stating the case for his wronged people. At no point did he mention the scores of white women and children killed or kidnaped by his savage warriors of the Oglala, Hunkpapa, Minniconjou, Brulé, Yankton and Sans Arc bands of the Dakota Sioux. Or, if he did admit these tragedies, the fact failed to reach his listeners through the lips of the Indian Bureau interpreters.

All that the American people understood was that here was a brave and noble red man who had been robbed and betrayed by the "white devils," and made to sacrifice his own people by signing the "notorious treaty" of 1868.

Public indignation was instant. The Secretary of the Interior was forced to alter the reservation clause. The Sioux, henceforth, would be free to "trade as they wished." This new triumph of the peace party meant one thing alone in Indian terms. From that time forward, the Sioux could come and go as they wished. The new "treaty" was nothing less than a guarantee that they could return to their old warlike way of life, riding and raiding where they wished, so long as they called it "trade." Red Cloud went back to his western home, not to plow, but to put on the war paint.

For the next three years, and into the fourth summer, that of 1874, the Sioux plundered and burned and scalped from the Dakotas down into Kansas, and westward from the Missouri River into the mining country of Colorado and far Montana. No settler, no prospector, no wagon party was safe. The north plains were "made bloody" by the Sioux, as the south plains had been ravaged in the years before by the Cheyenne and the Arapoho, the Comanche and the Kiowa. Nowhere on the frontier was this more true than in Red Cloud's own homeland of the Black Hills. Here, his fierce Oglala tribesmen, under such famed chiefs as Crazy Horse and American Horse, would not listen to anything but war.

Oh, they had a peace chief and a white-talker of their own, even as the Cheyenne had had in old Black Kettle.

The Sioux friend of the white man was named Spotted Tail, and he was old and wise and had been to Washington before Red Cloud. Spotted Tail prayed and pleaded that his people would listen to him in time.

"Hear the Great Father," he warned. "Obey his words. If he tells you to go home and farm the land, do that. For I have been to his great village in the East. We cannot fight all those people. Believe what I say. Obey your Father who lives in Washington!"

But the Sioux would far rather hear what Tashunka Witko or Nakpa Kesela had to say; they much preferred to listen to Crazy Horse and American Horse.

"Cover your ears!" these fighters cried. "Do not hear the old man! The white men have bought his tongue and they have split it in the middle like the tongue of a snake, and it speaks in two different directions at the same time. Ride with us. Stay free. Do not let the white men lie to you again. This land is ours! Are you all old women, that you will no longer fight for what is yours?"

So it came about that the peace party in the Indian

Bureau brought woe and distress to the very people they
intended to protect.

The public lost sympathy for Red Cloud's folk.

The newspapers and the politicians began to demand
some action by the Government to stop the raiding and
the pillaging of "innocent settlers and honest husbandmen."

Now it was the turn of the war party in Washington.

An expedition, it was announced, would be mounted
at once. Its purpose would be to "explore" the Black
Hills—the very heart of the Sioux country—seeking to
establish a wagon road through them, and to find a
location for the building of an army fort which would
"threaten" the warlike spirits of the "spoiled red children" throughout the length and breadth of their sacred
Land of the Spotted Eagle.

This expedition was to have results so dark as to be
beyond imagination at the moment. Wise heads, both
red and white, understood this and tried in vain to stop
any such foolhardy invasion of the treatylands which the
government had guaranteed in writing to the red man
"for as long as the grass shall grow."

It was no use.

Across the United States a hard depression had set in.
Times were very bad. The public could see no sense, at
all, in continuing to spend millions of dollars to pacify
the Sioux when white children were going hungry, and
white fathers could find no work, and white mothers
toiled long hours merely to put a scrap of food on the
table. Suddenly, the people had had their fill of the false
propaganda of the Indian Peace Party. Let Red Cloud
look out for himself! So far as the temper of the times
was concerned, he and his folk would not get another
dime of what was now openly being called "blackmail" to
stay peaceful. Let the Indians feed themselves for a
change. "Uncle Sam's children" were tired of taking care
of their red brothers and sisters.

As for the response of the Sioux to this hardening
attitude, it was too late for helpful change.

The red man never had understood the peace policy which sought to buy his friendship with food and gifts. In his view, such generosity was a sign of weakness and fear. The more he was given, the more he demanded, and the more he came to believe that the Americans were soft and cowardly.

Thinking this, he made the mistake of his red life.

The War Department moved swiftly ahead with its plan to invade the last sanctuary of the plains Indian, to drive a wagon trail through the Black Hills, a trail that the Sioux would forever after call "That Thieves' Road."

The department selected for the commander of this fateful expedition the most dangerous of all possible soldier chiefs for the purpose.

He was a man the Indians remembered.

Indeed, he was a man they had sworn never to forget, or to forgive.

His name was General George Armstrong Custer.

8. GOLD IN THE BLACK HILLS!

Fort Abraham Lincoln stood across the Missouri River from Bismarck, North Dakota. Custer had been named its commander in the winter of 1873, before the fort was finished. Now, in the spring of 1874, the new post was completed. The Seventh Cavalry had moved into its prairie home and Custer had returned from a journey eastward to fetch his lovely young wife, Elizabeth, to the far Dakotas to share his lonely command.

That spring was surely one of the happiest in the young general's life.

But the excitement which stirred him was not brought by "Libbie" Custer, alone.

Yellow Hair was high in spirit because soon he would be gone again into the Indian Country. Soon he and the Seventh Cavalry would be back in the saddle, riding out there where the Sioux warriors waited, faces smeared with black and yellow paint, fierce eyes watching for him who was only truly happy when the feathered bonnets were flashing far off, the trumpeter blowing the charge, the gray and the black and the bay horses of the Seventh Cavalry thundering into the chase. Ah! if he could but get one good fight from the red rascals this time!

He well recalled the past summer, when he had ridden up and down the Yellowstone River with General Stanley looking for some Sioux to defeat. The thought of it made his face flush. Not only had he not found the Sioux, but the Sioux had found him. Two separate times. And not only had he not defeated the red horsemen, but they had beaten him badly on both occasions. The second time Custer's command had barely been saved from a massacre by the timely arrival of General Stanley with the infantry troops. Moreover, Yellow Hair had suffered the added humiliation of being put under arrest by Stanley for disobeying orders!

Custer remembered something else about that Yellowstone march of 1873. That was the name of the Indian who had so nearly caught him and killed him. It was the famed Sioux chieftain, Rain-in-the-Face. How could he forget that Indian? Rain-in-the-Face had killed his two good friends, Doctor Holzinger, the veterinary of the Seventh Cavalry, and Balarian, the popular post sutler at Fort Lincoln, in the first scrape with the chief's Sioux war party.

Now, if Custer's luck would bring him another chance to meet that treacherous savage, things would be different! In fact, just let any of the Sioux try anything with the Black Hills column. Yellow Hair would show them. Those Indians needed a lesson. And the Seventh Cavalry were just the boys who could give it to them.

Forward, ho——!

The long line of troops and supply vehicles rolled out of Fort Abraham Lincoln on the second of June, 1874.

With Custer were ten troops of cavalry, the regimental band, two companies of infantry, one hundred wagons, three Gatling guns and a three-inch cannon, a herd of beef cattle to feed the soldiers, a corps of newspaper reporters, photographers and assorted guests from the East who had simply been invited along "for the sport" by the good-natured, high-strung commander of the Seventh Cavalry.

Custer well understood the need for letting the outside world know about his daring exploits and adventures.

Hence, the people of the press, and the cameramen.

Some of Yellow Hair's officers, the sober and older ones like Captain Benteen and Major Marcus Reno, said that the "Boy General" scarcely went to shave in the mornings but that he alerted the reporters to come along and see if he might cut himself.

But every great man has his critics.

Custer was so popular with the American public that even President Grant, who intensely disliked him, was forced to tender favors to the long-haired "hero of the Washita." Indeed, Grant had at first refused to even let Custer accompany the Black Hills Expedition, far from commanding it. But kind old General Terry and peppery Phil Sheridan had begged Grant to relent, and the tough old Civil War commander had given in against his better judgment.

"He is a vain fool," the blunt, cigar-chomping President was said to have growled in private. "And not one-half the soldier those blasted reporters are forever saying."

Custer could not have cared less had he heard the remark.

He had his command, the old Seventh, again at his back. Out toward the sunset, where the troops were heading, the Sioux waited. Now they would see how Yellow Hair repaid his debts. Now that haughty Red Cloud and that traitorous Rain-in-the-Face would get what was coming to them.

But the long days passed, the column wound onward and onward, and in all of the time not a single eagle-feather bonnet was spied from afar, not a solitary Indian ponytrack was seen by the eager scouts of the Seventh Cavalry.

At last, after nearly three weeks, the Black Hills rose along the southwestern horizon. The land commenced immediately to grow more fair with each mile. Soon the trrops were winding into the beautiful hills themselves, and their wondering eyes were seeing for the first time why the wild and savage red horsemen of the plains called these places "sacred."

Custer, always a man with a quick and sensitive eye for loveliness, be it in nature or in the slender graces of a young woman, could not contain his spirits.

"There is such grazing here," he said, "that its only fault can be that it is too luxuriant!" He found, also, "crystal streams of water so cold as to render ice undesirable even at noontime."

Tall grass and flowers grew to the knees of the riding troopers. Pine trees dotted the lovely meadows. Lakes and streams were everywhere. High clouds drifted in a sky "blue as angel's eyes." The air was soft and brilliant with sunshine, yet deliciously cool after the parching heat of the level plain which surrounded the Sioux paradise.

"I know of no portion of our great nation," rhapsodized the General, "where nature has done so much to prepare homes for the husbandmen and left so little for the latter to do as here. Nowhere in the States have I tasted cultivated berries of better flavor than those found growing wild here. Cattle could winter in these valleys without other food or shelter than that to be obtained from running at large."

But Custer was only getting started.

On top of all these unbelievable bounties of nature which had been discovered in the Black Hills, there was another gift of value positively staggering.

"*Gold*," proclaimed the reports sifting back to civilization from the leader of the Seventh Cavalry, "*is to be found at the very grassroots.*"

The first response to this was a thin trickle of men who were near the scene, rugged and tough westerners who had only to turn their pack mules toward the Dakotas to be "on their way." The real flood came when Custer, after sixty days away in the field, returned to Fort Lincoln to begin writing up his "magnificent exploration" for the magazines and newspapers of the country.

With that, the rush was on.

Hundreds upon hundreds of greedy whites poured into the sacred Hills in search of what the astonished Indians called "the useless yellow metal." The situation became ugly almost at once. By the early autumn the Government knew that, unless it took some drastic step, an Indian war would break over the *Pa Sapa* which would make the Washita and Palo Duro and Adobe Wells fights of the southern tribes seem as skirmishes. In a desperate move, Red Cloud was once more called to take the Iron Horse for Washington.

The proud chief, to save his people, consented to try this final time to make an honorable peace.

What awaited him in Washington stunned the Sioux.

It was this, no more and no less:

The Great Father had decided to buy the *Pa Sapa* from the Indians. All that Red Cloud might do for his people was to agree on a fair and fitting price for their beloved Black Hills. No, it was worse than that. All that the Sioux chief might do was to *accept* that price which the Great Father would *tell him* was fitting and fair!

Red Cloud looked at the Indian Commissioners, and could not speak.

What was there to say?

The white men had once more caught him in a *wickmunke*, a trap, and words would never again open its jaws.

Red Cloud knew it, every white man there knew it.

When the springtime came again, and the ponies were fat and strong with the new grass, there would be war.

9. WHAT CUSTER SAW FAR OFF

Autumn deepened in the land of the Dakotas. The short curl of the buffalo grass turned blue-brown, its winter color. The first ice storms, the beginning flurries of small-flaked snows drove across the naked prairies. The Sioux looked up at the leaden skies, listened to the last thin cries of the departing geese, high above the storm.

"*Wasiya* is coming," they said.

Wasiya was the Winter Giant, the Blizzard King.

When he commenced to blow in earnest, to bring the great drift-snows, then Mother Earth went to sleep. The animals sought their dens. The Indians gathered into their winter camps, pitching their snug buffaloskin tipis close together in some sheltered spot, where the people might help one another through the Time of the Big Cold.

And, for this time, the red brother was quiet.

The white brother, too, must bow to the fierce blasts of Wasiya's sub-zero breath. Even he must stay in his lodge and keep warm. His Iron Horses, his Talking Wires of the telegraph, his diggers of the yellow metal, his breakers of the Mother Earth, his Pony Soldiers and his Walkaheap Soldiers—all were forced by Wasiya to lie up and be at peace, even as the Indian.

And so, for a little while, the life was good.

But across the Big Muddy River, at Fort Abraham Lincoln, Yellow Hair Custer grew restless. He was bored with the games and charades, the costume balls and dramatic plays which made up the social life of an isolated far western army post in mid-winter. The

minuets, waltzes and Virginia reels supplied by the
regimental band were fun at first. Then the musicales
performed on the grand piano freighted by army wagon
for Libbie all the way from St. Paul relieved the
monotony of post life briefly.

But dance balls and piano recitals were scarcely fit
substitutes for summer campaigning.

Not for the General.

In truth, "Armstrong," as his adoring wife and close
personal friends called him, loved a party and the
gay-bright smile of a fair maid as well as any man alive.
Yet that winter at Fort Lincoln seemed without end to
Custer.

Something, he could not say what, lay in his mind and
would not leave it. When his young wife or his officers
would question him, he would deny that it was anything;
he was the happiest man in the world, he would insist, as
what reasonable man would not be with Custer's luck?

But once, when his brother Tom found him deep in
brooding thought, he sighed and looked far away toward
the southwest and the sacred *Pa Sapa*, the distant Black
Hills of Red Cloud and his betrayed people.

"Tom," he said, "if I were an Indian, I would greatly
prefer to cast my lot among those of my people who
adhered to the free open plains rather than submit to the
confined limits of a reservation."

"That's a strange thing for you to say, Autie." Autie
was Custer's boyhood nickname, and he did not hear it
much these days. But Tom and he were always very
close, and the Custers were sentimental people. "You've
always been on the other side, I would think," Tom
continued. "Why this sudden sadness for the noble red
man?"

Tom was not like Custer. He was a bigger man, and
much less keen of mind. He was also a heavy drinker,
whereas Custer never touched a drop of anything
stronger than the clean sparkling water of the mountains
and prairies he loved so much. Perhaps this crudeness of
the younger brother was what drew the General to

protect and cherish him. In any event, young Tom
Custer was his favorite chick, and the dashing leader of
the Seventh Cavalry mother-henned him on every campaign and in every camp they shared together.

"Well, boy," he now told Tom, "a man is not always
what he seems, is he? Not even to his little brother."

Tom wanted at once to know what that meant, since
he knew Custer did not always say what, precisely, he
had in mind.

"I mean," the General answered him, "that I think the
wild Indian of the American plains has led the finest and
noblest life of any man in history. He drinks the cold
wind, he is wrapped in the warm sun. He is brave, loyal,
generous. He lacks nothing that I admire, or would not
give my all, in another life, to share with him."

Tom frowned. "Are you saying that you wish you had
been born an Indian!?" Tom's frown changed to a grin, as
the absurdity of the thought hit him. "Hah! hah!" he
laughed, big hand slapping his thigh. "Oh, that's rich,
Autie! *You*, an Indian! Ho! ho! ho!"

Custer shook his head.

"Be serious a moment, Tom," he said. "I want to tell
you something."

There was that ring of iron in Cutster's voice which
men did not ignore. He was giving an order to young
Lieutenant Tom Custer, and the latter nodded and sat
down and waited.

Custer's voice softened at once, and he began to talk.

He asked Tom to look around the room. Did he notice
all the stuffed birds and animals staring at them from
every wall and corner? Did he not remember these were
all shot, and many of them mounted, by his famous older
brother? Well, suddenly, all of such youthful fancies as
stuffing animals seemed foolish. Custer was not even
greatly heartened by the recent publication of his first
book, *My Life on the Plains*, in which he told of the
hunting and taking of all those stuffed birds and beasts
which stared at him so remorsefully now.

Did Tom know, yet, how it felt to realize, overnight,

that boyhood and youth were over? That life had fled, like a thief in the dark, and left only middle age behind it? Did he understand that his great hero, the "Boy General," was a boy no longer?

Custer paused here to stride over and stand in front of Tom. He was smiling his old peg-toothed smile, but there was a plaintive quality to it.

"My dear little brother," he said, "look at me; I am thirty-five years old this winter!"

Tom shrugged. "You don't look any different to me, Autie," he said loyally.

"True," nodded Custer. "And to you I never will look any different. Thank you, Tom. But I know I grow old."

"What?" Tom cried. "At thirty-five? Custer, old? Hah!"

But the General was right, and Tom Custer had not the eyes to see it.

Custer's features were taking on the skully look of advancing time. His long nose seemed longer and sharper. His forehead glistened where the hairline had receded. His brows jutted out in a shelf over his pale eyes. His mustache seemed run to weed, flowing to cover his mouth and make his chin appear less resolute and bold. Beyond all, the famed yellow hair had thinned alarmingly. It was still glossy and of full curl behind the ears. But on top he was now combing long strands sideways to cover the growing baldness, and in the rear the legendary curls of "sunbright gold" did not now reach the collar, let alone fall almost to the epaulets, as in the glory days of the Civil War, or the Washita.

"Yes, brother," said Custer now, after long delay. "Old at thirty-five; and if you will bear with me, perhaps you will learn why."

Strangely—or so it seemed to young Tom Custer—the General returned now to his sad-voiced, gentle praise of the plains Indian. There was a spell, almost, in the way that he spoke. Even Tom Custer, that rough-roisterous fellow whose own opinions of the red brother were not fit to mention in polite company, felt the power and the sorrow of his brother's words.

The Indian, Custer began, was in many ways the most admirable of men. Kind to the old and the afflicted, gentle with the lost of mind, loyal to friend, devoted to all children, honoring the given word, punishing the broken vow, he was a man who did not understand the forked tongue of his white brother, and who believed until far too late that simple justice and the fundamental rights of humanity would prevail, preserving both life and liberty.

When at last he saw that this was not true, and that he must fight or die in the bondage of some reservation, the Indian had chosen his way with all of the dignity and pride which were the birthrights of his freedom.

If it was a harsh way that he had chosen, Custer continued, it was also a noble way. And it was necessary.

For there was now no time remaining to the Indian.

There was scarcely time for him to oil his rifle, run in his war pony, make his medicine prayers, say the sacred words to *Wakan Tanka*, his Great Spirit.

For the white man was demanding war or peace. And the peace could be had only at the price of slavery. For the red man, the latter course had become impossible. He knew that where freedom fell unfought for, there men died as if by their own hands. And for him, the Indian, his liberty was the same thing as his life.

Hence, when the white man insisted that the Indian go and stay upon a reservation, forsaking his freedom, the white man was condemning the Indian to death.

"That," said Custer, with a heavy sigh, "is why I am feeling old today, Tom, and not at all like a hero."

Tom Custer was not so crude as to fail to realize he had just heard a genuine eulogy. His older brother did actually admire the savage red horsemen of the plains. But neither was the young lieutenant to be touched by such tributes.

"Autie," he said, bounding to his feet with a laugh, "there's nothing wrong with you that a few weeks out trailing old Rain-in-the-Face won't cure! Come on, General, admit it, now. You'd rather fight redskins than eat!"

Custer looked past him, his glance once more seeking the western window of his study.

"No, Tom," he said, "you're wrong. It won't ever be the same again. Not after this spring. By that time the country will have realized that the Sioux will not sell the *Pa Sapa*."

He paused, going to his desk and picking up a many-paged document. He found the section that he wanted, turned again to Tom. "Let me read you something," he said.

". . . The United States hereby agrees and stipulates that the country north of the North Platte River and east of the summits of the Big Horn Mountains shall be held and considered to be unceded Indian territory, and also stipulates and agrees that no white person or persons shall be permitted to settle upon or occupy any portion of the same; or without the consent of the Indians first had and obtained, to pass through same; and it is further agreed by the United States that within ninety days after the conclusion of peace with all the bands of the Sioux nation, the military posts now established in the territory of this article named shall be abandoned, and that the road leading to them and by them to the Territory of Montana shall be closed . . ."

Custer returned the paper to his desk.

"That," he said to Tom, "is Article 16 of the Treaty of 1868, signed at Fort Rice with the Sioux and allied tribes. *That* is what we promised them. But what we are giving them, when this new spring comes, will be the greatest horde of white rascals that ever invaded any land. When our people understand that their Government is going to buy that land from the Indians, and the Indians be damned, there will be utterly no stopping the rush for mineral and ranching rights in the Black Hills.

And I, Tom, your own brother—I was the one who opened up that Pandora's box for the poor devils."

"Oh, nonsense!" said the irrepressible Tom. "Somebody had to do it."

"Wait," said Custer. "There's more."

He picked up a second document from his littered desk. Waving it briefly, he tossed it back among the other papers.

"Instructions just in from the War Department," he said. "When the big rush starts this spring, the Seventh Cavalry is ordered to stand by and watch. We are not to interfere, Tom, neither on the Indian side, nor on that of the whites. Do you understand what that is going to mean?"

"I can't say that I do, General," smiled Tom. "But then I never was any threat to the bright boys in the class!"

"It means, sir," said Custer, speaking with deadly seriousness, "the end of the Indians."

"Well!" cried Tom, relieved, not sensing, either, his brother's foreboding mood. "Good riddance to them, sir, and the sooner the quicker. Where's your tragedy in that?"

Custer did not answer him.

Instead he turned back to the window.

He stood there long after Tom Custer had left, staring into the winter sunset, a far-off light in his pale eyes.

Was he seeing into that future which awaited him along the sunlit banks of that other river where the tongueless dead of the Washita had promised to wait for him?

PART THREE

POWDER RIVER

10. THE VISION DREAMER— TATANKA YOTANKA

There followed, in that year of 1875, a period of strange quiet in the Land of the Spotted Eagle. From Fort Abraham Lincoln to far Montana and Wyoming, wherever the Sioux held sway, there were no major conflicts between white man and red.

The spring which Custer had feared would bring the showdown brought instead only puzzled reports from his scouts as to a peculiar scarcity of Indians.

Could it be because the buffalo herds had moved farther west? Were the Sioux merely following their food supply?

It was true that, with the coming of the new grass, a brawling flood of white goldhunters and homeseekers had struck the Black Hills. In this, the General had been precisely correct. But the Indians, instead of fighting the white invaders to the death, as both the army and the Indian Bureau had been so certain they would, seemed to have left the country with the buffalo and other wild game ahead of the renewed invasion of the hated "pale-eyes."

Might the do-gooders of the Peace Policy group have been right all along?

Was filling his savage stomach more important to the red man, after all, than defending his supposedly sacred lands and liberty?

Much white opinion now came to believe this. Newspapers proclaimed it. The Sioux were "getting out." They had just simply "run off and hid." They would "never stand and fight now." "The so-called 'Indian Wars' in the west," trumpeted one famed journal, "are as good as over."

But the country and the newspapers were wrong.

Far out across the plains of Montana and Wyoming, where the Powder River and the Tongue and the Rosebud and the Big Horn flowed, the Sons of the Spotted Eagle were gathering. The strange quiet and the peculiar scarcity of the Sioux in the sacred lands of the *Pa Sapa* were not things of accident. Nor were they evidences of surrender. The truth lay many long pony journeys from any such foolish white man's boastings as these.

For the Sioux had found a new leader.

He was a man who had risen steadily and with supreme use of talk to a position of power within their nation.

He was not a war chief, not a fighting man, but a leader of the people. In the ways of the nomad red horsemen of the high plains, in their names for such things, he would be called a medicine man. He was not tall and handsome like Red Cloud. He was not a great orator like Spotted Tail. Nor was he a hero to the Sioux such as the famed Crazy Horse. He was, in fact, a short and homely man of middle years. He wore no dazzling burst of eagle feathers in his warbonnet, but only a solitary black feather slanted through the long braid of his dark hair. Yet his was greater power than that of any war chief, for he could see into the future—his eyes were the eyes of a vision-dreamer, and the Sioux of all the seven bands gathered to him.

This man was of the Hunkpapa tribe, with the Oglala of Crazy Horse the fiercest of all the Sioux peoples.

The vision which he proclaimed was one which aroused the red heart, stirred the Sioux blood, called to the Indian pride of all the tribes—the Cheyenne and the Arapaho most importantly—to rise up and stand tall with their Sioux brothers in one last great war upon the white man.

The name of this man was Tatanka Yotanka.

But that is not the name by which the white men called him, and by which history was to remember him.

His other name was the one which came to turn the white man's blood cold.

It was Sitting Bull.

11. THE DECISION OF CRAZY HORSE

It was a beautiful autumn. The buffalo were sleek and fat. Their great curly coats were deepening for the winter. The September and October moons went quickly. The hunting was good. Well before the first moon of the Big Cold, December, the lodges of the Sioux were filled with a fine supply of buffalo meat. Many glossy hides had been tanned and made into warm sleeping-robes for the snug tipis. The buffalo—the Indians called him "Uncle Pte"—had , as always, supplied both food and bed to the red man. *Ha-a-u! Ha-a-u!*

Spirits rose. Thanks were offered to Wakan Tanka, the Great Spirit.

It was true that the Cheyenne and the Arapaho had not yet joined in Sitting Bull's plan for a last great battle against the whites. But neither had they rejected the idea. They were thinking it over, they said. They would make up their minds in the springtime. That was the time for war, anyway.

Who made war in the wintertime?

Sitting Bull was not angry. He was sad. What did it take, he asked the Cheyenne, for them to realize that they must fight the white man? Why did they not understand, by this time, that the white man broke all of his treaties? That he lied about everything?

Did not the Cheyenne remember what had happened to Makhpiya Luta, to Red Cloud, only the autumn before this one? How the white man had called him again to Washington and told him that they were going to buy the Black Hills then and there? How they had set a price upon the *Pa Sapa*, and Red Cloud and his people could either pay it, or get out?

Did not the Cheyenne remember that price?

Did they not remember the Indian Commission coming out to Red Cloud's country with its offers, when the Sioux chief had stormed out of Washington in rightful anger?

Let Sitting Bull remind them, then. That price was only $6,000,000 for outright purchase, or $400,000 per year for the right of the white man to hunt gold wherever he pleased in the *Pa Sapa*. Was not that a sorrowful enough thing for the Cheyenne to remember? Were they not stirred by Red Cloud's answer? Had they forgotten that, also?

Listen, then:

"I will not even consider such a price," Makhpiya told the white chiefs. "I demand a hundred times your amount, and moreover the Government must support the Sioux for seven generations to come. The Government has brought my people from their hunting grounds and made them to live upon their reservations like white men. It is only reasonable, then, that the white man shall pay all of the expenses and supply all of the needs of the Indian."

And did not the Cheyenne brothers of the Sioux recall also what followed, the saddest thing of all? How the white man had said to Red Cloud, "If you do not go home and do as you are told, coming onto the reservation and staying there, all rations will be withheld from your people until you consent." And how the once proud and haughty Red Cloud had surrendered to this wicked threat, and gone home and told his people he could fight no more for them. How he had said he could not see them starve, could not look into the faces of the women and the old people and the children asking him for food, and that they must then, all of them, do as the white man said, and go and live upon the reservation.

Were the Cheyenne going to let this same evil shame be brought upon their own people?

Or would they not, at last, come to their senses and join with Sitting Bull and Crazy Horse?

Was it not better, in the end, to die as men than to live as old women and cowards?

So spoke the vision-dreamer of the fierce Hunkpapa.

But the Cheyenne still said that they were not sure. It was a terrible decision to make. Give them yet a little more time. Perhaps the white man would relent. Perhaps he would show some gentleness and charity in his heart, after all, and let those Indians who were still free, stay free.

Did he not have most of the Indians already on the reservations, suggested Two Moons, the Cheyenne chief.

Of course he did.

Down in the south plains, the Cheyenne and the Comanche, the Kiowa and the Arapaho, were all coming in now.

The war down there was all over.

Perhaps it was all over up in the north, too. Did not Sitting Bull see this possible good thing? Why make war plans when peace might still be in the hearts of the white man? Wait until the spring, anyway. Then decide.

There was nothing that Sitting Bull or Crazy Horse could do about this Cheyenne refusal to fight, or to face reality.

And, silently, they despaired of support from their Cheyenne brothers—support which the Sioux must have, to win.

But where their own red kin could not convince the warriors of Two Moons, the white man would try.

And he did.

Upon the third day of December, 1875, a fateful letter sped from the Secretary of the Interior to the Indian Bureau. Its contents were secret, but they soon leaked out.

This is what the letter said:

> . . . Referring to our communications of the 27th
> ultimo, relative to the status of certain Sioux Indians
> residing without the bounds of their reservation and
> their continued hostile attitude toward the whites, I
> have to request that you direct the Indian Agents at
> all Sioux agencies in Dakota and at Fort Peck,
> Montana, to notify said Indians that unless they shall
> remove within the bounds of their reservation and
> remain there, before the 31st of January next, they
> shall be deemed hostile and treated accordingly by
> the military . . .

Now it was to be seen that the white man, too, had a
plan for war. But his plan would not wait for spring, or
for the Cheyenne. His plan was already under way.

It was in the coldest part of the winter. The camps of
Sitting Bull and of Crazy Horse (the "certain Sioux" and
"said Indians" referred to in the Secretary's secret order)
were far, far from the nearest agency at which they
might surrender. The closest of any of the Sioux winter
camps to the agencies was over two hundred miles away.
The big main camps of the Hunkpapa and Oglala were
even farther out across the snowy plain. It was a cruel
deception to tell those Indians that they must come in to
the agencies by the last sun of January. For the messengers who were sent out from the agency to bear this
order to the hostile Sioux had not even reached the main
camps when the January moon was finished.

Not one of those messengers is known to have found
any winter camp of the Sioux in time to permit the latter
to travel through the deep snows, even had they wished
to do so.

The Sioux understood this clearly.

They were not ignorant. They knew now that the
white man intended to destroy them. The white man
said, "Go to the agency at once, or the Pony Soldiers will
hunt you down and make the snow bloody where they
find you." At the same time, the white man knew that
the Sioux could not obey his order.

Now, certainly, the Cheyenne must join the Sioux.

But, to the amazement of the latter, the people of Two Moons still said no.

"That paper of the Grandfather's," replied Two Moons, "does not say anything about the Cheyenne. It names only the Sioux. We are still at peace. The Pony Soldiers will not bother our camps. It is the Sioux they want."

The Grandfather, or the Great Father, was what the Indians called the President of the United States.

Surely *his* word on a piece of paper meant what it said.

Of course the order was not from President Grant. But, in their direct, childlike way, the Cheyenne had come right to the truth. The President, the Grandfather, must know of the order, and so it became as his order, even so.

Sitting Bull was at first very angry, then alarmed.

A council of the Sioux was called to meet in the village of the Hunkpapa, high up along Beaver Creek. The chiefs, muffled in their winter robes of buffalo and wolf, came in by ones and twos and threes. All of the famous warriors of the bands still outside the reservations fought the great drifts and the bitter, terrible cold. All were there, save one. Makhpiya Luta—Red Cloud, one-time unquestioned head man of the Oglala—was not among the dark-faced leaders who gathered at the lodge of Tatanka Yotanka. He had gone upon the reservation, and he had taken many of his people with him. The council noted his empty place in the circle about the fire, and the elders nodded to Crazy Horse that he must take that place. He did so, and from that time the Oglala of the wild bands called him their war chief, and Red Cloud was forgotten and his name spoken no more.

All of the chiefs were allowed their turns to speak to the council, and to say what their particular bands would do: whether they would now try to go in to the reservation and surrender, or stay out in the snow and fight.

At last it came down to the time where only Sitting Bull and Crazy Horse had not spoken.

And it came down, also, to this: whatever it might be that these two great men would vote to do, that would be the vote, too, of all the others.

Sitting Bull, when the pipe was pointed in his direction, raised his hand. He did not rise, however.

"My chiefs," he said, "everyone here knows my heart in this matter. Let my Oglala brother speak for me."

All eyes turned upon Crazy Horse.

The legendary Oglala came slowly to his feet. He stood for a long moment without a movement. The firelight fell upon the red-bronze of his fierce face. It glittered within the inky black shadows of his eyes. It bathed in scarlet glow the red Hudson's Bay blanket which swathed his copper body. The silence in that lodge was a thing to be felt by the nerves. It made the skin chill.

Suddenly, from the ranks of the watching chiefs arose a deep sound. *Hun-hun-he! hun-hun-he!* it ran in a growling like thunder around the firelit ring of savage red faces.

Crazy Horse bowed his head.

It was the "courage sound," the guttural rumble that the Sioux men reserved only for the "moment of deepest respect," and it was the greatest tribute that they could pay a man.

"*Ha-ho*, my brothers," the slender war chief said. "I must thank you in my heart, for my words are not enough, nor will they come out of my heart. Let me only say that I will not fail you, nor ever forget that you are my people."

He paused, his slanted eyes, gleaming like hot coals in the shadows of Sitting Bull's lodge, sweeping the circle.

"I will not ask my women and my little children and my old ones who are weak and feeble to march that long harsh way through icy drift and blizzard wind to reach an agency where no food awaits them, and no real friendship, either," he said.

"Even as I speak to you here, the lodges of our people on this river, and throughout the other winter camps, are filled with agency Sioux who have stolen away and come back home simply to get something in their bellies more nourishing than the windy promises of the whites."

For the final time he hesitated, then concluded swiftly.

"I will stay out here and be free! I will fight the Pony Soldiers. I will die a Sioux, and I need no cowardly Cheyenne by my side to do that! That is what Tashunka says."

A vote was held at once.

Only one chief found his heart failing him. He Dog, a boyhood friend of Crazy Horse's, led his eight lodges of Sioux out of Sitting Bull's camp and over the deep-snowed ranges to join the people of Two Moons, and follow the path of peace.

For the others, it was the darker road.

With spring, and the new grass, war would come.

A-ah, katela! So be it!

Death to the Pony Soldiers!

12. THE WONDERFUL TONGUE OF THE WASICUN

In their buffalo-hide lodges the Sioux of the Tongue River free bands knew some brief happiness. The weather was very bad, even for that land of bitter snows, but there was plenty to eat and plenty of wood and dried buffalo chips to keep the tipi fires burning brightly. Visitors coming to the wild camps from the agencies during the February moon reported that the Pony Soldiers had been forced to turn back in an expedition they had planned from Yellow Hair's fort over in the Dakotas. The Pony Soldier chiefs had decided that the snows were too deep for white men to march from the *Mini Sosi*, the Missouri River, to the Sioux camps on the Tongue and the Powder and the Rosebud. Was that not interesting, the visitors asked, when the white man thought nothing of commanding the Indians to march through those same deep snows *from* the Tongue and the Powder and the Rosebud, to the *Mini Sosi?*

Ah, the *Wasicun*, the White Man!

What a wonderful tongue he had; it could wag in two separate directions at the same time.

What a pity, too, that the tongue of the *Shacun*, the Red Man, could speak only in a single line.

But, anyway, there was cause for thanks. The good friends and relatives from the reservations had brought welcome news. There would be no Pony Soldiers that winter. The people could enjoy the warm lodges. They could play with the little children. The women could cut and sew the beautiful moccasins and leather shirts for

the spring hunting parties. The men could while away
the smoky tipi-hours with their endless tales of great
fights and fighters of the past. All would be of gay heart,
as in the old days, before there were any soldiers.

Owanyeke waste, said the Sioux. Everything was good
to the eye, was pretty to look upon.

But the Sioux were only seeing what they wanted to
see; believing what their wild hearts wished to believe.

They were not remembering what had happened to
Black Kettle and his people in their happy winter camp
along the Washita.

The Pony Soldiers had not forgotten that lesson,
however.

When the troops from the Missouri River could not
get through the terrible snows from the east, other
troops were at once ordered to march from the south.

Of these troops the Sioux of Tongue River knew
nothing.

Yet the troops had gathered upon Fort Fetterman,
down in Wyoming, by the hundreds and hundreds. So
swift and so secret was the planning that, by the first sun
in March, the new soldiers were moving up the old
Bozeman Trail, toward Montana, and the Sioux still did
not know that they even existed!

The destination of those troops was the Wolf Mountains and the headwaters of Tongue River.

Their commander was a man feared and respected by
the Indians second only to Yellow Hair Custer.

He was called "Three Stars" and "Red Beard" by the
Sioux, General George Crook by the white men.

Crook's choice for the command of the winter march
did not pass unnoticed by his fellow officers in the West.

Nor, indeed, far back in Washington.

Of course, those loyal to Custer continued to insist
that it was only the deep snows which had kept their
"Boy General" from being given the chance to strike at
the Sioux.

But there were other whispers flying about the nation's capital, not so favorable to the leader of the

Seventh Cavalry. It was not the snows, alone, said these whispers, which had kept Custer from the command.

There was something else involved; something much more serious than the depth of the snowdrifts between Fort Abraham Lincoln and the winter camps of Sitting Bull's Sioux.

13.　THREE STARS AND THE MULE-SOLDIERS

The General had been in the East on leave, far from his post in the Dakotas, since the early fall of 1875.

He and his sprightly wife, Libbie, had been doing the town in New York, with Custer showing little or no disposition to return to the snows and the zero cold of the open plains. He continued to ask the War Department for extensions of his leave until, at last, it was February and Crook had been given the task of subduing the Sioux.

Only then did "Armstrong" seem to realize that he had perhaps been at play too long. He made immediate effort to reach Fort Abraham Lincoln and resume his command. But stronger fates outmarched him. No sooner did he arrive at his post than orders from the War Department came over the telegraph wires: General Custer must return at once to Washington to answer certain inquiries of the Congress.

These "certain inquiries" were what had caused the whispers to spring up and say that more than snow had kept him from his "last best chance to chase the Sioux."

Custer, in his honest soldier's way, had spoken loudly about corruption. In particular, one article said to be his pointed the finger of guilt at Secretary of War William W. Belknap—President Grant's soon-to-be-impeached friend. Graft, the taking of money for political favors, was the dark charge leveled in the article. Custer denied authorship, but Grant was completely angry with "the young popinjay" this time. He would not relent of his

59

directive calling the General back to the capital, despite
all efforts of Custer's powerful friends to get him "off the
carpet."

However, in his usual reckless way, Custer would not
retreat either. His subsequent testimony before Congress was ruled hearsay in its entirety. He was discred-
ited as a witness and excused from further testimony,
but *not* allowed to return to Fort Abraham Lincoln and
his command of the Seventh Cavalry. President Grant
might be, as his critics said of him, "a cigar-chomping,
whiskey-drinking old hellion," but he was something
else, too: he was one of the greatest professional soldiers
in American history, and he believed that he saw, in
George Armstrong Custer, certain weaknesses which
unfitted the Seventh's leader for command of so serious
an undertaking as the final capture or destruction of the
Sioux.

So it came to be that, while Yellow Hair languished in
Washington knowing that his great opportunity was
passing him by, Three Stars Crook, a man who did not
chase glory nor ghost-write articles accusing the President's cabinet officers of "selling Indian agency and
army post traderships," was marching through the snows
of northern Wyoming.

It was some time in the second week in March that he
struck the headwaters of Tongue River, and started
down that stream.

Between him and the camps of the Sioux lay only the
unbroken snowfields and the dark-timbered sentinels of
the Wolf Mountains. He crossed into Montana, still
undiscovered by the Sioux. His chief scout, Frank
Grouard, told him to keep going, to move even faster.
Crook nodded, and passed the order: forward, *ho*,
double time!

There was good reason for this trust in Grouard.

The dark-skinned scout was a half-breed of strange
beginnings. His father had been a Frenchman, his
mother a native of the South Seas. From her he took the
dark skin and the features which later were to save his

life, for finding him, as a young boy, with a wagon train
of white emigrants, the Sioux believed him to be an
Indian, and did not kill him. Instead, they took him to
the Hunkpapa camp of Sitting Bull, where he was raised
in the very tipi of the medicine man and vision-dreamer
who now led all of the Sioux in Red Cloud's place. To
Sitting Bull, Grouard was as an own-son. He was given
the name of Sitting-with-Upraised-Hands, and the nickname of "The Grabber." When, as he reached manhood,
Grouard had returned to the people of his white father,
it had been a great blow to Sitting Bull, and indeed to all
the Sioux. As yet, however, the Oglala and Hunkpapa
did not realize that The Grabber, whom they had raised
as their own blood, was actually working for the enemy,
against his fierce foster-parents—in the employ, even, of
the detested Pony Soldiers!

Hence, when, upon the cold and snowy morning of
the 14th of March, 1876, three young Sioux braves
halted their snow-caked ponies on a windy ridge above
the frozen Tongue, they received a very bad surprise.

It was shock enough to see, down there in the valley,
the long dark line of mule-mounted foot soldiers,
cavalry-men and army ammunition wagons crawling
northward along the river toward their winter camps.
But the more ugly discovery was yet to come.

The leader of the three braves was an Oglala. His two
companions were Hunkpapas.

Little Killer, the Oglala, owned a pair of army field
glasses which he had taken from a dead officer. Through
these, he now commenced to examine the rapidly
moving column of strange Pony Soldiers who rode mules
into his country in the dead of winter.

His first discovery was that Three Stars Crook headed
the enemy troops. That was enough bad news to bring
frowns and growls of uneasiness from the two Hunkpapa. But then the young Oglala made a hissing sound
and uttered the warning word, *a-ah!* and handed the
field glasses to one of the Hunkpapa.

"Look down there riding with Three Stars," he said. "See who it is that guides these *Wasicuns* against us."

The Hunkpapa took the glasses, focused them.

"*Howo!*" cried the Hunkpapa. "It is The Grabber——!"

The Indians then knew they were in very great trouble, and must act with all haste. Yet they must take great care, too.

"I will stay and follow the soldiers," said Little Killer. "The one of you must ride to warn the village of Sitting Bull, the other to carry the alarm to the lodges of Crazy Horse. *Hopo, hopo,* hurry now!"

"*Ha-a-u!*" said the Hunkpapa, and turned their ponies from the ridge and were gone down its far side, racing north.

Little Killer waited on the wind-blasted spine of the ridge until the last mule-soldier had vanished beyond the bend of the Tongue. Then he put the heels of his bull-hide moccasins into the shaggy ribs of his spotted pony, and sent him down the slope, into the valley.

"*Hookahey!* small horse," he said with fierce softness. "Let us go swiftly after them!"

14. THE FATAL TRAIL OF HE DOG

Little Killer followed the column of Three Stars Crook only a short way down the Tongue. Then, surprisingly, the mule-soldiers stopped. The Grabber had halted them.

The Oglala brave watched through his field glasses.

Grouard was excited. He kept pointing away from the Tongue, over the high country toward Powder River. That was very interesting, thought Little Killer. Over there on the Powder was the winter camp of Two Moons and those "peace lovers" of his, those Cheyenne who would not fight.

Was it possible that The Grabber was telling Three Stars to go after those Indians?

How was that possible? They were peaceful Indians.

When He Dog and the eight lodges of his Oglala had deserted the camp of Crazy Horse to go with the Cheyenne, it had been because Two Moons had already sent his word to the agent at Standing Rock that his people wanted peace and would come in to the reservation in the spring.

He Dog believed, through this, that if he were found with the Cheyenne, he, too, would be called peaceful, and his people would be safe from the soldiers. In the spring he planned to surrender with Two Moons and the Cheyenne. Now these soldiers from the south, from Wyoming, they must know of Two Moons' offer to come in when the snows melted. They had to know. Two Moons had sent his messengers to Standing Rock a long time ago. Something was very wrong here.

Presently, he saw the mule-soldiers turn away from
Tongue River. They went over the high country, toward
the east and toward Powder River. The Oglala young
man sat upon his pony, frowning.

At first he was glad in his heart that the soldiers had
not found the camps of Sitting Bull and Crazy Horse.

Then he thought, no, there is still something wrong
here. The Grabber had seen something else that Little
Killer did not know about. But Little Killer believed that
he knew what it was. It must be the trail that He Dog
had made, leaving the camp of Crazy Horse and going
over the hills to the camp of Two Moons. The Grabber
was a great tracker. He was better, even, than any
Indian. But he had certainly been fooled here. He had
thought that the trail of He Dog and his few lodges
would lead him to the main camp of Crazy Horse or of
Sitting Bull. And he had thought this because he could
tell the tracks of Sioux horses from those of Cheyenne or
Arapaho ponies. He was perhaps one of three men in all
the prairies and mountains who could do that. The other
two were Big Throat Bridger, a white man now grown
old, long gone from Montana, and Bloody Knife, Yellow
Hair Custer's favorite Indian scout, a full-blooded Arikara.

Yet, great tracker or not, The Grabber had guessed
wrong this time. He would not find the Sioux camps over
there.

If he led the soldiers along that line of old pony-marks
in the snow, he would come to the Cheyenne camp.

Well, what should Little Killer care about that?

If the Cheyenne were harmed, they had it coming to
them. Sitting Bull and Crazy Horse had warned them
again and again. But wait! Little Killer had suddenly
remembered something that caused his heart to beat
wildly. His own sister, Fair Morning, had gone to visit
relatives in the band of He Dog only three days gone.
She would be in that camp with the Cheyenne. What if
the mule-soldiers found her there. *A-ah!* Now Little
Killer knew what he must do; he must go faster than the

winter wind, over those same hills where The Grabber was guiding Three Stars. He must come to the camp of Two Moons before the soldiers did. He must get his little sister and take her away from there.

"*Ho, shuh,* small horse," he said to his pony. "Do not be frightened, but run as though *Yunke Lo* were at your heels. *Hopo, hookahey!* Let's go again!"

The shaggy mustang knew who Yunke Lo was. He was the Sioux god of Death. The pony did not like the sound of his name, and he leaped forward over the icy crust, ears back, eyes rolling.

"*Iho!*" cried Little Killer. "Run——!"

15. THE LEGEND OF LIEUTENANT MOORE

Late in the day of the 16th of March, Crook halted his troops in a deep and darkened vale of the roughlands.

Frank Grouard had found, just ahead, a place where many other ponies had joined those of He Dog's little band.

"Plenty of these new ones are Cheyenne," said the scout to Crook. "But that don't matter. They run together with the Sioux, specially in the winter."

"Now, Frank," said Crook, "we must be sure. We want the Sioux, none other."

"Nothing's ever a hundred per cent sure with Injuns, General," growled the famed guide. "Excepting that you can't trust none of them."

"How far behind then are we, Frank?"

"Closer than I thought, General. I found some campfires at yonder meeting of the trails. Some burning coals still smoking. I reckon your big village is just past them seven ridges due east there. That will put it in the loop of the river, under Sage Mesa. I know the place."

At this point Crook's two senior cavalry officers rode up—Colonel J. J. Reynolds and Captain Anson Mills. Mills was a good steady man, and careful with Indians, like Crook. Colonel Reynolds was neither steady nor a good hand with Indians. He frowned now, seeming very nervous. Captain Mills spoke with an easy, sure manner, however.

"What is it, Grouard?" he said. "The bunch we're looking for?"

"Yes, sir, I reckon it is. I can't tell you for certain sure, until I see their horse herd. I'll know the ponies of the Oglala of Crazy Horse's bunch, even in the dark."

"The dark?" asked Reynolds quickly. "You're not thinking of going after them yet today!"

"Depends on the General," shrugged the half-breed. "I can take you to that village yet tonight, providing you got the sand to follow along." Grouard did not like Reynolds. He thought the colonel lacked the essential quality of any fighting man—a stout heart. But Reynolds ignored the scout's scowling remark, turning instead to Crook.

The latter was still fingering his famous red whiskers. An Indian fighter who had faced all the major tribes in battle, from the bloodthirsty Apache of the Arizona desert to the Comanche of the Texas plain to the wild-riding Sioux of the northlands, he was thinking of his position there in that dark valley with night coming on so swiftly.

"Hmmm," said Crook to himself.

He looked up at the sky, sniffed the cold wind.

"Well now," he said, "I don't see any sense of sending all these weary infantry troops after such a relatively small band of hostiles as these would appear to be. I believe that I smell snow in that quickening wind, too. With a dark night, a rough and dangerous trail, the weather threatening to get worse—hmmmmm."

He paused, and Colonel Reynolds leaped eagerly into the "opportunity."

"I think you're absolutely correct, General!" he said. "We'll camp here and see what is to be seen in the morning, eh, sir?"

Crook cocked his head, bright small eyes gleaming.

"Why, now, Colonel Reynolds, sir," he said in that famous meek-soft voice of his, "I scarcely think that is what I had in mind, at all. I believe what I was going to suggest was that you take the cavalry troops of Mills, Egan and Moore, and go ahead and find that village for us—tonight. I will camp here with the rest of the troops."

Before Reynolds could catch his breath, Crook's voice changed. His words commenced to sing and hop.

Frank Grouard would go with Reynolds and guide him to the village, he ordered. The scout would make certain it was the camp of Crazy Horse's Oglala before any attack. If it was Crazy Horse, Reynolds was to wipe the village out, showing no mercy. But if it were some other Indians, they were not to be touched on penalty of courts-martial.

Getting Crazy Horse was the great thing.

Break him, and the back of the Sioux rebellion would be broken with him. Sitting Bull was not a war chief. He could not continue his resistance without Crazy Horse.

So spoke General George Crook at sundown of the 16th of March, 1876.

Colonel Reynolds only saluted and said nothing.

An hour after sun's last brief light had gone, with the rest of the mule-soldier camp snug and its fires banked for the night, the attack column moved out. Grouard went ahead of the chosen Pony Soldier troops, showing the way. The snow was coming in wind blasts that stung like shotgun pellets. The cold grew deeper with each numbing hour that the men marched eastward toward the Powder. But The Grabber never faltered, never slowed. All through that night the troops stumbled and cursed their way. But with daylight still not yet showing in the east, the half-breed foster-son of Sitting Bull had found the camp of the Indians for them. And more. He had shadowed up to within calling distance of the drowsing village and seen the horse herd. He had *seen* Oglala horses that he knew. This would be the camp of Crazy Horse. Grouard *knew* those ponies, *dead sure!*

Nor was even that all of the good discoveries.

While lying near the pony herd, the scout had heard an old news-crier walking through the village streets and assuring the camp in his rusty-creaking voice that "all was well." The crier had gone on to announce that the scouts which He Dog had ordered to go out and look for the mule-soldiers which the young Oglala, Little Killer, had reported to be coming from Tongue River, those scouts had returned only now. They brought fine news. They had gone a long way toward the Tongue and seen no mule-soldiers whatever. Neither had they read in the snow any sign of Pony Soldiers, or any other soldiers. Little Killer was a very young man. He could be excused for his mistake.

"*Waste, waste*," the old man had cried. "Go back to sleep, everybody. All is good in the night. *Waste* . . ."

Grouard knew what had happened.

The lazy scouts had not gone "far" toward the Tongue. They had gone only a little way. Had they gone only a rifleshot farther than they did, they must have discovered The Grabber's own tracks, and then, of course, those of the cavalry troops following so closely behind him.

But now the way was clear.

All Colonel Reynolds had to do was tell Egan and Mills and Moore to "Sic 'em!" and the village of Crazy Horse would be done for.

"It will be a beef shoot, Colonel," the half-breed said.

Reynolds knew what a beef shoot was. It was when beef cattle were issued alive to the Indians on the reservations at Standing Rock or Pine Ridge. The cattle were put in a pen where they could not get away, and the Indians would sit on the fence and shoot the poor brutes down with their rifles.

The Colonel shivered and was very much afraid.

But he could not turn back now.

"Captain Egan," he ordered, "mount the attack."

Egan sent Moore's troops to the north of the camp to block the Cheyenne from getting into the rocky hills. He and Mills went in from the south, his troops first, those of Mills to follow in reserve, in the drive to catch the Cheyenne between the jaws of another *wickmunke*, another Pony Soldier trap.

Egan's men charged bravely enough.

They were actually into the camp before an old woman, out gathering sticks for the morning fire, saw the dreaded figures looming through the ice-fog which blanketed the campsite.

Her hoarse cries brought braves, squaws, old ones, children tumbling from their warm sleeping robes in the manner of sowbugs from beneath overturned buffalo chips.

They all ran from the lodges in terror.

At that precise moment, a wind lifted the fog from the bend of the river. The Indians saw the hills all about them alive with the Pony Soldiers of Three Stars.

Yet He Dog, the Oglala visitor, and Two Moons, the Cheyenne village chief, were fighters. Rallying behind the young Oglala warrior, Little Killer, who had seized his loaded Winchester and ran into the streets naked but for his loincloth, they began to fight. Little Killer had shot six soldiers in the space of ten breaths. Egan's troops hesitated. Other Cheyenne were racing up now. The firing became furious at this spot. Frank Grouard, the hated Grabber, was among the first to go down, shot twice-through. The soldiers had not expected such ferocious and instant resistance by Indians who were sleeping in a peaceful camp. They commenced to waver, and soon came to a stop, half in and half out of the village.

"*Hunhe!*" shouted Little Killer. "They are afraid. Quick! Someone must go and get the women and children into the rocks. We have a chance now. See! Up there on the mesa! The other soldiers have lost their hearts. They are just standing up there, instead of attacking like these soldiers."

It was true. Young Lieutenant Moore was still up on the sagebrush flat of the mesa. He had not gotten into the rocks as ordered. He seemed to be afraid, and the Indians sensed it.

"I will get the people together, ready to rush for the rocks up there," yelled He Dog. "You hold back these soldiers down here!"

The Cheyenne redoubled their firing at Egan's troops, while the Oglala chief dashed to the rear. The soldiers began to retreat, then they stood hard and fast. But the time had been enough. He Dog was back now, and yelling that he had all the people ready to go for the hills and get into the rocks. There was a moment's argument about leaving the pony herd, the dearest possession of any plains Indian band. But Two Moons called out that no pony could travel fast through such deep snow. He said He Dog was right. They must run on foot.

"*Hopo! Hookahey!* Come on, follow me!" shouted He Dog.

The rush by the entire Cheyenne village to reach the momentary safety of the rocky hillside now followed.

Too late, the troops of Anson Mills came up in support of Egan's stalled command. Too late, young Lieutenant Moore tried getting into the rocks ahead of the leaping, bounding warriors of the Cheyenne. In the years to come, stories were to be whispered about the army posts of the West that the youthful Pony Soldier was a coward. That in all of the flight of the Cheyenne up that hillside, he and his soldiers did not fire one shot. But the truth was not in that story. The Cheyenne saw what it was that Lieutenant Moore really did, and they honored him for it forever afterward.

As the Indians came upward, their poor women struggling and falling with the papooses on their backs and in their arms, with other children crying out for lost parents but still pausing to help the old people who could not keep up, Moore shouted to his sergeants to pull the troops away and hold their fire. His men formed a funnel through which the entire village fled to the safety of the higher rocks. Lieutenant Moore not only did not fire a shot to stop those Indians, he actually sheltered them from gunfire from below. And, as the red men went by his position, the warriors all touched their brows toward him and called out "*Naonoatamo! Naonoatomo!* We respect you! We honor you!" Moore knew not a word of Cheyenne, but he understood the grateful cries as clearly as if they had been shouted in English. He raised his fringed cavalry gauntlet and saluted the escaping red men, and that is the way they remembered him in their legends.

Lieutenant Moore did not stand aside in fear that terrible morning above Powder River. It was not cowardice that guided his heart. It was the love of one man for his brothers.

16.   WHAT THE WHITE MAN PAID FOR
POWDER RIVER

As had Custer on the Washita, so now Reynolds on the Powder made a bonfire of all the Cheyenne lodges and blankets and food supplies. The red stain lighted the still leaden skies for miles. While the fires were yet leaping and the Cheyenne watched from the hillside, even again like the southern cousins eight snows before, the soldiers took the pony herd and retreated back toward Three Stars and the main force of mule-mounted infantry.

But Little Killer took some reckless young men of Two Moons' people, and went after the ponies. They sneaked in close and cut the wild Indian horses away from the soldiers, driving many of them back to the smoldering village.

Here the people mounted them and the Indian retreat started across the frozen hills, away from the place of the fight which they afterward called "Bloody Snow Bend."

Again it was Little Killer, the Oglala, who showed them the way. Little Killer and the older chief, He Dog.

"Follow us," they told the grieving Cheyenne. "We will lead you to the safe warm lodges of our people. The Sioux will help their Cheyenne brothers. Come on. Sitting Bull has a fine camp along Beaver Creek, over beneath the Blue Mountains. He will give food and fire to you. *Hopo*——!"

So they set off bravely through the bitter cold. More snow whipped down at them from the higher ranges. The temperatures plummeted below zero. Several of

the old people made their last ride that day, and in that
night which followed four small children also died of the
cold. But Little Killer and He Dog said they must keep
on. It was a far ride to the Blue Mountains. And who
knew if Three Stars would come behind them to avenge
the bad fight his soldiers had made?

But no soldiers came after them, and, with that second
nightfall after the shame of Bloody Bend, the people of
Two Moons topped the last ridge and saw before them
the winking of the guide-fires which the Sioux had
lighted to bring them in out of the bleak and stormy
night.

The Cheyenne survivors of the Black Night march
were given everything by the Sioux of Sitting Bull.

The hearts of the Hunkpapa were made to cry, they
said, at what the soldiers had done to their Cheyenne
cousins.

When his people were all being fed and had been
wrapped in warm blankets and were resting by the
Hunkpapa fires, Two Moons went with He Dog and with
Little Killer to see the chief of the Sioux who had saved
his village.

Sitting Bull said that what the Sioux had done was all
that one red man would do for another, nothing more.
But Two Moons shook his head. He told the Hunkpapa
chief that now his eyes were opened at last. Now he saw
that it was but a foolish dream to pray for peace with the
white man. The white man did not want peace. He sent
his soldiers to kill women and children in the dead of
winter—women and children of a tribe which had
promised to obey the Grandfather's order, and to come
in to the reservations.

Now let the white man know that the Cheyenne were
at peace no more. Let the Sioux brother know, too, that
from this fire, the people of Two Moons would fight by
the side of the Hunkpapa and the Oglala, until the end.

Sitting Bull thanked his Cheyenne brothers.

But he reminded them that there was still great
danger from the soldiers of Three Stars. He, Sitting

Bull, must move his camp as soon as the Cheyenne were warmed and revived. They would all go over and camp with Crazy Horse on Tongue River. As they went, scouts would ride out to all the winter camps of all the Sioux bands, calling their leaders to come to the camp of Tashunka Witko and meet there with Tatanka Yotanka, the vision-dreamer.

Two Moons agreed, saying his people would be ready.

Next day they marched, coming without incident to the Tongue and to the site of that great winter war camp where so much of Indian fate was to be forecast.

Present at the council, which sat three days later, were the Sioux White Crow, Gall, Two-Bull-Bear, White Bull, Grey Eagle, Old Bull, Elk Nation, American Horse, Yellow Bull, Black Moccasin, Paints Brown and Iron-Road-Walking.

For the Cheyenne, there were Bob-Tail-Horse, Hump, Comes-in-Sight, High-Back-Wolf, Yellow Nose and Half-a-Horse.

In the center of the circle, alone by the council fire, sat the vision-dreamer who had called them there.

The chiefs watched him as they waited.

Sitting Bull was a short, powerfully broad man. He had a very large head. His face was without much expression, wide of forehead and wide between the eyes. His eye-color was oddly gray, not black or brown like that of most Indians. Also the eyes were levelly set, not slanted or slitted in the usual Sioux manner. His hair was showing the silvered-snows of his considerable number of winters. Seeing him thus, none but a red man could have guessed at his enormous influence and power among his people.

And now he arose to speak.

What he said was brief, but all the chiefs remembered it.

"My brothers," he told them, "the whites are a great lake around us, and the Indians are an island in the lake's middle. We must stand together or they will wash us all away. These soldiers have come shooting. They want war. All right, we will give it to them."

Then it was the turn of Tashunka Witko, of Crazy Horse.

He, too made a picture never to be forgotten.

And he, too, kept his talk short.

"My chiefs," he said, "our uncle, Tatanka, has put the tongue to the words of angered sadness crying in the hearts of us all. A war will come now, and I will lead you in it."

The council then departed after one final instruction from the quiet-faced Sitting Bull.

It was an instruction which cost many a white man his hair. Shot away many a soldier's life. Lost many an innocent white settler his wagons, his horses, his milch cows, even his wife and his children, in the terrible months to come. It was an instruction which smashed Three Stars Crook and his thousand-man mule-soldier column completely to a halt, disorganized, beaten, afraid to move again. It was an instruction, finally, which was to run red with the blood of the Seventh Cavalry the sunlit buffalo grass of that "other river" which waited for Yellow Hair Custer and his gallant men.

"Swift riders will go at once to every hunting band of Indians yet free upon the prairies," said Sitting Bull. "At the same time, riders will go to every agency of the Sioux, Cheyenne and Arapaho to the sunward of the Big Muddy River. The riders will whip their ponies hard. When the ponies stagger at last into the prairie camps and the agency villages, the riders will leap from their backs and will rip open the entry-flags of each chief's tipi, speaking to him these words of Tatanka Yotanka:

"*'It is war. Come to the camp of Sitting Bull which then will be at the big bend of the Rosebud River. Let us all get together and have one more big fight with the soldiers!'*"

"*Hun-hun-he!*" roared the chiefs, deep voices bounding from the buffalo skins of the council lodge. "Let us die as proud men, as free men, as *Indians*——!"

Thus was named the true price of Reynolds' cowardly raid upon Two Moons' sleeping camp.

That price was not the destruction of the Cheyenne lodges and the death from cold of a few old people and little children at Powder River a few days before.

That price was the death of two hundred twenty-six helpless officers and men three months later.

For the name of that waiting "other" river was not the Rosebud or the Powder or the Tongue.

It was the Little Big Horn.

PART FOUR

THE ROSEBUD

17.   GENERAL GRANT SURRENDERS

All of this while, Custer had been back in the nation's capital fighting for his political and military life.

Not only had President Grant refused to let him return to his command, he also had issued direct orders to General Alfred Terry that Custer must not be permitted, *under any circumstance*, to even go with the troops of the Seventh Cavalry when that spring's great column of soldiers should march from Fort Abraham Lincoln.

It was no secret now, except to the unsuspecting red man, that a great expedition was to be launched against the hostile Indians as soon as the snow was gone and the prairies were open to travel by land and river.

General Crook had failed badly in his single-handed attempt to crush the Sioux. He had done worse than fail; in the order which sent Reynolds against the village of Two Moons, Crook had been responsible for getting the Cheyenne into the war on the side of the Sioux.

General Terry, an old rival of Crook's, saw in Crook's bad luck a rare chance to build his own reputation as an Indian fighter. There was only one flaw in the opportunity: General Terry was *not* an Indian fighter.

However, Terry knew where such a fighter was to be found.

The place was right in his own command at Fort Abraham Lincoln. The man was one who had chased more Indians—yes, and caught more of them—than any other cavalryman on the plains. And this did not exclude the famous red-bearded Crook, General Nelson A. "Bearcoat" Miles, Captain Anson Mills or any of the army's skilled western officers. The only problem was to convince President Grant that he, Terry, must have this particular "Indian hunter" by his side, if he were to do better against the Sioux than had Three Stars Crook.

Toward this end, two fateful letters were written in early May. By this time, President Grant had relented enough to permit Custer to return to his post. Indeed, the reckless commander of the Seventh Cavalry had proceeded there *without* permission, when Grant refused to see him personally in Washington. But the first week of May had begun with no word that Yellow Hair would be forgiven. And the latter knew that the time was already growing much too late for the troops to be setting forth against the Sioux. The ponies of the Indians would be too strong and fat, the Indians themselves too full-fed from the spring buffalo hunts, to make for an easy victory over them. So the two letters rolled eastward along the rails of the Iron Horse bearing seals and signatures warning of their vital nature.

The President was handed the communications from the West by special courier, and his bulldog jaw clamped down hard upon the ever-present cigar.

This is what he read:

HEADQUARTERS DEPARTMENT OF DAKOTA
SAINT PAUL, MINN., MAY 6TH, 1876
ADJUTANT GENERAL,
DIVISION OF MISSOURI, CHICAGO.
(*I forward the following: To
his Excellency the President
through military channels*):

I have seen your order, transmitted through the General of the Army, directing that I be not permitted to accompany the expedition about to move against the hostile Indians. As my regiment forms a part of the proposed expedition and as I am the senior officer of the regiment on duty in this department, I respectfully but most earnestly request that while not permitted to go in command of the expedition, I may be allowed to serve with my regiment in the field.

I appeal to you as a soldier to spare me the humiliation of seeing my regiment march to meet the enemy, and I not to share its dangers.

> (signed)
> G. A. CUSTER
> BVT. MAJ. GENL. U.S. ARMY

The second letter was only a brief note in support of the first. But it was eloquent and Grant understood this fact.

Sir:

In forwarding the above, I wish to say expressly that I have no desire whatever to question the orders of the President or of my military superiors. Whether Lieut. Col. Custer shall be permitted to accompany my column or not, I shall go in command of it. I do not know the reasons upon which the orders already given rest; but if those reasons do not forbid it, Lieut. Col. Custer's services would be very valuable with his command.

> (signed)
> TERRY
> COMMAND DEPARTMENT

When he had finished reading, Grant's cigar had gone cold.

His troubles were many in those latter days, and he was weary of them. He knew by this time that Belknap, his Secretary of War, was in a grave situation. He knew, too, that what Custer had said of corruption in the War Department was undoubtedly true. Himself as honest and courageous as any man alive, Ulysses Simpson Grant knew also when to admit a wrong, and when he must redress it.

General Terry wanted Custer.

Grant did not trust Custer, nor did he believe him to be a sufficiently good and careful commander for the moment's grave assignment—he had not changed his mind in that.

But he was too big a man, and too just, to think that he might unfairly damage a fellow soldier's reputation for reasons of personal dislike, or professional pettiness.

"Mr. Secretary," he sighed to the slender man hovering at his elbow, waiting for his reply, "you may telegraph General Terry and tell him Grant surrenders . . ."

"Custer's Luck" again!

In the face of all odds, Yellow Hair had regained command of the Seventh Cavalry. He would go with Terry toward the Rosebud, even as Crazy Horse would go with Sitting Bull.

The trumpets of the Pony Soldiers would blow in the same spring wind with the beating of the Sioux war drums.

Where would the two sounds meet?

And when?

18.   THE GIRL HE LEFT BEHIND HIM

The seventeenth of May, 1876, was a day as fine as springtime brings to the great plains country. The weather was clear, warm, heady with the smells of prairie flowers. The gates of Fort Abraham Lincoln were lined with cheering wives and children of the proud troops marching away to punish the hostile Sioux and Cheyenne. The regimental band of the Seventh Cavalry was playing "The Girl I Left Behind Me," and the officers' ladies on the verandas of their barracks homes waved linen kerchiefs and cried out farewells as confident as those of the enlisted men's womenfolk.

Of course the General's wife, the spoiled Libbie Custer, had to ride with the column that first day. She was a person, then and later, who never saw anything in her "Autie" but a knight-errant of purest snow-white purpose.

As for Custer, he treated his wife like a small child, embarrassing his staff constantly. But then he was "the General." Terry himself had begged the President to let him go along. This was G. A. Custer's hour of vindication, of triumph. If he indulged himself a bit during it, with such complete nonsense as having his doting bride tag along for a few miles, who might deny him the privilege?

Certainly not somber Major Marcus Reno, or competent Captain Frederick Benteen, who rode behind the Boy General and his "darling girl," sharing looks of disgust and, indeed, professional uneasiness.

It seemed to them, and to some other grown-up

84

officers of the Seventh Cavalry, that regimental bands and perennial child brides had little place in a column charged by the President of the United States with settling for all time the Sioux and Cheyenne troubles of the Far West.

But it was still Custer's hour, and he commanded it.

The camp that night, the first west of Bismarck and the post, was gay with the sound of music and laughter and of the troopers complaining with loud good humor of Custer having gotten them too far away to spend their money, before paying them. It was true, too. The General had had the army pay-wagon follow the column out across the plains, so that the men could not get drunk when given their pay.

The Boy General was not going to let anything interfere with his appointment with destiny.

It was whispered by his enemies—of which he had some even in his own regiment—that "Armstrong's" ambitions knew absolutely no bounds. He aspired, some swore darkly, to no less an eventual promotion than the Presidency.

It was even said that he thought to make of the present campaign, the stepping stone to that high place.

But if he had those who were not to be captured by his great charms, he had also the others who swore as strongly by him as his critics did at him.

Among these were Captain Calhoun, Tom Custer, Captain Keogh, Captain Weir, Captain Moylan and, of course, Custer's scouts, the faithful Arikara Bloody Knife and the white man Lonesome Charley Reynolds.

Next morning, darling Libbie and the pay-wagon turned back to Fort Abraham Lincoln. Custer and the Seventh Cavalry marched on, into a sunset from which they were never to return.

Libbie Custer may have been the last white woman to see those gallant soldiers.

Certainly, she was the last to wave them farewell.

19. FORWARD, HO! THE SEVENTH CAVALRY

General Terry's column from the Dakotas marched westward day after day. The line of his soldiers, led always by Custer and his Arikara, or "Ree," Indian scouts, and his Crow Indian scouts, stretched for over two miles.

Twelve troops of the Seventh Cavalry rode first. Then came three companies of infantry, a platoon of Gatling guns, and the wagon train. There were one thousand uniformed fighting men in that long and dusty line!

But no time was lost.

Four other journeys had Custer made over these same plains. He knew every prairie-dog hole and buffalo wallow from the Big Muddy to the Yellowstone. He knew the hostile Indians to be near the south shores of the Yellowstone, somewhere between the Little Missouri and the Big Horn. And he knew that, wherever they were, this time they would not escape.

The reason was that two other long columns of blue-clad troops were closing in upon the Yellowstone at the same time as the soldiers of Terry and Yellow Hair.

From the north, from Fort Ellis and Shaw, General John Gibbon, called "Red Nose" by the Sioux, was marching swiftly with four hundred hardened veterans.

From the south, Crook, recovered from his bad scare over jumping the Cheyenne of Two Moons by mistake, was striking once more upward from Wyoming. Three Stars had nearly eleven hundred men, and he was smarting from his blunder on Powder River. He was

looking for those Indians with "blood in his eye," and he
intended to find them. He had left all of his wagons
behind. His foot-soldiers were mounted on tough army
mules, moving almost as fast as his cavalrymen up into
the Indian country, skirting the Wolf Mountains, driving by forced march for the headwaters of the Rosebud,
and the Valley of the Yellowstone into which those
waters led.

The troops were now some three hundred miles apart.

But, as they were all marching toward the same point,
and toward each other, the distance diminished and the
soldier trap closed about the Indians with secret speed.

Or so the commanders believed.

On the 3rd of June, a party of scouts from Gibbon
found Custer's forward troops. Gibbon had reached the
mouth of the Rosebud eleven days before. There had
been no sign of Crook at the rendezvous. The big hostile
camps were moving around now. Some were on the
Powder, some on the Rosebud, some on the Tongue.
Especially on the Rosebud. But there were no Indians
whatever along the Yellowstone. General Gibbon would
respectfully wait for General Terry. But it was getting
very lonesome up there. Would General Terry please
hurry?

This news greatly excited Custer.

Suppose Gibbon or Crook should find those Indians
before the Seventh Cavalry got on the scene?

They had plenty of men between them to tackle any
number of plains Indians. Why, Crook alone, with his
cavalry and mule-mounted infantry, could whip all the
Indians in Montana and Wyoming put together! This was
a very serious thing.

The Seventh must not be late!

But genial, kindly General Alfred Terry was as com-
placent and unhurried as Custer was anxious and excited.

"Be easy, Armstrong," he advised. "We will get
there."

But in his mind General Terry was not so certain, nor

so satisfied. He had seen the sudden nervousness of
Custer at the news from Gibbon, and espcially at the
word that Crook was "on the loose somewhere and
unreported." Had Terry been wrong after all in forcing
President Grant to release Custer against his will? Was
this likable and charming young cavalry genius a reckless
and unreliable commander, as blunt old Grant feared?
Terry would have to watch him closely.

Watch him he did, nor was he reassured.

Two weeks of cautious marching followed, during
which Custer boldly disobeyed orders to make a scout on
his own forty-five miles up the Little Missouri with four
companies of the Seventh Cavalry. For such action, salty
old General Stanley had arrested him on the Yellowstone expedition of '73. But patient, fatherly Terry told
no one of his worries over the "irrepressible Armstrong,"
except his diary, and that was not read until years later.

But Terry did recall Custer from the front of the
column. First news the General had of this was when,
upon striking Powder River, the scout duty ahead was
given to Major Marcus Reno. Reno's orders read for him
to scout up the Powder, cross over to the Tongue, follow
that stream back down to the Yellowstone. But steady
Reno disobeyed his orders, too! Yet he had reason,
where Custer had none. Reno's scout party had struck
the broad trail of a big band of hostiles—at least three
hundred lodges, said Lonesome Charley Reynolds, who
was with Reno—and the trail was so fresh that some of
the pony droppings in its dusty track were still warm!

Now all knew that the big camps of the red men were
near.

They even knew, now, where the very biggest of
those camps must be.

Reno and Reynolds had followed that hot, three
hundred lodge trail far enough to see where it led. *Or
seemed to lead*.

It was beyond the Powder, beyond the Tongue,
leap-frogging the smaller Rosebud.

West it lay.

Due west, and straightaway, *toward the Big Horn!*

Terry now abandoned caution. He ordered the troops forward with all speed to hook up with Gibbon on the Yellowstone at the mouth of the Rosebud. It was June 17th when the Fort Abraham Lincoln column sighted the cross-stream camp of Red Nose Gibbon's Montana men. They were excited also to see, lying in the Yellowstone, off the southern bank—their side of the stream—the famed riverboat, the *Far West*. All flagging spirits of the long march from North Dakota now revived. Sore feet could no longer be felt. Aching seats no longer ached. Hoarse voices rang with cheers up and down the long line of the Seventh Cavalry, and Custer called up the regimental trumpeters to blow "Garry Owen," the battle hymn of the Seventh, as the sun-burned riders charged down into the valley to greet their brothers from far Montana.

But the good feelings took a little chill upon arrival of Gibbon from across the Yellowstone.

Crook was *still* unreported.

And the Yellowstone was still strangely bare of Indians.

Where was old Red Beard, old Three Stars?

And where were Sitting Bull and Crazy Horse and all those hundreds of hostiles supposed to be gathering in this country and swarming the hills of the tributaries of the Yellowstone?

Something was very wrong here.

Custer, of course, would have no part of such stuff and nonsense. What the devil did everyone expect of those Indians, those far-riding red sons of the plains and prairies? That they would have a welcoming committee down there at the mouth of the Rosebud waiting for the soldiers? Standing happily around at the anchorage of the *Far West* singing prayer songs and chanting good medicine poems for the white brother?

How ridiculous!

Those Indians would have to be hunted up. And right away, too. Even now they might be escaping to the west or south. After all, they had shattered Crook once before, and only three months and not very many miles from this same spot, too!

Somebody had to go after those Indians.

"General, sir!" Custer pleaded with gentle Terry. "Let me go ahead! We cannot lie here waiting for Crook to make his position known. We must at least *find* the Indians, sir, before they find us. Once they get the wind of us, General, then we will never see them again. Tonight. We can go in two hours!"

This was on the day of arrival, the 17th.

For three interminable days Terry hesitated. Then, upon the 21st, a signal from the steamer *Far West* announced that "General Custer is wanted aboard."

Custer knew that Gibbon and Terry had been on the steamer arguing strategy the entire day.

What did they now want of him?

He was rowed out into the stream and put over the low rail of the riverboat. A trooper showed him smartly to the Captain's quarters, where Terry and Gibbon were waiting.

Terry spoke in his patient reticent way.

The two commanders had spent the day going over all scout reports current to that hour and poring over the military maps of the Yellowstone, with the result that the whereabouts of the main Indian camps had been narrowed to two locations.

They were either directly above on the Rosebud itself, or they were over along the Big Horn, or its branch, locally called the "Little Horn."

As to the best estimate of strength of the combined Cheyenne and Sioux forces presently in the country, the scouts believed it could not exceed by far one thousand warriors.

At this point Custer's pale blue eyes flashed.

"Begging your pardon, General," he interrupted. "My two best men—the Ree, Bloody Knife, and Charley Reynolds, my chief white scout—have given me a slightly different count. They say no less than fifteen hundred fighting braves!"

Gibbon shrugged.

"In any event, General," he said to Custer, "there are not so many that a regiment of cavalry cannot handle them."

Again the pale eyes gleamed.

"That, sir, is correct!" snapped Custer. "*If* you are speaking of the Seventh Cavalry Regiment!"

Terry smiled and nodded. This fellow Custer had to be admired. Whatever doubts he may have given a man on the outward march from Fort Abraham Lincoln, to see him now, the light of battle in his thin face, the devotion to duty burning in those unforgettable blue eyes, ah! there was a cavalryman to ride with! No wonder the Indians feared him. No wonder the other officers in the army envied him. Here was a man to reckon with, and to remember.

"Well, General," the white-haired officer said softly to Custer. "I am pleased that you feel as you do. For General Gibbon and I have a little detail for the Seventh Cavalry, and I believe that you will find it to your liking, as well as suited to your particular experience."

He paused, enjoying Custer's visible high excitement.

"I am going to have General Gibbon use the *Far West* to ferry his men over to this side of the stream. They will then march up to the Big Horn, turning up that stream, south. The steamer will accompany them as far as it may find navigable water. I myself am too old for this sort of walking and will command from the *Far West*. Is that clear?"

Custer slapped the map-table with his folded gauntlets. His high voice rose higher still.

"Yes, yes, of course it is!" he cried. "But what of the Seventh? What of *me*?"

"Oh," said Terry, enjoying his small joke, "yes, you."

Again he paused, then waved his hand as if ordering a mere changing of the guard, or a barracks inspection.

"You, General," he said, "will take the Seventh Cavalry and go after those Indians whose trail Major Reno found upon the Rosebud. You will have your written orders in the morning. Good night, sir. Have a good sleep."

20.   THE RETURN OF
RAIN-IN-THE-FACE

Around the clock the hostile war camp at the Big Bend of the Rosebud seethed with activity.

Arrivals and departures were endless.

Warriors left for the trading posts and the agencies to barter for guns and ammunition. Others went to the peaceful tribes of west and south to trade for fresh war ponies. Riders traveled to all points of the Indian compass carrying the vision-words of Sitting Bull: *"It is war; come to the Rosebud."*

Old men started from the camp with empty pack trains, returned with ponies staggering under loads of dried buffalo beef, robes and blankets, new moccasins, harness, bullhide for war shields. Squaws trailed away with empty travois behind their pack horses, appeared again with the animals pulling bulging travois of agency-issued goods: flour, salt, sugar, army blankets, cooking pots, steel knives, axes.

And always the new bands of warriors kept coming, and coming, and coming.

The arrival of one such group of men answering the call of the Hunkpapa vision-dreamer was of singular importance. It impressed the people with the power of Sitting Bull's medicine. *Look!* they said. *See what he can do!*

The newcomers were a small band of Oglala, and they were agency Indians. There were no women or children with them. They were all young men, all heavily armed. In their lead rode a young giant of a Sioux, revealing in his carriage the bearing of a hereditary chief, and also something strikingly familiar in the lines of his handsome face.

As he brought his warriors into the great camp, he was recognized by an old Indian, also from the agencies.

"Jack Red Cloud!" cried the old fellow, and rushed to the tipi of Sitting Bull with the news. "Come out, Uncle, come out!" he cried to the medicine man. "See who your magic has brought to fight with us against the white man!"

Sitting Bull, who was within counciling with Crazy Horse, came to the door of his lodge. Behind him, Crazy Horse peered out to see the cause of the commotion. The young Oglala warrior rode up and saluted the two great men with respect.

"*Woyuonihan!*" he said.

They accepted his greeting, and Sitting Bull said quickly, "Where is your father? Has he sent you to us?"

The young brave shook his head.

"The old man has been to Washington and measured the big guns there with his eagle-feather fan," he said. "He warns we can win no victory against the whites. He advises our people to stay on the reservation. To cover their ears and not listen to the calls of my uncle Tatanka Yotanka. But I would not obey him. I am here. I am ready to fight."

So came the son of the great Red Cloud to join with the people his father seemed to have forgotten.

There was one other arrival, too, in that swarming camp, whose cause and case were of peculiar importance to the hold of Sitting Bull upon the gathering army.

This latter man came on the same day as Jack Red Cloud. Almost, in fact, he followed upon the heels of the magnificent young warrior. But this other one was no younger fighting man, no son of a great man. He was a great man himself, and he had an amazing and fateful story to tell.

Many moons ago, in the first of the new year—no, it was the old year, last year—this man had been seized by Custer's troopers when at peace in the agency store at

Standing Rock. The troopers had come in the night, guided by Lonesome Charley Reynolds, commanded by Yellow Hair's brother, Tom Custer. They had taken the man back to Fort Abraham Lincoln and imprisoned him there on the charge of having been the leader of the Sioux who killed Custer's veterinary officer and the sutler Balarian in the Yellowstone defeats of Custer in '73.

All these moons the man had suffered in that soldier jail, and only a few suns ago had he managed at last to escape. What? What was that? Had he actually been the chief who commanded those Sioux who whipped Yellow Hair on the Yellowstone? Had he actually killed Dr. Holzinger and Balarian, as Custer said? Was he guilty?

Guilty! *Ha! Iho!* Of course he was guilty!

But that was not what had made him angry. It was the fact that Yellow Hair had lied about the matter. He hadn't arrested him because of those killings. He had done it because of his shame and anger at being twice beaten on the Yellowstone by the Sioux under this same man. Yellow Hair had a small mind. He was not the great fighter that the Sioux believed him to be. This man, himself, had easily whipped him. Two times over! That was the message he now brought to all his Sioux and Cheyenne brothers—that Sitting Bull was right in his great vision—that the Indians would win a tremendous victory over the Pony Soldiers. This man *knew* that.

He also knew something else.

Something he had learned because he had been in prison right there in Yellow Hair's fort all the time Yellow Hair was getting his troops ready to march west. He knew all about how many troops there were, how good the men were, how many were old soldiers and how many green new boys—he knew everything about Yellow Hair's army. Including the most important thing of all. *He knew where that army was right now,* and he could take a big scout party to it at once, so that the plans of Sitting Bull and Crazy Horse might be made to set a *wickmunke* for those devils of the Seventh Cavalry that they would never forget!

So went the story, and so came to the war camp on the Rosebud the only Indian who had ever beaten Yellow Hair Custer in fair and open fighting: it was Rain-in-the-Face!

His story set the camp afire with new flames of bravery.

Any hesitation which had been slowing the minds or weakening the hearts of the people was now vanished.

The big scout party suggested and led by Rain-in-the-Face was sent out the following day. From the moment of its dispatch and subsequent finding of Terry's and Gibbon's armies approaching their rendezvous at the mouth of the Rosebud, no movement of Custer and his men was without the knowledge of Sitting Bull and the Sioux War Council.

This was something never understood in the white man's stories of the great fight.

And it was something that made the Indian medicine strong as the blood of the bull buffalo.

But it was well that this was so, for within the week of Rain-in-the-Face and Jack Red Cloud's having found the hostile war camp on the Big Bend of the Rosebud, the Sioux had need for strong blood. If they had discovered the approach of Yellow Hair without his knowledge, someone else had discovered the approach to their war camp without *their* knowledge.

It was upon the bright and sunshiny morning of May 16th that the Indians found this out.

That was the morning upon which a small band of scouts—Elk Nation, Little Wolf, White Bull, Yellow Nose—came racing down the Rosebud from upstream —*the opposite direction* from which the Sioux had been watching the approach of Yellow Hair and Red Nose Gibbon.

These scouts were wildly excited.

Three Stars Crook was coming from the south! He was less than one pony ride away! *Hopo, hookahey* ——!

Tashunka Witko, Crazy Horse, the great strange man of the Oglala, at once asked for more information. He knew how his own people were. Always exaggerating. Always making a big story out of a little one. Like small children.

"You," he said to White Bull, "you tell me. You are of the blood of Sitting Bull. You would not lie to me."

White Bull replied that he and his three companions did not lie to anyone. Three Stars was just over the hill, just up the river. Why would he be there but to fight?

"Yes," said Crazy Horse, "but we have easily beaten him one time already. We and the Cheyenne of Two Moons did it on Powder River *without* any warning. Why, then, are you all so excited now? That is my question."

White Bull drew himself up to stand tall and proud.

"You have a good question, my chief," he said. "And I will give you a good answer for it. Yes, the Cheyenne, with old He Dog's help, did rally and beat back the mule-soldiers that other time. But that was different. This time Three Stars comes riding with Indians helping him. In front of the mule-soldiers we saw over two hundred of the cursed Shoshone scouts, led by Washakie. *Now* do you say we are too excited? *Iho!*"

Crazy Horse apologized. This was dark news indeed. It was the first the hostiles knew that the Grandfather in Washington had at last agreed to let the Pony Soldiers employ Indians to fight against Indians. For a long time the people who were the friends of the red man had succeeded in preventing this inhuman use of red brother against red brother. Now the great fighter understood that all of the days that followed would be different than Sitting Bull had said. When Indian fought Indian, the end could not be far off. But he would not say this to White Bull, or to any of the people. He *must* believe in the vision of Tatanka Yotanka, and so must the people.

"All right," he said to the four scouts, and to the warriors who were now rushing up from every part of the camp. "Let everyone get ready. I will lead the fight myself."

But his heart was not good within him when he said it.

Crazy Horse was seeing a vision of his own now.

It was a dark dream, and in it the bodies of the fallen which lay everywhere upon the ground were not the bodies of white soldiers.

They were the bodies of Indians.

And among those bodies Crazy Horse saw one that he knew better than any.

It was his own.

21. THE RETREAT TO GOOSE CREEK

The battle with Crook next morning on the Rosebud was a wild Indian fight from first to last.

It began with the four scouts who had discovered the return of the mule-soldier chief, given the honor of leading the charge. The Sioux and Cheyenne, by acting so swiftly to strike before they might be found, caught Crook entirely by surprise. The red-bearded general and his men were not ready to fight. They were, in fact, spread all over the little meadow in which they had camped for the night. Every soldier's mule and every officer's horse was unbridled and grazing. The men were lying about on the ground resting. Parts of the command were on both sides of the river. The Indians should have had a sweeping and terrible victory.

But they made the mistake of underestimating Crook.

The four scouts, peering over the hill in the forefront of the red attack, were excited.

"Look!" cried Yellow Nose. "Look down by the spring there. Old Three Stars is still braiding his whiskers!"

Sure enough, there was General Crook taking his ease by the side of a lovely little fount of water. He was carefully weaving his famed beard into two queues, tied with ribbons! This was to keep the whiskers from blowing in his face in the attack he was expecting to make on the Indians later in the day. He always did that before a fight, the Sioux understood. He even used the same mirror for good luck. This was a polished frying-pan bottom. It was being held up for him now by an enlisted man, so that he might see if he were ready to mount-up his mule-soldiers and lead them into battle.

"Yes," said Little Wolf. "And see also that he wears his canvas tent as usual, *iho!*"

This was the Sioux or Cheyenne description of the patched army fatigue uniform which this great general wore on his campaigns. Along with his braided red beard, it was his trademark, letting the Indians know that he had surely come to fight, not just ride through their country.

"The men have all eaten their breakfasts," commented Elk Nation pleasantly. "Isn't that a nice thing? You know that a man always dies more happily with a full stomach."

White Bull scowled. They were wasting too much time.

"*Hopo!* come on," he ordered. "Let's get back, or someone will start the charge without us."

But they were already too late.

Washakie's Shoshone scouts, out early in the dawn, had just returned to the halted column. In the process, they saw the four scouts turning their horses from the hilltop.

They charged the four hostiles, chasing them hard.

And when they rode over the top of the hill, there on the far side, they saw the thousand warriors of Crazy Horse waiting to pounce on Three Stars and the mule-soldiers.

The Shoshone hated the Sioux.

Instead of running back to the white soldiers, they instantly attacked the entire Indian army. The hostiles were disorganized by this charge of over two hundred fierce men of their own blood, armed with repeating Winchester rifles.

They became momentarily scattered and the Shoshone scouts were then able to retreat to the column and find that their brief bravery had given Three Stars time to get most of his command into the bluffs and protective rocks of the river.

From there, the hostiles tried in vain to dislodge

them. The fight raged for hours and until late in the day, when, at last, the weary soldiers began to draw back from the rocks. They were breaking and would be running in full retreat in another few minutes. It was then it happened.

Out of the hills on the far side of the river, behind the attacking Indians, a cavalry trumpet sounded high and clear. Amazed, the red horsemen whirled to see, splashing across the shallows of the Rosebud, Captain Anson Mills and eight troops of Pony Soldier cavalry. *Aihai!*

They had not yet realized that Mills and the horsemounted Pony Soldiers had separated from Crook. Now they discovered their carelessness too late. Mills had been dispatched to find their village while Crook and the mule-soldiers fought by the bright-watered spring. *That* was why they had so easily unbraided Red Beard's whiskers—not because old Three Stars was becoming soft in his brain.

Well, enough blood had flowed anyway. Old Three Stars had been hit very hard. He was in no condition to be helping Yellow Hair Custer and Red Nose Gibbon. The Indians could now turn their eyes on the *real* enemy, on Yellow Hair and the Seventh Cavalry. *Hopo! Hookahey!* Ride back to the village. Get ready for the big scalp dance tonight!

The Sioux and Cheyenne pulled away from their chase after the fleeing mule-soldiers of Crook. They knew Captain Anson Mills for a fierce and hard fighter, and those Pony Soldiers of his looked mean and angry. Away went the red warriors, shouting, yelping, crying their war cries and blowing their eerie chants on the eaglebone flutes which were the "bugles of the red cavalry."

The battle which was to become known as "Crook's Fight on the Rosebud" was over.

But its effects were only beginning.

When Sitting Bull heard of the outcome of the clash between Crazy Horse and Three Stars Crook, he forbade any great celebration. "This is not the fight of my vision!" he warned. "In that dream I saw hundreds of white soldiers all dropping suddenly dead in rows around my feet! Today you killed but a few, although wounding many. Listen, now, to me. The place for the great fight is not this river, not the Rosebud. I will lead you now to that other river!"

The warriors were disappointed, but they obeyed.

The medicine of the Hunkpapa vision-dreamer was too powerful to stand against. Moreover, Tashunka Witko, their great war chief, would hear of no argument against his uncle, Tatanka Yotanka. He believed Sitting Bull's vision, he said. All who were of the same heart must come with him, must go and move the camp to that other river. Right away!

When he spoke, not one warrior, or one squaw, not even one child or an old person, turned away.

"*Hun-hun-he! Hun-hun-he! Hun-hun-he!*" they cried as one.

And the great camp in the Big Bend of the Rosebud River was broken that same evening, and moved off through the black hours of the night even while Three Stars Crook was ordering his beaten and frightened mule-soldiers to retreat all the way south to Goose Creek, where they sat in fear for seven weeks—licking their wounds and lying to themselves about what had happened to them.

The only question that Crazy Horse ever made to Sitting Bull's order to move the war camp away from the Rosebud came when the great lines of pack horses and mounted people were streaming out of the Big Bend, not yet knowing their destination.

"My Uncle," said the war chief, pulling his pony in beside that of the medicine man, "where is that other river that you would have me lead the people to? What is its name?"

Sitting Bull nodded, and spoke.

"Its name is the Greasy Grass," he answered. "That stream which the white man calls the Little Big Horn . . ."

22. FROM THE ROSEBUD TO THE GREASY GRASS

The march of the hostiles toward the Little Big Horn was a thing such as no Indian then alive had seen.

The first dawn was the 19th of June.

The course lay through the most beautiful of all the prairie uplands, the northern foothills of the Wolf Mountains. The summer grass stood high, brushing the moccasins of the riders. Groves of yellow-green cottonwood trees sheltered the splashing waters of the mountain streams. Fragrant pines covered the ridges and mesas. Upon the lower hills were brilliant stands of oak and sycamore, of alder and aspen. Near the water, always, were the slender white trunks of graceful birch. Above all loomed the distant high peaks of the "Shining Mountains," the magnificent snow-clad Big Horns.

Through this paradise moved the Sioux and the Cheyenne with all the lordly pride of hereditary owners.

In the lead, with Crazy Horse, rode Dull Knife and Two Moons, the principal Cheyenne chiefs. Sitting Bull, whose own Hunkpapa people had already removed to the Little Big Horn before the fight on the Rosebud, had held back to accompany the Oglala and the Cheyenne. He rode behind the three fighting chiefs, where all the people might see him and know that he was with them.

Next came the warriors of both tribes mounted on their finest ponies, their buffalo lances splendid with dyed eagle and heron feathers. After them came the vast concourse of pack animals loaded with tipi skins, lodge poles, robes, blankets, pots, pans, spare weapons—all the housekeeping supplies of the wanderers of the high plains. With these animals were all the squaws, old people and young children, together with the scores of yapping curs which always infested every Indian village, moving or still. Lastly, came the immense pony herd of the combined bands. There were three thousand animals—blacks, bays, grays, pintos, chestnuts, roans, whites, buckskins, every color and size and shade known to horsedom. On all sides of the column and in its rear rode the Fox Lodge soldiers of the Oglala Sioux—the Indian policemen who guarded and controlled every large march or movement to the people.

The squealing and kicking of the ponies, the braying of the pack mules, the yelping and fighting of the dogs, the cries of children, yelling of squaws, war-chanting of braves, and shouted orders of the Fox Lodge police—all created a din which might be heard for miles.

The dust raised up into the clear summer skies towered hundreds of feet high. The marching Indians stretched over the low foothills and meadowland valleys for a distance of three miles!

And these were but *two* of the many bands of hostile red horsemen forgathering at the word of Sitting Bull upon the banks of the Greasy Grass.

This fact was impressed upon the Indians themselves when, late the following afternoon, June 20, they straggled over the final rise and saw below them the shining waters of the Little Horn.

There before their startled eyes lay the greatest Indian camp in all *Shacun* history.

To the southeast, upstream toward the Big Horn Mountains and the scarps and gullies of the Rosebuds, were pitched the lodges of the Hunkpapa, together with the Two Kettle, Santee and Blackfoot Sioux bands. After them, going downstream toward the Yellowstone, were the Minniconjou Sioux and the open space reserved beyond them for the Oglala. Next came the tipis of the Sans Arc Sioux and the Cheyenne, the giant encampment stretching both ways beyond the reach of the sight of the staring red chieftains upon the rise.

But merely those Indians and their animals in view below were of numbers beyond counting. Crazy Horse was stunned.

"Uncle," he said to Sitting Bull, "I had not imagined the true power of your medicine. I cannot even *think* about so many warriors to lead into battle. And the horses! They outnumber the buffalo and the birds and the fishes. *Howo!*"

Sitting Bull nodded. "There have never been so many red men of fighting age brought together in one place before," he said. "In the way our people count such things, you and I must know that there are at least two warriors for each lodge."

"*Wan howo!*" muttered Crazy Horse. "Four or five thousand men of battle age!"

"Yes, and among that number two thousand must be called *real fighters*, men who have seen war before this."

The two leaders fell silent, looking down upon the great camp which they had called together.

What their thoughts were in that moment, no white man might say. But what that great camp meant to the white man was a thing no mind might doubt, red or white.

The grim prophecy made so long ago by Captain Benteen on the night before the Washita attack on Black Kettle was being fulfilled. Counting, in the Sioux manner, five inhabitants of all ages for each lodge along the Little Horn, the numbers in that vast camp were almost precisely what Benteen had said would one day wait for Custer.

There were ten thousand Indians gathered along the sunlit banks of the Greasy Grass.

All Yellow Hair had to do was to find them.

PART FIVE

THE LITTLE BIG HORN

23. "IF THE TRAIL LEADS
TOWARD THE LITTLE BIG HORN . . ."

The Seventh Cavalry marched away up the Rosebud on the 22nd of June, 1876.

Custer had commanded "light marching order."

This meant no tents, no swords, no personal trinkets, not even any blankets or other bedding. The troopers would sleep in the ground, or on their saddle-blankets, or sit up in their overcoats. Custer's sole concern was catching up to the Indians.

Toward this end he ordered the Gatling guns—deadly weapons of rapid fire—left behind.

Each trooper took only his bridle, halter, picket rope and pin, nose-bag for his mount, twelve-pound sack of oats across saddle-cantle, and his knapsack of field rations.

The weapons were 1873 model Springfield trapdoor carbines, caliber .45-70, for the enlisted men, .45 Colt revolvers for the officers. Custer carried a special custom-made rifle in addition, as did some of his staff and the newspaper reporter invited to go along "for the ride" by the high-spirited leader of the Seventh Cavalry.

Owing to a review of the Regiment held for General Terry and General Gibbon, the departure was not taken until noon. The day's march was thus but twelve miles, Custer halting the column at 4 P.M. The camp was in a deep flat surrounded by high bluffs. The cliffs were of yellow clay, the only cover a rough type of bullbrush. Officer and man alike wondered why Custer had ordered such an early halt, and in such desolate surroundings. They soon found out.

For the first time the General now revealed to his staff what the written orders of Terry were.

"Gentlemen," he said, "let me read you the pertinent parts of our instructions:

"Lieutenant Colonel Custer, 7th Cavalry;
Colonel:
The Brigadier-General commanding directs that as soon as your regiment can be made ready to march you will proceed up the Rosebud in pursuit of the Indians whose trail was discovered by Major Reno a few days since. . . . You should proceed up the Rosebud until you ascertain definitely the direction of the trail. . . . If it leads toward the Little Big Horn . . . you should still proceed southward . . . to the headwaters of the Tongue, and then turn toward the Little Big Horn. . . . The Column of Colonel Gibbon is now in motion for the mouth of the Big Horn . . . it is hoped that the Indians . . . may be so nearly enclosed by the two columns that their escape will be impossible. . . .
Very respectfully,
E. W. Smith,
Captain, 18th Infantry,
Acting Assistant Adjutant-General

"So you see, gentlemen," smiled Custer, folding the orders, "we are supposed to get above the Indians while Gibbon gets below them, and so come together as to crush them between us."

He paused, looking at his officers, the famous peg-toothed grin lighting his thin face.

Major Reno, that sober and unsmiling man, could see nothing of great humor in the moment.

Neither could Captain Benteen.

"You're not thinking to add something of your own to those orders, are you, General?" the latter asked.

"All in good time, Captain," he laughed, "all in good time."

He would say no more, and dismissed the officers.

"I think," said Benteen to Reno, as they walked away, "that he has stopped early today to give us strength for what he intends to do wrong tomorrow."

Major Reno only nodded and said nothing.

He had discovered that big Indian trail. His scouts had followed it a long way and returned to tell him that they promised it would lead to more Indians than any cavalry regiment would want to fight. Even the Seventh Cavalry.

He had spoken these worries to Custer, and been waved aside. Reno was a professional soldier. He said no more about it at the time, nor would he now.

"Well," said Benteen cheefully, "one thing's sure; we won't have to wait until tomorrow for a fight. We are going to be battling these pesky mosquitoes all night long! Did you ever see so many of the brutes, Marcus?"

"I never did," agreed Major Reno, brushing away the singing clouds of insects which swarmed the bottom-lands at day's end. "But never mind. Men who march with Custer are not still long enough to worry about mosquito bites."

The next day proved Reno to be correct.

The start was made very early, and Custer's orders to the troops tightened the nerves of every man.

No one was to leave the line of march, not even stray from ranks to pick a flower or toss a pebble in the stream.

There would be no discharge of any firearm whatever.

All commands were to be issued by officers' voices, never by trumpeter or by brass-lunged sergeant's yell.

There was not even to be any loud talk or jollying among the men. On the vastly silent plains the human voice could carry to great distances, and the sound of a white man's tongue was sure giveaway in Sioux country.

The troopers were even forbidden to whistle!

By these signs all in the command understood that the regiment, this day, had passed within the lines of the red enemy. Yellow Hair was away from the control of Terry; he was on his own now, and the men sensed that

Custer believed the quarry would be sighted at any turn of the river.

Just before noon the first "Indian sign" was discovered.

The column came to a halt while the Ree scouts of Bloody Knife examined the marks of the travois poles and unshod pony hoofprints in the soft earth of the riverbank.

"Maybeso two day," said Bloody Knife. "We go quick."

When the regiment started on it was with a tingling of skin and those quick, wordless glances men give one another when hunting dangerous game that is near, but not yet discovered. Without command, the intervals between the troops were closed up. The pace of the horses was quickened, along with the breathing of their riders.

During the afternoon, three deserted campsites were found along the Indian trail. At the last one, come up to just at sunset, Bloody Knife felt of the leaves which were on the willow and alder branches cut by the squaws to make the shade shelters or wickiups of the Sioux.

"Leaf still limp," he said. "Curl up but no dry yet."

"Lieutenant Cooke," said Custer to his adjutant, "pass the order to camp here. We have come far enough."

The weary troopers were soon on the ground, too tired to wander. A few, with their officers, bathed in the nearby Rosebud. Captain Benteen, who was trying to catch a trout for his supper, scolded them good-naturedly.

"What is this man's army coming to?" he asked. "Bathing before dinner on an Indian campaign? La-de-dah!"

So ended June 23rd.

The regiment had marched thirty-three miles on that day.

They were forty-five miles from the Yellowstone, as far again perhaps from the Little Big Horn.

But these distances were not what disturbed Captain

Benteen, nor what brought him to seek out Major Marcus Reno.

"Major," he said, when he had found Reno in the twilight of the June night, "are you thinking what I'm thinking?"

Major Marcus Reno glanced about to make sure they were alone. He was a more cautious man than Benteen. And perhaps a wiser one. Satisfied now, he nodded slowly.

"Do you mean about Custer disobeying General Terry's orders?" he asked.

"Yes," replied Benteen. "We were not to follow this Indian trail if it led toward the Little Big Horn. We were to circle wide and come in above the Indian camp."

Reno puffed at his pipe and nodded again.

"Yet here we are," he said, "following the Indian trail. I'll admit I don't like it."

"Marcus," scowled Benteen, "Custer is not trying to *meet* General Gibbon on the Little Horn. He is trying to *beat* him there!"

Major Reno shook his head, puzzled and perhaps a little fearful, but loyal still to his commander.

"I can't believe that, Captain," he said. "I simply can't believe Armstrong would risk the regiment like that."

Benteen was silent a moment. When he spoke, his voice was hard and his eyes were angry.

"He *would*," he said. "You'd better remember that, Major. It may save your scalp."

24. BLOODY KNIFE'S DARK WARNING

Next morning the march resumed straight along the Indian trail toward the Little Big Horn.

At midday a very large campsite was discovered. Bloody Knife, raking in the coals of one of its cooking fires, picked out a black ember. Squatting, he blew upon the bit of charred wood. It commenced to smoke, and then to glow.

"Injun stay here last night," he said, looking up at Custer. "Heap close now. Watch out. Go slow."

But Custer did not "go slow." He ordered the pace of the march increased. However, at the insistence of Lonesome Charley Reynolds, his chief of all scouts, he did send out the Ree and Crow Indian scouts well in advance. What those scouts returned to report about mid-afternoon was chilling.

They had covered many miles but seen not one Indian.

The grass, though, far around on all sides, had been eaten short. An immense pony herd had been pastured here not twenty-four hours since. "Thousands of ponies," said Curley, the handsome Crow Indian scout. Great care must be taken from this point. Clearly, there were ten-times-ten the number of Indians ahead than anyone had suspected.

Custer was not pleased with Curley's words.

He did not like to be "warned" by anyone. Especially when in front of his officers, as was the case then.

Moreover, Curley was not of his staff, but loaned to him by General Gibbon.

"What does Bloody Knife say?" he demanded of his own scout, and turning his back on the Crow.

Bloody Knife was as ugly a man to look at as Curley was handsome. His attachment to Custer was that of a totally faithful dog; he followed the General like his shadow, by day and by night. But now he had to shake his head.

"Me say same Curley," he replied. "Too many Injun up there." He pointed toward the Little Horn. "Crow Injun hate Sioux. Curley no lie to you. Too many Sioux. *Iho!*"

Bloody Knife's mother had been a Sioux squaw, his father an Arikara brave. Bloody Knife knew the Sioux as he knew his father's people. Custer's frown deepened. His drooping mustache seemed to quiver with indignation. His pale eyes darted uncertainly at his waiting officers.

"We will go forward!" he announced stubbornly.

Lonesome Charley stepped forward, moving in front of Bloody Knife and Curley.

"Begging your pardon, General," he said, "but I don't think we will. Here is something else we found in the trail up ahead. It was stuck on a pole atop yonder rise."

As he spoke, the white scout handed Custer something which looked like the pelt of a dead animal. It was reddish brown in color. The hair was long and unmistakably wavy. Custer scowled angrily.

"By heaven, this is a white man's scalp!"

"It is," said Lonesome Charley. "Maybe we had better slow down a bit, General. We've made twenty-eight miles today. It's certain we will have a big fight tomorrow, or next day at latest."

"Very well' answered Custer, in his quick way. "Pass the. order, Lieutenant Cooke. Tell the men to make small fires and cook their rations before dark. All fires will be put out and the ashes spread while it is yet daylight."

The grateful troopers dismounted. Long before darkness fell they had put out their fires and scattered the ashes and embers so that no rising sparks or tell-tale columns of white woodsmoke would mark their halting place.

Before retiring, some of the officers gathered with Captain Benteen to share a canteen of whiskey one of the group had brought along from the Yellowstone. It was then about 8 P.M. The canteen was still half-full when Custer's trumpeter, a popular immigrant youth named Johnny Martin, stepped out of the surrounding blackness to inform the officers that General Custer wished the regiment to be formed up immediately: a night march had been ordered.

Benteen and the others groaned helplessly.

Custer had evidently thought better of his earlier decision to be cautious and listen to Lonesome Charley. The General was a man who must have his way, come what would. And his way that fateful night was to drive the Seventh Cavalry in a single-file blind march straight on toward the Little Big Horn.

The start was made just after 10 P.M.

For six hours and until 2 o'clock the following morning, the regiment stumbled and felt its way through the pitch darkness. Then Custer called the halt. The men tumbled from their mounts. They lay down in their overcoats where they were, and slept on the bare rocky ground. Before them, only a short distance, was the long ridge which was the divide between the Rosebud and the Big Horn. With first daylight Custer and his favorite white scout were on top of that ridge. Before the exhausted troopers were fully awake, the General was back in camp and calling his officers to him. It was still so early that the sun was not even into the hill-locked basin where he had halted the Seventh. Its first rays were just tipping the high ridge, and spilling over into the valley of the Big Horn, beyond.

When Reno, Benteen, Keogh, Moylan and the others had answered Adjutant Cooke's summons, and were gathered in the misty dawn about Custer, the latter spoke quickly.

When excited, he had a stammering way of speech, and he was stammering now.

Bloody Knife and Curley, with the very best of their Ree and Crow scouts, had been up on the ridge all night. He, Custer, with Lonesome Charley Reynolds, had joined them there just before sunup. The Indians all said that in the gray predawn they could see the hostile camp along the distant banks of the Little Big Horn. They said it was twelve or fifteen miles away, and the biggest camp any of them had ever seen or heard of in the stories of their people.

Here Custer paused to interrupt himself.

"But you know how Indians are," he smiled. "I stared through my field glasses for half an hour up there, and could not see one sign of any Indian camp. Indeed, I could not even see the Little Big Horn!"

At this, Bloody Knife, squatting on the ground nearby, raised his dark hand. He said something in the deep-growled tongue of the Sioux, and Custer turned swiftly to Lonesome Charley Reynolds.

"What did he say?" he demanded of the white scout.

"He said you would find enough Indians over there on the Little Horn to keep you fighting for two, maybe three, days."

Custer laughed. He was at once his old confident, optimistic self. He put his hand on Bloody Knife's shoulder.

"Never you fear, old friend!" he said. "We will get through them nicely in one day——!"

25. THE PATHS OF GLORY

The Seventh Cavalry climbed the divide and passed over it at about 8 A.M. Before them lay the valley of the Little Big Horn River. Custer was excited.

Captain Benteen and Major Reno, with the other officers, had not seen this view from the divide before.

As they now saw it spreading below them, some of them did not like the situation, at all. The reason for this was that the country ahead was a series of rough ridges and gullies. It looked like a rumpled bedsheet covered with scraggly brush and tall grass. High bluffs of red and yellow clay loomed everywhere. These were washed by the rolling, rough waves of the brush and grasslands. Nowhere could the officers see the channel of the river itself.

Was this what Custer had seen from the crest at daybreak?

Was this *all* he had seen?

Were the trusted Indian scouts of the Seventh Cavalry leading the Pony Soldiers into a trap?

Or had their wonderful eyesight *really* been able to see the stream and the campsites of their wild cousins, where the inferior vision of the white man could not?

Major Reno turned to Bloody Knife, who was riding nearby.

"My friend," he said to the Ree scout, "you must not lie to me. Did you see the camp of the hostile Indians?"

"*He-hau!*" growled the red man. "Yes, me see."

"Then," said Reno, "will you please point the place out to me?"

The white officer thought that he had caught the scout in a trick, for Bloody Knife scowled darkly. But the Ree was only showing his pride.

"Why you think me lie?" he demanded. "Me serve you Pony Soldier long time now. Tongue of Bloody Knife not follow two trails, like tongue of snake, or tongue of white man."

"I apologize," said Reno soberly. He was a good man. He lacked Custer's high spirit and dashing charm. He did not have Benteen's wit and good humor. But Major Marcus Reno was an honest and capable cavalryman. His greatest "fault," unlike the handsome leader of his regiment, was that Major Reno never said more than he meant, or promised the impossible.

Now Bloody Knife stopped scowling, waved his dark hand.

"Me understand," he grunted in his deep voice. "You good Oak Leaf Chief. You careful. You afraid. You smart!"

Even Major Reno had to smile.

Was the Indian telling him that he was wise to be afraid?

That it might be good policy to be a coward that coming day?

Reno lost his brief smile.

"Do you see the camp of your wild cousins now?" he asked Bloody Knife. "Can you show it to me from here?"

Bloody Knife pointed to the west, and a little to the north. Following the direction of his finger, Reno could at first see nothing. But then the Ree uttered one grunting word, "smoke," and the officer at once made out the hazy thin blue curls of hundreds upon hundreds of tipi-fires rising in a line which entended for miles. He turned back to the Ree scout, his sober face pale.

"Was General Custer able to see that smoke?" he asked.

Bloody Knife shrugged.

"Me show him," he said. "Him may see, maybe not see."

Major Reno thought Custer must be told of those smokes immediately. He could not gamble with Bloody Knife's word for the matter.

But when he had ridden forward along the line and found the General, he could not get him to stop long enough to look at the distant smoke.

"Major Reno!" laughed the commander of the Seventh Cavalry, "I was looking at those campfire smokes before you were awake this morning!"

"Yes," said Reno, not smiling back at Custer. "But did you *see* them?"

Custer scowled for a moment. He did not like to be thus questioned by his officers. He always invited them to state their opinions freely, but he nnver took their advice, nor really welcomed it. Yellow Hair followed his own orders.

"Go back to your troops, sir," he now said, "and leave the worrying to me."

But Major Reno did not move.

"General," he said flatly, "do you intend to attack those Indians today?"

"What do you mean by that?" challenged Custer.

"I mean," answered Major Reno, "that General Terry told you to wait for General Gibbon to get into position below this camp. General Terry said we were not to attack until the twenty-sixth, when Gibbon should be ready."

"Well, sir?" cried Custer. "Come, come, say what you mean, man! I've no time for guessing games."

"What I mean, General," replied Reno bravely, "is that this is only the twenty-fifth. You're a day early for your *appointment* with General Gibbon, sir. You should wait for him."

"Hah!" grinned Custer, trying to pass off the unpleasantness of the moment. "Can we help it if old Red Nose is so slow of foot? The Seventh Cavalry was given a job to do, Major. I suggest you get back to your men and help me to get on with that job. Lieutenant Cooke——!"

He turned his horse away from Major Reno, calling

again for his adjutant, Lieutenant Cooke. The young officer dashed up, wheeling his horse and saluting smartly.

"Order the column forward at once," said Custer. "We shall follow the course of that small drybed stream ahead." He pointed to a gully which began nearby, and ran all the way down the divide into the valley below. "Tell the officers to order extreme quiet in ranks. Have Captain Benteen take the advance. He's been spoiling for action."

"Yes sir!" said young Cooke, saluting again. "Beg pardon, General, sir," he added. "What's the name of this stream we're to follow down to the Little Big Horn?"

Custer looked a moment at the frowning Major Marcus Reno.

Then his famous peg-toothed grin spread over his sun-tanned face. The pale eyes danced. Custer was a man incapable of holding resentment. His heart was as gay and brave as his never-failing ambitions.

"Well, sir," he answered the youthful lieutenant, "Lonesome Charley Reynolds tells me that the Sioux call it Sundance Creek. But I think we will change that in honor of the day. For the purposes of the Seventh Cavalry, let's call it Reno Creek. The major needs a little encouragement, eh, Marc?"

Reno sighed and nodded his head in agreement.

He could not resist George Armstrong Custer. And few men could. Now he managed a wan smile, and a small wave.

"General," he said, "you know that if you order me to ride off the top of this mountain, that I will do it."

"Nonsense!" laughed Custer, spiritedly. "Nothing that drastic, Marc. All you need to do is lead your men down Reno Creek to glory and to a colonel's eagle! Think of that, sir!"

What he meant was that, if the battle went well and many Indians were killed, Major Reno would be promoted to Colonel Reno as a reward for his loyal services and blind obedience.

But Major Reno could not think of it that way.

He saluted Custer now, and rode back to his men, as any good soldier must.

Yet he was not thinking of Custer's promise to promote him to colonel. He was thinking of that other part of Yellow Hair's statement. The part about following the banks of Reno Creek to *glory*. And that is what made faithful, steady Major Reno seem to be afraid.

The night before, during the rest halt between 2 A.M. and sunrise, when the Indian scouts had gone to the high divide, Custer and Lonesome Charley Reynolds joining them later, Captain Benteen had come over in the thinning darkness to visit Reno.

Benteen had still been with Reno when the Crow scout Curley, a particular friend of Benteen's, had drifted in through the growing grayness of the predawn. Reno had been startled by the handsome Indian's appearance. But he was far more startled by what Curley had to tell his good friend, Captain Frederick Benteen. It was concerning what Yellow Hair had just told all of the Indian scouts up on the divide.

Curley could scarcely believe his ears. He had been so astonished that at first he could not think what to do. But Curley had been to the schoolhouse on the reservation. He was more *civilized* than the other scouts. He knew more about the way the white man thought.

So it had been that when he heard what Yellow Hair promised the Indian scouts, he believed that the officers in the camp below should know of the promise.

For that reason, Curley had slipped away from the divide and come back ahead of the others. This was his story:

When the daylight began to come and Bloody Knife and the Ree and Crow scouts had said they were able to see the great hostile camp of "the three thousand smokes," Custer had refused to believe them. When the Indians then warned that he would find more hostile warriors than any regiment of Pony Soldiers could fight,

Yellow Hair had still refused to be halted, or even made to go slow.

"Nonsense!" he had cried, in his high-voiced way. "You are seeing things! Your eyes are strong but your hearts are weak! Come along, now. Did you ever lose a fight following me? Oh no, you say? Well, then, let's go!"

But the scouts had just stood there.

Then Yellow Hair could see that he must tell them something more than just to follow him. And he had done so. He told the Indians, both Rees and Crows, that he was putting everything important to him into this one fight with Sitting Bull and Crazy Horse. He said that if he won the fight, if he defeated the Sioux champion, Tatanka Yotanka, the famous medicine man of the Hunkpapa tribe, then a great thing would happen.

It was that Yellow Hair would be made the Grandfather—the President of the United States!

If his brave friends, the Ree and Crow, would go with him and run off the pony herds of the Sioux and Cheyenne, Yellow Hair would not forget their people when he sat in the Great White Lodge in Washington.

This story, which was never to be proved, had stunned Major Reno at the time. But with his customary loyalty to Custer, he had put its report aside as "Indian imagination and lies."

Yet now, riding back along the advancing column of the Seventh Cavalry, he was not so sure.

In truth, he was not sure, at all.

Had Curley lied to Captain Benteen? Was the handsome young Crow only showing Indian imagination? Trying to impress his friend, Captain Benteen, with his faithfulness?

Or was it true that Custer had promised great rewards to his Indian scouts because he could see he had made them nervous and afraid by his own rash desires to win a great victory for the Seventh Cavalry? To make a glory-ride which would make Yellow Hair Custer the next Grandfather in Washington?

Steadfast Major Marcus A. Reno did not know.

But in that quiet June morning before the Battle of the Little Big Horn, he was thinking of a line from the famed poem, Gray's *Elegy;* and it was not a happy line.

What was it Custer had just said—to follow him down the pathway of Reno Creek to glory?

And what was it Gray had said so long ago:
The paths of glory lead but to the grave . . .

26. FOLLOW THE FLAG WITH THE BIG RED "7"

Custer halted the advance only part way down Reno Creek toward the valley of the Little Big Horn.

Officers looking at their watches noted the time to be 10:30 A.M. No sooner had they made this observation than they were startled to hear the bugler blowing Officer's Call. It was the first time in two days that the General had permitted a trumpet to sound. Something big must be afoot.

When they had ridden to where Custer awaited them, they found the commander of the Seventh in excellent spirits.

"Gentlemen," he announced, "we have been discovered by the hostiles. Our Indian scouts have seen their warriors riding along the bluffs above for the past half hour. Undoubtedly these braves were drawn by the dust our horses have been raising in descending the dry water-course. By this time they will have returned to arouse the camp. Since there is no more need for silence on our part, we will proceed in battle readiness. Any questions?"

It was much too late for questions. All of the officers knew that, and none of them answered Custer.

"No questions, sir," said Adjutant Cooke, saluting.

"Very well, Lieutenant." Custer's words were sharp with the ring of command. "Have Trumpeter Martin sound the advance."

Shortly, the Seventh Cavalry was moving forward again.

But mile after mile passed and no sight yet of the Little Big Horn River, or of the vast Indian encampment said to cover its banks. Eleven o'clock passed. Noon drew near, and Custer became nervous. He feared that the Indians were fleeing.

"Captain Benteen," he ordered, "take three troops and the ammunition mules and proceed to the left. Watch for the Indian village. If you see it, pitch into it."

Benteen gave over the advance to Custer, took his three troops, about a hundred and twelve men, and the pack mules carrying all of the spare ammunition for the entire regiment. As he went into the rough country, he turned to Captain Gibson and said that he did not think it wise to leave Custer. He added that it seemed very foolish to have the ammunition all with one group. Captain Gibson said that he agreed, but that Custer was commanding the regiment.

"Let's hope," replied Benteen grimly, "that he is still commanding it tomorrow at this time."

But the rough-humored captain would have felt even more grim uncertainty about Custer's leadership had he been able to hear the next order that Yellow Hair issued.

No sooner were the troops of Benteen's column out of sight in the rough hills to the left, than Custer instructed Major Reno to take a like number of men—three troops —and advance to the right, on the south side of the dry streambed.

"I will stay on this side, Marc," he said. "In that way we shall have three columns spreading out, and the Indians cannot get away from us."

Reno saluted and rode away with his three troops.

Like Captain Benteen, his thoughts were not pleasant ones. But he kept them to himself. It was his duty to do so. If he should show uncertainty, then his men would see this in him, and they would become uneasy and afraid.

Moreover, Custer's five troops of the Seventh Cavalry were in plain view on the far side of the dusty streambed. There seemed no hesitation in the General.

In truth, none of the men in the ranks seemed to fear any danger, or to suspect a defeat. Of course, none of them knew what Major Reno knew. It had not been told among the troops that the regiment's Indian scouts had reported "*three thousand tipi-smokes*," or "*enough Indians to fight for two or three days*," or had advised Yellow Hair to "*go slow and be careful.*"

All the men in the ranks knew was that the big camp of the hostile Sioux and Cheyenne lay somewhere just ahead.

That being so, they also knew that when their general had found the camp, it would be the last bugle call for old Sitting Bull and that wild-riding fool of a Crazy Horse.

When Custer went after an Indian camp, it was the end of that camp.

So, with the officers worried, the commander absolutely determined to push ahead with all speed, and the troopers convinced that no amount of Indians could stop the Seventh Cavalry, the regiment swung to saddle for the last time.

The clear brass notes of Bugler Martin's trumpet shrilled through the early afternoon.

The "Forward, hos!" of the officers sounded down the long lines of blue-clad, dusty troopers.

The men cheered. Even the horses were excited. They snorted and plunged and kicked up their iron-shod hoofs. In the lead, General Custer's long-limbed thoroughbred "Vic" pranced and whirled and pulled at the reins. Vic was a beautiful stocking-footed sorrel horse, fit mount to carry Yellow Hair, the "Boy General," into battle.

Custer wore his famed black felt hat, with rakish wide brim curled up on one side.

He had donned his fringed jacket of Indian buckskin, and the bright scarlet neckerchief which was his fighting "good medicine charm." High boots reached above his knees. His gauntlets were of yellow leather, fringed nearly to the elbow. He rode, as always, with the grace

of the born horseman. Here was a cavalry commander to
follow! A commander who, in all the fierce and bloody
campaigns of the Civil War, had never lost a battle flag
or a single gun to the enemy. A commander who had
more courage than a lion, more luck than a Mississippi
River gambler. Here was a leader who always won!

Forward, ho! Forward, ho! Follow the dust of the
Seventh Cavalry. Follow that maroon-and-white regimental pennant, proud with the big red "7" upon its
centerpiece! Never fear, never falter. Follow George
Armstrong Custer to glory and to gallant victory. Forward, ho! Forward, ho!

The horses moved now at a spanking trot.

Their bright blue saddle blankets with the orange
borders flashed in the summer sunlight.

The riders leaned eagerly in the McClellan army
saddles.

Their rough service boots were tight in the oxbow
stirrups, their hands were sweaty upon the bridle-reins.

The gray horse troop, the black horse troop, the bay
horse troop, the sorrel and the white—all moved more
swiftly to follow Custer toward the last bend of Reno
Creek. Around that bend the valley of the Little Big
Horn would open wide. The Indian scouts had just
returned to tell the General this. All straightened in
their saddles, took a firmer grip on Springfield rifle or
big Colt .45 revolver, as this news swept down the long
lines of the Pony Soldiers.

The Indian camp lay only around the bend!

Then, suddenly, the bluffs of Reno's Creek spread
apart.

The first troops rode into the meadowlands of the
Little Big Horn, following Custer. As if by command
—where there was no command—all the crowding
soldiers of the Seventh Cavalry brought their lathered
mounts to a halt.

Before them were perhaps fifty hostile horsemen
riding wildly back and forth not two hundred yards away!

But that was not what halted the troopers. It was what

towered beyond those first brave Indians, and beyond the great curve of the Little Big Horn. It was a column of dust which rolled upward as if from some great volcano, staining the June skies red and yellow with its angry swirlings. It continued to grow larger as the troopers sat and stared at it.

Each man had the same uneasy question in his mind.

If the fifty Indian horsemen they had just discovered in front of them could raise the dust they were raising putting on their little show for Custer and the Seventh, how many *other* Indian horsemen must be raising that great dust cloud beyond the river's bend?

"Holy smoke!" cried one excited trooper to his nearby comrade. "There must be ten thousand of them up there!"

His companion nodded. He was feeling his first fear.

"We'd best start praying, Ben," he said. "And mighty hard . . ."

27. THREE COLUMNS JUST LIKE THE WASHITA

When Custer saw the fifty Indian horsemen dashing away toward the banks of the Little Big Horn, he ordered his Indian scouts to pursue them and cut them down.

But the Ree and Crow scouts, although they far outnumbered the fifty hostiles, would not go.

"Him little bunch Injun only decoy," Bloody Knife told Custer. "Them Cheyenne. You follow Cheyenne, you find Sioux waiting. Heap many. Curley, him say all Hunkpapa this end village. Stay back, be careful!"

But Custer was furious. He ordered the scouts to have both their ponies and their rifles taken away from them. Doing this, he intended to punish them. What he did, instead, was to save their lives.

It was here that the Crow scout, Curley, announced that he would go no farther with a man "whose head is spinning."

He meant that he thought General Custer was behaving as a crazy person, that he had lost his senses.

Lonesome Charley did not tell the General what the Crow scout had said. He did not even dare tell Custer that Curley was quitting the Seventh Cavalry.

For his part, Custer dismissed the matter of the rebellious Ree and Crow scouts. "Let them go," he ordered Lieutenant Cooke. "We must continue forward."

"But General, sir," objected Cooke, "what of the

hostile ponies? Our Indian scouts were supposed to run them off."

"Let the ponies go, too," commanded Custer. "We are wasting time here. Those Indians will get away from us. Here, quick, I want you to ride over to Reno with these orders."

Cooke at once spurred his horse across the dry streambed.

"Major Reno, sir!" he called, dashing up to that officer, "the General sends his compliments. He wants you to ford the Little Big Horn. Once across, he directs that you shall take as fast a gait as you deem prudent and charge afterward, and you will be supported by the entire outfit——!"

Cooke turned his horse, galloped back up the streambed of Reno Creek toward Custer's waiting troops. Meeting Captain Keogh on the way, he stopped and the two officers watched Reno's troops go forward and disappear around the bend of the Little Big Horn. They started on, but before they reached Custer, a lone horseman thundered up shouting for them to wait. It was a scout from Reno. The major had already found the Indians! Just beyond the bend. They were everywhere among the trees of the riverbottom. Beyond the trees, the major could see the tips of the buffalo hide tipis by the hundreds. This was without question the great camp they had been looking for. Were General Custer's orders still the same?

Cooke told the scout that he should tell Major Reno that Custer had already given him his orders. He was to attack!

Meanwhile, Cooke would race to Custer and tell him what Major Reno had found beyond the bend. If there were any new orders, any change of the battle plan, a messenger would be sent at once to Major Reno's column.

And there began the mystery of the Little Big Horn.

Cooke did ride hard for Custer, and Captain Keogh with him. But no man knows if they ever relayed to

Custer the information from Major Reno. And no man knows why Custer then did what he did. For, instead of following up with his main force of five troops to support the three troops of Major Reno, General Custer ordered his command to cut *away* from the Little Big Horn. He led his troopers *out from behind* the troopers of Major Reno, and left Reno's men to their fate. The only possible guess which could be made, was that Yellow Hair had decided to make a big circle and strike the hostiles on the flank, while Reno fought them from in front. It was his favorite Civil War cavalry tactic. It had brought him many victories in that war. Also, it had worked upon the red man. Did Custer think of the Washita in those moments before leaving Reno unsupported to lead his own men into the buffalo grass beyond the river, and into history? Did he remember that he had split the Seventh Cavalry into three columns then? Had struck the Cheyenne of old Black Kettle from three sides at once? Had killed them after that like shooting tame cattle in a pen? Had won the greatest Indian Fight victory up to that time?

Ah! no man would ever know.

That is, no man left behind with the commands of Reno or Benteen would ever know.

For when General Custer took his five troops of the Seventh Cavalry into the rolling hills beyond the Little Big Horn that silent, sunlit afternoon, he galloped into eternity.

Neither Reno nor Benteen, nor any trooper with them, ever saw him alive again.

28. CHIEF GALL CLOSES THE HUNKPAPA TRAP

Major Reno waited uncertainly for Custer's reply about advancing past the bend. But no answer came from Custer.

What had happened to Lieutenant Cooke?

Had he not delivered Reno's message? Had the Indians gotten him? Had he given Custer the message, and Custer chosen to ignore it? And aside from Lieutenant Cooke, what had happened to Custer? His troops should be advancing behind those of Major Reno. Reno should be able to see them by now. But he saw nothing behind him.

Ahead of him, it was another matter.

Reno and his anxious officers looked hard at the vast cloud of dusty brown-yellow haze striking skyward beyond the bend. The small band of Indian horsemen which had met the main column of the Seventh Cavalry had disappeared around that bend by now. They were hidden, with their fellow warriors of the main camp, beneath that dust cloud, no doubt.

"Sir," said Captain French, "we had best do something."

"What we had best do," added Captain Moylan, "is to hit the Indians while we still know where they are—in front of us."

"I agree, I agree," echoed young Lieutenant McIntosh.

Major Reno looked at his three officers. He looked at his two scouts, Bloody Knife and Lonesome Charley

Reynolds, loaned to him by the generous Custer only minutes before.

"The captains are right," said Lonesome Charley. "We can't stay here. The Indians will get behind us."

"Too many Injun," rumbled Bloody Knife in his deep voice, and said no more.

Major Reno sighed as though a heavy weight were upon him.

"All right," he said wearily. "Let us go forward."

The three troops of Seventh Cavalry moved ahead at the trot. As they neared the edge of the rising cloud of dust, they began to hear the chirruping, wild war cries of the Sioux and the Cheyenne. The Indian voices were so many and so confusing coming through the thick yellowish dust that the soldiers did not know which way to look for the enemy. The noises of the warriors seemed to be all around them, like a swarm of angry red bees.

"Reynolds," said Reno, grim-lipped, to Lonesome Charley, "we have struck a hornet's nest."

"They are buzzing right bad," agreed the white scout.

The next moment a breeze stirred down the valley of the Little Big Horn, lifting the skirts of the dust cloud.

Before them, Reno and Reynolds saw more Sioux and Cheyenne than they had thought to be in the entire four-mile camp of the hostiles.

All of the yelling, swift-riding braves were mounted on fine ponies. All were painted for war. All had good rifles. Many of them had new Winchester repeating rifles. These were far better weapons than the old Springfield carbines carried by Custer's men. It was immediately evident to anyone who knew Indians that Yellow Hair had *not* surprised the hostile camp that sunny June day along the Greasy Grass.

Lonesome Charley and Bloody Knife understood this fact at first glance.

It took a high plains horseback Indian hours to prepare for battle. To put on his warpaint. To select and bridle the pony he would ride in that day's combat. To oil his gun, and to load it, and to fill his warbag with extra

ammunition. To smoke his good medicine pipe and
arrange his good luck battle-charms. To say his Indian
prayers to the red gods of his people. To Wakan Tanka
for the Sioux. To Maheo, the Allfather, for the Cheyenne. And then, finally, to offer war chants to the
heavens, so that the bullets of the Pony Soldiers would
fly wide of their marks, while those of the Indians would
be guided directly to their targets.

The two scouts with Major Reno's troops, thinking of
these things which both knew to be true things, exchanged dark and foreboding looks.

"Major," said Lonesome Charley to Reno, "we had
better get out of here, *right away!*"

But he had no sooner issued the hurried warning than
his companion, Bloody Knife, flung up his arm, pointing
ahead.

"Too late," rumbled the Ree scout in his deep voice.
"Injuns all around. No go back. Fight here, or all die."

The white officers could see that the hostile horsemen
were not waiting for the Pony Soldiers. They were
starting out around both sides of Reno's little band of
troopers. In another few moments they would be, as
Bloody Knife had just said, "all around." Then it would
be impossible for Custer to come to their aid. Something
must be done.

"You have got to charge them, Major," said Lonesome
Charley. "That will pull them back together and give us a
chance to fall back toward the General."

Reno nodded quickly. He was not a brilliant nor a
dashing officer. Neither was he ambitious. He did not
like to see his men die. Nor did he like to think about
dying himself.

But he was no coward.

"*Forward, ho!*" he shouted to the troops, and himself
led the advance toward the screaming red men.

For several minutes the Indians retreated. Reno and
his three troops moved forward until they were in the
clear of the bottomland meadow of the Little Big Horn.
Now, for the first time, they could see the countless

lodges of the camp running beyond eye's reach, northward, downstream, where General Gibbon was supposed to be coming with his infantry.

Oh, if Custer had only waited one more day!

How simple it would have been to catch and crush
those Indians between the Seventh Cavalry and Gibbon's foot-soldiers and his artillery cannon!

But Custer had not waited, and Major Marcus Reno
and his little command of a hundred and twelve men
were fighting for their lives.

Suddenly, and just as the sweating, frightened men
thought the red foe was fading back, was giving away,
Bloody Knife again pointed dramatically down the valley.

"Hunkpapa!" he shouted. "Heap many!"

Out of the tipis at the upper end of the great village
now streamed a new horde of painted, half-naked
horsemen. Lonesome Charley Reynolds at once drove
his pony to the side of Major Reno. He told the white
officer that he must instantly begin to fall back toward
Custer. But once more his advice was delayed too long.
The Hunkpapa horsemen, led by Chief Gall, had already cut around the left flank of Reno's line of troopers.
The soldiers on that side were beginning to retreat
before the mighty Hunkpapa fighter. In a moment they
would be running, not just retreating, and then the
Indians would be able to shoot them down like galloping
buffalo, helpless, pitiful.

"What can we do, Reynolds?" cried Reno. "I can't hold
those men from breaking over there."

Lonesome Charley called to Bloody Knife in the Sioux
tongue, and the two scouts spoke swiftly, back and forth.

"Bloody Knife says you must fight your way to those
trees in the bend of the river," the white scout told
Reno. "If you can get into the trees, the Sioux won't
charge you like they will out here in the open grass."

"Someone must go and tell Moylan over there on the
left," answered Reno. "We must not start away without
telling him."

"I'll go," volunteered Lonesome Charley. "Bloody Knife can stay with you."

The white scout spurred his pony away.

The next moment, the Sioux had renewed their attack upon the middle of Reno's thin line of riflemen, and upon the right flank of the line, where Captain French commanded.

The first of the Seventh Cavalry's soldiers began to fall from their rearing, plunging horses. Against the one hundred and twelve men of the Reno battalion there were now no less than *ten* hundred hostile Indians riding in vengeful fury.

In ten minutes of blasting gunfire, Reno's command suffered eight dead and seven badly wounded.

The troopers were beginning to panic.

Where was Lonesome Charley Reynolds? Why hadn't Captain Moylan come in from the left flank as ordered?

Were they all dead over there?

Major Reno could not answer these terrible questions. He waited as long as any officer would dare to wait for the white scout to return, or for Moylan's troops to appear. Then he turned and told Lieutenant McIntosh that they must go without the others.

"I'm sorry, McIntosh," he said. "But we must leave them."

The young lieutenant answered him with an angry, accusing look. He said nothing, only wheeling and ordering the men to get their horses and be ready to go *fast*.

Reno watched the youthful officer without anger of his own.

He knew McIntosh believed him to be a coward.

To Bloody Knife who stood beside him, he said quietly, "Do you agree with the young man, my friend?"

The faithful Ree scout shook his head, dark eyes flashing.

"Him easy be brave," he said. "Much hard lead retreat."

29. MAJOR RENO'S RACE FOR THE RIVER

Major Reno started his troopers toward the trees in the river's bend. When the soldiers were moving, he left the lead and went back to encourage the stragglers in the rear.

The men were dismounted now, leading their horses. In this way they would not offer such inviting targets for the howling red marksmen. The Indians were riding in so close by this time that the white soldiers could see the sunlight strike the gleaming teeth in their dark faces, as they cursed the white man, firing again and again into the ranks of his desperate retreat. It was a moment to break nerves apart.

But Bloody Knife's great calmness and remarkable bravery helped the terrified troopers to steady down and stay together.

The Ree scout would not get off his pony. He kept the little animal between Major Reno and the war-hooping enemy, thus sheltering the white commander with his body and that of his horse. He had been told by Yellow Hair Custer to go with the Oak Leaf Chief, Reno. This was his duty. He would perform it to the death. And that death now struck him. A Sioux bullet screamed in out of the rolling gunsmoke. It burst against the Ree's head, showering his blood down upon Reno. The startled officer cried out and staggered back as the stricken body of the Indian scout crashed down upon him.

For a moment he did not appear to realize what had happened.

He seemed to be paralyzed by the death of the Ree scout. He could not give commands. Lieutenant McIntosh, little more than a boy in years, rushed up and shouted for the men to remain calm, not to panic and begin running.

"Every fourth man will lead four horses," he ordered. "The other three men, thus freed, will fire their rifles as we retreat toward the river timber. Yonder comes Captain Moylan's troop, men! We are all together now. Let's go, lead out!"

The men ran stumbling and firing back toward the Indians.

The Sioux rushed in behind them, returning the fire. The nearest Indians were less than a stone's toss away. In those last few yards they were not firing, but were trying to get up close enough to the fleeing soldiers to use their war axes and buffalo lances upon them.

Major Reno was among the last three men of his command to reach the trees in the river's bend. Before he could get under cover, White Bull, a great Sioux warrior and nephew of Sitting Bull, ran his pony up behind the white officer and struck him with a war axe. Reno went down, and did not move.

In a display of great bravery, young Lieutenant McIntosh ran out and dragged his commander into the cottonwoods.

The troopers, somewhat protected now, began to get a hard fire into the yelling, wheeling Indians. The red horsemen were packed so closely together that the bullets of the cavalrymen took a heavy toll among them, and very quickly.

First Chief Gall, and then White Bull, called their Hunkpapa away from the cornered Pony Soldiers. The warriors withdrew out of pointblank rifle range. For a precious few minutes Reno's shattered troops could gather their wits and their courage. In the brief lull, during which the Indians continued to fire constantly from long range, the major recovered consciousness.

His first act was to call for Lonesome Charley

Reynolds.

With Bloody Knife gone, the white scout was the only one left to counsel troops in escaping the Sioux trap.

But Dr. De Wolf, one of the regimental surgeons, who was bandaging Reno's scalp-wound, shook his head.

"I'm sorry, Major," he said. "Reynolds is dead. He was killed after he carried your retreat order to Moylan. We also lost six more troopers getting over here into these trees. Hold still, please, sir. You must let me finish."

Reno staggered to his feet, pushing the doctor away.

"Moylan!" he shouted. "Moylan, where are you?"

Captain Myles Moylan, happy-go-lucky Irishman and Reno's second-in-command, came up through the drifting powder-smoke.

"Yes sir," he saluted. Although his face was blackened with grease and powder-grime, and dried blood stained his blue blouse, he was still grinning, still fighting. "What can I do for you, Major? Would you like thirty days leave?"

Reno was a man without much humor. He did not smile now at the Irish captain's small joke.

"Moylan," he said, "tell the other officers we are going to run for the bluffs across the river. Have every man get to his horse and mount-up immediately. We have a moment now while the Indians are readying for their final rush. That's an order, Moylan. Hurry. We have no other chance."

So it came about that Major Reno made the fateful decision to strike across the Little Big Horn and try to reach high ground. His men were remounted and galloping out of the cottonwoods for the crossing of the stream before Gall and White Bull realized their intention. Then the Indians came after them in a great whooping charge of blazing Winchesters and neighing, lunging war ponies.

There were less than one hundred soldiers now.

Many of those remaining were wounded, or without weapons.

Behind them came the hundreds upon hundreds of

the war-bonneted Hunkpapa Sioux, screaming their
hoarse-throated war cries. It did not seem to the white-
faced, sweaty and blood-stained troopers of Reno's
battalion that any of them would ever reach the river
alive.

30. "BENTEEN, COME QUICK—
BRING PACKS—!"

General Custer led his troops away through the hills toward the lower end of the great Indian village. His orders were for a fast trot and no bugle calls or other unnecessary noise. When one of his officers rode up beside him to question the matter of leaving Reno without the promised support, the General laughed happily, thin face flushed with excitement.

"What better support can I give him than to strike these rascals on one end, while he smites them on the other?" he cried. "Don't you remember how it worked on the Washita, sir?"

The officer saluted and said nothing.

He remembered all too well how it had worked on the Washita. On the Washita, Custer had abandoned Colonel Elliott much as he had just now left Major Reno —without advising either commander of his change-of-plan.

Returning to his own troop, the officer prayed that *this* time the strategy would work less tragically.

But if some in those five troops of Seventh Cavalry now jingling rapidly through the rough hills beyond the Little Big Horn knew doubt of their leader's wisdom, there were many more who still had complete faith therein.

None of these felt a greater trust in the General than Custer's young favorite, Trumpeter John Martin.

Johnny Martin, the regimental bugler boy, was not yet twenty years old. Born in faraway Italy, young

141

Martin—his name had been "Martini"—could neither speak nor understand English too well. But he loved his new country and he worshiped General George Armstrong Custer.

Riding now at the General's side, the immigrant boy reflected the prevailing attitude of his fellow-troopers in the Seventh Cavalry. They were tired from the long night march which had brought them to the Indian camp. They wished the General might have waited one more day and permitted them to rest up for the fight. But they had no fear and no doubt of their commanding officer's ability to whip the Sioux.

If the General said that now was the time to hit the red devils, then "forward, ho!" and get the job over with!

Presently the column turned to its left. Custer had seen a high place up on the river's bluffs. The view should be splendid from up there, giving a long sighting of the valley and of the enemy village.

He was right as usual.

When the command halted behind the edge of the high bluff, young Johnny Martin went forward with General Custer and Adjutant Cooke to the very lip of the yellow clay cliff.

Below them the huge hostile encampment spread along the opposite side of the river. To the surprise of the bugler boy the Indians did not seem to be stirring or aroused. He could see the distant tiny brown dots of the figures moving about their camp chores without haste. As if to confirm the boy's thoughts, General Custer, who had been examining the village through his field glasses, put down the glasses and turned to Adjutant Cooke, voice crackling.

"Lieutenant!" he said triumphantly, "we have got them this time——!"

Lieutenant Cooke, the adjutant, seemed to frown slightly. Johnny Martin wondered if he were worried about something.

"Will we wait here for Reno to attack?" Cooke asked. "Or go on?"

Again Custer laughed happily.

"Wait?" he said. "Listen—" He held up a fringed gauntlet, cocking his head up the valley. "Don't you hear that?"

As Cooke strained to hear, so did bugler boy Martin.

Whatever it was that Custer had heard, or that his adjutant, Lieutenant Cooke, now heard, Johnny Martin heard nothing. The wind was moving away from them, and the immigrant boy could not identify the distant "pipping noise" which came to them there on the high bluff. But it was a sound both Custer and Cooke knew all too well.

"There's your answer!" cried the General. "Let's go!"

The command turned back from the bluff. The pace was the gallop now. They had come two miles from leaving Reno to his fate. They sped now a third mile before coming to a long ravine which split the bluffs and led downward steeply to the river. Here Custer once more halted the five troops.

"Trumpeter!" he called to Trooper Martin. "I want you to take a message to Captain Benteen. Ride as fast as you can and tell him to hurry. It's a big village, and I want him to be quick and to bring the ammunition packs."

The boy saluted and turned to depart.

"Wait!" called Adjutant Cooke. The young officer knew that the bugler boy spoke poor English, and might mix up the vital message to Benteen. "I will write that order down for you, Johnny."

He took a note-pad and hurriedly scribbled the message to Captain Benteen which was to become one of the most famed documents in American frontier history. Handing the small piece of paper to Trumpeter Martin, he put his hand on the boy's shoulder, spoke very seriously.

"Now, Johnny," he said, "ride as fast as you can to Captain Benteen. Take the same trail we came down. If you have time, and there is no danger, come back. But otherwise stay with your company."

Johnny Martin saluted again, and turned his horse.

In a few minutes he passed the high bluff where Custer had viewed the camp. And where, perhaps—no man will ever know—he and Lieutenant Cooke had heard the distant sounds of Reno's battalion firing at the overwhelming Sioux.

The boy spoke to his galloping brown horse, encouraging him to more speed. For now, to Trumpeter Martin's *own* ears, the sounds of Major Reno's desperate rifle-fire was coming, and in a continuous, unmistakable crackling volley.

"Run hard, horse!" shouted the immigrant youth in his native tongue. "Something very bad is happening!"

Before long, Johnny Martin came again to the valley of the Little Big Horn. His heart leaped. Out across the meadow, coming from the far side, he saw a column of horsemen riding in troop formation. These must be soldiers! No Indians rode together like that. The bugler boy spurred his mount over the open grasslands, standing in his stirrups and crying out for the soldiers to wait. Hearing him, the officer at the head of the galloping column halted his troops.

Johnny Martin slid his weary mount to a halt, a prayer of thanks on his lips. He had found Captain Benteen!

When Benteen had read the message from Custer, he handed it silently to his fellow officers, who had just galloped up.

The officers read the hastily scrawled note.

Then they, too, fell silent.

Were these the last words of Yellow Hair Custer?

. . . BENTEEN, COME ON—BIG VILLAGE—
BE QUICK—BRING PACKS. P.S. BRING
PACKS . . .

Benteen folded the paper, put it in his breast pocket.

"If we are lucky," he said to the waiting officers, "we may just be able to reach Major Reno on the bluff above those trees in the river bend ahead. There is no chance whatever of reaching General Custer *four miles farther down this valley*. Back to your commands, gentlemen. We will run for Reno's position."

Trumpeter Johnny Martin, remembering Lieutenant Cooke's orders should danger threaten, stayed with Captain Benteen.

Thus the angels touched an immigrant boy upon the shoulder.

31. IRON CEDAR SEES THE GRAY HORSE TROOP

Iron Cedar could scarcely believe his eyes.

The great warrior Gall had dispatched him to this high point on the bluff where he could serve as a lookout for more Pony Soldiers, while Gall finished off the frightened troops which had fled the river trees and taken refuge on the hill across the Greasy Grass.

Iron Cedar could not know that these were Major Reno's soldiers which Gall had cornered on the hill. Nor would he have cared. His job was to make sure that no other Pony Soldiers approached to bother the Hunkpapa of Gall and White Bull.

That is why his slanted black eyes were now so wide.

Down from the eastern slopes of the river, away down there by the tipis of the Cheyenne, the Sans Arc, the Oglala and the Minniconjou, *more* Pony Soldiers *were* appearing!

In that far view—three or four miles—even the keen eyesight of an Indian was strained. But Iron Cedar saw that one of the troops coming down from those far hills to threaten the other end of the camp was mounted on light-colored horses. Those could be gray horses. And Iron Cedar, and every Sioux warrior of note, knew with which leader rode the Gray Horse Troop of the Seventh Calvary. *That was Yellow Hair Custer coming down from those far hills!*

Now, surely, Iron Cedar must report such an exciting thing to Chief Gall and the Hunkpapa. Even though the other Pony Soldiers were not in a place to interfere with the finishing of the soldiers trapped on the hill, would not Gall want to know where Yellow Hair was? Would he want all the glory of fighting Custer to fall to the Cheyenne? Or even to his own Sioux brothers of the Oglala or Minniconjou bands?

Iho! It was hardly possible.

Away went Iron Cedar, sweeping down into the valley on his fleet pony. Racing up to Gall, he gave him the news. Gall and White Bull had almost gotten the soldiers on the hill down to their last bullets. They could tell this by the reduced rifle-fire of the surrounded troopers. In a few more minutes those trapped Pony Soldiers would all be killed. But also in a few more minutes, the Cheyenne or Oglala or Minniconjou might have met and defeated Yellow Hair! That would never do.

With a wild yell, Gall called his best fighters to him.

Down the grassy valley the Hunkpapa drove their ponies, war cries echoing. Many others of White Bull's warriors also went with the Hunkpapa chief to be in on the killing of Yellow Hair.

On the hill above, Reno's soldiers, doomed but the moment before, saw the Indians leaving them to race off upvalley. The weary, sweat-stained troopers rose from their shallow-dug rifle-pits and hiding-holes, giving thanks to God. In the same moment of divine help, they saw Captain Benteen's column leave the far side of the valley and gallop toward their side.

The troopers could not know that Trumpeter Martin had just found Benteen with Custer's last message. Neither could they know that Benteen had decided to stay with Reno on the hill, and was even then rushing over the meadow to join them. The troopers with Reno would never know, either, that it was Iron Cedar's message to Chief Gall which was just as fateful as Johnny Martin's ride from Custer. And perhaps even more so.

For if the Hunkpapa had not been called away by Gall's jealous pride to make certain that Crazy Horse, Crow King, Bob-Tail-Horse, Roan Bear and the other famed war chiefs did not grasp all the credit for destroying Yellow Hair, Benteen could never have crossed the valley and lived. Or, had he done so by bloody sacrifice, he would have found no single trooper of Major Reno's command still alive to greet him.

But the heart-felt cheers of the Reno survivors which met Benteen's exhausted but uninjured command were stilled almost as they rose from the parched throats of the rescued.

Even as Benteen's troopers, with the pack train of mules bearing the desperately needed ammunition, fought their ways up the hill through the remaining Sioux, a great quiet fell upon the valley. The Indians, themselves, stopped firing.

Far down along the river, borne upward faintly upon a rising current of the afternoon air, came the sound of thin and ragged rifle-fire. And it was not Winchester fire. Those were Springfield carbines firing. Seventh Cavalry guns.

"God help us," said a white-faced trooper softly. "That's the General down there. They have got him . . ."

32. "THERE WAS NOT TIME TO
LIGHT A PIPE . . ."

Custer began the descent to the river. Adjutant Cooke,
looking at his pocket watch, noted the hour: 3:30 P.M. An
air of tense confidence was shared now by officer and
man.

The General had caught the lower camp napping.

With his swift wide circle out away from the stream,
he had completed the same fatal surprise tactic with
which he had destroyed the camp of Black Kettle on the
Washita.

All that remained was for his troops to press down the
wide gully ahead, charge over the river, unite with the
troops of Benteen which must soon appear on the other
side. Then the combined commands would turn and
drive through the helpless Indians to meet the troops of
Reno. The camp would be split in two parts, the people
put into panicky flight, the warriors forced to surrender.
The victory would be Custer's. And, with the victory,
who knew what other prizes?

What actually followed is known only to Indian eyes.

Red tongues, alone, can tell the tale.

Custer, the Indians say, came down the slope nearly
to the Little Big Horn. The place was at the fording of
the river where Medicine Trail Creek enters the mother
stream.

It was a true thing, also, that the camp at the lower
end was helpless. Most of the warriors had rushed off up
the river to help the Hunkpapa kill the Pony Soldiers of
Reno. If Yellow Hair had come on down that slope and

charged the camp, the Indians would have fled in wild
fright, ending the battle. But then a strange thing
happened.

Four Cheyenne warriors appeared in full fighting
dress.

They were Bob-Tail-Horse, Roan Bean, Calf and
another whose name was never remembered. In all of
the confusion of running squaws, crying children and
frightened old people caused by the sudden appearance
of the dreaded Yellow Hair, these four Cheyenne rode
straight out toward the ford, and toward the five troops
of Custer's Seventh Cavalry.

For a reason no man was ever to know, the supreme
courage of the four warriors riding directly into his
troops brought Custer to a halt. He ordered the cavalry
to stop on the lower slope of the hill, before ever they
reached the river.

It was probable that Yellow Hair believed the four
Cheyenne were only the tempting bait in an ambush of a
hundred times their number of warriors waiting hidden
behind the lodges. In any event, his halt upon the hill
was a terrible mistake. It permitted Iron Cedar the time
to see the Gray Horse Troop from afar. And it gave Gall
and White Bull time to bring their Hunkpapa down from
the Reno fight. Thus, when the General did order the
advance resumed, there were hundreds of warriors in
front of him, and he could not get across the ford.

Indeed, he never reached it. The hills all about were
suddenly black and swarming with Sioux and, before the
Seventh could retreat, half of Custer's command lay
dead or wounded on the lower slope. The surviving
troops were huddled about their commander midway of
the hillside. They cursed their Springfield carbines, and
threw them away, and fought on foot with the big Colt
revolvers. Ammunition was nearly gone. With every
burst of Indian fire, white men fell.

Custer stood hatless in the June sunlight.

His golden curls glinted.

In his hands was his beautifully engraved rifle. Again

and again he fired with it. Each time an Indian screamed, whirled around, pitched from his rearing pony and lay still.

Others of the officers and men of the Seventh Cavalry did what they might. Only heroes were left now upon that bloody hill. The unsure, the weak, the faint, had died in the first wild assault of the Sioux.

Now only Yellow Hair and 115 of his 231 troops, scouts and civilian followers remained.

Upon the north hill a lean warrior wearing a single eagle feather and a black wolfskin cape directed the fighting. Who could miss that handsome face? The panther's grace and fearlessness? It was Tashunka Witko, Crazy Horse, who was tearing at Yellow Hair's left flank. He, and his Oglala.

To the south, the gully was not so much one channel but a series of rough breaks and shallow dips in the hillside. Here were the Hunkpapa, led now by Gall and White Bull, and the Cheyenne with Bob-Tail-Horse, Two Moons and the rest.

In front of Custer the lower slope crawled with Minniconjou and Sans Arc Sioux and with a mixture of all-comers and all bands—in total, some two thousand warriors at this late stage in the fight.

Strangely, now, perhaps in wonderment at the courage of the Pony Soldiers, the host of Indian braves rested their fire, watching Yellow Hair and all that was left of the Gray Horse Troop—the last of the gallant Seventh Cavalry alive upon the upper slope.

In the lull, Custer called his officers and his men to him. He was not yet wounded, although caked with filth and powder grime, as were all the troopers who came now to his call. Those who were not dripping and dark-stained with their own life blood, were covered with the blood of comrades no longer there. As those in the inner ring, near the General, listened to his words, those upon the outside of the circle kept firing to hold the Indians back.

Custer's head was high.

His voice was firm. He raised it scarcely a tone. He spoke to the men as comrades, as brothers-in-arms, and not as a commanding officer to troops about to die.

"Boys," he said, standing straight as the shaft of a buffalo lance, "we are going to reach the top of this hill. We are going up there, and you know why. Let us go like men—like Seventh Cavalrymen—and we shall all meet again upon the other side. God bless you. God keep you all . . ."

Some of the men were weeping.

Others stood for that small instant of eternity there in the sunlit stillness above the Greasy Grass, dry-eyed, but filled with the fierce sharp pain of pride.

They could not speak, could not reply to Custer. Nor were they given time to do so by the Sioux.

A tremendous burst of renewed Indian rifle-fire came from the command of Crazy Horse upon the north hill. With the furious rifle-fire came a thousand-throated scream, and the great mass of Oglala horsemen swept in toward Yellow Hair and his remaining men. Upward the valiant survivors fought their way on foot. But with every step of the way, soldiers fell and did not rise again. When Custer began that last retreat up the slope, he had one hundred and twelve troopers with him. When he came to bay just below the hilltop he had struggled to reach, less than sixty men still stood in a desperate ring about their gallant leader.

Half a hundred lives had been lost within ten minutes.

All there with Custer in that panting, smoke-grimed circle knew that Yellow Hair and the Seventh Cavalry had come to the last stand. But the General's fiery heart would not falter.

His unforgettable voice rose above the battle one more time.

"Stay together, men!" he called. "We are almost to the top. See there where the sun strikes the grass of the crest!"

But the sun was setting for the Seventh Cavalry.

With a final wolf-pack howling of war cries, Crazy Horse and four hundred Oglala warriors drove their painted ponies in upon the huddled knot of white troopers. From the opposite side, Gall swept in with the Cheyenne and the Hunkpapa. The last of the Seventh disappeared beneath the shrieking red wave. In the very center of the Indian tide, Yellow Hair Custer, shot through the breast and bleeding from the mouth, struggled once more to his feet. His big Colt revolver was in his right hand. He fired one, twice, three times. A swinging Oglala war club struck his shoulder, knocking him backward over a dead mount of the Gray Horse Troop. He again reeled upright, then fell to his knees, the big Colt leveled across the body of the gray horse. Suddenly he saw the Indian ponies blot out the sky above him, and then the dark red faces snarling down. He fired upward into the dark faces and into the bodies of the leaping ponies, and that is all that he was aware of —and that is the way that he was found—with his revolver empty and still aimed at the enemy—a Sioux bullethole through his left temple and into his brain.

It was just a little after four o'clock in the afternoon.

Custer's great fight upon the eastern slopes of that far river called the Greasy Grass was over in less than an hour.

As for the final end, that dark moment of the charge of Crazy Horse and his Four Hundred, only an Indian could know how swift was Yellow Hair's last thought.

"After that," the old warriors say, "the fight did not last long enough to light a pipe . . ."

33. SILENT LIES THE SEVENTH

"Sir," said Captain Weir to the wounded Major Reno, "for the final time I beg of you to permit me to take D Troop and go down toward that firing."

The captain was speaking of the distant rifle-fire which many of the Seventh Cavalrymen on Reno's hill believed to be from General Custer. The time was then nearing four o'clock. Most of the attacking Indians were still away down the river with Gall and White Bull. There might yet be a chance that a single troop could slip from the hill and make a scout for Custer and his five troops before the hostiles returned.

But the wound in Major Reno's head made him dizzy and faint. He could not command his senses clearly. For the past hour Captain Benteen had been in actual charge of the defenses. It was the latter who now urged the suffering Reno to grant Weir's request, "before the cursed Sioux come back at us in force."

Reno refused. He insisted that no man leave the hill.

If they could defend their position only until nightfall, they might survive. Tomorrow was the twenty-sixth, the date when Gibbon and Terry were due to arrive. Surely, with first sunlight, they would hear the buglers' calls, see the pennants flying.

Weir and Benteen exchanged hopeless glances.

"Major Reno, sir!" repeated brave young Captain Weir, "did you hear me, sir? For the last time, please! Give me your permission to take D Troop and make a scout for the General."

But Reno only pressed the bloody bandage on his

head and groaned. Benteen, standing nearby, looked at Weir and shook his head. It was no use. The major was not listening.

Captain Weir leaned down to face Reno, who was sitting on the ground propped up against a stack of pack-saddles.

"Major, I am going now. You cannot stop me. If you will not authorize me to take D Troop, I will go alone. I, and any man brave enough to come with me."

Reno finally looked up at him.

"I forbid you, or any man, to leave this hill," he said.

But Captain Weir only turned his back and went to where his horse was standing. His lieutenant, a youth named Edgerly, ran up to him and begged to go with him. But Weir told him he was now in command of D Troop, in Weir's place, and must remain with the men. Before the young officer could reply, the captain put spurs to his mount and dashed off the hill and down the spine of the long ridge which led toward the lower Indian camp, and toward the sound of the distant rifle-fire.

Yet when Captain Weir could defy Reno out of loyalty to General Custer, then why could not Lieutenant Edgerly disobey Captain Weir for the same reason?

Two tough sergeants came up to the youthful officer, seeing him start for his horse.

"What do you think you're going to do, Lieutenant?" they asked. "Follow the Captain?"

"You two men stay here and hold the troop together," answered Edgerly. "There will be no officers when I am gone."

"Yes, sir," saluted the two hard-faced sergeants. "You can surely trust us, sir. Can't he, boys?"

The question went to the weary, powder-burned troopers of D Troop who were now coming up to see what was going on.

"Oh, yes sir!" chorused the soldiers. "We wouldn't think of following the Lieutenant when he follows the Captain!"

Edgerly turned and rode off after Captain Weir.

Immediately the two sergeants swung to their saddles.

"D Troop, mount up!" bawled one of them, and the valiant men ran for their tethered horses and got to saddle.

"Forward, ho, D Troop!" shouted the other sergeant, and away down the ridge went every able-bodied trooper in the company of Captain Weir and Lieutenant Edgerly. The two officers, hearing hoofbeats, turned in their saddles. But what could they say? What could any officers say to men like that? What could be said, was said by Captain Weir in a voice that was choked with feeling.

"All right . . . God bless you, boys," he said. "Let's go and find the General——!"

But they were not to find Custer that day.

They advanced down the ridge as far as they could, being shot at by Indians every step of the way. And being in danger of being cut off and killed to the man at any moment.

Finally they could ride no farther.

A mile or more away they saw a sunlit, silent slope of the river where many Indians were riding around and around on their ponies shooting arrows and rifles into some motionless objects on the ground. They could hear no other fire now than that coming from the sharp bark of the red men's Winchesters.

But there was no fight going on upon that distant field.

If the firing they had heard before had been that of Custer, then Custer was no longer on that field.

Had he been there?

If so, where was he now?

Weir and Edgerly discussed the matter with their sergeants.

None of them mentioned the possibility of a defeat for the General. It was agreed that Custer had found the Sioux too strong for his small force, and turned back. Most probably he was making another circle to find

General Gibbon or General Terry and rush with them back to help Reno and Benteen.

They even took cheer in the notion that the General would soon come charging back up the valley with reinforcements.

But the Indians were now leaving the sunlit slope in the distance and returning toward Reno's hill. Weir and Edgerly started back, but were frightened to learn that the Sioux had gotten behind them. Were they cut off?

Only the fact that cool Captain Benteen now appeared leading a column of troopers along the ridge toward them saved their lives. Joining up with Benteen, the combined troops fought their way back to the hill, and the fortifications they had dug there. There the fight raged anew, its red fires raised up again by the return of Gall and the Hunkpapa, and of Crazy Horse and the Oglala, and of Two Moons and the Cheyenne. Suddenly it seemed to the troopers on the hill that all of the Indians in Montana were charging at them up every side and slope of their high bluff. They were saved only by the fact that darkness fell, and the Indians went back to their camps to light the victory fires and start the scalp-dances. The men on the blackened hill tried not to think about where those scalps might have been taken that day.

All night long the wild fires leaped and the war drums boomed in the great hostile encampment.

But there was no rest for the soldiers on the hill.

Hour after hour Benteen and Weir and Moylan and the other officers drove them to the task of scraping more rifle-pits in the flinty earth of the bluff-top. They used spoons, tin cups, spurs, knives, their fingernails —anything with which they could dig a shallow depression which might hide their bodies from the Indian bullets which sunrise would surely bring in blazing showers. The only real tools on the hill were three spades and two axes brought in by the pack train. All of the horses and mules were put in the center of the circle of shallow rifle-pits and tied there so that they could not be stampeded by the Indian fire. When the first streaks of the summer dawn of June 26th lighted the east, Captain Benteen went to Major Reno, and crouched beside him.

"Marc," he said, "we've done all we can. Before they beat us, they will know they've tangled with the Seventh Cavalry." He paused, looking off through the gloom. "What do you suppose has become of Custer?" he asked.

Reno shook his head, but then spoke hopefully.

"I think he is all right. He will be coming into our lines as soon as the daylight lets him see where we are."

"No," said Benteen, "you're wrong, Marc. The talk among the men is that he's gone on and deserted us. They are cursing him plenty, believe me. As for myself, well, you know what I think of the General."

"Yes, I know," answered Reno softly. "But it is you who are wrong. Custer would never leave us."

"Oh? What was it he did to Major Elliott on the Washita?"

"Elliott was dead. Custer knew that."

"We all knew it—later on."

"Please go and have one more look to the lines," ordered Reno, straightening. "They will be back at us any moment."

Even as he spoke, the day broke over the eastern hills and the Sioux were screaming their war cries and once more forcing their ponies up the slopes of the bluff.

Soon they stopped charging and took sheltered places from which they fired into the soldier positions on top of the hill. Hour after hour the fire continued. And every hour more soldiers died, more were torn by wounds, more began to lose all hope and to pray for a merciful, quick death.

Then a strange and uneasy thing commenced to occur among the Indians. The soldiers began to hear the blowing of cavalry bugles down in the war camp. Straining to see, they made out some of the half-naked warriors riding about tooting the trumpets. Others of the red warriors were wearing uniforms and parts of uniforms of U.S. Cavalry troopers. Here and there an officer's hat was seen, or a blue coat with gold epaulets on the shoulders. Where had the Sioux gotten these things?

It was a dark question, and the men upon the hill would not try to answer it.

The fight continued all that day, the Indians charging the hill, the soldiers pushing them back, but always the action ending with the red men dug in a little nearer to the hill's top than they had been before.

With the second darkness the soldiers buried their dead and moved their rifle-pit positions into a smaller circle. This was very easy, now, for there were so few to dig for, and so few to hide. Volunteer patrols stole down to the river to bear up water that the dying might drink, and the living might drink also, and so live a little longer.

They knew now that Custer was not coming.

Or that when he came he would be too late.

One more hard charge by the hostiles in the morning and the Seventh Cavalry would be no more.

But that charge never came. Unknown to the men upon the hill, the column of Terry and Gibbon had been sighted by the Indian scouts late that second afternoon. Even as the warriors were making their last wild rides to overrun the hilltop, the squaws were taking down the lodges and the young boys were running in the vast pony herds. When daylight of June 27th dawned pale and clear, it revealed to the wounded heroes on the hill two sights of equal joy and wonder.

Far to the southeast, fingering off through the hills of the Rosebud and of the Greasy Grass, the black lines of the retreating Indian camp crawled like distant, fleeing ants.

Nearer at hand—much nearer—marching up the river from the north, came the long blue lines of the United States Infantry. Their bright pennants fluttered in the morning sun. The brass notes of their bugles blended with the hoarse braying of the pack mules and the rumble of artillery wheels.

The sleepless Seventh Cavalrymen watching from the weathered bluffs above the deserted hostile camp stood and cheered to the man, tears streaming down their gaunt faces.

These were the troops of Red Nose Gibbon and General Terry, come at last!

Reno and Benteen were saved.

The Sioux were scattered to a thousand prairie winds.

But wait.

Where was Custer? What had happened to Yellow Hair?

The question was answered an hour later when an advance scout from Gibbon rode up to the rifle barricades on Reno Hill.

General Custer and all of his five troops of the Seventh U.S. Cavalry had been found upon a grassy slope four miles below—every officer and man stripped naked, lying still-eyed and silent in the summer sunlight, at peace forever along the banks of the Little Big Horn.

34. CRAZY HORSE COMES IN

For nine months following the destruction of the Seventh Cavalry, the Sioux of Sitting Bull and of Crazy Horse wandered the outer plains like lonesome wolves.

The Cheyenne had left them. Two Moons, Dull Knife and the other principal chiefs were talking peace. They said that the white man would surely come with more new Pony Soldiers than a cloud of locusts to avenge the death of Yellow Hair. And there were many rumors and stories flying about the prairie to support such fears.

American Horse, the great Oglala, had been killed . . . His forty-eight lodges had been burned . . . Three Stars Crook was back up from Wyoming . . . General Nelson A. Miles, "Bear Coat" Miles, was marching up the Yellowstone with a huge force . . . Red Cloud had been removed from power by the white man . . . Spotted Tail was now the head chief of the agency Indians.

Then, late in the autumn, came news of a terrible blow to the wild Sioux. The Cheyenne had been broken in battle.

General Mackenzie had captured and burned to the snows the main village of Dull Knife, head chief of all the Cheyenne. In the fight, the war chief, Last Bull, leader of the fierce Cheyenne Dog Soldiers—the tribe's best fighters—had been killed. Dull Knife had surrendered to the whites. Little Wolf, that unforgiving warrior, had fled with the few Cheyenne survivors who would not surrender to live on an agency.

But when Little Wolf sought to join his people with

the Oglala of Crazy Horse, Crazy Horse turned him away.

Yes! it was true.

Tashunka Witko, fighter of fighters against the white man, had said that he would now go in. The defeat of his old friend Dull Knife had decided him. Crazy Horse was taking final counsel with his fellow Sioux, even then, before sending word to the agency and to Spotted Tail that the Oglala were ready to surrender "when the new grass comes again."

Angered, Little Wolf returned to the agency and offered his services, and those of his free Cheyenne, as scouts to help the soldiers hunt down Crazy Horse and Sitting Bull!

It was the beginning of the end, when Indian thus turned upon Indian. The melting of the snows would finish the red man.

Many of the Sioux could not believe these tales. When spring did come at last, they traveled to the village of Tashunka Witko to hear the words from the war chief's own lips. When they arrived, they heard even more than they had been told of bad news.

Not only was Crazy Horse going to surrender, but Sitting Bull had fled the country!

Iho! it was a true thing.

With two hundred lodges of his Hunkpapa people, and some of the Oglala people who would not go in with Crazy Horse, the vision-dreamer of the Little Big Horn had escaped northward into Canada, "the Land of the Grandmother."

There the hated Pony Soldiers could not follow them.

There they would try to make a life like the old free life in the United States. It was better than slavery. It was better than starving on a reservation. *Woyuonihan!*

Unable to believe their ears, the visiting Sioux gathered at the great red and black lodge of Crazy Horse to hear his final speech.

They knew, as they came there, that Spotted Tail had been there before them. The old man had come from the agency to plead with his hostile brothers to give up the hopeless fight. He was gone back, now, afraid to linger too long among the wild and fierce Oglala. This speech of Tashunka Witko's which they now would hear was the war chief's answer to the old man's plea for peace.

What would he say? What would his Oglala people do?

"My brothers," began the dark-skinned warrior-hero, "our Uncle Spotted Tail has told me there is no use to fight any more. We have no remaining chance to beat the Pony Soldiers. But what I say here is for myself. All of you must do what your own hearts say to do."

He paused, the firelight marking his sorrowful face.

"I have fought long," he resumed, "and I love this Land of the Spotted Eagle. But I am tired, and the soldiers are too many now. I am all done. I am going in. I have asked our Uncle Sitting Bull if he would surrender with me. He said that he would not. That he did not wish to die just yet. He has gone to the Land of the Grandmother. His trail is broad and easy to see. Those of you who wish to may follow it. But my home is here on this Montana soil, and to the east, in the *Pa Sapa* sacred to our fathers. I will not run away. I am going in to the agency. I gave my promise to follow Spotted Tail along the road to peace."

The Sioux went away and smoked their pipes and thought of the decision to be made.

Next morning all of the lodges came down. Half of them traveled to the east, toward the agency, with Crazy Horse. The other half went to the north, toward Canada and the people of Sitting Bull.

For four moons, May to September, Crazy Horse lived without trouble at Red Cloud agency. Then his beloved wife, Black Blanket, sickened. The warchief was arrested while trying to take her to the doctor at nearby Spotted Tail agency. He was escorted under guard back to Red Cloud by Major Jesse M. Lee, agent at Spotted Tail and a true friend of the red man.

As twilight drew down, they approached the agency

with its soldier barracks and bayonet-armed sentries.
Major Lee for the final time warned the great warrior to
be careful, that there could be grave danger for him
here.

Crazy Horse only nodded and continued riding
straight toward the agency. It was dark when he got
down from his horse and shook hands with the soldier
chief who met him outside the office of General Bradley, who commanded the troops at the agency.

The soldier chief seemed very nervous.

The Indians sensed the officer's uncertainty. The best
friends of Crazy Horse among them came to stand by the
proud Oglala war chief. They were Swift Bear, Touch-
the-Clouds, High Bear, Black Crow and Good Voice.
They looked hard at the officer.

"Excuse me," said the latter hurriedly to Crazy Horse.
"I will tell General Bradley that you are here."

When he came back out of the general's office, his
face was drawn tight. His eyes would not look at the
Indians.

"The General says that if you will come with me," he
instructed Crazy Horse, "not a hair of your head will be
harmed."

The war chief hesitated. He looked at his friends.
They shook their heads quickly, for they were suspicious
now.

But Tashunka Witko was not afraid.

He shook hands with the soldiers who had marched up
suddenly to escort him. But he had no idea that the little
building toward which the soldiers then took him was
the guardhouse of the agency troops—the jail.

When he saw the iron-bound door swing open, revealing the bars of the prison rooms within, he gave a great
cry like some wild animal at the closing of the steel trap
upon its tortured legs.

Crazy Horse became then like an animal.

He wheeled about and broke free of the soldiers. He
had seen the white man's "iron house." No power on
earth could put his free wild spirit in such a foul and

filthy cage. He ran toward the outer darkness, but only a stride or two.

The bayonet of one of the soldier-guards struck him through the back. He stopped and straightened slowly. Some of his Indian friends took hold of him to help him stand. But he shook his head, deep voice moaning like a hurt beast.

"Let me go, my friends," he said. "Can't you see that I have my last wound . . ."

The Indians took their hands away. They shrank back from him, as coyotes from the growling of the king wolf.

The war chief turned slowly and began to walk toward the soldiers who had bayoneted him. He took three proud steps. Then, without another sound, he slid forward down into the dirt of the prison-yard, shirt and leggins already black with life-blood.

Touch-the-Clouds ran up to his leader's fallen body.

"Let me take him to the lodges of my people," he pleaded with the soldier chief. "You have killed him here. Let him die with his own kind."

"Carry him into the guardhouse!" shouted the soldier chief to the troopers. "And clear this yard at once!"

But Touch-the-Clouds would not move.

He reached down and gently lifted the body of Crazy Horse.

"Where my chief goes, there I go," he told the officer. And, turning, he bore the stricken Oglala toward the iron-bound doorway. The soldiers parted to let him pass. The officer, touched by that Indian dignity which the treachery of the white man had never weakened, bowed his head. Two other figures followed behind Touch-the-Clouds and Crazy Horse. And these, too, the soldiers permitted to pass; they were the aged parents of the dying war chief.

The guards cleared the yard of all other Indians. The post surgeon hurried up through the lamplight. After a while he came out of the guardhouse, and spoke to the waiting officer.

"The bayonet entered both kidneys," he said in a low voice. "There is nothing to do for him."

In a small bare room inside the jail building of the Pony Soldiers at Red Cloud Agency, Crazy Horse lay dying.

There was no bed, only a pile of army blankets upon the cold stone floor.

With their faces to the wall, his parents were crouched praying to the Great Spirit, crying the words of the chant for the Fallen Ones, the Katela Song of the Sioux People.

By the blankets crouched Touch-the-Clouds, his hand holding the hand of his dear friend. He could feel the coldness coming into the dark fingers of the war chief.

"My chief," he said, "is there something you would have me tell the people? Anything at all, Tashunka?"

He saw the slender face move, the lean head nod slightly.

"*My brother,*" whispered Crazy Horse, "*I am bad hurt; tell the people it is no use to depend upon me any more. . . .*"

With those words, he was gone, and the story finished.

Crazy Horse, last war chief of all the Sioux, was in the arms of Wakan Tanka. Sitting Bull, the vision-dreamer, had vanished into Canada. Yellow Hair slept along the Greasy Grass. The war drums thumped no more upon the Powder or the Rosebud. Then, truly, could it be said, and softly:

The Battle of the Little Big Horn was ended.

ABOUT THE AUTHOR

WILL HENRY was born and grew up in Missouri, where he attended Kansas City Junior College. Upon leaving school, he lived and worked throughout the western states, acquiring the background of personal experience reflected later in the realism of his books. Presently residing in California, he writes for motion pictures and television, as well as continuing his research into frontier lore and legend, which are the basis for his unique blend of history and fiction. Four of his novels have been purchased for motion picture production, and several have won top literary awards, including four of the coveted Spur Awards of the Western Writers of America. Mr. Henry's most recent books include: *From Where the Sun Now Stands*, *The Last Warpath*, *Reckoning at Yankee Flat*, and *Chiricahua*.

WILL HENRY

ALIAS BUTCH CASSIDY

No one would make a more unlikely outlaw than young George LeRoy Parker, grandson of a Mormon bishop. But at sixteen Parker throws in with Mike Cassidy, a shrewd old bandit who sees something in the boy nobody else does—the courage of a cougar and the heart of a renegade. Old Mike teaches the kid everything he knows, and before he is done there is no outlaw more feared, hunted, or idolized than George LeRoy Parker. . . .

___4516-8 $4.50 US/$5.50 CAN

A BALLAD FOR SALLIE

JUDY ALTER

Longhair Jim Courtright has been both a marshal and a desperado—and in Hell's Half Acre, the roughest part of Fort Worth, he is a living legend. His skill with a gun has made him a hero in some people's eyes . . . and a killer in others'. As soon as young widow Sallie McNutt steps off the stage from Tennessee, her refined manners and proper attire set her apart from the other women of the Half Acre. And it isn't long before something else sets her apart—someone wants her dead.

___4365-3 $4.50 US/$5.50 CAN

Dorchester Publishing Co., Inc.
P.O. Box 6640
Wayne, PA 19087-8640

Please add $1.75 for shipping and handling for the first book and $.50 for each book thereafter. NY, NYC, and PA residents, please add appropriate sales tax. No cash, stamps, or C.O.D.s. All orders shipped within 6 weeks via postal service book rate. Canadian orders require $2.00 extra postage and must be paid in U.S. dollars through a U.S. banking facility.

Name_____
Address_____
City_____ State_____ Zip_____
I have enclosed $_____ in payment for the checked book(s).
Payment <u>must</u> accompany all orders. ☐ Please send a free catalog.

WILL HENRY

YELLOWSTONE KELLY

Yellowstone Kelly is an Indian fighter and scout like no other. The devil-may-care Irishman can pick off hostiles and quote the classics with equal ease and accuracy. Even the mighty Sioux fear him. Most of them. Sitting Bull's main war chief, the dreaded Gall, fears no man, and Kelly has something of his that the warrior will gladly kill to get back—his woman.

___4364-5 $4.99 US/$5.99 CAN

Dorchester Publishing Co., Inc.
P.O. Box 6640
Wayne, PA 19087-8640

Please add $1.75 for shipping and handling for the first book and $.50 for each book thereafter. NY, NYC, and PA residents, please add appropriate sales tax. No cash, stamps, or C.O.D.s. All orders shipped within 6 weeks via postal service book rate. Canadian orders require $2.00 extra postage and must be paid in U.S. dollars through a U.S. banking facility.

Name_____
Address_____
City_____State_____Zip_____
I have enclosed $_____ in payment for the checked book(s).
Payment <u>must</u> accompany all orders. ☐ Please send a free catalog.

WILL HENRY

WHO RIDES WITH WYATT

"Some of the best writing the American West can claim!"
—Brian Garfield, Bestselling Author of Death Wish

They call Tombstone the Sodom in the Sagebrush. It is a town of smoking guns and raw guts, stage stick-ups and cattle runoffs, blazing shotguns and men bleeding in the streets. Then Wyatt Earp comes to town and pins on a badge. Before he leaves Tombstone, the lean, tall man with ice-blue eyes, a thick mustache and a long-barreled Colt becomes a legend, the greatest gunfighter of all time.

BY THE FIVE-TIME WINNER OF THE GOLDEN SPUR AWARD

____4292-4 $3.99 US/$4.99 CAN